Charlotte has been writing from a  several novels in both the science- published internationally by R Macmillan. These include Fury, Book One of The Cure series and Avery, Book One of The Chronicles of Kaya.

She studied a Masters of Screenwriting at the Australian Film, Television and Radio School, and is the author of the Australian Writer's Guild award-winning screenplay *Fury* – adapted from her novel of the same name. She now lives in London, writing novels and working on both film and television projects, as well as the upcoming graphic novel *Skin*.

Also by Charlotte McConaghy

Fury: Book One of *The Cure*
Melancholy: Book Two of *The Cure*

Limerence

Charlotte McConaghy

First published by Momentum in 2016
This edition published in 2016 by Momentum
Pan Macmillan Australia Pty Ltd
1 Market Street, Sydney 2000

Copyright © Charlotte McConaghy 2016
The moral right of the author has been asserted.

All rights reserved. This publication (or any part of it) may not be reproduced or transmitted, copied, stored, distributed or otherwise made available by any person or entity (including Google, Amazon or similar organisations), in any form (electronic, digital, optical, mechanical) or by any means (photocopying, recording, scanning or otherwise) without prior written permission from the publisher.

A CIP record for this book is available at the National Library of Australia

Limerence: Book Three of The Cure (Omnibus Edition)

EPUB format: 9781760302238
Mobi format: 9781760302245
Print on Demand format: 9781760302337

Cover design by Matt O'Keefe
Edited by Tara Goedjen
Proofread Lauren Choplin

Macmillan Digital Australia: www.macmillandigital.com.au

To report a typographical error, please visit momentumbooks.com.au/contact/

Visit www.momentumbooks.com.au to read more about all our books and to buy books online. You will also find features, author interviews and news of any author events.

For my friend, Rhia.

We require that all things be mysterious and unexplorable, that land and sea be infinitely wild ...

Henry David Thoreau

Chapter 1

Josephine

I used to imagine that in the heart of the earth it would be warm. But in the deep dark it is cold. The space grows smaller each day. The walls creep closer and the silence seems to petrify all in its path like the ancient ghostly trees within the dead forest. We've become like the rats whose claws *scratch scratch scratch*, the hated creatures who flee below to hide. We are hunted and cowed. Forced into the cold dark corners. They wish to make us small, the smallest things in the world, too small to fight. Once this was where I belonged. Under the floor of the world with all of you, my family. With you, Luke Townsend. Once I was content to be small because it meant being alive.

But now I think I'm done with being hunted.

Now I think I belong in the sky with the other predators.

*

December 15th, 2067

Luke

The cold of the tile floor makes my muscles stiff. There are metal bracelets around my wrists and they cut into my flesh more by the day. I have no veins left – the army of scientists has started searching between my toes for places to inject me. When they've ravaged the veins there they'll move to my eyeballs. That'll be nice. I swing between perfect clarity and hazy confusion, between mind-altering rage and mind-numbing boredom. Sometimes what they give me makes me sick, sometimes it makes me hallucinate or try to scratch my wrists open, and sometimes it makes me strong. What gets to me most is the light. I live now in a room of perpetual glare and cold white tiles; I exist outside of time. There's no escaping it, not even when I bury my face in my arms. My head and eyes, so used to the dark of the underground, ache.

A tone sounds from somewhere above and I sit up on my hard bed. The tone means it's time for testing. Through the glass door of my cage I see four men approach along the white hallway. Two scientists and two Bloods. I stand and go to the chute. My head's quite clear today, which is a pleasant surprise.

"Bruce, my man. You're looking peaky. Did you get enough sleep?"

The scientist's name isn't Bruce, as far as I know, but since he didn't tell me what it actually is I decided to name him. I've named them all even though they never say a word to me that isn't an instruction.

"Cuffs on," Bruce tells me calmly. Everything he does is calm. Larry, on the other hand, is easily ruffled. He's twitchy.

I take the cuffs from the chute and lock them around my already manacled wrists, then place the second set around my ankles. "How's Marie? And the baby? Did I tell you I decided you've had another baby? Well, you have. And she's a crier. Maybe that's why you look so dopey today, Brucey."

"On your knees, face the wall."

I face the wall and crouch to my knees. The door slides open behind me and I feel the two Bloods take hold of me. They yank me to my feet and steer me into the hall. I shuffle along at a snail's pace. There's a gun between my shoulder blades, aimed right at my heart. There's a second at the base of my spine. Cameras watch me from every few meters and gas vents will dose us with a knockout sedative if I so much as blink the wrong way.

Still, as I pass Larry I lunge at him and snap my teeth like a Rottweiler. He gives a yelp of alarm and I grin. It earns me a whack on the back of the head. Not hard enough to knock me out of course, but hard enough to hurt.

We move through the facility and despite the pain I count the doorways and turns as I always do. I have most of this place mapped out now, but there's still an east wing into which I've yet to be taken.

"Hey Brucey, can I have some more of the green stuff? That was a fun day. I bet you use that shit on yourself, don't you? Take the edge off the numbness?" Surprise, surprise, he ignores me but I keep going. I always keep going. "I bet Marie hates living with a robot. Bet she's desperate for a bit of passion, huh? Some life? Do you make her laugh? Or cry? You can't, can you? You're not even a real person. You're a fucking drone, mate."

We arrive at the lab and I'm hooked into the machines and then strapped to the upright bed. It's very Hannibal Lector-y.

The scientists start injecting and extracting. They usually take blood and piss and shit and hair. Sometimes they take bone marrow. Once they took a piece of my kidney and a chunk of liver. I think they would pluck my heart from my chest if they could. Maybe they intend to.

Of all of this, the worst day was when the birds left me. That was how I knew they'd cured the blood moon from my heart. I've never felt so lonely.

Bruce approaches to swab my mouth.

"You want saliva?" I ask him, and then oblige by spitting on him.

He recoils. I wonder if they've given me anything infectious. I hope so.

One of the Bloods punches me in the face but I'm laughing and hardly feel it. His blows are nothing. All of this is nothing. It's funny, actually. It's so far beneath what matters to me that they are specks of dust on the bottom of my shoe.

I laugh because they can prick and prod and steal little pieces, but they've taken nothing real from me. Not my rage. Not my sadness. They certainly haven't taken my sense of humor. And here's the secret: there's no survival without laughter.

Today is a big day for me. Today is attempt number twenty-eight.

I've already worked out how to get free of the cuffs, and I can use the Bloods' weapons against them. The problem has always been finding a way out of this damn place. The security is unlike anything I've come across and each time I get free I wind up sprinting blindly into one of a million dead ends.

I'll get there in the end though. I'll find a way out, no matter how long it takes.

Because I know one thing. If Josephine Luquet has yet to rescue me then something immense is stopping her. And I sure as hell intend to find out what.

*

I wake some time later. I have a pounding headache and a very sore jaw. Obviously whatever they gave me knocked me out before I had a chance to get free of my bindings. That's attempt number twenty-eight in three months, failed spectacularly.

"Lukey."

I blink at the sound of the voice. My heart rate spikes. In the bright tile room I struggle to sit upright. Confusion and a concussion make me dizzy.

"You're okay," the voice says.

I know this voice. I never thought I'd hear it again.

They must have given me some very strong hallucinogens because when I finally manage to settle my eyes upon the figure sitting in my cell with me, I recognize him straight away. The sandy hair and big brown eyes. The slightly crooked teeth. The tall, slender frame and lanky crossed legs.

It's my brother, Dave. My dead brother.

A woozy breath leaves me and I decide that I'm not able to deal with this today. I rest my head on my knees and squeeze my eyes shut. Go away. Please.

I hear him rise and cross to my side. My skin prickles.

And then—

He touches me, this hallucination. A hand on my shaved head. It's warm and gentle. "It's okay, mate," he says softly. "I'm alright. You're alright."

It's a mighty ocean wave striking my tiny body and slamming it way down into the deep. It's all the air from my lungs and the thoughts from my mind. Gone is the laughter. It must be a lie. They've finally found a way to breach my walls and brutalize me with a monstrous trick.

It takes all my courage to open my eyes, turn my head and look him full in the face. He is older and wearier and different. And that's how I know he's real.

"What …?" The single word leaves me in a breath and then I'm weeping and clinging onto him and burying my face in his too-skinny chest.

"You're dead," I tell him. "You're dead."

"I'm not. I promise."

My big brother. He smells like my big brother, this creature in my hands.

My heart.

"How."

He doesn't answer. He waits for me to gather myself. It takes a very long time. Seemingly hours of scrabbling in the dark for an answer, of fearing when I will wake from this dream, of dreading when he goes again.

The raw edge of it all can't remain raw. In full survival mode, my mind starts making it numb. When I've stopped crying and moved into a space of numb dull *what the fuck*, Davehe goes back to his spot on the floor. He looks so much smaller than I remember him. So much older.

"You didn't kill yourself."

"No."

"So what happened? Where have you been?"

"Here."

I stare at him. "For eleven years?"

He nods once.

A shiver of horror runs down my spine. "What ... I didn't know. I didn't know or I would have come for you." This is a more ferocious truth than any I've yet known.

Dave shakes his head. "That's why they told you I was dead. So you'd never look."

"But ... *why?*" I'm not even close to making sense of this. I can't fit any pieces together.

"To use me. To punish me."

"For what?"

"For leading the protesters."

"But you stopped protesting when they cured you."

Dave shrugs blankly. "Shay wanted a subject. For the future cures. Who better than the man who'd been so publicly defying him?"

"Jesus. So he brought you here and tested you for eleven years?"

"On and off. Mostly I have time to myself."

"To stare at a white wall?"

"I don't live in the lab anymore."

"Then where do you live?"

"Within the Gates."

I wait for him to continue explaining but he's tight-lipped. "Dave, man, you're not making this easy on me. Start from the beginning."

So he does. Softly and calmly. He tells me of how he was snatched by the Bloods and brought here to be experimented on. After a couple of years he was moved into the cloistered community of the Gates, which is where the twelve Ministers live with their families and never leave the safety of its guarded walls. Dave says he knows Prime Minister Falon Shay, that he has been watched like a good little puppy and every so often returned to the lab for further experiments.

He says he has seen the way the people fear Shay, all of them, even the Ministers who serve him. Dave says it is not only fear of the man himself that makes them acquiesce to his every order, but fear of the plague that ruptured the world one day returning. It was Shay who ended the first sweep of disease, quarantining us behind walls. It will be him who protects us from another. Or so he says.

Last of all Dave explains how he's the only human in the known world to have been given all three cures.

"*Three?*" I demand. There are two cures – one for anger and one for sadness. The cure for anger was given to the public years ago but Josi led the resistance to destroy the sadness cure on two occasions before it could be administered to the remaining public. Since then we haven't heard a word about it. I didn't think anyone had successfully been injected with both the anger and the sadness cures.

But Dave nods.

There's a pit in my stomach because of the way he's looking at me. I can feel it, suddenly. A gaping absence in the air between us. A yawning grief.

"What's the third?" I ask softly. But I know, I think.

Dave frowns and laces his hands over his knees. His eyes look hollow as he says, "A cure for love."

*

December 16th, 2067

Luke

There is still no sense in it. No way to take the enormity of such a thing and fit it inside me. But I'm extremely good at compartmentalizing, so that's what I do. I put my shock and my emotion into boxes with heavy padlocks and I determine to deal with them later. When it's less … When it's just less.

We talk for hours. Well, I talk and Dave listens. I tell him about my life. About my Blood mission to spy on Josi. About escaping to the West and joining the resistance community of the Inferno. About the discoveries we made under the brutal sun of a scorched world. How the Furies aren't a horror story, but all too real, created by Shay's scientists and set free to spread their rabid disease throughout the last remaining humans. A sea of monsters swells out there beyond the city wall, scratching to get back in. I find myself speaking of poor dead Anthony Harwood, Josephine's therapist, and of Raven, too. Raven the dark-haired, dark-minded, utterly mad beauty. I speak of our flight into the tunnels on that bittersweet night more than a year ago. I speak of what came after, of lives lived under the ground. I tell him about the blood moon and the birds that I see even though they are extinct, and about my own brutal stupidity. I tell him of the terrible, terrible mistake I made and the lies that led me to here. And last I give him word of our parents.

I watch his face as I explain about Mom's laughter and Dad's builder's hands trembling unnaturally. I see no hint of emotion. He's not empty, exactly. Not cold. Just calm. I'm not sure if he feels nothing at all or just nothing with any strength.

"You remember them, right?" I ask.

"Of course. And you, Lukey."

"We've missed you." Words can be so, so small.

"I'm sorry you went through that. I know it must have been difficult." He hesitates. "I … tried to get back to you, in the beginning. But I was unequal to the task."

I squeeze my eyes shut. I keep thinking my tears must be spent and then I feel more. "I should have come for you. I should have come." The heart of it. The shame of it.

*

We are quiet now. My thoughts have shifted to our escape. I thought I was determined before. I wasn't. I will tear down the walls of this place to get him free. I'll die to do it.

It occurs to me slowly, a result of the drugs they have me on. "What are you doing here? In my room."

"I wish I knew. I woke up here."

I frown and consider why they might have put him in with me after taking such means to ensure I thought him dead. There is purpose to everything Shay orders. I can only imagine it means he thinks I'm never getting out of here and wants to torture me with the truth.

But if he thinks that he doesn't know me at all.

And, as it turns out, he doesn't know Josephine Luquet.

Sometimes I think nobody does.

*

An alarm sounds. It's not one I've heard in the three months I've been cloistered here. Smoke fills the hallway but none of it seeps through the airtight, unbreakable glass sealing us in. Dave and I are on our feet.

"This ever happen when you were here?"

"Nope."

I smile.

"What are you so happy about?" he asks.

"You'll see."

There's nothing in here to use as a weapon. Just the manacles around my wrists.

"Have you kept up your training?"

He glances at me like I'm a lunatic. "No."

Now that he's standing I can see how weak his body is. What happened to my mammoth giant of a brother, the one whose strength I envied so badly? That man is gone and this one looks frail. "Then stay behind me."

Figures move within the smoke. Someone appears before the glass, clad in gray with a hood and mask to cover their face. Whoever it is, they are heavily armed with automatic weapons. They place small charges on all four corners of the glass and then motion for us to move back. Dave and I go for the far corner and crouch low with our fingers in our ears. I squeeze my eyes shut and try to shield my head. A high-pitched sound slices through the world and the glass shatters. I feel a burst of pressure slam me back against the wall and my ears go.

Within the soundless world I get to my feet. Smoke swirls around the masked figure. A Blood appears and attacks. He isn't prepared for the knife that sheathes twice between his ribs and drops him to the ground.

As the smoke is sucked back up into the vents the figure removes the mask.

Standing before us is a young woman with long black hair and impossible eyes. She's lithe like a cat as she spins to take out a second attacking Blood with as much ease as the first. I see a finger missing on her left hand. I see a terrible, ugly scar along her throat, as though someone has cut it open and sewn it clumsily back together. I see disfiguring burns on her right ear and jaw. I am heartbroken by all these things that I see.

Because what I don't see when she looks at me is the girl I remember.

"Is he with us?" she asks softly with a glance at Dave.

I nod.

"Let's get on with it then."

I haven't seen her in three months but she barely looks at me as she strides down the hall. There is something hard in the set of her mouth and chin, something broken in her dual eyes.

We follow her through the impossible layers of security she has somehow managed to disengage. At one point she swings the enormous machine gun off her shoulder and takes out three more charging Bloods.

"Who the hell is she?" Dave asks.

And I say on a breath, "She's my wife."

Chapter 2

March 2nd, 2067

Josephine

I can't even see the hand in front of my face. I stumble blindly forward and flail about until I manage to trip and land with my shoulder hard against the tunnel wall.

"Owwwww! Dammit, where *are* you?"

"That'd defeat the purpose of the exercise."

I whirl toward the sound of his voice. "Stuff your exercise up your butt."

He whistles low and soft. I follow it as he moves, and despite my lack of enthusiasm I whistle back.

The idea is to keep track of each other through sound. We're honing our ears because when you live in abandoned underground tunnels, ninety percent of which are pitch black, you have to be able to function without sight. Most days when we have time we come down here to search for and find each other in the dark. It's even less fun than it sounds.

In the silence I can hear my breathing and more faintly his. Something makes a light *swish* and then the *clack clack* of tiny scuttling rodent claws. The soft tread of footsteps picks up speed. He's trying to escape me but he won't get far.

I hurry after him and realize too late that he's stopped. We collide and I feel him trip into the wall. He catches me against him and our lips bump clumsily.

"Hello, darling," he murmurs against my mouth.

"I could be anyone down here. You could be kissing a stranger."

"So could you."

I shake my head a little. Run my tongue over his lips. "I'd know the taste of you anywhere."

I feel his smile and then he kisses me properly. In the dark beneath the world. Even though in the tunnels above there are a hundred resistance members wondering where we are, wanting to ask us things, needing our help, our attention, our opinions. Even though our time is hardly our own and everything we do now is to create and build and maintain. Even though.

Because this is why we fight. For these stolen moments together. For this search in the dark.

Behind us I hear a new sound. This one is different. *Scratch scratch scratch* it goes.

The Furies have smelled us.

*

The route back takes us past the northeast gate. I reach for the lighter to light the oil lamp hanging on the wall. It illuminates the snarling monsters in the tunnel beyond. They will never stop trying to reach us. We erected these gates to create a safe living space – we have sections of tunnel for sleeping, eating, cooking, bathing and training. None of the gates have yet been breached and I pray they never will, because if even one Fury gets into our home, blood will spill.

Luke and I pause to watch the ravenous creatures. They've been down here as long as we have – they followed us here, after all, drawn by the scent of our flesh. Their skin has paled more than ours; the lack of sunlight has turned them even more to things of nightmare.

Hal once said we all have wilderness inside us. We all have an animal to tame. I look at the Furies and think they must live so deep in their wild that they'll never find their way out.

I try often to spot the humanity in their bloody eyes. I never do, and I hate them for it, even though it's not their fault.

"Come on." Luke takes my hand and pulls me down a different tunnel. I carry the torch aloft to light our way and it flickers against the concrete walls.

I miss the daylight. But I'm glad to have a home we've built for ourselves, a safe place the Bloods won't find us. The thing about living amid the Furies is that Blood technology doesn't distinguish us, so they have no idea that the rebel fighters they seek are hiding right beneath them.

Up a ladder and into the next level of tunnels we climb. To our right stretches the labyrinth of tunnels that makes up the sleeping barracks. Lumpy mattresses, either made or stolen, line the floors, more than a dozen in each stretch. To our left curves the long dining hall and the kitchen we built from stolen materials and a hefty dose of ingenuity. Most of these tunnels we live in connect to the abandoned subway – presumably there was once an industry down here, one made to keep those trains running. But the rusting carriages have long since been discarded to decay; like the skeletons of giant metal beasts.

Above us is dead farmland. Old uninhabited homesteads we picked clean in our first weeks here, endless sloping land with nothing left in its soil to grow. It'd be nice to live in those farms, but the Bloods would find us before we could even think to utter *home, sweet home*. Farther north is the city wall rearing up into the sky. The boundary of where human souls are allowed to stray. We lived beyond that wall last year, way out west, but we dare not now – not with thousands of Furies waiting out there for us.

Luke and I head now to a place we named the arena. We have to climb almost to the surface to reach it.

The kids are gathered and waiting when we arrive. A loud rabble of *boos* sounds at our tardiness.

"Yeah, yeah," Luke laughs. "Positions."

The arena is a massive water silo, long since abandoned like everything else in this rural area. It's as wide as a city block and four floors high. We've drilled tiny holes into its roof to allow natural sunlight to stream in, plus we built seats up around its edges. Spectators can watch our training bouts from above like in one of the old coliseums.

This training session belongs to the kids. Not only the few who survived the Fury attack on the Inferno, but those we plucked from the city above. A month ago we destroyed a holding facility containing a dozen fifteen-year-olds waiting to be given the cure. They've all dealt with it differently, being snatched from their lives and their families. Some pine for home, others haven't missed it for a second. But they are all, without exception, in agreement: not a single one of them would choose to return to a city that would cure them of their feelings.

Luke starts running the warm-up on the mats. I spot Teddy standing apart from the others and walk over to him. "Yo."

"Hey." His fist clenches. I've noticed he does this a lot.

"You should participate, Teddy."

"I can't." He's small and wiry. At fourteen he looks twelve. But there's something interesting hiding beneath his surface, a mind ravenous for knowledge. Most of the time I find him tucked in a corner with his nose in a book, or tapping away at the computers in our tech room.

"It'll keep you alive."

"I wasn't built for this."

We watch the scuffling teenagers throw each other about on the mats. I should force Teddy to join in, but I don't have the heart to. I sort of know what he means. None of us should have been built for this but I guess we were, some more than others.

I get Teddy to help me with the drums. Since the cello Luke and his father Tobias built me was such a hit, they have taken to building more instruments. I requested a couple of drums for the training sessions and Tobias worked painstakingly until they were perfect. Together Teddy and I make a beat on the bongos and as the thumping sounds fill the silo I feel the energy lift. Luke and I worked out last year that music is a good way to help you get out of your head and into your body. Sometimes it's the best way to learn to fight. I still remember the bruises I had from those first few months with him and don't envy these kids. The least I can do is whack some drums for them.

Luke giggles as two boys – Alo and Lawrence – attack him simultaneously and try to wrestle him to the ground. He flips them both onto their backs and crows with victory.

Henrietta asks him to show her the floor work and I roll my eyes. She's sixteen, her hormones are running rampant and she fancies herself madly in love with Luke. He wisely gets Will to show her, much to her disappointment. Meanwhile poor Will hops to the task eagerly: everyone in the tunnels can see how much he adores her, except Henrietta herself. Oh, the delights of adolescence.

Teddy and I pound away, making up new and more complicated beats. We glance at each other and grin. I like the boy and it's not rocket science to figure out why: he's an outsider even amongst the outsiders.

"Do you miss your family?" I ask after a while.

Mutely he shakes his head.

"Why not?"

There's a long silence. "They forgot how to love anyone but themselves."

I sigh. "Do you miss above?"

Another head shake. A hesitation. "I like it down here. Except for training."

"Would you get rid of training?"

"No. I'm not a complete moron. But I think we need more classes."

I consider this. We recently set up a few classes for the kids. We only teach what we can, of course. I give classes on history because I can remember reading a bunch of it. Tobias runs a workshop on building and engineering. His wife Claire does first aid. Brigit and Luke run the cooking shifts and Pace does a very rudimentary class on basic science with the occasional guest appearance from bio-chemist Dodge, who mostly just ends up further confusing everyone.

"What would you add?"

"Computer sciences? Basic IT training? Chemistry, mathematics, physics, philosophy, economics—"

I snort. "And will you be the one kidnapping university lecturers from above to teach these classes or will I?"

He shrugs. "I could. Teach, I mean."

I look at him properly and forget to keep drumming. "Seriously?"

Teddy blushes and can't look at me. His fist clenches. "A bit, at least. It's gotta be better than nothing. I don't really want to be surrounded by a new society made up entirely of moronic thugs who only know how to beat each other up."

"Gee, thanks."

"Not you."

I smile. "Okay. You're on. Write up a proposal for the classes you want to teach and I'll set them up for you."

He ducks his head but the edges of his lips curl. "You, too. You could be doing more than you are."

My eyebrows arch. "I can't remember the last time I had five seconds to myself but it's really gratifying to know I come across as a lazy ass."

"Just with your class, I mean."

"How so?"

"You tell us facts. Heaps and heaps of facts. And don't get me wrong, it's pretty cool that you can remember them all. But nobody else can – not when they aren't applicable to anything. And anyway what good are facts about the past unless you're using them to help plan the future?"

"Whose plan would that be?"

"Yours."

"Why mine?"

"Because you're the leader of the resistance."

"But why should I be teaching my plan to anyone?"

He frowns. "You want it to be secret?"

"No, Teddy, what I mean is – shouldn't you be allowed to develop your own opinions on what future life should contain?"

"Yeah, but you aren't challenging us to do that either. Have you even been to one of your classes? You just bang on about the dates of this invasion and that war and when the vaccinations for polio or Spanish flu were discovered. Half the kids sleep through it."

I belatedly return to drumming. "You make me feel very inadequate sometimes, Teddy."

He chuckles and ducks his head.

"*Excusez-moi*," Luke interrupts us. "But would the two of you kindly get your backsides up here?"

"We're on music duty."

"Training duty trumps music duty. Come on."

I jump up and pull a reluctant Teddy behind me. "See? Philistine," he mutters, then makes his body go limp so I have to drag him onto the mats. By the time we've made it the other kids are all laughing. Training isn't particularly rigorous today.

*

March 3rd, 2067

Josephine

I walk through the dark tunnels and listen to the sound of my boots clipping softly on the ground. I listen to the *drip drip drip* echoing off every surface and the endless *scratch scratch scratching*. My skin prickles but I'm not sure why. My senses feel heightened. I can smell so much, all things I never thought to even have a scent. The air is unusually hot and it makes me imagine that the tunnel surrounding me has slipped incongruously down through the layers of the earth to its center without any of us noticing. We shall soon burn.

When I reach the arena my kids are here, all thirty-two of them. They're training with gusto, the raucous explosion of limbs a frenzied thing. As I look more closely I start to see that their faces don't look quite right. One has the bloodstained muzzle of a lion, another has the enormous liquid black eyes of a seal. I turn to see a long gray elephant's trunk curling from the nose of a boy and the sharply curved beak of an eagle where a girl's mouth should be. From them come rabid snarls or monkey screeches or the call of a hooting owl. I watch feathers ruffle and scales ripple and fur scatter as terrible claws rake. They are beasts grappling and fighting all around me. I will them away but they grow wilder, the noise swelling until it forces me to my knees—

*

I wake disoriented. Quiet reigns. Except … The snarling is still there. As consciousness slowly returns I recognize it as the distant sound of the ever-present Furies. I roll onto my back and stare at the ceiling, which I can't actually see in such heavy dark. Luke's body is too warm beside mine so I disentangle his limbs from me and throw off the sheet. I can't stop listening to the creatures at our doors, *tap tap tapping* to be let in.

"We have to do something about them," I murmur. "We can't live like this."

Luke makes a muffled *huh* sound.

"Pest control."

"Go back to sleep."

But I can't. Because on top of the snarling scratching hissing there's another sound, even more grating. "Is that dripping?"

"Josi, no. Just ignore it."

"Those little bastards!" I'm up and reaching for the lighter so I can light the gas lamp on the floor at my side. It illuminates a small circle, in which I can see Luke groaning and burying his head under the pillow.

I climb off the awful homemade mattress on the floor and pull a pair of track pants over my undies, then I carry my lamp out into the tunnels. Sure enough, when I reach the lavatories I find that the hose has been left trickling a steady stream. When we first got here we built rows of pit-toilets over an opening that drops down into a lower tunnel, into which we do our business. But you don't want that getting too full, for painfully obvious reasons, so we have to come in here every now and then and burn it all away. Only problem with that is the ventilation, so we use the same process we use for some of the cooking fires: a system of smoke flutes that divide and spread the smoke up through the ground at various points, ensuring it doesn't ever create a plume big enough to be visible to Blood surveillance.

It reeks something fierce in here so we rigged up a flushing system to at least keep the toilet seats clean while we wait for the pits to fill up. With a roar of frustration I turn the trickling hose off at the tap and then stride into the kitchen.

I grab a huge pot and a wooden spoon (both stolen, everything is stolen, we are the princes and princesses of thievery), then I take the garlic wreath from its hanging spot above the pantry shelves. As I'm heading for the barracks I spot a second circle of light near the entrance to the arena and take a detour, curious about who might be up so late.

It's Will, of course. He has his lantern perched on a wall bracket and he's doing what he does best: painting. He doesn't notice me peering at his art. The tunnel walls are littered with his work and I feel something immense in my chest every time I glance at one. This painting, like all the others, is a sort of impressionist work of light and shade and color, and amidst all this are two willowy, skeletal figures smudged in gray. I always think of them as ghostly landscapes and though many down here find the bleakness depressing I never see anything but hope in the luminous quality of them.

"Nice."

Will jumps about a foot in fright and clutches his heart. "Jesus, Dual. Don't do that!"

"Sorry. This one's gorgeous."

I perch my chin on his shoulder and we look quietly. I imagine we are the two figures in the endless landscape of browns and grays and ochers. Earth and sky are the same and I feel us fall into both and walk and walk and walk, never able to find their end. Even though I imagine this I know it's not me at all that he paints. It is Hal. Always Hal, his truest friend, killed last year by the Furies.

"What are you doing up?"

"I'm about to interrupt your peace," I warn him.

Will laughs. "God you're relentless."

"Only because the toilet bandit is too."

"I gotta see this."

We share a grin and then I put my game face on. With my pot in hand, I march through first the boys' sleeping barracks and then the girls', whacking away and shouting at the top of my lungs. "Up! Up! Up!"

There is a chorus of horrified groans. I don't let up until every one of the brats is out of bed and following me into the arena.

"Line up!"

They all line up sleepily. I catch a few *what the hell* looks.

"A tap is a very simple concept," I say. "Because evolution has kindly given you opposable thumbs, you are able to twist one until the liquid stops running. Indeed, you can even twist it far enough to ensure it doesn't drip. Are we agreed that this is a task even the most pathologically distracted of you are able to complete?"

They mutter an unenthusiastic *yes*.

"So then who is the Neanderthal incapable of turning the goddamn toilet flusher off?"

No one says a word. A few of them snicker.

"Do we all remember what happened last time it didn't get turned off? The toilet overflowed and the sleeping areas got flooded with feces!"

More laughter and a few groans of memory.

"Me being the optimistic kinda girl I am assumed that this would have taught the toilet bandit a lesson, but I guess that was giving you too much credit. You've got one last chance to own up or every single one of you gets punished."

"How are we meant to know who did it?" Lawrence asks. He is *always* the first to speak, the last to shut the hell up. On his chin sits the day's five o'clock shadow, which I know drives him crazy – at sixteen he's the first of his friends to deal with the endless hair growth, and goes through more razors than the girls combined. "If we knew we were doing it, we wouldn't do it," he points out smugly.

"The clues point to a conscious decision to leave the flusher running," I reply. "Whoever the culprit is, they're premeditated and pathological." Out of the corner of my eye I can see that some of the adults have risen from bed to watch in amusement. Luke is leaning against the opening of the silo with folded arms and a smile. I feel momentarily guilty for having woken them with my pot bashing but return to the problem at hand.

"Come on. Step forward and be cleansed by the truth. We're not leaving until someone does."

A few murmurs and rustles go through the group and then finally Coin steps forward. We call him Coin because he's the best pickpocket around – he can pinch you anything you want without a soul being the wiser.

"It was me," he sighs, brushing his long blond hair behind his ear as his neuroses demands he must every time he speaks.

"Hallelujah! Why?"

"Because it grosses me out. Those toilets are never clean enough."

"He's got OCD," Malia giggles. "Ligit." She is tiny, a human in miniature, and she's also Coin's girlfriend. The two of them spend all of two seconds a day not glued to each other's mouths.

I raise my hands to the sky. "Yessssss!" The month-long mystery is solved and now I can return to being a normal human being. I sink to my knees and hug Coin around the waist fervently. He rolls his eyes and starts laughing and then so is everyone else as I lay the garlic wreath around his neck.

"I dub you King of the Crapper. You get toilet duty for a week. Everyone give it up for the King!"

A mighty cheer goes up and two of the other boys lift Coin onto their shoulders. I jog over and switch on the ancient iPod and speakers.

"Can we go back to bed now?" Henrietta asks.

"Screw bed. Let's dance!"

Suddenly the silo is filled with the thumping base of a dance track. The kids give another cheer and immediately everyone is dancing, including the adults. I am immersed in a sea of moving limbs. We love to dance here in the tunnels. We take every opportunity we can get, even if it's the middle of the night, even if it's first thing in the morning, or right in the middle of building something or cooking something or punching something.

In this sea I am reminded of my dream. And though compared to some of the nightmares I've had it ranks pretty low on the creepy scale, I feel inexplicably disturbed by it. If I half close my eyes I can almost see the flap of a set of wings or the flick of a furry whisker or the dart of a long reptilian tongue.

Hands take my waist and Luke is behind me and we dance close. He holds his watch up to show me the time. 12:32. Into my ear he says, "Happy birthday, kid."

Today I turn twenty-two, and for once I just want to act my age. So we dance all night because why not?

*

September 22nd, 2067

Josephine

My veins are empty. The percentage of fluid that is meant to make up a human body is on average sixty. I think I have dropped well below that. I think I might be steadily drying out and very soon I will be at zero percent. I will be a shriveled husk of a creature preparing to become dust, the very same as what she is lying upon. I will dissolve into the ground and the sky. Into a world of endless, endless dust.

When my eyes worked better I saw dust in every direction. When I could taste I tasted it in my mouth and nose. When I could hear more than the sluggish thump of my slow heart I heard it swirling on currents of wind. My skin, now too raw to distinguish sensations, felt the dust flick and press and coat it. There's no water left in this world. There is certainly none left in me. My mindless mind takes up residence in the ocean but I don't have the imagination to keep even it filled. Instead it turns swiftly to a dry bed of salt.

I am done. Turned inside out and wrung dry. I'm at my end and I have no power to forestall it any longer.

The hands that appear above me are unfathomable miracles. They trickle fresh cool water into my parched mouth and somehow I am returning to the edge of life once more. I can't make sense of it until I see the eyes above and recognize that every blood vessel in them has burst. The red of them is the brightest thing in this yellow gray world.

The red is how I remember where I am.

And I wish simply that I'd been left to die after all.

*

March 3rd, 2067

Josephine

I groan aloud and lick my cracked lips. My mouth feels like it hasn't tasted water in weeks but has instead devoured something foul and furry.

"Water," I croak.

I hear the jarring sound of Luke's laughter as he holds a cup to my lips. I drink greedily and slump back on my pillow.

"Whyyyyyyyy."

"Not feeling too hot today, are we?"

"If you even so much as think smug thoughts I will kill you."

He laughs again and passes me some painkillers for my pounding head. I manage to sit up slightly.

"Think you'll puke?"

"Don't say puke."

"Knock knock!" someone says loudly from the entrance to our little bedroom. Pace is the culprit.

"Shhhhhh."

"Happy birthday, you look like rubbish," she says cheerfully. Glimpsing the amount of metal piercings in her face makes my eyes sore. "I'm here to make a deposit."

Luke jumps up to receive the small child. Pace spends a moment kissing her son's cheeks then waves to us. "See ya, losers."

"You're welcome," I mutter. "She better not be off on another date."

"With who? She's already slept with every unattached human of the male variety in the tunnels."

"And one or two of the non-male variety."

Luke carries Hal to the bed and lays him between us. I kiss his chubby fingers happily, instantly feeling a million times better.

"I'm sure he's part Viking," Luke says. Hal is enormous for his age and has a mane of thick blond hair. Just like his father. Luke's large hand rests on the boy's chest, feeling the heartbeat.

"Can we steal him? Pace wouldn't mind too much, right?"

"Nah. I don't think she's very attached."

The birthday celebrations got particularly rowdy last night. I got carried away because I've been pretending not to mind that a certain person isn't here. Not that I could care less about birthdays. But down here it's impossible to ignore when someone's missing.

I clear my throat. "I think it's time to get Shadow."

Luke shakes his head. "We don't have the intel. Surveillance needs another month at least. Nor do we have any of the equipment."

"So we'll get the equipment and make do with the intelligence we have."

"We gotta wait, Josi. It's not like other missions. It's a death trap."

I meet Luke's green eyes. "We've waited six months already. We can keep waiting and waiting forever and it might never make a difference. We have actionable information now."

He watches me intently in that assessing way of his. I'm not sure what he sees. Besides a revoltingly hung-over newly twenty-two-year-old.

After a while he just says, "Trust me, not yet."

So I nod and I trust him.

*

Will has a gift for me, despite clear rules to the contrary. He's picked it up on one of his missions above, and when I see it I gasp aloud. It's an ancient looking book on birds called *Migrations*.

Once upon a time there were birds in the world. It was they who delivered a plague that wiped out most of the world's population. It was birds who then died of the same thing, one after the other, and if any survived they were shot down in fear, every single one, every single species.

All but the chickens, because our appetite for them outweighed even our fear of plague.

Once upon a time there were birds in the world but now the only ones that remain are locked in cages and then eaten.

Will opens this precious book and eagerly shows me a section on the migration paths of wild geese, reading aloud about how geese fly in a V formation. Because their leader must cut the path for the others through the air currents, they work harder than the rest and allow the others to fly in the slipstreams they create. After a long shift at the front, the leader falls back and the freeloaders migrate to the front of the V to take over the more difficult work. They can travel huge distances like this, working together in a cycle. Or, they could, when they were still alive.

"There's heaps of cool stuff in here like that," Will says, closing the book and handing it to me.

"I love it." And I do. Even if it makes me sad.

There's a feast to celebrate. I had no idea but it was obvious everyone was acting shiftily. The eating tunnel is long and narrow and slightly curved. We don't usually eat together because there isn't enough room, but tonight everyone crams in to present me with a massive flan-type thing that looks like a cake but isn't, of course, because we can't cook a cake. Luke's done an awfully good job with whatever this creation is. They sing me happy birthday and cheer when I blow out the candles and it's very sweet but I can't shake this awful nagging feeling in my chest that I'd hoped this year would finally be the year I got to spend with family, at least one member of it. It's ungenerous and ungrateful but I really, really want my dad.

"You okay?" Luke murmurs in my ear as Claire starts dividing the long flan into enough portions to give everyone a taste. Actually, it may be more of a smell than a taste, but still.

I nod and smile.

Lawrence, Alo, and Coin have made up a song to sing me while Malia accompanies them (quite poorly) on the guitar. It contains lots of jokes about my so-called obsession with toilets.

Afterwards I play my cello. I pluck the strings and fill the tunnels with bluegrass. Sara plays her fiddle and Henrietta her recorder and despite wanting newer electronic music the kids all seem to forget how old these songs are and instead just enjoy them.

Twang, go my strings, deep and vibrating. The music is lively but my bass notes feel heavy. As I play I watch Luke and his parents. He sits between them and all three are tapping their feet. He says something that makes them both smile. Tobias' hands shake and his son reaches over to take them in his own, to squeeze them tight as though he can gentle them still. The sight makes me ache. Just as the sight of Hal in Pace's arms does. She is dancing with him, spinning him around and bouncing him to the beat. There's this thing in her now that seems to cry out in sweet freedom. He has unburdened her somehow from whatever difficulties her life held.

I watch them all and I play and I feel lonely. I shouldn't. I have so much. So much life and love and friendship. A few short years ago I was truly alone but now I'm surrounded by people and I've never felt so lonely and it's such a sick thing, a hateful thing. I don't understand it.

I don't think I was built to be happy and the thought makes me ashamed.

When we finish I duck out to go to the bathroom and instead make my way blindly back to my room. I sit on the edge of my lumpy mattress in the dark and relive those last moments.

I've done this a thousand times. Remembered the exact look in my father's eyes as he held Falon Shay to the ground and shouted at me to go, *go*! And Luke pulling me out of that building and into the chaos of the night in time to escape the explosion that should have killed him. Might have killed him. But if the minister got free then maybe Shadow did too. Maybe, maybe, maybe.

I asked him once if he had family and he said he had, a lifetime ago. A wife and a daughter, both dead. I wonder now as I do every damn day why he thought me dead. How did the events that brought me alone to a rough dirt road near the wall when I was two unfold? How could it be that my mother was the wife of the Prime Minister, and why does that minister think Shadow murdered her? How did she die, and why didn't Shadow take me with him when he left for the west? There are way too many questions and they're making me crazy. I'm lost in them, when I shouldn't be lost at all, I should be found.

I rest my head in my hands. That's how I am when I hear Luke lighting a match. He climbs onto the bed and sits behind me, threading his arms around my shoulders and waist. His lips find my hairline, my jaw, my ear.

"I can't watch you like this any longer. Let's get Shadow back."

I swallow. "We don't have the intel, or the equipment. I can't ask you to do it."

"But you're going, aren't you?"

I nod slowly. His question makes clear something I hadn't quite realized myself. I am going, of course I am. "It's smarter for you to stay here. You're too needed to risk."

Luke tilts my face so we're looking at each other in the candlelight. He smiles a little. *How silly you are*, this smile says. *You go, I go*, it murmurs.

It feels as it did the first time I loved him. How does this happen? This endless maddening ardent love? How could it still feel like those first frenzied days or weeks or months? After all these years and all these lies I still adore him to distraction. When I was a child I was experimented on and made a slave to the violence of the blood moon. Once a year adrenalin flooded me and ravaged my body and nearly killed it. This feels the same. This feels like too much intensity to handle, like it must surely eat away at me and leave me destroyed.

My mouth finds his and I taste him. His hands pull at me, at my soul, removing me from my clothes and my sadness.

"This is going to kill us both one day." I'm not sure if I've said it or thought it or wished it or dreaded it.

Luke pulls away to look at my face. His hand takes my chin, then gently encircles my throat. His eyes hold the same thing that's in my chest and he understands, he feels it too and he's a creature from my dream, one of the wildest ones.

Chapter 3

December 16th, 2067

Dave

I'm a piece of wood that was once twisted and gnarled through with knots and dips and grooves and edges. I had sharpness and smoothness and roughness. A living breathing throbbing thing. I was ugly but I was beautiful in my ugliness. Gloriously, beautifully ugly.

Now I have been sanded down until there is only smooth. I am evenly surfaced and weighted and round. I am perfect. A sphere of wood dropped into a tiny tank of water and left to peer out through the slow blur and wonder what's on the other side of the glass.

*

The girl is wild. I know it instinctively because I know she's all the things I'm not. Her calm is as far from mine as fire is to smoke. Seemingly so close, so similar, and yet formed of a completely different elemental makeup.

My brother sits somewhere in between, or perhaps he's not even on the same spectrum: he has no calm whatsoever.

He is a beating heart without ribs for protection. Without muscle or even skin.

We follow and do as the girl says. As Luke's *wife* says. She gets us free and through the city to a safe house I have no idea how they managed to obtain. Her capabilities are immense and she is seemingly without compassion for human life. Or at least for Blood life, these soldiers of the Ministers, men and women made more deadly than any on the planet. There's no difference between them and us, in truth – they are just people, after all – but maybe she doesn't know that yet.

I'm weak and Luke is flagging after having been so consistently drugged for three months. There are others in her group – resisters, presumably – but they flit in and out of our vision and then disappear entirely. All of a sudden Luke and the girl and I are alone in a small living room. I peer around at the dark, windowless space. Outside her people will be sweeping and watching for any danger, keeping the safe house safe. I know this instinctively, not because I know anything about rebel groups or sweeping and watching or keeping safe houses safe.

I see Luke try to hold the woman but she removes herself from his touch and turns to me.

"Who's this?"

"I'm Dave," I say, when Luke doesn't.

She looks at her husband. He doesn't even have to nod for her to understand that yes, it's the Dave he's mentioned, the brother Dave.

Her face shifts. It was lovely in its ferocity but now as she smiles a true smile it becomes beautiful. I feel no stirrings of desire, not even the base, primitive ones most people left in the world would feel when faced with beauty of this nature. Warm, tugging beauty.

I offer her my hand but she hugs me instead. I return the hug easily and hold her as tightly as she holds me. When she lets go I let go. She looks at me without blinking so I look at her without blinking.

Here is the secret to human behavior: not emotion, but mimicry.

"It's an honor to meet you," she says softly. Her voice sounds scratchier than it might once have been. Maybe whatever cut her throat damaged her vocal chords. "I've heard a lot about you."

Luke is crying again, I see. He wasn't a crier as a child. I can't remember him ever shedding a tear beyond the age of about three but he has wept almost consistently since we met. It stirs something, but only very vaguely, like an awareness of pity, perhaps. I know I don't wish for his pain – in fact I would go to great lengths to prevent it, I think – but I can't detect anything that goes beyond that.

This has become a daily exercise for me. The cataloguing of emotions, motivations and thoughts. An intellectual process of understanding what I am capable of now, and perhaps what kind of thing I am in general.

"You're his wife," I say belatedly.

"Josephine Luquet."

I must be exuding some kind of confusing blankness because Luke takes the opportunity to explain about my three cures.

She doesn't react at first. It doesn't seem to sink in. Then she says very softly, "Love?"

Luke nods. I watch the look that passes between them.

"Impossible," Josephine says. "No injection can cure love." There is a short silence and then she adds, "Only life can do that."

Limerence

*

Some time later her eerie-colored eyes fall on me. This time there is none of the genuine joy with which she learned my identity. This time she is like the wolf with whom she shares her heterochromia.

"Why were you put in the cell with Luke?"

"I don't know."

She doesn't believe me. "We need to search you for trackers."

Luke doesn't protest. He lifts my shirt over my head and tosses it in the corner, then runs his fingers over every inch of my chest and arms, looking in my armpits and through my hair, inside my mouth and nostrils and even my eyes. Next he tells Josi to turn around so he can search my legs and groin. I don't feel any embarrassment but I can tell that he does. He hands me a clean set of clothes to change into and then Josi runs a hand-held piece of tech around my body to look for anything inserted under the skin. It comes up clean.

We sleep, or at least pretend to. I lie awake and listen to them whispering to each other in the dark.

"It's too risky to take him below. There's no way it isn't some kind of trap."

"I'm not leaving him up here."

She doesn't reply at first, then says, "I'm happy for you. I am. But he's dangerous."

"He'd tell me if there was a plan."

"He might not know about it."

"Come closer. Why am I not touching you?"

I hear something moving.

"Josi. What's going on? Where did you get these wounds?"

"I'm fine."

I can feel the tension in the air. It makes me uncomfortable and I find myself slipping into a memory of Livvy. I think of her often, my ex-girlfriend, the one who was scoured clean of her heart and soul by the very same cure that makes me calm. I think of her now just to see if my heart will stutter back into beat but it never does.

Only life can do that.

Pity swells in my teeth. Poor Luke. It may not be obvious to him yet but it is to me: while he wasn't looking his wife fell out of love with him.

*

December 17th, 2067

Luke

It's a slow process getting back to our tunnels. One of the first things we did was set up protocol to ensure no one follows us or happens to witness us vanishing below ground, which means going in the opposite direction to where we live. We head to an aqueduct in the heart of the drug-fucked suburb, the Crimes-Are-Us suburb, a place so rife with basic human crumminess that it's perfect for hiding our comings and goings. Only problem is that this is the kind of place where if you blink too slowly you get stabbed for no conceivable reason. Once we're below ground it's a matter of following the tunnels home. We've set up cage doors and alarm systems at intervals to notify us if one section has been breached by Furies, and there are fail-safes to ensure that no more than one section could go at a time. The rest of the group Josi brought to rescue me is made up of six resistance members, and they've divided into two groups that will stagger their journey. Basically it's a big pain in the butt to get home, but I couldn't be happier to be free.

Once we're below, Josi opens each gate by scanning her prints and retinas. We make our way slowly beneath the expanse of city, avoiding the rats and listening for any sign of Furies. There shouldn't be any in the tunnels we've cleared for travel but it's better to be safe than sorry. Moving in the dark is second nature to Josi and me after a year underground, but I can hear Dave stumbling and tripping like he secretly got wasted before the journey.

At about halfway it's safe to use the motorbikes chained at one of the gates. The noise won't be heard above but if there are Furies nearby it'll definitely alert them to where we are. Every time I silently pray to the universe for the gates to hold firm, I feel my heart rate rise. One of these days, surely, one of the gates will give, and after the nightmare of the Inferno, when Furies stormed our compound and killed hundreds, I am filled with dread at the thought. All we can do is keep checking and fortifying our defenses.

Josi and I take a bike each and Dave hops on behind me. He feels too light as we whizz through the tunnel. My mind races ahead to imagine how Mom and Dad will react to this. I need to give them some kind of warning. I can't predict how their cures will allow them to feel.

I don't think about how Josi's behaving toward me. I don't.

It happens with about three miles left to go. I'm glancing down at the stretch of ground illuminated by my bike's headlight when I hear an engine rev. My eyes shoot up to witness Josi skidding her bike wildly around a turn. The wheels fly out from under her and she hits the ground sideways. I lose sight of her around the bend and hammer my brakes on without losing my own grip on the wet ground. Water flies up from beneath me in a great arc. Then I'm around the bend in time to see Josi disappear between the wall and her bike.

My heart lurches but I'm moving without thought. I angle my headlight at her before I stop the bike and jump off. Dave is slower to dismount and I have to make sure I don't drop the heavy thing on him before I dash over to Josi.

She's already crawling her way out of the wreckage. "Furies," she pants.

I immediately spin to check our surrounds but I can't see or hear any. I frown and jog back the way we came, to the bend where Josi wiped out. If she says she saw something then she saw something. Only I can't work out what as I listen. There are no footsteps approaching nor are there the growls they emit when attacking. There's just that cold, eerie stillness of the tunnels.

I jog back to see Dave helping Josi out from under the bike. She looks beat up and bruised but on high alert, her gun already aimed into the dark.

"What—" Dave starts but Josi hisses at him to be quiet. She has her eyes closed.

Without opening them she swings her gun directly overhead and fires twice. Sparks rain from the metal but it works – we hear the distinct scuffle of many sets of feet in the tunnel above.

"Yep, there's a crapload of them," she comments. "How the hell did they get in there?"

"I dunno but we gotta warn the others," I say. In the group behind us is Will, Blue and Henrietta, and if those Furies find the opening farther along then this tunnel will be swarming in no time.

"You take Dave ahead and I'll scout back to reroute them," she says.

"We don't split up." That's the rule. We have teams for a reason and she knows it.

Her eyes dart to Dave pointedly. I know what she's saying – in terms of safety he's pretty much a burden rather than an asset. But what my eyes say is even simpler: you go, I go. Dave'll be alright. He's a Townsend and we don't go down easy.

Before either one of us can cave the sound of the second group of motorbikes roars down the tunnel.

Fuck. Our bikes are directly around the curve. There's zero visibility and this corner's already a death trap. Josi and I sprint to haul our motorbikes out of the way but hers is mangled so badly it's difficult to maneuver. Before I can shout at her to leave it Will's bike zooms around the curve, clipping its back wheel on Josi's. The boy goes flying over his handlebars like he's been shot out of a cannon. Meanwhile his bike flattens Josi's and scrapes it along the wall of the tunnel at high speed. For the second time in minutes she is dragged along somewhere between them, showered in red sparks and billowing smoke.

And that's when the ceiling caves in, raining Furies upon us.

In the chaos I see that Henrietta and Blue have managed to stop their bikes in time to avoid yet another collision. I grab Dave and shove him behind me, trying to peer through to where Will hit the ground. Thankfully he's struggling woozily to his feet, badly banged up but not dead, not dead.

Josi isn't moving.

"Don't let go of the back of my shirt," I bark at Dave and then start fighting my way through to her. My fist smashes skulls and jaws and shoulders and ribs. I hit anything moving – Jesus, there must be at least fifty of them and I've never felt so bone-weary. Whatever shit they pumped me with yesterday has decided to take this moment to make my limbs weigh an extra thousand pounds.

Bullets explode from barrels. We don't fire guns in the tunnels unless as a last resort. Too much risk of them either ricocheting, accidentally hitting one of us or drawing more Furies to the fun. But they're sure as hell being fired right now, which means someone is panicking.

I reach Josi and haul a Fury off the bike pinning her. She's awake and looking up at me calmly. "Deal with them."

I want to get her out but I don't have time so I do as she says. Thrusting Dave out of the way I use the long hunting knife Josi passes me to slash through the carotids of every Fury I face. The bullets are still hailing chaotically and there's a very real possibility that one of them is about to pop through my head.

Behind us the third group of resisters arrives and their weapons finish off the remaining Furies.

But someone's still firing.

I look over to see Henrietta sending bullet after bullet into the already dead bodies piled before her. I skirt around behind her and say her name loudly. She doesn't answer so I reach swiftly for the gun, forcing it down and twisting her wrist so she's forced to drop it.

"Hey," I say, taking her face and forcing her dazed eyes to me. "It's over. You're okay."

She nods shakily and I let her go. Blue and Eric are hauling Josi out from beneath the bikes. Her feet give out beneath her and she nearly hits the ground before they catch her by the arms. Dave watches them calmly, apparently unbothered by the fight. Will is leaning against the wall with his eyes closed – he's in pain but I have to check on my wife first.

"Jose, you okay?"

She nods but her teeth are gritted tight and there's sweat beading her forehead.

"What's the damage?"

"Left leg."

I look and see a gruesome gash along her thigh. Blood has already pooled around her foot.

"Seen worse," Blue comments, because he's a dickhead and all he ever says are very dickheadish things.

"I'm good," she says briskly. "Let's move out. Will, you good?"

He nods. Henrietta has managed to gather herself and is now supporting him. I don't know what his injuries are but I hope he can make it home. "Blue, get Will home on a bike," I order.

Blue settles the smaller boy on behind him and revs off into the dark. It's a measure of how out of it he must be that Will doesn't argue.

"Josi, you ride too."

She shakes her head. "Can't bend it enough to ride."

"I don't want you walking on it. Eric and Alo, can you carry her?"

Josi ignores that and sets off, brushing past Eric and Alo as they offer to lift her. I can see how badly it costs her to walk but she does so without a sound.

"There's nothing to prove!" I protest. She knows that – we don't do more than we can because it's a quick way to endanger yourself and others. We ask for help. We rely on each other. But Josi just walks off alone into the dark, leaving the rest of us to hurry after. She leaves a trail of blood that seems to get thicker and darker as we walk.

Something really messed up has happened to her. What scares me is that I can't remember if I should know what it is.

In my head there's a whole chunk of time missing from when I got captured. From around the blood moon.

*

Dave

One of the things that remains is intellect. Another is instinct. Logic, reason, problem-solving. And survival. The survival instinct is the most intact, oddly. I feel it all the time in a way I never used to. Perhaps love made me complacent. Perhaps sadness made me immobile, anger made me blind.

Now I see so clearly all the endings and they are all here, under the ground. This is where creatures come to die, I am sure of it.

And fear… That never goes away. No matter how much else gets stolen.

Chapter 4

March 5th, 2067

Josi

I dream there are wolves at the door, *tap tap tapping* to be let in. But when I open it there is only a mirror. My reflection has blue and brown eyes and long, sharp teeth. The real wolf gazes back at me.

*

The preparations for the mission to rescue Shadow are underway. Luke is focused on about a million different tasks and it's impossible to get two words from him. I'm waiting on Teddy to present me with an idea he had about the tech, but that won't be for another hour or two. I check my watch and realize it's time for my history class with the dreaded teens. Truth is, I mostly feel like one of them. I certainly don't feel like an adult.

All thirty-four of them are sprawled on the mats in the arena, looking up at the spots of sunlight in the distant roof. The silo isn't particularly class-like, but it's comfortable on the mats and big enough for everyone to spread out. I join them and hesitate, thinking about how Teddy 'gently' broke the news to me that my class is boring and useless. Thanks, Teddy.

"You okay?" Will asks me. He doesn't have to attend the classes but he always does. I think his brain is as bored as mine sometimes gets. The poor guy is in that awkward place between adolescence and adulthood. He's eighteen, which makes him older than any of the other teenagers, and he's certainly a lot more experienced, but I don't think he feels like he fits in with the resistance fighters from the Inferno either. Ever since he lost Hal, and Pace had a baby to contend with, he's been at a bit of a loss. I wish I had more free time to spend with him. He's grown close with Eric, at least, Hal's ex-boyfriend, but Eric tends to get swallowed up by relationship drama.

"Yeah, I'm good," I answer. "I'm just ... Is my class boring?"

Nobody says anything.

"I'm going to infer from that awkward silence that the answer is yes."

"It's just hard to remember for normal people," Georgie assures me kindly. She's thirteen, precociously smart, and the sheer volume of the questions she asks could fill the sea. "Not that you're not normal!"

"Okay, so what can we do about it? Do you want to make it more of a conversation? Got any questions you want to ask?"

"About what?"

"Anything, really."

"Can we have more free time?" Lawrence asks, flashing a disarming smile.

"You get plenty."

"What about a holo projector? We could set it up to play movies. Make a film club."

"When I said 'anything, really' I meant 'anything, really, within the bracket of history'."

He sighs, scratching that beard of his.

"But that's a good idea," I add. "I'll look into it."

"Are we criminals?" Georgie asks abruptly.

I blink. "Well, I'd say that since every single one of our possessions is stolen – yes."

"Aside from that. Can it really be criminal to remove yourself from the politics of society? Or from society full stop?"

"Law says we have to be cured," Alo puts in morosely. "Avoiding that's the biggest felony there is." He's a very beautiful boy, a Greek renaissance painting of a young Narcissus. With golden skin and hair and pale blue eyes he's the crush of every adolescent girl in the tunnels, as well as some of the boys. Only problem is he's the most mournfully earnest creature anyone's ever met.

"Bigger than murder? Rape?" Georgie asks as though the words don't fit in her mouth.

"Apparently." He shrugs and sighs.

They look at me. This isn't really what I had in mind, but I sigh and figure that it must be what they need: someone to give them the answers straight up, without holding any punches. Or at least to challenge them to find their own answers, as Teddy put it.

I consider my response. "Once we let the rule of law reign. It was what governed each of us, even those in power. It kept us culpable, and equal – in theory. It gave us the right to elect and remove our leaders. But when those at the top no longer abided by those laws, and our power to denounce them was lost, the rule of law no longer governed us. That's what's called a totalitarian regime. It renders its citizens powerless. Which is why we had to remove ourselves from it, or our denial of their rules would have seen us killed without consequence."

"But that's so wrong," Coin says, obsessively pushing his hair behind his ear. He's taken to wearing his Crapper King garlic wreath all the time now, and he stinks. At least it's put a temporary hold on him sucking face with Malia, who refuses to go near him until he takes it off.

I nod. "I believe it is. That's why I'm here. I don't recognize their authority over me, or their right to inject me with permanently altering drugs. Which classifies me as a rebel and a threat."

"What about us? Is that what we are?"

"Fuck yeah!" Lawrence grins and a few of the others cheer.

I look at Georgie, who doesn't share their excitement. "You are whatever you choose to be. You're not here against your will. You don't have to be involved in any of our actions. You have every right to return to the city above and rejoin their society."

"And be cured."

"That's the choice. I wish I could offer you a life less dangerous, less criminal. I wish I could offer you what you deserve. But this is the only alternative I have for now. It's yours if you want it."

She nods and turns thoughtful. I hope she never discovers the lie I've just told her: there's no going back, not for any of them.

"Why'd they do it?" Henrietta asks and the rest of them fall silent at the pained tone of her voice. Her eyes are bordered in black kohl and peer out from beneath her jagged blond fringe. She is effortlessly stylish, even down here in the dirty pit of the world. "Why did they do this to us? To our parents?"

My chest feels heavy. She seems much younger than she usually does, trying tirelessly to seduce Luke. Now she just seems vulnerable and I have a fierce urge to protect her. All of them.

"Power and opportunity make cruel creatures of even the best of us," I say. "When the plague wiped out most of the world there was a power gap. The ministers saw it and filled it. I can't imagine they were cruel people to begin with. But the more power you have the more you want. They built a wall to protect us but it became a cage and made us unruly. We wanted out."

I see a few of their gazes dart up to the pieces of sky they can glimpse; I see the longing in every minute detail of them.

"The Ministers discovered a simple way to calm everyone down, and it must have seemed like such a good idea. Just keep them all calm. It's better for them, for us, for everyone. But forcing someone to be calm is the ruination of them. Calm is a choice – real calm means peace, not emptiness. By taking parts of us they made us into the kinds of creatures we have never been, not even in the very beginning of humanity when we were wild things evolving to possess logic and reason and inference capabilities. Even before all of that we had feeling: it was vital to our survival because without it we couldn't have evolved."

I look around at each of their faces and realize they are listening more intently than they ever have.

"But isn't it true that by removing emotion we have higher mental capabilities?" Alo asks.

I shake my head. "In the era of the Romantics it was believed that in reason versus emotion, the wise chose to be ruled by their hearts. It was all the rage to be swept away by feeling. But scientists began to study the relationship between the two and it was understood that a healthier way to live was to find a harmonious balance: the mind and the heart should work together. This is when you're most intelligent, functional, the most able to seek and achieve fulfillment. They called it having 'emotional intelligence'. Psychologists understood that thinking about emotion didn't mean you had to forego feeling deeply – the twentieth century was an age of understanding things. It led to more intense exploration, until it was discovered not too long ago that it was possible for certain signals in the brain to be redirected or blocked altogether, potentially cutting off one entire facet of feeling – the ones that caused unhappiness and violence."

"It seems like a good idea until you do it," Lawrence mutters.

"So they went from one end of the spectrum to the other," little Georgie says, one of her many questions only not framed as one.

"Yep."

"But what about real medical conditions?" Alo asks. "What about people who actually need to feel less?"

"Who do you mean?"

"Well, Coin, for one."

"Hey!" Coin protests.

"Seriously, man," Alo says kindly. "Last night you were so anxious you got in and out of bed thirteen times. So is he meant to just put up with that because it's part of feeling?"

I shake my head. "Mental illness is not normal feeling. It's illness. There's a very big difference between treating an illness and shutting off an entire line of healthy emotion. Coin, I want to talk to you after class, okay?"

Coin nods glumly, flashing Alo a glare, who shrugs apologetically.

"Can we go back?" Henrietta asks. "Can we turn them back, I mean? The cured?"

I rest my elbows on my knees and lace my fingers together, biding time before I have to answer. I'm not sure what to tell her. The truth, I remind myself. "I don't know."

I see a shadow of yearning pass her pretty face. She's thinking about her parents. I see the same thing in Will's eyes as he gazes at her, or something similar, at least.

"Have you ever killed anyone?" Lawrence asks, startling me.

"What?"

"You and Luke are always off on missions with like forty guns each and sometimes you come back all wounded and sometimes you come back without as many people. What are you doing up there? Do you kill people?"

Christ, I'm starting to regret this whole venture. I rub my eyes. "We go above to get supplies. It takes a lot to run this place. And we have to steal ninety percent of it. We also go above to run resistance missions, like the one that freed you from the holding facility."

"And you fight the Bloods?" He sounds impressed.

I nod.

"Have you killed any?"

I nod again.

"No way."

They all start asking questions at the same time: How did you do it? How many? Are they scary? Aren't they meant to be impossible to fight?

"It's not glamorous. Or something to be proud of. We only kill Bloods if they're trying to kill us. And we never kill the cured."

Liar. You're a disgusting liar.

"What's the difference?" Henrietta asks. "Why's it okay to kill a Blood and not a cured person?"

I crack my knuckles. "It's not. It's just that the Bloods are the soldiers."

"So now it's a war?" Alo asks. "They never killed us. They just cured us. They kept us from getting sick. And now you go up there and make things dangerous. You're the ones who brought killing into it."

Everyone's getting impassioned but it's their right to. It's their right to be angry and to have an opinion.

I let Alo's words sit a moment and I make sure my voice is even when I respond. "Sixty-one. The number of people murdered during the scientific trials for the sadness cure. All children. All without families or homes, taken because they wouldn't be missed and then erased from records. Seventy-eight. The number dead from the trials of the anger cure. Not one of them reported or publicized." I lean forward. "They think nobody misses them but I do. *I* do. I have each of their names burned into my memory and sometimes I say them aloud."

"Okay, sorry—"

"Ten thousand: roughly the number of suicides since the cures were first administered twelve years ago in 2055. *Ten thousand* people who felt so inhuman, so lost, so *wrong* inside their own bodies that they had to get free of their skin. They had to get out and they couldn't come down here and hide from the cure. They could only die."

His face has gone very pale. None of them are moving anymore.

"You think they haven't killed because they don't tell you they've killed," I say softly. "But they have. They've killed thousands of innocent bodies, and they've killed millions of spirits."

Alo drops his eyes.

I close mine and take a breath. My hands are trembling with fury. I am a flame of it. Flashes of memory flicker through my mind, cold labs and needles and other children crying and my voice getting lost.

"You okay?" Will asks and I open my eyes to see that he's beside me.

I nod and look at the kids. "I'm angry. Sometimes I get so angry I can't breathe and sometimes I get just as sad."

Alo clears his throat and can't look at me. "Why is that such a good thing?"

"Because it's who I am. I also get really, really happy."

There's a silence. Some of them are watching me while others are lost in thought.

"I should make something clear. Killing is never the right response to killing. Just because they've used a method that causes casualties doesn't mean we should. But shit happens up there. Things are hard to predict. People are violent when they get in each other's way." I shake my head. "It comes down to how far you're willing to go to do what you think is right, and how you can justify the death to yourself. We all have to decide how much violence we can live with committing."

"How much can you live with?" Lawrence asks.

"Why do you wanna know about me so much?" I ask, exasperated.

"Because you're our leader."

"I'm one of them." By default.

"Everyone knows it's you, Josi."

I frown, unsure why this bothers me.

"So maybe stop hammering her with personal questions," Malia mutters. Lawrence rolls over and pins her down, smothering her cheeks with kisses. She grumbles and shoves him off, smoothing her red hair off her face. Instead of rising to the bait, Coin simply rolls his eyes. Thankfully the goofing has broken the tight spell we're under and I feel everyone relax a little.

"Come on, Josi, how much?"

I shoot Will a plea for help but he just shrugs. "Answer your disciples, oh wise leader."

I spread my hands. "I can live with a lot, I guess."

"Why?"

"Because I used to run, and hide, but I started to hate myself so now I fight." I shrug. "Besides, I think you only know where the line is when you cross it."

"And by then it's too late, right?" Alo asks flatly. I need to have a proper chat with him when I get back. The kid is usually pretty angsty but this is more than usual. "Where's your line? How'd you know you crossed it?"

They're not about to let me out of it. The desperate need to quantify the unquantifiable. They plead with me to make the inexplicable understandable. And I swore to myself that I would try to be honest with them, even if it's scary. You grow up fast in the tunnels with the sounds of the Furies to haunt your sleep.

Where's your line, Josephine Luquet?

"I'm not sure I have one," I admit.

*

After class I pull Coin off to the side. "You okay?"

"I'm fine." He touches his hair.

"If you need help, I'll take you up there and find you treatment." I don't know how I'll do this, but I'll be damned if I let him suffer.

"I'm okay," he promises, except there goes the hair tuck. "I just get stuck sometimes. Have to do something until it's right. But everyone helps get me out of it. Malia especially." He glances over his shoulder to see his girlfriend waiting for him, strumming her guitar very badly and winking at him.

"If it gets worse, or you just don't want to deal with it anymore, promise you'll ask me for help, okay? Promise, Coin."

"I promise! Chill!" He grins, gives me a quick peck on the cheek and then dashes off to wrestle the guitar free of Malia's hands.

"Get away from me, King Crapper," I hear her telling him as she pushes his garlic-wreathed face away from her.

Will and I walk to the tech room together. We're quiet until we pass by one of his paintings. The colors of this one are deep reds and burnt oranges and it always, always makes me stop to look. There are five figures instead of two. I'd never dare ask who they are, but I secretly hope they're us. Will, Hal, Pace, Luke and me. Lost in the land on fire. Our lamps throw flickering light and shadows over it, bringing it to life.

Will laughs a little. "How you do indulge me."

"I'm not! I stop here even when I'm not with you."

"Come on, dual-eyes." He grabs my hand and swings it like I'm a two-year-old. "That was a really good class."

"They didn't learn anything about history."

"They learned a lot about life."

As I ponder this he adds, "You know I'm coming above with you, right?"

I smile at him. "Thank Christ for that."

*

"Check it!" Luke grins as we enter. The tech room is narrow and dark. We don't light it because of the danger of open flames, and because there's enough light emitted from the multiple flashing screens. The stolen tech in this room could run a 747. This is where most of our generator's power is used – here, the infirmary and the kitchen. I have no idea how anything in this room works. I do know we have surveillance on a bunch of places above, and use wirelessly connected networks to open doors we're not supposed to and read information that isn't ours. Luke's pretty good with the tech and Will has always been great, but the real genius among us is fourteen-year-old Teddy.

What Luke is imploring me to check are contact lenses. I'm impressed even before he makes me put them in my eyes – contact lenses were ruled illegal years ago so I have no idea where they got these. The real excitement happens when I blink them into place. What I'm looking at – Luke's grin – flashes up onto a large holo screen before us.

"Woah."

I move my eyes to Teddy and there's two of him in the room.

"For starters," Teddy explains, "they give you normal looking eyes. But the fun bit is that we're able to see everything you see. Plus they're programmed to deliver information to the scanners, so if you get scanned they won't know who you are."

Teddy hands me a tablet with the information of my false identity. As I look down at it, it flashes onto the screen in my peripherals and makes me dizzy.

"Ugh, this is disorienting. Can I take them out?"

Once they're safely back in their case Teddy shows me what else he's managed to create and program: fake fingerprints.

"You're the gadget man from a Bond movie!" I laugh.

"What's a Bond movie?" Luke asks.

"Oh, boy. You're in for a treat when we get home."

"The prints," Teddy prompts. "We only have one for each of your thumbs so don't let any of your other fingers get scanned."

"And two for Luke?"

"Nope. Just two."

I look at Luke. Things just got scarier. "So where am I going that needs fake prints and irises?"

"A party."

"Come again?"

Luke changes the feed and suddenly we're looking at a large map projected onto the wall. "This is the Gates. A walled community designed for the ministers and their families—"

"I know what the Gates is. Everyone does."

Luke clears his throat. "It's more professional if I do a general summary of the mission, so if you could not interrupt me in the middle that would really help, thanks."

I hide a smile. "Sorry."

"*As I was saying.* Most of the members of the Gates don't ever leave. There are at least fifty Bloods on guard at all times, security is very tight and almost impossible to penetrate. Sometimes high-profile prisoners are kept within a facility there – this is where a lot of scientific experimentation is also carried out. As we know, Falon Shay hated Shadow for personal reasons, so it seems plausible that he'd have him detained in a place he could come and go from without fear of the resistance."

"Well done. What's the plan?"

"On Saturday night the ministers are holding an annual event. We're going to place you inside, under the cover of that event, Josi."

"Okay, to do what?"

"To access Shay's personal security information, which we'll need to locate Shadow. Once you've relayed it to us we can infiltrate and get him out."

I frown, peering at the map. "So … wait, the event is at his house? That seems risky of him."

"To him discretion is more important than the risk."

"Why? What's the party for?"

"It's for him and the other ministers to act like a bunch of assholes."

"Huh?"

"They bring in a bunch of cured women to entertain them."

"Ew."

"Yep."

"How do you know this?"

"I went to one, after I was made a gray."

My face crinkles in revulsion. It hits me belatedly. The obvious reason I'm the only one going in. "You want me to be one of those women?"

Luke nods. "I know it's gross, but it's a prime opportunity. Our team will be there, surrounding the perimeter. I'll be in your ear the whole time and we'll see what you see. I can't go with you because a lot of those guys would recognize me."

"Won't I be recognized too?" Shay knows exactly what I look like.

"We're working on that," Teddy assures me.

Luke points to a section of the map. "I'll be close the whole time, in these underwater tunnels, waiting to give you a way out."

"So I find Shadow and take him to meet you there?"

Luke shakes his head. "We can't get him out on Saturday – we're just getting his location. Then we regroup and work out how to extract him another day."

"But I'll be *inside*. We won't have that opportunity again."

Luke's eyes narrow. "How are you meant to locate and retrieve him on your own, Josi?"

"I'll figure that out while I'm in there."

"No way. Poorly planned, improvised missions go down in flames and get everyone killed. Just be patient. We'll get there eventually."

I sigh. "Okay, so I go in posing as an emotionless whore for a bunch of creepy lechers and sneak around until I stumble upon top secret information, and then I have to – what, avoid them for the rest of the night until I get dismissed? This is sounding a bit ridiculous, gang."

The second I get sent in there I'll be accosted by a bunch of dirty old dudes who want to do god knows what with me, and the likelihood of me being able to avoid that is low, by the sounds of the security involved.

Luke stares at me and the same thing obviously occurs to him because he says, "Yeah, true. Let's plan for another night."

"Hang on, I didn't mean that. I just meant …"

"You said she'd be okay because everyone in there will be so wasted they won't know what's going on," Teddy reminds Luke.

"That's a good point," I agree. "While they're messed up I'll get the codes or whatever it is and then go straight to the tunnels where you'll be waiting to swim me to safety."

"You're not a strong swimmer."

"Cheers."

"It might be a long way."

"Well then, it's a good thing I have my big strong boyfriend to rescue his poor weak little girlfriend."

"Shut up." He laughs.

"We're not going to be able to infiltrate the Gates twice," Will pipes up for the first time. He's been staring at the map and listening to us in silence. "Getting the information now, then going inside again to get Shadow? No way."

"That's my point!" I say.

"So what if we take someone to trade with Shadow?" Will suggests. "That way Shadow gets sent to us."

We go quiet, pondering it.

"I'm not sure there's anyone we could take that Shay would want more than Shadow," Luke points out. "He hates him a lot."

"What if it was his son?"

My eyebrows arch, intrigued. Teddy types the name in and we're met with a file photo of Zachariah Shay, aged 19. He has brown hair like his father, coal gray eyes and a gruesome scar pulling at one edge of his mouth. He's strange looking, and something about him unnerves me despite how young he is.

"How would we get him?" Luke wonders aloud. "He sure as hell doesn't leave the compound. He's probably more highly protected than Shadow."

"But he's not a prisoner, which makes the difference," I say. "He'll have the freedom to move around inside. And while the party's raging I can duck away and find him."

"*If* you find him – and that's a big if – how are you gonna get him to go with you?" Luke asks.

I shrug. "I'll think of something."

He groans. "I really don't like this reckless side of yours."

"Sure you do." I grin. "You're the one who taught me that lateral thinkers see opportunity everywhere. That boy is a neon sign." I look at the picture again and can't help thinking about what we could do with a boy like that.

"That's what worries me," Luke mutters. "Things that seem too good to be true usually are."

I shake my head. There's something in the picture I'm having trouble looking away from. Something in the boy's eyes. Something, I realize, that reminds me of my own child protection photos as a kid.

"He's miserable," I say.

"So what?"

I don't know. I chew on my lip as I study him.

"He's gonna change things for us," I murmur eventually. "I want him."

Chapter 5

September 17th, 2067

Josephine

It's hot. I don't know where I am. Pain holds my head captive and I'm not sure I can open my eyes. In fact, I think they're swollen shut. The sound of footsteps is all around me. I can't see so I concentrate on what I can hear. Breathing. Lots and lots of breathing. There is a huge group of people surrounding me. A chill runs down my spine as I feel myself being lifted off the cold ground. I'm carried and the hands that hold me have fingernails that puncture my flesh. I know they're not my people because they're not talking. There are no voices being raised to give orders or ask questions. It's too silent with only the rustle of limbs and the thump thump of my blaring pulse.

Where's Luke? My head's too fuzzy and I can't remember what happened or how I got here—

The wall. I remember the wall. And Luke didn't come. He wasn't answering Teddy's radio pleas, which means something went wrong on his end and god what if he's hurt *what if he's dead*?

I'm carried a long way with this terrible fear in my heart. I can taste blood and bile in my mouth. I count the seconds so I can work out how far I'm being taken but it's a stupid endeavor because I have no idea where I started. I know the scent and feel of the tunnels, and I know that this isn't them. I'm above ground somewhere, but I can't think of how that's possible. It lasts a long time. I move in and out of consciousness. I vomit from the nausea of being carried and the pain in my head. The mess goes all over me but my carriers don't stop or comment.

Finally the air outside grows cool enough for night and we stop. There's a crack and a sting on my face. Someone has slapped me.

"Wake," a deep female voice commands.

I manage to open one of my eyes just a crack. Enough to let the dim inky light of twilight fill my head.

Enough to see the moon high above, just a wink of it. It hangs red, tinged with blood, and I understand all at once, like a blow, how this has happened. It all comes back to the blood moon.

*

March 6th, 2067

Josephine

It occurs to me as we're driving through the city that not one of us raised a moral objection to kidnapping a young man and using him as a hostage. I feel slightly bad about that, but to be honest it doesn't weigh on me too heavily, which is probably a more concerning fact. Oh well.

Luke, Will, Henrietta and I park the car in the underground parking lot and take the lift up into the department store.

I have my contact lenses in and my thumb pads on, but none of the others have anything to protect against random scans so we're sticking to Murder Mall, as we call it, because it's pretty much filled with drug addicts likely to murder you and funnily enough the Bloods don't bother with much security down this way. I guess they figure it's already down the toilet so there's no point wasting time policing it.

Today's agenda is a rather hilarious use of our time: I need to find a dress for the event. Despite how silly it sounds, Luke has assured me that I'll need to look smoking hot to even be allowed near the Gates. Shallow, chauvinistic scumbags that they are. So I've decided to have fun with it. I figure the year of being twenty-two is my year of being young.

Henrietta is with us for today's mission – she's never been above ground on an op before – because I needed some help with the dress. Also, Will begged us to let her come since he's madly in love with her in a not-so-secret actually-totally-obvious way. For my part I would have preferred pretty much anyone else since she keeps mooning really obviously over my boyfriend.

On the escalator Luke drapes his arms around my shoulders from behind. "I used to shop here when I was a kid. It smells just as bad as it did then."

"Huh. I used to steal here. We're made for each other."

He grins. "What did you steal?"

"Anything I could get my hands on. It was all very Oliver Twist-ish. I've got quite nimble fingers."

"Oh yeah? Can you pick pockets?"

"*Please.*"

"Prove it, hot shot. Bet you're not half as good as Coin."

"This seems like a very dumb game to be played by hunted fugitives."

"Chicken?"

I can't help laughing as I scan the shoppers around us. As we walk off the escalator I spot a bedraggled man following a woman chatting away on her phone. He has about fourteen bags in his hands and looks bored to tears. I angle toward him and eye his tattered jacket. One of the front lapels is slightly more raised than the other – his wallet's inside a pocket there.

"Keep your eyes on me," I tell Luke under my breath.

"Not a problem."

I walk up to the man and brush close enough to gently graze one of his bags. As he turns to see me I let my foot slip sideways and I hit the ground awkwardly. He almost trips over me but manages to catch himself. I wince in pain and he puts his bags down to help me.

"Sorry," he says even though he didn't do anything.

"No, god, I'm sorry. Klutz."

With him bent down to help me I spy the wallet inside his jacket. I look up and meet his eyes. He's not expecting it. People don't meet the eyes of strangers. But I hold his and while he's distracted I brush closer and pluck the wallet straight out of his jacket. It goes swiftly into the back of my jeans where he won't spot it. I help gather his bags for him and apologize again. As he walks past me I flash the wallet for Luke to see, then turn and swiftly drop it into one of the man's shopping bags, all while he's none the wiser.

Luke gives me a slow clap as I return. Will and Henrietta look impressed.

"Redirection, my friends. Never doubt me again."

"Never, my little street urchin."

We wind our way to the formal dress section. I grab the first few I spot and then see Henrietta's unbelievably withering glance.

"What's wrong with these?"

She stares at me as though it's just become apparent that I'm a sewer monster. Which I suppose I am. Her family is very, very wealthy. She's much better equipped to deal with this than I've ever been, so I sigh and put the dresses back. "Come on then. I'll wear whatever you choose."

Her nose crinkles. "In here? I'd have to have a gun to my head."

"Let's pretend you do. Because if I don't look good enough to get into this party then I'm going to come home and murder you."

"What about this?" Luke suggests, holding up a cream lace dress.

Henrietta of course smiles and nods. "Nice choice, Luke."

"*Nice choice, Luke*," I mimic.

He smugly hands the dress to me. Henrietta also pulls out a plunging black gown and a weird red tutu thing. "Try these so we can get your color palette."

"It's very important to get the color palette," Will agrees, deadpan.

"It *is*! I don't know, you're all cavemen."

Will does an excellent impression of an ape and jumps around the aisles, much to our amusement. I catch Henrietta turning away so we won't see her smile. Thankfully there's no else in this section of the shop.

I try the dresses on. The tutu is first. It's see-through so you can see my underwear. Oh well. I fling open the curtain and strut out with some faux sexy moves, bending over and snapping back up, flashing a pout and sticking my butt out. Luke pisses himself and Will whips his phone out to film me acting like an idiot so quickly that it goes flying from his hands.

Hen groans. "Good god, no."

"This doesn't look good?" I ask as I thrust my pelvis.

"*No*," is the resounding answer from all three.

With the next dress I stick my leg out first. Luke whistles. When I emerge it's with a shimmy of my breasts, which nearly fall free of the skimpy black fabric. There's a mannequin next to us and I sexy dance against him, licking his plastic face. "This is what I have to do tomorrow night, right?"

There are tears in Luke's eyes he's laughing so hard.

"I really, really hope not," Hen mutters. I am determined to get a laugh out of her.

"Do that awkward bending over thing again," Will tells me. "This is getting projected in the arena when we get back."

I bend over but my butt knocks the mannequin and it crashes into a rack of dresses. Even Henrietta can't help laughing as I awkwardly lunge to catch it and manage to rip the seam of my dress above my hip.

"Now we're talking," Luke says.

"You are a concerning level of perverse."

The last dress is the cream lace he found. I emerge without any theatrics because I don't want to rip it too.

"Yep. That's it," Hen says.

Luke nods somberly.

Will snaps a few pics. "You'll be prom queen for sure."

"It's not too ... covered?" I ask. "Not that I want to be uncovered but I thought the idea was to seduce people ...?"

"Oh, honey," Hen sighs. "Don't you know anything? Seducing men has nothing to do with showing skin. It's about class, mystery, elegance, being absolutely aloof and completely un-gettable. You put your body on display and you're basically hanging a sign around your neck that says 'easy'."

I blink. How the hell does a sixteen-year-old know that? "So … really? This is it? I thought you'd drag this out all afternoon."

"When it's right, it's right," Hen says.

I look down at the dress. It's form-fitting with a high-neckline, long sleeves and a straight skirt that hangs to the ground. The whole thing is made of lace. I suppose it is quite beautiful. I feel very unlike myself in it. I don't think I've ever worn a dress. Like, actually ever.

"Quick, Oliver, stuff it in your purse and let's get out of here," Luke says.

I roll my eyes, get unchanged and pay for the dress the old fashioned way. The good thing about Murder Mall is that it accepts illegal cash. It's very cheap, being a knock-off and all, which Hen takes great offense to.

"You know you'll need heels, right? At least six inches."

"Six inches? What the fuck?"

"Oh, please. I used to do eight easily."

I look at Luke but he nods, the traitor.

So we get shoes. I hate them more than I've hated anything. Well, no. That's an exaggeration, but I do hate them a lot. They hurt and make it almost impossible to move.

"From now until that party you wear those," Hen tells me. "You sleep in them, shower in them, eat in them. Except don't actually shower in them, obviously. But you have to try and get used to them because you're embarrassing me right now."

"Can't I just get lower heels?"

"No one at that party will be wearing heels under six inches."

"So what?"

She shakes her head and is done with the conversation. I buy the damn things and then we head back to the safe house.

We have a couple dotted throughout the city, all properties owned by imaginary citizens Will tricked the system into accepting. This way we don't have to worry about the houses suddenly becoming occupied by real drones. We keep cameras surveying them even when we're not here and when we arrive we spend most of our time suspiciously sweeping the area and jumping at every sound.

I decide to have a bath because there's endless hot water and nothing pressing to do this evening. And best of all: windows to the sky. It's bliss. I sink into the scalding hot water and look at the darkening twilight. I think of all the baths I've laid in. Given it's one of my most favorite things to do I've been in very few. The best bath of all was the one in Luke's city apartment. Thinking of that bath makes me think of that bathroom, which makes me remember the time he walked in on me naked when we'd known each other for about three days. I was so desperately uncomfortable in my own skin then. I'd never been naked with anyone – I'd barely been naked with myself. My body was a shameful secret. And then he appeared and made it so much worse and so much better. He was a revelation; *I* was a revelation.

There's a soft knock on the door.

"Yeah?"

"Can I come in, baby?"

"Of course."

Luke enters and closes the door behind him. He looks down at me and smiles, then sits with his back against the bath. I run my wet fingers through his hair.

"You and your baths," he murmurs.

"Me and my baths."

"I'm giving the adolescents a chance to really stew in their hormones together."

"Pleasant."

"I think she likes him."

"Are you out of your mind? She likes *you*."

"That's just posturing. I'm telling you, he's growing on her."

"She not …"

"What?"

"Enough for him."

"Enough of what?"

"I dunno. Strange enough. Kind enough."

"People aren't always what they seem. She's had it tough."

"We all have."

"What's your problem with her?"

I shrug. "She just thinks she's better than everyone."

"She's a child, Josi. She's been taken from her parents and her extremely privileged life and presented with sewers."

"And freedom."

"Yes, and freedom. Attitude is a survival mechanism. And don't you think she's been really solid?"

It's true. She has. She's taken to the tunnels with admirable aplomb and not a word of complaint, and she's always the first to plead with us to be brought above for a mission. "She's brave," I allow. "I don't know why I'm so hard on her. Sorry."

"She reminds me of you."

"*What?*"

"You last year. Bitching and moaning about everything just to make people hate you as much as you hated yourself."

"I did not," I say weakly.

"Uh-huh."

"Anyway, you were in a coma for most of that."

"But I heard many, many stories."

"Oh, good."

He laughs a little. I move my fingers over his scalp, massaging it gently. "I'm nervous about tomorrow," he admits. "I don't like sending you in there like this."

"It was your idea."

"I know, but I don't know what the fuck I was thinking."

"You were thinking that I'm capable of dealing with it, because I am. Want to get in?"

He shakes his head. "I've got meat in the oven."

"Let it burn." This is blasphemy. Not only because Luke loves food – cooking it, eating it, serenading it, probably marrying it – but also because we practically starve in those tunnels most of the time.

Luke looks at me. Our eyes lock. He climbs in and holds me as he plunges under the surface, pulling me down with him. I open my eyes underwater. We are wrapped in each other's arms and he's looking at me and with tiny bubbles leaving our mouths we kiss.

Eventually we have to resurface for air. We bob up and rest on the slippery bath.

"I wish we could stay under forever."

"Me too," I agree.

"When will the world stop needing us?"

"I'm not sure it does."

"That's because you underestimate the impact you have."

"Sometimes I want to leave," I say. "I imagine building a boat and sailing with you until we find a new place. Or just walking. I picture us walking out and out and out."

"What would we find?"

"I don't know. Just … quiet. I used to imagine you swimming out into the sea until you were nothing but a speck on the horizon."

"When did you imagine that?"

"When I was in the asylum. I missed you like a limb cut off." He swallows. His hand moves to my jaw. "You never say it."

"Say what?"

"That you love me."

I close my eyes so I don't have to look into his too-green ones. "Josi."

"I feel it too much that I'm afraid to say it."

"Darling," he murmurs roughly.

I open my eyes. "But you know, right? You know I do."

He nods a little. "I know."

"Sometimes I miss you even when you're in my arms. I'm scared of how much I love you."

Luke lets his lips touch mine, but I move away because I'm anxious. "Psychologists say when it's this intense it's not real. They think it's limerence, not love, and that it will burn out just as fast as it arrived."

"What's limerence?"

"It's the sickness of love, the madness of it. The soul destroying, obsessive passion of love. Doctors called it unhealthy, a kind of fugue state we needed to break free of. They said that couples who suddenly fell out of love with each other didn't love one another at all – they were just limerent."

Luke thinks about this and the look in his eyes constricts my chest. He runs his hands down my stomach to my thighs and then in between them. "Maybe it won't last forever but the sad ones who've never felt it must be the ones who say it isn't real." His fingers slip inside me and I gasp. Against my mouth he says, "I think I'd rather be limerent than anything else in the world. I think limerence is how love begins and maybe how it stays."

*

Later he gets out to deal with dinner but I stay immersed in the water. My body is a prune, so wrinkled I could be ninety years old. I look at my fingers and imagine myself at that age, I imagine loving Luke this much so long into the future. I think of the intensity of it and wonder how it can possibly last.

It does feel like a fugue state, sometimes. A kind of madness all too similar to the one that crept inside me on those dark nights of the blood moon. And like that madness, it seems to me in this moment that whether or not this fugue state ends or lasts, such a thing could be very dangerous and very powerful. It could even be a weapon.

The sad ones who've never felt it must be the ones who say it isn't real.

Chapter 6

March 6th, 2067

Luke

I pull the smoking tray of pork and leek sausages out of the oven and swear loudly. It is such a treat having meat that I can't believe I let it burn.

"They're still okay," Hen tells me, peering over my shoulder.

I shake my head. Okay is disappointing. I wanted us to have one nice meal, just one, that wasn't made up of damper or rice or pasta. At least all the vegetables will be tasty. I drizzle them in a garlic dressing and scatter some slithered almonds over the top.

"Where did you learn to cook?"

"This is not cooking. But my parents taught me."

"They must have been well off, cooking food like this."

"Not at all. Later there was a period in my life where I could afford to buy any food I wanted."

"Must have been nice." She sighs. "I had a similar period."

I look sideways at the girl. Josi's still in the bath and Will is doing a perimeter check so I have a moment alone with Hen. "Money doesn't mean anything real. I love good food but I love freedom more."

"Well, obviously. Only sometimes it doesn't feel like we're free at all."

"Why's that?"

"We live with the rats and the monsters and we're always worried about getting caught or killed."

"It won't be like this forever."

"So how's it going to be different?"

"We'll make it different."

"How?"

I hesitate. We don't talk to the kids about our big plans. The ones that include taking out an entire government. Because they scare even us. They're unwieldy and difficult to grapple with, they have an unknown outcome and they're more than likely to get us all killed. But something about Henrietta craves big, even the scary big.

"By changing the way this city works."

"Are you going to seize control?" she asks. "You'd be a perfect leader."

I shake my head. "There can't be only one leader and even if there could be, it wouldn't be me."

"That's stupid. There's no one else it could be."

I don't respond. I don't like the idea of that.

Hen lowers her voice. "I'm not sure Josi's up to this. I could go. I'd blend in better. I'm more comfortable in that kind of situation. My parents took me to functions all the time."

I glance at her as I slice tomato for the salad. "You're sixteen. They wouldn't let you anywhere near that kind of party."

"I wouldn't look sixteen."

"Hen. There's no way in hell. There's also no need. Josi's got it covered."

"She's not—"

"She was messing around in the shop but she takes ops seriously. She'll do whatever she has to." I add with a smile, "And if you think she's not the most beautiful woman on the planet then you're out of your mind."

Henrietta blushes and immediately walks out the back door, presumably to find Will.

Despite my confidence I'm worried too. Not about Josi's abilities but about the danger of sending her into a pen of starved perverts. It makes me queasy.

As I set the table she emerges with dripping wet hair and flushed pink cheeks. She looks relaxed and not the slightest bit nervous about tomorrow. We sit down to eat and they're all very good about oohing and aahing over the food, even though in my opinion it's nowhere near up to scratch.

I look around at the little safe house. Its layout is quite similar to the house I grew up in, which is only a couple of blocks away. Apart from the millions of security cameras set up everywhere here, the house feels familiar and I can almost imagine that the four of us are a different four: a mother and father and their two sons sitting down to eat dinner.

"Here's to last suppers!" Josi announces, raising her wine.

Nobody follows suit.

"I'm kidding. Jeez, lighten up."

"At least we can take comfort in the fact that even if you do die tomorrow one of the other universes will hold the you that doesn't," Will offers placidly.

"Come again?"

"The multiverse theory."

Henrietta rolls her eyes. Will sees it and looks crestfallen.

"Explain," I prompt him. I've heard of it but can't wait to hear his explanation.

He shrugs it off.

"*Explain*," Josi and I say together.

"It's the theory that because of the rapid rate of expansion of our universe, one day in billions of years all matter will be wrenched apart, leaving a massive void of emptiness. But this emptiness will make way for more big bangs, the births of new universes. And if this is true, it essentially means that when our big bang occurred, there were probably a whole lot of others beside it, giving birth to many many parallel universes wherein any and all possible outcomes occur. So if you choose to do the mission tomorrow in this universe, there's also one where you don't, and a whole different set of events are spurred. The multiverse."

My eyebrows arch, impressed. Josi is more than impressed – I know she loves this idea but for Will's sake pretends she hasn't heard it before.

"That is so so so cool," she breathes.

Henrietta nods tightly as though she can hardly admit to liking such a nerdy thing but does anyway.

Will smiles.

"But surely all these other universes wouldn't be identical to ours," I protest. "I mean, there probably are a bunch out there, but surely there wouldn't be versions of us in them. The simple fact of us being here in this one is like the luckiest thing ever when you think about how many millions of animals had to survive and breed in order for humans to evolve and then how many had to survive to preserve our exact ancestry. Thousands and thousands of generations led to us, and not one of them died before they could have a child. That's just crazy. And miracles like that don't happen more than once."

"Who says? If there are *infinite* universes then there must be a whole bunch that reach our births and then splinter off differently," Josi points out. "Maybe we're in some but not all."

It's a strange thought. I'm not sure I like it, actually, but Josi's eyes are alight with the idea of her alternate selves. I wonder what it is that she imagines for them, and what she could regret so much about this reality.

"Maybe in one universe I'm a concert cellist." Josi grins. "Nah, that's too boring. I'm a trapeze artist. Or a hot air balloon pilot. And I sail around the clouds of the world, walking the high wire at dazzling and never-before-seen heights."

"Maybe we all have bat wings and sonar clicking capabilities," Will suggests, the weirdo.

"Ooh, yeah, and we fly around clicking blindly at each other until we find our families," Josi agrees.

"Maybe everyone gets to eat whatever they want, whenever they want," I say. My imagination is much more boring than theirs.

"And swim in the ocean. Maybe we'd all have sealcoats we could shed when we come ashore, like the sea folk," Josi says wistfully, reminding me of when I told her that story while swimming in the ocean. She turns to Hen. "Come on, what would your multiverse alter ego be like?"

Henrietta fidgets uncomfortably. "Maybe … she'd be a queen."

"There you go!" At least my imagination is better than Hen's.

We laugh and keep playing. I grab a brush and tackle the knots in Josi's hair, since she refuses to bother with it herself. It's become our nightly ritual, one I spend most of the day looking forward to.

*

As tomorrow draws closer, Josi tosses and turns in bed and makes it impossible for me to sleep. I pull her against me and hold her limbs so she can't move.

"Deep breath in, let it out slow," I murmur.

She does so, again and again, and I feel her heart begin to slow.

"Let your mind settle and hold on an image."

Sometimes this is the only way she can get to sleep. If it works it won't last long before her nightmares wake her again, but then we'll just try the meditation once more.

Softly she says, "Maybe in one universe we never evolved from animals. Maybe we're all wild beasts in that one, just as we started."

In the corner of the room I see the shadows of flying birds. I don't see them often, but when I do it's an all-too-painful reminder of the blood moon and its hold over me. The one I choose to keep hidden from Josi. The one I have to deal with again in six months' time.

"Maybe in that universe there are still birds," she says, as though she has seen the shadows herself.

I watch the flutter of wings and reply, "Maybe."

*

March 7th, 2067

Josephine

Teddy has done his job well. When I arrive to wait at the gate with the other women someone scans my eye and thumbprint, and my identity appears in their records as cleared for work tonight. Half a dozen Bloods escort us inside to where a small bus waits to carry us through the winding streets. Lush greenery lines the roads, while trickling fountains and modern sculptures are dotted through stretches of immaculate lawn. White fairy lights dangle from trees. The buildings are a mix of modern and old architecture, and are all bigger and more regal than any that still exist in the city. I'm still gazing around at it all when we arrive at a circular driveway. It takes us around the biggest fountain yet – oddly it's shaped like the molecular makeup of DNA – and stops before the entrance of what looks like a palace.

Here we are searched for weapons *again*, scanned, and ushered inside. The carved ceilings are so high I can barely see them. It's like a museum. We are lined up on either side of a huge gold staircase and I see the other women plastering smiles on their faces, sticking their chests out and tilting their knees. I copy them exactly, even down to the slightly vacant look in their eyes.

"Okay team, Dual's inside Shay's house," Teddy says in my earpiece. He's watching the whole thing from the tunnels, and linking all our teams together.

"I'm directly below," Luke informs us. "It stinks like shit down here, unsurprisingly. I'm about to go underwater so I'll be radio silent for the next twenty minutes."

"We've circled the perimeter and locked onto heat signatures," Will says. "All looks quiet, no unusual activity from the guards, no movement within."

I, of course, say nothing because it would get me instantly killed. Bloods watch us so closely I can sense the woman beside me growing nervous simply from the scrutiny. They are all very beautiful, and Hen was right – all are covered elegantly from neck to wrists to toes. Some even have head scarves. Their gowns are worth a million times what mine is and even I can tell that just from glancing. They look and smell of wealth and class and confidence.

The only thing I've got going for me is that I happen to be quite a good actress and an excellent liar. I set my spine straight and my face almost entirely blank, but not quite. The key, it seems, is to still be a human, just one caught between obedience and disdain.

The men arrive and champagne flows freely. We mingle in what can only be described as a ballroom, for god's sake. The chandelier glitters while trays of unbearably expensive food are offered. The whole thing reeks of decadence and I hate them all so much I can hardly focus.

"Bloody hell," Teddy says in my ear. "So this is how the other half live."

"Not half," Will reminds him. "Less than one percent."

"True. One one-hundred thousandth of the city's population, actually."

I circle slowly, not wanting to speak to anyone directly and trying not to catch anyone's eye. Falon Shay has yet to arrive. He always comes last, according to Luke (who, it turns out, came to *three* of these nights, cheeky bastard), which means I have time to get out of here before he shows up and recognizes me.

The speed with which things start to unravel astonishes me. Before I can blink, cocaine is being snorted and men are kissing women or pulling them into corners or spare rooms or just groping them where they stand. Gambling tables are opened and a man shouts at another, play-acting a fight. There is a performance being enacted around me and it's one of emotion. A parody of emotion, of huge hand gestures and lifted voices and cackling hysterical laughter. It is the trend, I realize, to be full of feeling, to be overt with it, to advertise its presence as a means of stating their position in this world. They are rich and high-born and pure-blooded and just *better* than the rest of us, so they're the only ones who've been spared the cure.

I'm sickened by it; I have to get out.

Near the door I'm stopped by an older man with meaty wandering hands and it reminds me so much of the time I was attacked in a casino bathroom that I almost have a panic attack.

"Where are you scurrying off to, little mouse?"

I take a long, slow breath and look him in the eyes. "Just the bathroom to freshen up."

"You're fresh as you are. Fresh and un-plucked, by the looks of you."

Ew.

"On the contrary," I say. "I've been plucked so many times I might as well be a harp."

He stares at me and then his face twists with distaste. "How vulgar."

"Indeed! Unforgivable, in such esteemed company. Excuse me while I wash my mouth out with soap."

Teddy and Will are both laughing as I make my way toward the bathroom.

"I'm in place," Luke suddenly pants. "The water is mighty cold, so if you could move things along, my darling, that would be greatly appreciated."

"Looking for a way out now," I mutter, since there's no one in this hallway.

"Just so you know, certain appendages may have frozen off by the time you reach me. Very necessary appendages."

"Necessary for who?"

"For both of us – trust me."

"Gross," Will comments.

"Stop distracting me," I scold Luke.

"Sorry."

"Dual," Will suddenly exclaims. "We've got eyes on Zachariah."

"Where?"

"He's with his father in the grounds."

"What? Why? What are they doing?"

"Dunno. Talking by the looks of it. Standby."

I reach the bathroom. Inside there are a couple of other women retouching their makeup or doing lines of blow. There are toilet cubicles, for crying out loud, like we're not in someone's house. I shut myself in a stall and gather my breath. No way to escape out of the bathroom as there aren't any windows. I decide to actually pee, then head out and wash my hands, all the while waiting for Will to tell me what the hell's going on.

"I like your dress," a woman tells me kindly. She's a tall redhead, beautiful and willowy. Her dress is scarlet and made of such fine silk it looks like rippling water.

"Thanks. Yours is beautiful."

She looks at her reflection and I see sadness in her black-rimmed eyes. I want to ask her why she's here, why she'd ever subject herself to such a thing but I already know the answer: she has no choice. Some of the others like it, I can see, but not this one. A great well of compassion swells inside me and I want to reach out and touch her, just for a moment, but I think it might unnerve her more than anything. Instead we stand silently looking at our reflections and putting off the moment we have to go back out there.

"Is this your first time?" she asks.

"Yes. You?"

She shakes her head once.

"Does it get worse than this?"

A single nod. She looks at me properly. "Don't be frightened. I'll watch out for you."

I smile at the simple kindness. The drones, these brain-damaged drones, they never stop surprising me. "Thank you."

"Dual, he's going inside with his dad. I repeat, Zachariah is attending the party."

Shit. That changes things.

"Abort," Luke tells me. "Shay will recognize you. Get out of there right now."

"We're ready to detonate the distraction when you say so, Dual," Will tells me.

"No," I say clearly. A couple of the women look at me like I'm mental. I go back into the stall. What do I do, what do I do. My purse contains make-up, but no matter what I do it won't make me look like a different person.

Okay. So the theme is emotion for the men, self-containment for the women. They're all completely covered up. Maybe I can use that. I look down at myself. My dress is long. It could stand a trim.

"What's going on, Dual?" Will asks. "We're waiting on your go."

"Do not move," I say softly. I hike up the end of my dress and see if there are any seams I can use. I don't have anything sharp so I use my fingernails to unpick the hem. I'm lucky it's such a badly made dress because the split at the side unravels and I use my teeth to make a rip. It's way harder than I imagined to get a whole strip free – the material doesn't just tear easily apart like it does in the movies. I have to really work at it and by the time I've got something usable, my fingernails are all broken and one of them is bleeding. I fold the strip so the edges aren't visible and then I tie it around the bottom half of my face. It covers my nose and mouth and I slip the ends into my elaborate braid. When I emerge I use my eyeliner to drastically darken my eyes and subtly change their shape. To my relief, I look utterly unlike myself.

As I head for the ballroom once more I get a few surprised looks but nobody questions me about the covering – I am simply trendier than the rest. Ha!

"I'm going back in to find Z," I tell the others and then I'm inside again. In the ten minutes I spent in the bathroom, everything has gone to chaos. I see a couple having sex right there on a chaise longue.

"Good god," Teddy mutters in horror as he sees what I see.

At the edge of it all, Falon Shay and his son watch. Their gazes are equally cold, equally hard. They don't speak to anyone or to each other and they look every bit father and son. I circle around, keeping them in sight at all times. A woman bumps into me and spills champagne down my dress but I ignore it and keep moving. My ass and breasts get groped multiple times. Grating laughter deafens me and the smell of perfume is dizzying. Someone gives a roar of triumph at the blackjack table and I see a girl trip and fall heavily but no one stops to help her. It's fucking insane. I swing her way and stoop to help her stand. Her heels are spiked weapons.

"No wonder you fell on those things," I murmur.

She gives an embarrassed laugh. "Thanks."

I'm up and moving again. I have to gamble on myself now. I edge into Zachariah's line of sight. He sees me. I let our eyes meet and linger. I let my eyebrow arch. Then without stopping I walk straight past him and through a curtain. He might not follow, but then again he might.

He does.

We're in a smaller room, draped in a veil of smoke. A piano is being played and several people lie around on the floor in various states of undress. I move through another door and keep moving faster. Zachariah follows me through several more rooms until finally I find an empty one. It has tall glass windows overlooking the beautifully maintained gardens. I stop to look out. Hear him enter the room behind me and pause. Then he makes his way to stand beside me.

Neither of us says anything.

"Dual, what the hell's going on?" Luke demands.

I reach up and remove my earpiece by pretending to fiddle with my earring. It is abruptly silent.

"The party isn't to your taste?" Zachariah asks softly. He has a rough voice, as though he doesn't often use it.

I shake my head and remain silent. We stand for a long while. I've put out my fishing hook with its bait and now I wait patiently as he circles it.

"This is my first time," I admit softly.

"Mine too."

"How do you like it?"

He doesn't reply.

I let the pause stretch. "You look just like him."

In the reflection of the glass I see his mouth twist bitterly and know that if I play this right I have a chance.

"Wouldn't he love to hear you say that."

"I don't know, would he?"

"What's your name?"

My cover name is Anne. I say, "Dual."

"That's unusual. Why are you called that?"

On impulse I reach up and carefully remove my two contact lenses. I'm playing a very, very dangerous game here and the others must be losing their minds with worry.

Limerence

But with the two lenses sitting delicately on my fingertip, I turn and show Zachariah my real eyes.

"That's why."

He gazes at me. His scar is very white in the rosy light, his eyes very dark. He has a narrow, thin mouth and a hooked nose. A nose with a very obvious break in the bridge, a break I saw in that photo of him. I wondered then who might have broken that nose, and I think I might know.

I let my lips part. Hold his gaze and allow him to see something in me, a shift, a thought chasing its way across my gaze, a moment of unsettled surprise. Let him see how startled I am at the effect he's having on me. Let him think I'm at his mercy.

I swallow and drop my eyes. "I know they're illegal but people think me too strange like this."

"Strange is beautiful," he murmurs.

"Not to anyone else." I look at his scar. "But I think I see what you mean."

A little color comes to his cheeks.

I reach up and remove my face covering. "It's like a cage in here. A lovely cage, but a cage nonetheless."

"You have no idea."

"Have you ever left?"

Zachariah shakes his head. And just like that, he takes the bait. "We could leave right now. Have an adventure." There's a terrible yearning in him.

I think my suspicions are correct: I think he hates his father.

I let my eyes light up but make sure to keep any expression from my features. "How? Won't we get caught?"

He shrugs, angry all of a sudden. "Maybe. Probably. I'm not sure I care."

"You might not, but I'd be killed."

"I'd never let that happen!" he exclaims. "You think I'd ask you to leave and then let you get killed for it? You think I'm some kind of monster?"

I shake my head slowly.

"Forget it. It was stupid. You're just one of my father's women."

I frown and step away from him.

He notices it with hawk-like perception. His gaze narrows on me. "Did that offend you?"

"Of course."

"How?"

I shouldn't be capable of feeling offended. Not if I'm cured. But I lay down my biggest piece of bait, the riskiest of all. Leaning close to him, I let him see a sudden storm in my gaze. "Here's the secret to it," I whisper. "I'm human. Wouldn't you like to be?"

Zachariah leans in too, searching me, trying to understand.

"Wouldn't you like to *live?*"

"More than anything," he says and I feel his breath on my lips.

I'm teetering on the edge of crossing a line here, and I think of what I told the kids. *I have no line.* For Shadow, I can't have one. So even though this is a cruel game I let our lips brush very lightly.

Then I pull away, squeeze my eyes shut. "I just wanted to talk to you. I wasn't supposed to … This is dangerous."

He takes my arms tightly. "Who *are* you?"

I shake my head.

"Who are you? What are you doing here?" His voice breaks a little and he looks close to losing it. He must be bound so tightly, all the time. It must be a nightmare having Falon Shay as a father.

So I say, "I'm here for you, Zachariah. To set you free."

*

March 8th, 2067

Luke

It's getting very, very cold in the water. I have only enough room in this little air pocket to try and keep my head and shoulders above the surface. My frozen fingers clutch at the metal rungs of the ladder and if I move them at all I have the feeling I'll slip below and be too cold to swim back up. I won't have a chance to, either, because the water is moving very fast. Josi's been offline for way too long now and I'm starting to prepare myself to go in after her. But I linger because she wouldn't take her earpiece and contact lenses out unless she had a good reason. I just hope Shay hasn't taken them out for her.

"Anything?" I ask Teddy through chattering teeth.

"Nothing yet. She's still offline."

"I've got nothing unusual about the heat signatures inside the house," Will offers. "People are still 'mingling', if that's the word we're going with."

"I think you need to get out of that water," Teddy tells me.

"Can't yet." I can't go back without Josi and I can't climb up into the Gates until I'm sure she needs help. Rushing in there now could put her in more danger.

I grit my teeth and try to flex my hands. My right one has never fully recovered from punching through glass; I struggle with it every day. It's unusual for me not to have complete control over my body, not to know its exact capabilities. But this hand, much as I hate to admit it, is an unknown element. Sometimes the fingers won't bend properly, sometimes it loses its dexterity, sometimes it aches or twinges or freezes. I am as frightened of this damaged hand as I am of the virus in my blood that is preparing to transform me. Right now my hand's frozen around a rusting metal ladder rung.

"Woah woah woah," Will says suddenly. "I've got two Bloods moving toward your tunnel entrance, Luke."

"They'll probably walk straight by."

"Standby. They're moving erratically."

"How so?"

"Back and forwards. Swinging around. They're looking for something. Don't respond – they're right above you now, man."

I have to move. My fingers ache as they let go of the ladder and reach for my gun. I do it left-handed – I do everything left-handed now. I have a silencer on my weapon but obviously it will still make a considerable noise.

"Do they use heat detection tech?" Teddy asks.

I don't respond, but they do.

"They shouldn't be able to pick him up down there 'cause his body temp's so low," Will argues. "I'm too far away to take them out, Luke, so get ready. I think they're sniffing around for you."

Turns out he's right.

The Blood swings open the hatch and points his gun in my face. "Drop your weapon in the water."

I sigh and do it.

"Ascend slowly and without any sudden movements."

I force my aching muscles to climb up the ladder and emerge from the tunnel. One of the Bloods hauls me out and slams me to my stomach. He grips my wrists together and I hear him getting cuffs out. When they touch my wrists I yank them and roll fast. He comes down on top of my chest and takes the bullet intended for me in his shoulder. I haul him up and ram him into his companion, who fires twice more into the Blood's body, knowing exactly where to aim so that the bullets will cut through his flesh and into mine. Luckily I'm already moving and the second bullet only grazes my ribs. My right fist, which is only good for punching these days, crosses heavily into the shooter's jaw. I hit him again, much harder in the temple. The pain doesn't affect him but I've hit the nerve to his eye and now he's blind in one. I use the momentary distraction to smash the gun out of his hand. Then my knee is in his groin, his chest, his guts. My hand sweeps to the knife at my belt and I slice it through his throat. The second Blood, who's been shot three times, is bleeding on the ground but he's still alive, so I cut his throat too. Then I drag them both to the tunnel and drop them into the water to be swept away in a current of freezing sewage.

"They're down," I say softly. "Anyone see us?"

"You've got more coming your way."

Shit. This is Josi's way out. If it's compromised she'll be stuck. I grab the Blood's fallen gun and climb back down the ladder. This time I leave the hatch open and I use it as a bunker, aiming my weapon across the lawn for any sign of movement.

"Any news on where Dual is?" I ask.

"Nothing yet."

"Which direction are they coming from, Will?"

"Your three o'clock."

I swing to the right.

"Oh fuck," Will breathes. "Not just three o'clock. Eight and eleven, as well. They're all around you. I'm gonna blow the bomb."

"No – you blow it and this whole place goes into lockdown. We don't know where Josi is and if she can make it out through that."

"They're closing in, Luke. Too many for you alone. This is what the bomb was for – a contingency plan!"

"For Josi, not for me!" I snarl. "*Standby.*"

I can see them now. Just shadows in the distance, moving behind trees and bushes. I line one up in my sight, let the air out of my lungs and fire. The person drops. I spin quickly to take another behind me. Then swing to eleven. If I can force them to keep taking cover then I might slow their progress but every time I do I use my limited ammunition.

Bullets are raining upon me. Several ping off the metal hatch lid and grass is bursting around my head. I keep firing back as heavily as I can. The magazine change will be a problem. As I come to my last bullet I duck down, free the empty mag and slot the new one into place as quickly as I can with a very stiff hand. But this has given the Bloods time to sprint closer. When I open the hatch again there's one bearing down on me. I shoot him in the neck, then spin to shoot the one directly behind me in the chest. A bullet whizzes by my ear. A boot kicks me in the side of the head, making my earpiece whine painfully. I kill the man but almost simultaneously a smoke bomb explodes above me. My only option is to retreat once more into the hatch so I won't pass out from the gas. I wrench the painful tech out of my ear and try to work out what to do. I'm now alone and perched in the water, trembling with cold. I have three bullets left and my right hand is seizing around the ladder. The second that hatch opens either the gas will knock me out or the Bloods will kill me.

Basically I'm fucked.

My only option is to escape through this tunnel and pray, *pray* that Josi won't try to come this way before she gets in contact with us again. Awkwardly I pull my wetsuit over my skull and shove the breathing hose into my mouth.

That's when the hatch swings wide above me and I realize I'm too late.

*

Josephine

Zachariah and I run across the lawn with our heads low. My heels are in my hand, obviously. No sane person tries to run – *anywhere* – in heels. I can hear shots being fired in the direction we're headed, which is bad. But despite this, despite the danger or maybe because of it, my pulse is racing a mile a minute and I have that excited thrill beneath my heart that always starts when I'm on a mission. I hate to admit it because it's so passé, but I think I've become an adrenalin junkie. I really like doing dangerous crap.

We scurry to a halt when we reach a line of trees. Beyond them is chaos. Luke – presumably Luke – is hunkered down in the tunnel, hatch open, firing and being fired upon. I can see gunmen pressing closer as he struggles to protect all sides.

"It's our way out," I tell Zachariah, who hasn't said a single word since agreeing to escape with me. That's a whole other issue I don't have time to tackle. He could definitely be a trap or a trick or a spy but I don't have any other option right now and I've gone too far to turn back. Besides, there's no way we'll find Shadow without him.

Someone moves behind us and I whirl in time to see the butt of a gun leveled at my face. I strike it sideways with my wrist; it fires right next to my ear and I go painfully deaf. In the silence I move into the attack, sending a right cross straight into the Blood's sternum. Ribs crack beneath the blow but he's still moving forward, sending a fist into my stomach that *feels* as though it should be heard, it hurts so much, but it's still oddly silent as I hit him hard in the throat, then in the eye. He goes down onto one knee and I send my bare foot into his groin, then smash him over the temple with the butt of his own gun. It takes a lot to get a Blood agent unconscious, and even through this punishment he's still woozily struggling to rise.

I turn to see Zachariah crouched over the dead body of a second agent, his gun still aimed at the man's gruesome mess of skull. I grab his arm and try to help him up. He looks at me slowly, blinks eyes that have shifted to empty.

"It's okay," I try to tell him but I can't hear my own voice.

He points behind me to where a smoke bomb has gone off. Before I can second-guess myself I wrench him forward through the gray smog. I can't hear or see now. We run fast and low for the hatch and the world is eerie dancing smoke. My eyes stream with it and I can't stop coughing but thankfully it's not sleeper gas.

I spot the hatch, but just as I'm about to reach it, the smoke clears to reveal several figures. Falon Shay has a knife at Shadow's throat. Bloods surround them, their weapons pointed at us. Zachariah and I freeze.

As the smoke evaporates almost entirely I meet my father's eyes across the short distance. His hands are cuffed and he is gaunt with pain from whatever they've been doing to him, but I can see a lot of things in his eyes that make me think he might not have been cured yet. He stands as straight as he always did, his shoulders square, his jaw set.

They're saying things but I can't hear them. One of the Bloods opens the hatch and I watch Luke climb out, hands raised. He spots me, spots Shadow and the minister, takes it all in and then says something short.

I see fear flash through Shay's eyes. Without another word he sheathes his knife into Shadow's abdomen. It happens in slow motion. Soundless and terrible and unstoppable. My eyes fly up to Shadow's and I see nothing but dull shock.

Before anyone can react, the earth trembles. A mighty crack seems to rend it. We're all thrown from our feet, every one of us. I still have my weapon and in the chaos I roll onto my side and try to find Shay in my sights. Too much is happening. There are literal cracks in the earth now. The ground ruptures and I see fissures sucking people in. I can't work out where Shadow is. I barely stop myself from sliding down an incline to one of the cracks.

Then I spot Luke dragging Shadow toward the hatch. They're both bleeding. Bloods are behind them, struggling upright. From the ground I shoot one man in the head, then another. Someone takes hold of my shoulders and pulls me to the hatch. I don't stop firing, trying to give Luke as much cover as possible. Where's Falon Shay? He's always squirming his way out of trouble, the scumbag. I can't see him – only floating dust and debris. I think there's ash falling from the sky. It looks like snow.

It's Zachariah who's pulling me, and we reach the hatch just behind Luke and Shadow. They climb in and we follow. There's an awful whining sound in my left ear. My head pounds.

Below me, Luke is fitting Shadow with an air tank and hose. I grab the third and hurriedly try to fit it.

Zachariah is saying something, shouting it. Luke is shaking his head. He looks at me, makes a motion with his hand, easily read as *leave him*. He points at the three mouthpieces. We don't have a fourth. I look up at Zachariah. His eyes plead with me; the desperation is as loud as a scream.

Please, his lips mouth.

I make a decision I'll probably come to regret: I nod and pull him down into the freezing water with me and we're off. Pummelled along at a breakneck pace, freezing cold water above and below and I have no idea which way is up but I've somehow managed to hold on to Zachariah's hand and he's holding on to mine and I pass him my mouthpiece and we're flying.

Chapter 7

March 8th, 2067

Josephine

We get wounded a lot. Basically, if everyone comes home from a mission unscathed it's some kind of creepy miracle we don't trust. Therefore we keep gurney beds at different spots in the tunnel, which is how we come to be currently sprinting through the underground systems with an unconscious Shadow nearly careening off his wheeling stretcher every time we round a corner.

I am so so sick of running through these damn tunnels while someone's life is seeping out of them in a red sticky trail. I'm so sick of being chased by Bloods and Furies and our own mortality.

But.

But at least we have him. Shadow, aka Phillipe Luquet, aka my long lost father, is finally free of the fucking Prime Minister and here, with me, within touching distance. After six months of not knowing whether or not he's *alive*. This feels like the much bigger miracle.

*

It's the second time Claire has patched Shadow up. Last time it was in her home, with a bullet in his guts. Now a knife has tried to do the job, and this time she doesn't have Rabbit to finish his medical treatment for her. This time Claire's on her own.

At least that's what I think until someone else steps forward.

The infirmary is in chaos. People are running around trying to deal with getting Shadow to a table, getting the right medical supplies, arguing over what to do and basically just getting in each other's way. Claire is panicking for the first time since I've known her. I can see her looking at the wound and not having any idea what to do. I can feel myself leaning toward a panic attack of my own and Luke is roaring at everyone to shut up and get out of the way and then—

"I can operate on him."

We all turn – seemingly all four billion of us – to see Zachariah.

"Who the hell are you?" Pace demands at the same time several other mouths voice the same query.

"You're not going anywhere near him," Luke says. "In fact, you're coming with me."

"Wait."

Luke pauses to look at me.

Zachariah and I exchange a long gaze. My heart is pounding its way out of my chest. "You know how?"

"It's the only thing I know."

"Yes. Okay. Do it."

"Josi! He's the minister's son, for god's sake!"

I turn to Claire. "Can you do this on your own? Honestly?"

She giggles: her cure short-circuiting. Quickly she snaps her mouth shut and shakes her head.

"Zachariah, do it. But if he dies, you die."

He nods once, not remotely perturbed by my macabre ultimatum.

Turns out Luke's been shot but it's shallow, so he sits nearby to be tended to by his mother. I stick to Zachariah's side, watching every move he makes and passing him the things he needs. I want to see precisely what he's doing so I can remember it in case something goes wrong. He has extraordinary hands; the way his fingers move is more delicate than anything I've ever witnessed. Flesh is knitted back together with the tiniest stitches, the most nimble and tender of touches. It takes hours to repair everything but he doesn't stop or even pause for a break. He doesn't ask for water and he doesn't stretch his own muscles. He just works and works and works and when he's finished Shadow is whole again.

And I think even if he betrays us, even if this is a trap, it will have been worth it. For me, anyway.

*

My ears are still ringing hours later. I have one of the worst headaches of my life and no matter how much aspirin I down it won't ease. I'm still wearing the filthy, ripped white dress and my five tons of eyeliner have made their way over the entirety of my face. I need bed, badly, but first I have a matter to attend to.

In the middle of the arena is Zachariah, both his ankles tied by rope to either side of the silo. He can't go anywhere like that, so he's sitting calmly on the mats. Around him stand Luke, Will, Pace and Eric. Blue is lurking to the side because he gravitates to any drama like a gossip leech.

Luke moves to meet me apart from the others. "How'd you get him to come?" is the first thing he asks.

I shrug.

"Josi, I don't care what it is, I just need to know what tactic you used."

"I gave him the idea of freedom."

"And he just went for it?"

"I'm persuasive."

"Did you let him think he could have you?"

"*Have* me?"

"Yes."

"I'm not a possession."

"Did you or didn't you?" he snaps.

I sigh and nod.

"Did you kiss him?"

"Sorta."

Luke considers. "Okay, you're not trained for that kind of manipulation but it's something we could use to get him talking. Let him think there's still something between you and that you're working on getting the rest of us to trust him. Keep it subtle."

"He wants to be here. We don't have to manipulate him."

"Josi, he's a hostage and he's going back once we figure out what to trade him for. While he's our captive we gotta squeeze him for all he's got."

"By making him believe I like him?" I ask. "This sounds more like something you'd be good at. You've got the experience, after all."

Luke gives me a pained look that seems to say *please, not now*.

I bite my tongue, too tired to argue. We go back to the others in time to hear Pace say, "I reckon we should cure him. Serve the posh little bastard right."

"Shut up, Pace," I snap. "No one's doing anything to him."

She is taken aback at my tone but doesn't say anything.

I look at Zachariah. "Thank you," I say, and there's no manipulation in it, only genuine gratitude.

He nods once. His eyes dart between Luke and me and I can see him trying to work out who fits where and whether or not he's been played.

"Come on. Bed," Luke orders everyone and then I'm alone with our hostage.

"There'll be guards at the entrance," I warn him. "But you can sleep. No one'll hurt you."

He nods once more.

"Sorry about the ropes. I didn't …" I sigh and just about forget the English language.

"I get it. You have to be careful. Get some sleep, Dual."

"My name's Josephine Luquet."

Zachariah extends his hand and I shake it. "Pleased to meet you, Josephine Luquet. I always kind of figured you'd change my life, but I never thought it would be like this."

I pull my hand out of his, uncomfortable with the things he seems to mean. I let my expression grow firmer. "Don't make me regret bringing you down here, Zachariah Shay. These are the only people I love, and if you endanger them the world will get very ugly for you."

He nods and I can see in his eyes that he believes me.

I can see in his eyes that he might even fear me.

I wonder when I became a person to be feared.

*

March 9th, 2067

Luke

My sleep is fitful. My ribs are killing me and I can't stop thinking about the young man we brought into the tunnels. I've got a bad feeling about him. It was too easy.

Without Will's bomb – the power of which we sadly underestimated – we'd be dead now, and that's a direct result of not having a solid plan. Or much of a plan at all. We barreled in there without any info and a really unpredictable failsafe, and we did it because I can't say no to Josephine Luquet.

"It worked and we're all alive," she mutters halfway between dreaming and waking, knowing the exact reason I can't sleep.

I don't reply. I just lie here and worry about the next time something bad happens to someone she loves, because it apparently means the rules go out the window.

*

I keep dreaming about Doctor Meredith Shaw, the smudge of her dark hair and the white of her pale hand as she opened the gate to the Inferno and was swallowed up by a swarm of Furies. I keep dreaming about how small she looked in the distance, the shape of her and the terrible leaden weight of my own feet in reaching her. I dream again and again of not being able to stop her in time. Sometimes the tragedy of her loss is what wakes me, other times I hate her for the inexplicably violent act of opening that gate, and other times I wake with the undeniable knowledge that we can't keep living like this: we have to exterminate the monsters trying to eat us.

Because once again there are enemies within who might want to let them.

*

This morning the tunnels are abuzz with news of Shadow and Zachariah. We've got people rotating on guard duty for the hostage, bringing him food and water and escorting him on trips to the toilet. He's been utterly silent. As far as I know he hasn't spoken a word to anyone since he saved Shadow, and even then his words were solely reserved for Josephine. His gaze is one of the cruellest I have ever seen, and I've started thinking it might be a blessing he hasn't spoken whatever dark thoughts fill his head. As for Shadow, Mom is monitoring him closely but he still hasn't woken.

Josi spends the day at her father's side. I spend it patrolling and checking our fortifications, as I do every day. I spend it cooking tonight's meal with some of the kids and thinking thinking thinking. Training has been called off while Zachariah is held in the arena. We need a better place for him but the rest of the tunnels are usually filled with people and at least with the silo there's only one way in and out, and we can keep a constant eye on him.

I lie out the loaves of dough and then slide them into the single brick oven. Unlike the other fireplaces, we built this one by filing bricks at specific angles so they'd sit firmly together in a circular shape without needing any mortar. The roof of the oven has a dip in it, and by lighting the fire slightly to the side of this, the heat moves in a circular motion to ensure it cooks everything evenly. And best of all – there's no smoke. I leave Coin and Malia to watch the timer and make sure the bread doesn't burn.

"No making out," I warn them. "I do not want a repeat of what happened last time, got it?"

They mumble in agreement, remembering the twenty loaves they let ruin while distracted by each other's mouths.

I visit Dad in the storeroom. He's always in here doing inventory. He likes to keep busy and when his Parkinson's is bad he can't build or repair anything so he just comes here to be near all the supplies. It must be really shit to live down here and not be physically well enough to keep active. I mean, it must literally be like the most boring thing ever. I shudder at the thought. At least most of us can go running through the pitch-black stinking damp tunnels, but he just has to ... *be* in them.

"We need anything?" I ask him.

He pokes his head up from behind a stolen street sign. I have no idea what we'll use that for, but it'll be something. *Everything* can be used down here. "Nails. Always nails."

"Got it."

"Superglue. A larger drill bit. New electrical cables – it's not good to use the same ones forever, Lukey, they short out the generators."

I nod. It's always the same list. We do what we can, but food, medicine and warm clothes take priority. "You heard about the new kid?"

"There's always a new kid."

"This one's the prime minister's son."

"So he is. You're kidnapping people now are you, son?"

I don't know what to say to that. There's only one lamp lit in here and the space feels oppressively cramped within its glow.

"What do you plan on doing with him?"

"We'll get information. And we'll trade him for something we need." Even as I say this I know it's not true. There's a pit in my stomach because the kid has seen too much. He knows where we are and that means he can't go back to his dad. As far as everyone else is concerned, he'll be traded, but I have to bear the burden of the truth.

"Like chattel."

I sigh. "Yes, Dad, like chattel."

"What do you think the boy wants?"

"I don't care what he wants."

"What a fine leader you will make for the new world."

I shake my head, abruptly annoyed. "I won't be any kind of leader. It's not my job."

"Why's that?"

"Stop being obtuse, Dad."

He gives a wheezing laugh. His shaking gets worse. I try to help him into a chair but he pulls away from me. "Leave it."

"What do you want from me? I'm doing my best."

"I don't want anything from you. I want plenty of things *for* you, my boy."

"Like what?"

"Honor. Integrity. Courage."

The blow lands and it hurts. "I'm trying to get us out of these tunnels. I'm trying to win a war. He's an asset. Honor's got nothing to do with anything anymore."

Dad walks slowly around the table and puts his trembling hand on the back of my neck. He holds it tight enough to pinch my skin and I can feel that shake shake shake in my bones. "Slow, my boy," he says. "Slow right down. You rush, you hurt people."

"He's our enemy."

"Only if you make him so."

"It's like you're living in a little fantasy bubble down here. People are gonna get hurt no matter how fast or slow we go.

We're enemies of the regime. We plan to overthrow it. Do you think that'll happen with hugs and kisses?"

"Kidnapping a boy and holding him against his will is not doing your best, Luke. It's crossing a line."

I stare at him, and then I leave.

*

I'm more rattled than I realize by the conversation with Dad. At dinner I forget to eat until Eric flicks me in the side of the head and declares his intention to steal my portion unless it gets hoovered within ten seconds. Instead of eating it or giving it to his greedy black hole of a mouth, I take it to the arena.

Zachariah is lying on his back but sits up when he hears me. I put the plate in front of him and sit down. He doesn't eat, just looks at me with those weird black eyes.

"So here's the thing," I start softly. "You went with Josi pretty easily, which, as I see it, means one of three possibilities. Either you saw an opportunity with her. She's a beautiful woman. Maybe you've never met anyone like her. She likes you. You're young, lonely. I get it. Possibility two: you just wanted to get the fuck out of that place with its perfect lawns and water fountains and falseness. I get that too. Or possibility number three: you saw an opening, you took it. Your plan is to leave here and tell your dad exactly where we are, what we're doing, and how to kill us." I lean in a little closer. "Believe it or not, Zachariah, I get that one too. I understand about money and influence and status and power. I understand the roles we fit into. I understand misplaced certainty."

His expression doesn't shift in the slightest.

"I don't mind which it is, mate, I just want you to tell me. You won't get hurt no matter the answer."

Zachariah tilts his head and gives a soft sigh. An exhalation of breath. It's a funny thing, that little sigh. I wonder if he has any idea how young it makes him seem. I wonder if that was his intention.

He says, "You think you're in charge down here, don't you?"

My eyebrows arch in surprise.

Zachariah smiles. "You're not."

Scratch that. He doesn't seem young anymore. And it's not that there's malice in him. It's audacity. An arrogance he could hardly be expected to have avoided, growing up in the place he did.

I tell him simply, "I know exactly who's really in charge, and I'll follow her until my corpse has become the dust that a world of free, uncured people walk upon."

*

I find Josi by Shadow's bedside and sit with her for a while. The poor guy looks pretty ragged. He's about half the weight he used to be and his skin has a sallow tinge. I feel like we're forever waiting at someone's bedside. Forever burying our dead.

"Whatever you want to do with Zachariah, we'll do," I tell her softly.

Gently she reaches for my cheek. Smiles with her eyes. "We protect these kids. I think that matters more than anything. More than getting out of the tunnels or destroying the regime. I think it *has* to matter more."

"And you think he's a kid who needs protection?"

Josi bites her lip and turns back to Shadow. Sometimes a darkness falls over her and she goes missing in the past. I hate feeling like I can't follow her back there, can't even grab her hand to help her return. She murmurs, "Zachariah looks like I used to, don't you think? When violence was the only thing I'd come to expect from people?"

I stroke her hair and we sit in silence for a while. "Can I take you somewhere?"

"What about Shadow?"

"We won't be long, I promise."

*

I leave her at the armory to get us some weapons while I check the tech room for the surveillance camera I set up. It looks clear. Teddy's in here, scrolling through a security feed of somewhere in the city. Ensconced in the flickering blue light, he hardly notices me.

"Hey, kid, can you do me a favor?"

"As long as it's difficult. I'm bored out of my mind."

"No such luck, it's super easy."

Once I have him set up I return to find Josi waiting at one of the cages. She passes me two guns, a knife and a belt of ammunition clips. She's similarly armed. We climb up a ladder and into a new set of tunnels. These ones snake farther out and under the city wall. We follow them, turning left if we hear signs of Furies to the right, or vice versa. Eventually we snake our way into the beyond and emerge in the mouth of a tunnel that protrudes out the side of a cliff-face. We stand at its edge and look at the view.

Before us stretches the ocean. The sun has set and the sky is impossibly filled with stars. So many they're dazzling, a sparkling velvet roof to the world, and in its midst a brilliant silver full moon.

"Oh my god," Josi breathes at the sight. "Luke …"

"Swim?"

"Is that a trick question?"

We attach ropes and start climbing them down the crumbling cliff.

"Is it safe out here?"

"I've spent the last five weeks setting up security and watching for signs that Furies come anywhere near here, and as far as I can see they haven't. Plus I have Teddy on surveillance."

"So he'll be watching us swim?"

"Er … yes. But he's under strict instructions not to perve."

She laughs. "Gross."

We make it to the sand and run to the water's edge. Hopping while wrenching my boots off, I nearly fall on my ass. The sand is cool and coarse between my toes. It reminds me of a tiny beach on the opposite coast of the continent, the beach that helped me bring Josi back to life. The ocean, I think, is the one thing that has the power to save her from her depression, the never-ending plight of it. And maybe it saves her from more than that, too, from the weight of the tunnel walls and the clarity of her memories and the blood staining both our hands and from everything, everything she needs saving from.

I take off all my clothes and Josi laughs again. "What?"

"The poor kid'll have a heart attack."

"Only if you get naked too. Go on. Give him a thrill."

Teddy can't really see us – we'd just be black dots, given how far away the camera is – but I don't tell Josi that. She strips off in a rush and pelts into the water with a shrill gasp of delight.

I follow and surprisingly the water isn't as cold as it looks. The air above is so frigid that sinking below the surface is actually a relief. I hold my breath and stay under as long as I can. The sea is calm and the small waves do nothing but gently rock me. When I rise for air I see Josi floating on her back. The water's so salty it's easy. In the dark she's a silhouette. A tiny shape in the wide expanse of sea. Her own shadow.

"Another me has gills and scales," she murmurs. "She breathes salt."

I float on my back too and try to make shapes in the stars. I don't know any constellations, not one, but I still like the idea that there are secret stories in the spaces between them.

"Who loves the scaly, gilled you?"

"The scaly, gilled you," she says as though it's obvious, which I suppose it is.

We lie there thinking about these strange, creaturely versions of us. To me they sound monstrous but she's always seen the beauty in monstrousness.

Her long black locks of hair reach out in snakelike tendrils. I swim closer and let the tips of my fingers brush against their ends. My hand feels less stiff in the water, less distractingly sore. She talks so often of living in the sea and for the first time I can imagine enjoying it. If it stayed like this always, gentle and dark and soothing, then I might love it. If it stayed just me and her, I might die for it.

"Josi?"

"Mmm?"

"I gotta ask you something."

She sits up and treads water. We aren't touching but she's close enough that I can make out her face in the moonlight. "You sound ominous."

"Hopefully not. I just …" I let out a breath. I've been thinking about this for so long that I can't believe I'm finally here, that I've reached this point without any idea of what I'm going to say. "I keep thinking about the moment I first saw you."

"You mean when you were stalking me like a total creeper?"

"Yeah."

"Okay. So when was that?"

"Well, my memories don't normally have the clarity of yours. But I remember this one so clearly it's weird. I was sitting on this uncomfortable low wall enjoying a cigarette before you so cruelly made me give them up. I was really annoyed with you for just being you, basically. I was so annoyed by the watch op. I'd been waiting for you to come home for hours—"

"Tardy old me."

"And then you appeared. There were so many drones around that I only caught a glimpse of you at first. I thought I might not recognize you from your picture but I did. I knew you straight away. You were wearing ripped stockings and boots and your hair was in this messy braid and you wore a hoodie that was about three sizes too big for you. You were so thin. You pushed your way out of the crowd and plunged across the busy street and walked straight into my line of sight and you had this look on your face, and you were just barely mouthing something, like maybe you were singing under your breath or reading a book from your memory or something crazy. And you were strange and beautiful and awkward. And I felt …" I stop because I can't find the words. My chest is so swollen, the sky so enormous.

"Luke, you're embarrassing me."

"Just listen. It was like I ... I was ... I just *knew*, Jose. I never knew I'd been waiting but I knew then. I thought *here she is*."

She smiles but I can tell she feels awkward about being complimented, or maybe just about the sentiment. I laugh a little, reaching for her waist and pulling her against me. Our bodies are evolutionary triumphs, in this moment they're as wondrously creaturely as our monstrous counterparts. "I'm nearly done," I assure her softly.

"There's *more*?"

"Marry me."

She stares at me. It's so quiet in this infinite night. Just the waves crashing on the shore behind us and the beat of our pulses. I think, abruptly, of my brother.

"Life's so short," I murmur. "Let's get married, Josi."

I could watch the world burn if I had to; I've always known it. But I could never leave her. There are things that matter and then there is Josephine.

For the first time in my life I think she might feel the same way.

Because she says, "Of course," and I taste her salty lips.

Chapter 8

August 1st, 2046

Luke

The spade is giving me blisters. I sit back on the edge of my hole and survey it. It's about three feet deep and four wide. It takes a considerable amount of time to dig a hole this big; I'm pretty proud of myself. Within it the earth is rich and a little bit moist, but it's too dark to see much else. I imagine wriggling worms and roots of trees and maybe ancient fossils and pieces of buried treasure. Anything could be down here. There could be a *body* down here, for all I know.

Dave's lying behind me, plucking at the strings of his guitar. He's too good at it to be normal, not good enough to be special, as he puts it. He's always plucking the same tune, over and over as though it's somehow engraved in the pads of his fingers. I'm sick to death of it.

"Don't you wanna help?" I ask.

Dave snorts in that dismissive way of his. I don't really get how he can be so content not to know things, things like what lives beneath us, what's under this grass, this earth, what's deep within it. Doesn't he ever want to *find* anything? I do like that he's keeping me company, though. The backyard's a little too big to be entirely comfortable at night. And maybe he finds things of his own in the strings of his guitar. That's what Dad says, anyway.

"Luke!"

Uh oh. It's the voice of an insane person.

I drop the spade in the hole and shoot to my feet. Mom is storming across the lawn and she looks mad. Like, proper mad.

"What the hell are you *doing*?" she demands.

I blink and look around at the dozen or so holes in the backyard, thinking it's rather obvious what I'm doing. "Digging."

"I can see that. The implied question was *why*?"

I shrug. "To find something."

"Such as?"

"Anything. There's bound to be something under here, right?"

She stares at me with that crazy look in her eyes. Even though I'm used to it, it's still a pretty freaky look. "He's dug up the whole damn garden! Why didn't you stop him?" she asks Dave.

"Stop him?" my brother repeats like she's spoken another language.

Mom shakes her head and pinches my ear to get me back inside. "In the bath. You're filthy. And then we're going to have a serious discussion about why you feel it's necessary to be the most badly behaved nine-year-old on the planet."

*

August 28th, 2046

Luke

I dump the freshly removed alternator on my bedroom floor and drag Dad's toolbox over. With a screwdriver I start taking the pieces of metal apart, unscrewing all the little nuts and screws, prying the cylinder thingy off. I pinch my little finger but after I suck on it, it stops stinging. I have to get it completely apart. I have to get at what's inside so I can see how it works. It's important that I know how it works, because this lump of metal moves a *car*.

The back door slams shut and I hear footsteps.

Uh oh.

"Claire?" I hear Dad call.

"Bedroom!"

Dad's footsteps go past my room to reach his and I hold my breath the whole time, praying he won't look in here.

The walls in our house are as thin as paper, Dave says, so I can hear their conversation easily.

"The alternator's gone from my car!" Dad announces quizzically.

"What?"

"It's vanished."

There's a pause and I realize I've gotten engine grease all over the carpet. That's when Mom screams. "LUKE!"

*

October 3rd, 2046

Luke

Let it be known that Dave is an excellent model airplane flyer. He doesn't hit anything, he just zooms smoothly through the air, looping and spinning and avoiding all manner of obstacle. But where's the fun in that?

"Can I have a go?" I ask for the fifth time.

He sighs and hands the controller over. If I nag him enough he usually gives in. He's pretty good like that. The plane dips wildly as I struggle to work the buttons and then it swoops back into the sky.

I spy a tree. There are plenty of trees in our backyard, but the one I have my eye on is a particularly good one. Nice and solid, big enough to do considerable damage.

I angle the plane straight at the tree and press the accelerator.

"Careful!" Dave shouts, just as the plane smashes into the trunk.

Its pieces fall fabulously, no longer attached to each other but free to flutter in spectacular arcs. I drop the controller and sprint to the wreckage.

"Luke!" Dave yells in frustration. "This is why I didn't want you to have a turn!"

I'm too busy gathering the parts and peering inside them. I don't get what his problem is – the plane is way more interesting now that you can see how it works.

Mom inevitably arrives, alerted by Dave's big mouth. I'm dragged inside by the ear with a lot of scolding about how expensive that plane was and how it was Dave's birthday present and not everything is mine to destroy and lots of other things like that which are probably totally true and I do start to feel really bad that I wrecked something of Dave's but I just don't really get what the problem is. It's not like I tried to stop him from playing with the pieces – I'd gladly share them with him. We could have rebuilt the plane together, once we'd figured out how.

Mom puts me in front of the TV and tells me that if I move she's going to bury me in one of the holes I dug. Then she turns on a wildlife program but I hate sitting still and she knows that. I start fidgeting with the rug, tearing off the bits of wool at the end even though I shouldn't. I just can't stop myself.

My eyes alight on the holodrive under the TV and it occurs to me that I have no idea what it looks like inside. Overwhelming curiosity strikes and I unplug it. I have to break one side of it in order to get the top off but once I do I can see in to all the hardware and wires. Interesting. There's one wire in particular that piques my interest. I follow it to the chip panel but then decide that to really work it out I'll have to strip the plastic casing off.

I don't realize at first that Dad's sitting on the couch behind me, watching between sips of beer. Our eyes meet. I freeze red-handed. But Dad lifts a finger to his nose and pointedly shifts his attention to the TV.

I start stripping the wire.

"Luke! What—?" Mom catches sight of Dad. "Why are you letting him do that?"

"I dunno. He's curious," is Dad's reply.

"For god's sake! You both deserve to be buried!"

*

October 9th, 2046

Dave

My little brother happens to be three years younger than me, a thousand times smarter, the most annoying person to have ever existed and also my favorite in the world.

Basically, if you want to keep any of your stuff you have to think of brilliant hiding places where he won't get his grubby hands on it. I've got things stashed all over the place, but Mom hasn't come around to my tactics yet – I think she still holds out hope that he'll learn to behave himself, which is about as likely as me growing wings. Poor, sweet, naïve Mom.

When I get home from school I dump my bag in our bedroom and see Lukey fiddling with the electric chip of Mom's new tablet. He's totally lost to the world and hasn't even noticed me.

My eyes widen. "Jeez, you must really have a death wish."

"Nah, I've got her wrapped around my little finger." Lukey looks up at me with a sweet, innocent expression. "Would you kill this face?"

I crack up and he grins wickedly.

"Boys?" Mom calls as she arrives home from her shift at the hospital.

"Quick!" I exclaim, lunging for the electrical bits and trying to shove them under the bed.

The door opens. "Hello, my darlings – hey, what is that? What are you hiding?"

We're sprung. Mom sees the broken tablet and the crazy eyes arrive. "That's for my work!"

"I did it," I tell her.

"Funny, kid. You're very funny." She looks at Luke. "If that's broken you're in trouble."

"'Course it's not broken."

"They're *always* broken. And this time I'm taking every single thing out of this room and locking you in it. There won't be anything you can get your hands on and you'll be forced to use your imagination for once."

"That's child abuse!" he protests.

"Yeah, probably."

*

This time Mom actually goes through with her threat. Lukey and I watch in astonishment as she pulls everything from the room. Like, *everything* everything. It takes a lot of effort and I think we both keep expecting her to lose interest in the punishment before she finishes. No such luck.

Me and Mom and Dad sit down to dinner. We can hear him moaning from the empty room.

"You can't do this!" his little voice calls. "It's a form of torture!"

I see Mom hiding her smile by stuffing her mouth with salad.

"It is pretty mean." Dad grins.

"He's a terrorist," she replies. "He's methodically destroying everything in this house, piece by piece."

Lukey starts singing at the top of his voice. "*Woe is me, I've been given no tea!*"

I have to breathe deeply to stop myself from laughing. We are all staring very hard at our meals.

Lukey's voice gets louder. "*And when my family found my bloated corpse, they all keeled over and died of remorse!*"

Mom looks at Dad. He looks at me. I look at Mom. We all look at each other and then without anyone going first we're all suddenly just laughing and laughing and my guts hurt and Dad's got tears coming out of his eyes and then Mom wheezes, "See? He's becoming a wordsmith already."

*

When I go to bed it's to find Lukey lying on the floor, banging his feet repetitively against the wall. There's nothing left in here except two beds and an empty desk. Even the closet has been locked shut.

I've covertly been to the garage, to one of my genius hiding spots. Without a word I thrust my favorite game console and a screwdriver at Lukey. He stares at it in surprise.

"What's this for?"

"Just don't tell Mom."

"But this is your favorite!"

"Yeah, you owe me, weirdo."

We share a grin and before I've even climbed into bed with my book he's already started unscrewing the console.

It drives Mom spare, but secretly I kinda think it means Luke's going to be something special one day. And like I said, he's my favorite person. I'd take him over any of our stuff any day. Plus it's really funny when he gets caught. Just ask Mom and Dad – they laugh more than any people I know.

*

November 1st, 2046

Dave

It's stopped being funny today.

Because today whatever this curious thing within my little brother is made him cut open his own arm just to see what was inside.

When we get home from the hospital he's already bouncing around like a maniac again. His arm's stitched and bandaged and the doctor said he's fine, but the rest of us feel heavy with what he did. We're not laughing now, of course we're not. I feel a little freaked. I want to shake him and make him stop and listen but he never will.

Mom takes us all into the backyard. I don't know what this is about but I remember their conversation in the hospital.

I was in the room with Lukey, trying to keep him entertained while we waited for the doctor to discharge him. Mom and Dad were in the hall right outside so I don't know why they thought we couldn't hear, or maybe they just didn't care.

"It's too early," I heard Dad say.

"Do you want him to keep digging? Because soon it'll be his legs and his stomach and then it'll be his chest! He won't stop!"

I didn't hear what Dad said.

"He needs something. An awareness of his body, at the very least. Respect for it."

"It's brutal, Claire. He's only nine. I promised myself I wouldn't put either of them through what Dad did to me."

"This world grows more brutal by the day. What do you think will happen when he tears his way out of our house, and wants to tear out of the city? What happens when he tears his way out of his own damn body, Tobias?"

The doctor came then so we didn't hear any more. But I kept thinking about how hard Mom's voice goes when she's scared. Lukey only gets the stern parts of her, or the amused ones, but when he's not looking I see the softness under her frowns. I see her vulnerability. Since Luke cut himself she's been way more scared and soft than ever before, and that means it comes out as angry and loud.

Now we're standing in the backyard in the dark. A mozzy lands on my arm and I slap it. Mozzies always get me more than anyone else in this family. Dad says it's because my blood's the sweetest.

"It's your decision, boys," he says now. "Would you like to learn to box?"

I bounce on the balls of my feet. "*Yes!*"

Lukey makes a face. "Not particularly."

"Why not?"

"It's boring."

Dad walks over to Luke and pins him onto the grass in between two of his holes. Lukey wriggles in surprise. "Dad!"

"Listen to me," Dad says in a soft voice I've never heard him use before. "You are not invincible, my boy. You are very, very fragile."

I think to myself that I will never forget him saying that. Because when I look at my brother's face and see that he's finally listening, my chest fills with relief. I think maybe Mom and Dad have just saved Lukey's life.

*

June 12th, 2052

Luke

Even though I turned fifteen yesterday I'm still not half the size of Dave. I catch myself looking at his body all the time, feeling envious of the strength of it, the speed and the muscle tone. He's always flexing his biceps to annoy me. He loves wrestling when we're not out the back with our gloves on, because when we're out the back with our gloves on I beat him every time, no matter how much tinier I am.

School sucked balls today and I'm really ready for training. Instead of going through the house I cut round the back: I'm not in the mood for a lecture from Mom about something or other. Just to make my day worse I arrive in time to find Dave making out with his girlfriend. Sighing, I lean against the side of the house and wait for them to be done. The hours that Dave and Livvy have spent kissing could probably date back to the Big Bang, so I'm not holding out hope it'll be any time soon.

I'm at window level now so I can see into the kitchen. Mom's sitting at the table with a woman I've never seen before. She's wearing a black suit and has very dark skin, and not even the suit can disguise how tall and athletic she is. I see it straight away: there's motion in her stillness.

I strain to hear what they're saying.

"It's unusual to see intellectual scores this high in someone equally physically elite," the woman says.

"But it pays well?" Mom asks.

"Extremely."

Something pummels into my chest and scares the shit out of me. It's a pair of boxing gloves, pressed there by Dad.

"Eavesdropping, boyo?"

I clutch at my heart. "God, Dad."

"Come on. Training."

"Who's that lady?"

He shrugs in this very casual way. "Friend of Mom's."

I don't believe him for a second but I dump my schoolbag, take off my uniform shirt and pull my gloves on. "Let's do this, bro!"

Dave extracts himself from Livvy's mouth and bounds over to me. "Stroppy, are we? You gotta get laid, kid."

"Shut up!" I hate it when he talks about me getting laid in front of Livvy because she always smiles as though I'm some little kid they both laugh about behind my back.

We put our mouth guards in and soft helmets on. Then Dave and I touch gloves and get straight into it. He's always leaving himself unprotected, the idiot. I go in for the attack and hit him a few times in the ribs, just to warm him up. He may be bigger and stronger but he's slow as shit and lately he's always distracted by his girlfriend.

We go a few rounds and then I start really laying into him. For the sex comment. For bringing Livvy to our private trainings. For not being around as much. For growing up without me.

"Get your hands up, Dave!" Dad shouts. "Christ."

But Dave's got no hope. He puts his hands up and I just punch him in the guts. He moves them down and I punch him in the face.

"Push back, Dave! Get your head up!"

But he doesn't, and he doesn't even seem to be trying that hard.

"Stop, stop, stop. That'll do."

Dave and I both spit out our mouth guards. He's bleeding from a cut on his eyebrow. I grin and lift my gloves high, dancing around like a bit of a prick. Dave doesn't get offended though – he never does. He just laughs.

"What's wrong?" Dad asks him.

Dave shrugs. "I told you I'm not into it anymore."

"Dave's a pacifist," I tease.

He shrugs again, sharing a look with Livvy that makes me think that's exactly what he is.

Dad pulls Dave's gloves off for him and starts putting them on his own hands.

"Woah, big Daddy's in for it now!" I crow.

As I wait for him to do them up I can't help looking back at the kitchen window. The woman's still there with Mom, only now they're both standing at the glass and watching us.

"Who is that?" I ask, not of anyone in particular. Nobody answers me.

Instead Dad just attacks with a full-on blow to my face that I only manage to block at the very last second. Jeez. I spend the next few minutes moving as fast as I can to avoid Dad's mammoth punches but pretty soon he lands one in my guts and I hit the ground, winded.

"Not so cocky now are we, pal?" Dave asks from the side.

I'd give him the finger if I could.

Instead I look up at Dad, who's standing over me like an ancient Viking god of war or something. He does this every now and then to remind me, to make sure I never, ever forget.

"I get it, Dad," I tell him.

He nods and helps me get my gloves off.

I do get it: my fragility.

*

After dinner I find Dave in the bathroom, looking at himself in the mirror. He has his shirt off and there are a bunch of bruises darkening over his chest and stomach. I drape my arms around his shoulders and grin at his reflection.

"Get out of it."

"Sore loser, as usual. Who was that lady here?"

"Dunno. No one."

I frown, zeroing in on his eyes, which won't meet mine.

"You do know. Who was it?"

There's this long, weird silence. It's like Dave doesn't know what to say, but he always knows what to say so that can't be it. After a minute he reaches up to clasp my arm still draped around him.

"You're different," he says.

"To what?"

"To us."

I try not to let that hurt. "Meaning?"

Dave turns around so he can look me in the face. "Meaning there will always be people who are gonna try to make you into something, or push you, or use you. You're gonna have people pulling at you all the time, bro. They'll want so much of you because you have so much to give but the thing is that you don't *have* to give anything. You don't have to."

I don't understand what he's talking about. My skin feels hot. "Who was she?"

"I tried to stop them. They wouldn't listen."

My heart's beating funny in my chest now. My guts feel tight. "What the fuck are you talking about?"

Dave takes my chin and it's way too intense and I don't know why the hell he's doing this and then he says, my big brother, "I love you best of all."

"What? Fuck off."

I push him away, hard enough that he hits the edge of the sink and winces. Dave starts to leave the bathroom but in a panic I reach for him and pull him into a tight hug. He clutches at me and I know something's really wrong. I can feel it in his arms, his strong, strong arms.

*

December 17th, 2067

Luke

I'm thinking of this, all of this, right now as we stagger our way home. I'm in his arms again, my big brother's arms. We're supporting each other because I'm weak from being held captive in the lab and he's just weak. Years of our lives are rushing through my mind and I just keep thinking how stupid it was that we were always afraid for me, for the little brat who couldn't keep still, the boy who liked to pull everything apart, the one who got taken away by the Bloods. We were always so sure that one day my own voracity would get me killed, but in the end it was Dave we should have been worried about. Dave who got lost when everyone was looking instead at me.

*

There is hatred in my guts as we reach the infirmary. Pure self-loathing. If I'd watched him closer, if I'd been a better brother I would have seen him get stolen, I would have stopped it or gotten him back. I would never have accepted the lie of his suicide, I would have known in my heart that it couldn't be true and I would have saved my parents from having to endure the death of their son. Instead I hated him for leaving me.

Josi read me a Leunig poem once, the first lines of which I can't forget and I don't remember it very well, but one piece of it really stuck with me. It was about suffering *lifeache*, about having a life that was sore, one that hurt to move.

This was how I came to see my mother in the days and weeks and years after we were told that Dave had killed himself. Her whole life ached; she could hardly bear it. She was silent. She grew still as a sarcophagus in her tomb. She hurt too much to move.

It was my father who began to move more than any body should move and who made the sound, who wailed with a noise I'll never forget. There are no words for that sound, except to call it animal. Wild animal grief. The end of life. The beginning of something much less.

For my part, I dissolved. My favorite person had left me as I'd always feared he would. I scattered and vanished.

Now he's here in my arms once more and it's a miracle, it is, only he doesn't feel like my brother. He doesn't feel like my Dave. If only I'd held him tighter back then, when I had the chance. If only I'd never let him go.

*

We arrive to see Zach inspecting Josi's gruesome leg and to see Mom taking Will's blood pressure. Dave and I stop in the entrance and I find I have no voice. I feel panicked and excited beyond words.

It's Dave who speaks up.

"Hi, Mom," he says.

"Get over here and help, Luke," she answers.

Dave and I glance at each other. "I'll come back?" he asks me softly.

I shake my head and we shuffle farther into the room.

"Mom," Dave says again.

"What?"

He starts laughing a little. It surprises me so much that I laugh too.

And that's when Mom goes rigid. She's hearing two of the same voice when there should only be one. Her whole body tenses. She has a stethoscope in her hand as she turns and makes this high-pitched sort of yelp and then she just stares.

I don't remember the poem's cure for lifeache. I'm sure it was beautiful. I'm also sure we've found our own, here in this grotty smelling tunnel. Here in the look that passes between mother and son, between two people who have been altered and changed and made a little less than they used to be. And less though they may be, the look they share reaches up through the ground above us, through the earth and the sky and through the roof of the world and it finds a space for itself in the things that last forever, in the things that cannot be stolen. It is beyond love, beyond any ability to cure love. And when Dave takes her in his arms and holds her I can see the evidence of him, of his soul or spirit or whatever it is that makes him *him*; I see it still there in the tremble and strength of his hands as he holds his weeping mother who laughs when she's supposed to cry but who is crying now, finally.

I can do nothing but sink onto the edge of a bed and watch them. I think I have lifeache too. My whole life is sore. It hurts too much to move.

Chapter 9

March 15th, 2067

Josephine

I play to Phillipe. I've been playing to him for hours. In my head I've decided he's going to be Phillipe and not Shadow, just as I'd want him to call me Josi and not Dual. I think the Inferno names are a shield and you shouldn't have shields among family.

What a bizarre thought. I can't shake this uncanny feeling that it must not be true. I'm not a person who has family, certainly not parents. It doesn't seem real that this man could be related to me. I keep asking myself why he never told me. He must have known I was his daughter. And in all that time he didn't say a word. It makes me think, of course – the persistent whining rumbling nauseating thought – of my mother. But she's too big an ache so my thoughts slide away from her to easier things.

Like the cello made by my very own boyfriend. *Fiancé*. (God, what a trip.) In my hands this homemade cello lives and breathes and in its hands I do the same. I'm more returned to my strange dreams, my otherworldly imaginings. I keep thinking of these other versions of me; I can't stop.

I wonder if once upon a time they all got engaged to Luke in the ocean at night. I wonder if any of them did. I wonder if they are each as stained as I am or if they escaped that fate somehow; I wonder if they fear sleep.

People come in and out of the infirmary to listen to me play. Luke spends as much time as he can afford sprawled on the bed next to Phillipe's, reading and listening to my long slow notes. Claire hovers a lot, checking the patient endlessly and sometimes humming along. Zachariah checks on him too, now that he's no longer tied up in the arena. He says the wound is infection-free, which was the biggest concern. He's also explained that Phillipe is still unconscious because of the state of his body before the stabbing. From the spaces between Zachariah's words I can gather it was a terrible six months for my father. The young surgeon sits in the corner and watches me play. I get the feeling his dark eyes see a lot. Pace brings Hal here when she wants him to fall asleep. The only one who doesn't seem to be enjoying it is Phillipe, who won't wake up no matter how hard I musically beg him.

Tonight it's quiet. Everyone else is already in bed or on watch duty. It's just Phillipe and me. I've played him some very rowdy Prokofiev and some schmaltzy Debussy but now I put my feet up on his bed and rest my aching shoulders in a moment of silence.

"So you don't like any of that, huh?" I murmur. "I wonder what you do like."

"I have a request."

I turn to see that Luke has returned. He was here not long ago but he left to go to bed. I've lost track of time – I think it's very late. "What are you doing?" I ask softly. "Go get some sleep."

"I'm bored with sleep." He lies on the second mattress and rests his arms behind his head.

"What's your request? If I have to play Ennio fucking Morricone again for you I'll chop my ears off." I'm fairly sure he's the only cello composer Luke can remember, or else he just really likes the cheesiest of all cheese.

But instead he says, "Do you know Elgar?"

My head whips around to him. I stare, I can't help it. I think some part of my spirit has broken free and floated up into the sky. "What?"

"It's okay." He shakes his head to dismiss the idea.

"Luke." I clear my throat. "How do you know Elgar?"

"You know it?"

"The cello concerto?"

Now he looks unsure. "I think so."

"Why do you want me to play that? I've never played it for you before."

"But you know it?"

I nod slowly.

Luke breathes out. I wait, feeling strangely adrift. He's never once said a single word to me about a classical piece of music, never so much as hinted at having heard any before he met me.

"I used to know it well," he murmurs. Then, "It was Dave's favorite. He played it day and night for about a year straight."

The little piece of me finds its place. It's too strange a coincidence, or maybe it's simply an example of the undeniable grace of the world. I so easily forget it.

I try to explain but my words come out poorly. "I first heard Elgar's concerto being played by a woman called Jacqueline du Pre. I saw this old black and white video of it when I was eleven. I wasn't supposed to be on the computer but my foster brother had left it open so I stumbled upon this ancient recording and I think ..." I shake my head and smile. "It was the end of me."

Luke looks at me through narrowed eyes as though he can't quite believe what I'm saying.

"She died," I say. "She was the most wonderful thing, this marvelous thing. She had this mad passionate affair with her conductor and then she got multiple sclerosis and had to stop playing when she was only 28 and she couldn't move and her soulfulness was trapped inside this withering body until she died ... And I just remember ... It was such a tragedy to me at eleven." I meet his eyes. "Her playing Elgar was the loveliest thing I've ever heard. It's my favorite piece of all."

Luke closes his eyes and rests his arms over his face. It's too sweet, too bitter. Ships passing each other in the night. I miss his brother as though he was my own flesh and blood. Now more than ever I feel connected to him, to this shared desperate love of a piece of music. I'm not sure the profundity of such a thing can be expressed or believed if it isn't experienced; I think maybe poor Dave is the only one who might understand how it feels.

"Play it?" he asks.

I wipe my eyes. "I can't. I've never played it before."

"Why not?"

I shake my head – I don't know.

"Why?" he presses.

"I'm scared of it."

Here's my secret: I've never played it, not a single note of it, but somehow it's playing inside my heart on a constant loop.

He doesn't argue or tell me not be scared, he just nods a fraction and lets me be scared. And I decide that I will play it for him as a wedding present. I will. When, and only when, Phillipe has woken.

December 17th, 2067

Josephine

My leg hurts like skin and muscle and flesh being peeled off bone. Which is what's happened. Zach is repairing it. He recommended pain medicine, or failing that, liters of alcohol, but I've eschewed both. I don't feel comfortable enough to lose my senses. So instead I have fire and grinding bone and raw screaming nerve endings in my right leg. I keep my eyes closed. I think of the sky. It's not pain like I've come to know pain, after all. Anything's bearable until it's not and then you die.

Luke and his brother arrive at the infirmary. They've made it home safely and I'm glad. Luke and his brother. *His brother.* Whatever else I've become incapable of, I'm not incapable of a flicker of true joy. Here and then gone again, but here just for a moment. Pain has other ideas about any moments I might be feeling. I clench my jaw shut tight as red-hot pokers plunge into my body.

"Sorry," Zach murmurs. His hands are very gentle, as far as I can tell. His eyes are more so. I don't want gentle.

I don't want anything.

I glance at the brothers, looking at their mother. They're very different in appearance. Luke is a head taller, broader wider stronger, all the things one might want to be. Dave is worryingly lean. They have the same hair color, the same jaw lines, the same mouths. Not the same noses or foreheads, not the same eyes. Dave's are hazel, more brown than his brother's green ones. I don't know why I'm lying here making an inventory but I am. Maybe I'm making it to stem the pain of my leg but more likely it's because Claire has turned and seen them. I'm making lists of unimportant things because I think it might be too much to see her first glimpse of her dead son.

When she hugs Dave, Luke sits down on the end of my bed. He sits like he just can't stand anymore. I could reach to touch him. I should. Of course I should. Once upon a time my hands would have known to do that before my mind formed the thought. Muscle memory. But now they stay clenched in my lap, now they want nothing less than to touch him.

My eyes catch sight of my missing finger and I feel a sharp stab of panic that rears me backwards. I don't move an inch but inside my body I have reeled and recoiled and shuddered. Nothing passes my face but beneath the planes of skin and bones and cartilage I am breathless and panting. This roof is way way way too low and these walls are closing in. The tunnels are unbearable: I don't belong here.

I don't reach to touch my husband.

No music plays within me. I'm silent inside.

I'm even silent when Tobias finally hobbles his way into the room and his face is too much, his bright brilliant wail is flung free of his lungs, his tears and his sobs and his shaking shaking endless shaking. Dave reaches in time to catch his fall; Tobias trembles so violently that he can't hold himself up but his son is there. They both slump to the ground and they're holding each other so they're both shaking and all I can hear is "My boy, my boy, my boy, my boy."

Luke doesn't move from his spot at the end of the bed, he just watches.

And that's when Dave looks up over his father's shoulder. But he doesn't look at his brother, strangely. He looks at me.

He tries to communicate something, some silent message, but I can't interpret it. I'm no longer the sort of person who can read such messages. So we just stare at each other. Two lost, vacant souls, drowning.

I think of Elgar's cello concerto, I think of Jacqueline du Pre: I can't help it. I think of how, when Dave was dead, that piece bound us together. I think of how transformative it was for me as a child, how formative it was for me as an adult. I think of how it connected me to this dead man, to this part of Luke's family that was beyond Luke, to something that was even more than him, to something that was his brother.

And I see in Dave's eyes now that he wouldn't recognize it. His soul wouldn't know the concerto, not like it once had.

What's more, nor does mine.

The tragedy is all those marvelous notes and all that heart being sliced free of their connection to our bodies and left to soar up and away and gone. The tragedy is immense; I don't feel even a scrap of it.

*

March 16th, 2067

Josephine

"Ummmm ... I've been hearing some very concerning rumors about you."

I turn from washing dirty dishes to glance at Pace languishing in the doorway. "What?"

"Offensive rumors. The kind I might have to denounce friendship with you over."

"I'm distracted and not really in the mood for this, so could you get to the point please?"

"People are going around saying you're engaged," she announces.

My eyebrows arch and I quickly turn back to the dishes. There are six other people on clean-up duty, and they're all studiously pretending not to hear this conversation. I can feel their gossipy ears waggling for more info.

"Answer!" Pace commands.

"Jesus, chill *out*." I scrub a tray with burned dough stuck to its edges.

"I don't believe this."

"I didn't say anything!"

"Your silence screams, traitor."

I turn to face her and spread my hands. "How am I a traitor?"

"We're meant to be single sisters in solidarity forever!"

My mouth falls open. "You had a *baby*. I see you about point five percent of what I used to."

"I'm still single!"

"And sociopathic, apparently."

"Are you really?" she asks seriously.

I hesitate. A thought grabs me and I find myself striding out into the dining room. Everyone is still lurking, listening to Malia play her guitar (still terrible, even after dozens of lessons) and Blue telling some stupid story about Batman that he ripped off a movie.

I climb up onto one of the tables, my heavy boots rattling the wine cups. "Excuse me!" I shout.

I've never yelled on a table before, and nor to my knowledge has anyone else, so they all turn curiously to see what's got me acting like a loon. My eyes search the faces and spot first Claire, braiding Georgie's hair (she has a weird thing about braiding hair and will launch guerrilla braid attacks if you aren't careful), and then Tobias, whistling while he reads a book in the corner. I spot Luke sitting among Alo, Coin and Lawrence and playing some kind of sicko game where they flick a coin into each other's knuckles as hard as possible for no conceivable reason. They all look up at me and I start to laugh a little. Slowly at first, and then harder.

"She's lost it," I hear Eric say placidly.

I shake my head and try to get a grip. I have music playing in my heart. I always do. Today it's sweet and happy.

"Just one thing," I say. "For all of you who've been angling to get me into bed – you know who you are, it's at least ninety percent of you – you can now consider yourselves failures and give up."

They stare at me quizzically. The comedy hasn't landed well.

I say, somewhat awkwardly, "I'm getting married."

There's a pause and then Lawrence shouts, "To who?" and the rest of the tunnel explodes into laughter and applause.

People are reaching out to pat Luke heavily on the back and give him rough hugs. He grins shyly, shaking hands and returning the hugs. I watch him and the mess of sound and movement turns to a blur around him. I see the duck of his head and the warmth of his expression, I see the fall of his hair and the dimple in one of his cheeks and the scruffy beard he's been growing. His eyes finally find mine. Over the distance I wink and he smiles a smile I could die for.

"I will not be involved in the wedding in any way," I add. "Masochists need only apply for the job."

In the shadows by the door I spot Zachariah and feel a pit of sudden guilt in my stomach. I push through the excitement and follow him into the quiet dark. I can hardly see his face.

"Sorry," I blurt. "For not telling you."

"Why would you need to tell me?" His voice is cold. Way colder than it's been with me. It makes me think of his father.

"Look, I'm not gonna play games around this. You and I had a connection when we first met and I took advantage of it. I let you think something might happen between us when I'm not available for that. I'm sorry. It was cruel."

Zachariah's head tilts. His eyes are black hollows. "So if you were available it would be a different story?"

"But I'm not."

"But if you were." He says this like a statement, not a question. Like he thinks he's been given an answer and he likes it.

I shake my head quickly. "Zachariah ..."

"Call me Zach. I'll be here." Then he disappears down the tunnel. I'm left staring after him and feeling distinctly uneasy about the exchange.

"You okay?" Luke asks from the doorway. I have no idea how much of that he heard. I nod and we both look at the empty darkness.

"He makes me nervous," Luke admits.

I clear my throat. "Why?"

"Aside from you, I don't know what he wants."

I realize he's right. Which makes Zachariah the most dangerous person down here.

*

"I'm kidding, we're not having a wedding, obviously," I say an hour later in Claire and Tobias' bed-tunnel.

"What?" Luke asks. They're all looking at me in very concerning way.

"We're not having a wedding," I repeat.

"So we're not getting married?"

"That's not what I said. We'll do the equivalent of going to city hall and signing a contract or whatever people do."

Now they're looking at me like I'm an alien species.

"Are you out of your mind?" Claire asks me.

"I don't think so, but it sounds like you're about to tell me otherwise."

"You're having a wedding," she assures us. "For the sake of the world, you're having a wedding."

I can't help laughing. "Why would we want to get married in these tunnels?"

"Why wouldn't we?"

"They're depressing as hell and we don't have the resources."

Claire brushes this off. "We'll scrounge."

"Don't argue," Tobias tells me out of the side of his mouth. "She might murder someone."

"Well, I'm not being involved," I say, raising my hands in surrender.

"I will be," Luke offers. There is a distinctive light in his eyes. It's very much like eagerness. "I have a bunch of ideas."

I share a grin with Tobias and then head for the door. "Okay, I'm on patrol. See ya."

"Josi," Claire forestalls. She follows me to the door and then pulls me out into the tunnel. I can't see the freckles on her nose in this light but I know they're there. She takes my arm tenderly. "I have a lot of inefficient neural pathways and blocked emotional triggers. I'm an altered model. But they could take away every single thing I am and I'd still know how much I love you."

I suck in a startled breath; it catches in my throat.

Claire reaches for my face and holds it in both hands. "He was worse than we are," she murmurs. "Before you. He was a machine. Now he's a man."

I swallow and whisper, "I was a monster and now I'm a woman."

"We love you, sweetheart."

I nod and it's the second time she's said it in thirty seconds and I still can't say it back. I'm too uncomfortable. She doesn't mind, I don't think – she smiles and kisses me and goes back inside. I stand in the dark for a little while.

Instead of going to my patrol I go to the infirmary. Zachariah is here – he's always here – but I don't speak to him tonight. I go straight to Phillipe and shake his shoulders.

"That's enough! Wake up! I'm tired of not having you."

"Josi, wait," Zachariah says but I've spent too many hours waiting at bedsides. When Luke was dying I spent months waiting for him to wake up.

"I'm not going to do this anymore," I tell my father.

And he opens his eyes.

They're black like neither of mine.

"He woke a little while ago," Zachariah informs me.

I sit down hard. As relief replaces shock I take Phillipe's hand. Mine is shaking.

There is a gentle thing in his gaze, something infinite as we stare at each other. There are things I hate him for, things I can't forgive him for, questions I need to ask. But right now they fade away and instead I'm just grateful to have him here and alive and awake.

"You're a jerk for not telling me," I say.

Phillipe sighs. Squeezes my hand. "There's the obstinate, rude girl I know."

"That's not very nice."

"I'm not very nice. Nor, as I recall, are you."

"I'm nice."

He makes a face.

"I'm nice," I repeat more firmly. "No thanks to parenting."

"You're a whole lot of things no thanks to parenting." He removes his hand from mine and I just stare at it lying there. It feels like a much bigger rejection than it is. "I didn't tell you because it wasn't real. Maybe once. But not for a long time."

"What are you talking about?"

He shakes his head and won't meet my eyes. His gaze is clouded with pain and memory. "I'm not going to be your father, Josephine. And I'm not trying to hurt you, I'm just managing your expectations." Then he makes a breathy sound. "I'm tired. I'll sleep."

I nod faintly. He closes his eyes and rolls away from me.

I feel surreal. I almost wake him up again, but instead I watch him drift off.

"We have nothing to do with our parents," a voice says and I turn to see Zachariah again.

I have to clear my throat before I can reply. "I wouldn't know."

"We don't. They don't get to choose."

"Choose what?"

"The things that hurt us."

*

It feels kind of like being the runt of the pack, the one that gets left to fend for itself. As I walk through the tunnel I try to convince myself that it doesn't matter – I made it this long without family. And I guess I'm marrying into one now anyway. Phillipe Luquet can stay in that bed until he rots of bedsores, for all I care.

I spot an orb of light and follow it to Will. He's working on a new painting, this one undoubtedly of the ocean. I sit with my back against the opposite concrete wall and watch as smudges of grays and whites and blues form a vast unknowable landscape. At its center he forms a round smudge of red, a thing with edges that seem to throb in the candlelight.

"What's that?" I ask.

Will steps back to survey it. He shrugs as though he doesn't really know. "Sea's heart."

"I didn't know it had one."

"'Course. Everything does." He sinks down beside me. "Do you know I think Raven loved the sea as much as you do?"

I immediately wrap my arms around myself. *Please don't make me think about Raven.* "How do you know?"

"Just noticed. She was always watching it from the wall."

"You notice more than anyone else."

"Nah."

My thoughts stay with Raven for a few too-long minutes. Her death is one of the greatest regrets of my life. I didn't try with her. Sure, she was a bitch, but she'd been through some truly horrible things in her life, and she was *strong*. It's so easy to forget how strong, but in fact she spent her life protecting that settlement. She did whatever it took. She was a woman who truly had no line she couldn't cross. And I led her to her death and left her there alone.

I can't help thinking we were more alike than I knew. Only problem was that when her boyfriend betrayed her he did it with malice in his heart, whereas mine did it with love.

"Do you think I'm making a huge mistake?" I ask.
"With what?"
"Getting married."
Will snorts. "What's bothering you?"
"I dunno," I sigh.
Will snatches my hand to stop me from picking my nails incessantly.
"I can't give him children," I admit finally. "My body's too messed up from all the experiments they did." Only to Will would I be able to say that.
"Do you think he cares?"
I nod.
"But do you think he cares more than he loves you?"
"Not right now. But one day he will."
"Maybe one day we'll be dead."
"Actually definitely one day we'll be dead."
"Precisely."
"He tells me all these stories about how it was for him growing up. Their family was bursting with love. After that there's no way I'll be enough for him. He'll need what he had growing up. Hell, *I* need what he had."
"Which is what?"
"Numbers. More than two. A group of love."
"And what are we?"
I turn to look at him in the dark. There is suddenly a wound and I'm the one who's inflicted it. "Of course," I say. "Sorry. Yes. You're family."
"We're all family. Which makes this the biggest group of love there's ever been."
I nod, feeling awful. "Sorry. I love you."
"I love you too, loser. So get married and be quiet."
"I will."

He's still holding my hand and gives it a squeeze. "If I see any errant babies I'll pinch one for you."

"Cheers."

There's a long silence and then he repeats more softly, "One day we'll be dead."

Maybe for most people it's a pretty empty statement but for us, for those in the tunnels with the hungry beasts at our doors, it feels like it will probably be sooner rather than later. Which makes him right, more right than he knows. I'm surrounded by family. A wedding is what we need, all of us.

Chapter 10

September 29th, 2067

Josephine

We lie pressed together to survive the cold. We huddle and shiver like dozens of mammals whose body heat is needed to live upon. We touch like family might. Like creatures of a kind, the closeness tender and intimate.

But really they are monsters and I'm a ghost and we are all waiting out here to dissolve.

*

April 1st, 2067

Josephine

Today there is a wild wild wind. It picks me up and dances me through the sky. Today it rushes through my heart. Because once upon a time I didn't believe in love and now he's waiting for me at the sea cliff.

I walk past the people who make up this strange, motley family of ours. Shadow is here, leaning on crutches. I don't have the space in my heart to be angry with him for whatever he's incapable of offering – I'm already too full. This cliff is crowded with people I love. I feel their presence but I can hardly think, hardly breathe, hardly *be*. It seemed so silly to me that he wanted me to walk down an aisle to where he waited but now I think I understand the significance. It feels like a choice to make, an action to take. It empowers me and prepares me, this short walk to him. This too-long walk to him.

The sky above is very dark. Far out on the horizon a bolt of lightning strikes the ocean. I didn't know this was where we'd marry – he surprised me with the sea and the sky and he looks so handsome with tears in his green eyes.

I reach him and he takes my hands and suddenly it's as though we're alone on the windy cliff. The only two left in this world, just as it felt when we first met. There are words we're supposed to say but I can't wait. I kiss him and in his arms the rain ruptures the sky. It's dark with it. We are drenched to the bone and I can hear nothing but the roar of it around us. A storm I can feel through every inch of my body; the spark of it alights all the places we touch.

I pull away just a little. Enough to whisper in his ear. "I love you, my darling. Beyond life, beyond death."

"And I you," Luke whispers back, and we are married.

*

December 17th, 2067

Luke

There's a gaping dark beneath my feet and I'm just hovering. I'm hovering right above it. It's sucking. Jesus I can feel it sucking at me. She won't look at me. And there are all those terrible wounds on her body. That body I know better than my own. The one I've kissed and touched and fucked and loved for four years. It's mine. Her body is *mine*. I feel sick because she won't look at me and she's always looked at me and I've always seen a thing in her eyes that makes me know she's mine. Even when we broke up, even when she hated me for lying there was that thing in her eyes that I could sew into my soul and rely on but it's not there now it's not fucking there and I don't know why *I can't remember why.*

*

Life has been incomparably large today. I've watched both my parents greet their son after eleven years. We're all shell-shocked and without a clue what to do now. It seems like it should be obvious but it's not. It's like when someone dies, everyone sits around feeling lost. This is the same, but without the absence. Dave's so calm that it's making the rest of us uncomfortable. Mom has no idea what to say and Dad keeps making awkward jokes and meanwhile I can't concentrate on the magnitude of it all because my wife is acting like a stranger. She should be here but she's not.

I settle Dave into Mom and Dad's little sleeping-tunnel with a big bottle of whisky. They all sit down to talk but there's a long silence. I feel very selfish for asking, but I'm about to lose my mind and can't help it. "Do you know what's happened with Josi since I've been away? Has she been acting weird?"

Mom erupts into laughter, which is not a good sign. I look at Dad instead, starting to feel nervous. His hands shake, followed by his shoulders and back. "She hasn't been here," he finally admits in the halting, trembling speech of his disease. "She disappeared the same night you did."

Oh Jesus. "The *whole time?*"

"She came back less than a week ago. Found out that you were gone and went straight up to bring you home."

"And she didn't tell you where she's been?"

They shake their heads. I look at my brother for something, anything. He was always the one I looked to to make me feel better because he did it so effortlessly but all I see in his eyes now is pity. *Pity,* like he knows something I haven't yet worked out.

"I have to …"

"It's fine, go," Dave says. "I have a lot to catch up on with the folks."

I give them each a kiss on the cheek and duck out into the hall.

*

I can't remember that night, the night we both disappeared. I can't remember anything around it but I can feel it. Josi used to say she could feel the blood moon without having any memory of it. Now I understand what she means. Something bad happened and I'm responsible for it.

She's not in the infirmary which means Zach let her walk on the damaged leg. She's not in our bed-tunnel, or the dining hall or the kitchen or the arena. I find her, instead, gazing through the cage at the waiting horde of Furies. They aren't snarling or growling, they're just staring back at her. It's disturbingly quiet.

"Josi?" At the sound of my voice they erupt into their usual hideous noises.

Josi brushes past me and heads back through the tunnels. There's a brace around her leg and a crutch in one hand. I don't think she should be walking on it at all, given that I was very recently able to see its bone.

"Josi. Stop. Wait."

Finally she stops. We're only a meter from the opening to the kitchen and if there's anyone in there I'm sure they'll hear us but I don't care I can't think I'm only a question awaiting an answer.

"What happened?"

She looks at me. Slowly. And it's not as though there's nothing there. It's just ... calm. Everything that's there is calm.

I feel myself lurching forward and grabbing at her in terror. I take her arms and we meet the wall behind her and I'm asking *did they cure you* over and over because I'm so sure in this moment that they have but she says no, *no*, enough times until I hear it.

An unsteady breath leaves me. My hands tingle as I drop them. "Sorry. Sorry, darling. I thought ..." I shake my head and try to calm down. "I haven't seen you ... It's not ... What's happened?"

Josi studies me. Her one blue eye is very bright. There's no expression in her face. "Do you have time missing from when they captured you?"

I swallow. Nod. My guts churn with guilt: another of my goddamn lies come back to haunt us. Fifteen months ago I told her I'd taken the antidote for the drug that made first Josi and then me a slave to the blood moon. But I hadn't. I wanted the power it afforded me, the one that would allow me to kill Falon Shay. I craved the blood moon. What is it about me that lies and lies and lies? I hate that piece. I wish I could kill that piece.

"How much do you remember?"

I know the answer to this question well. I've spent the last three months lying in a white cell thinking about it. "I remember being in the city. Then nothing until I woke inside the lab."

Her eyes narrow fractionally as she processes this.

"That's a big chunk, isn't it? What happened? How did I get taken?"

She's very careful as she forms her words. I can see it. "I don't know. I wasn't there."

"Josi ..."

"Luke. Honestly. Just leave those days behind. It'll be better, I promise. They're over."

"I need—"

"Take a breath."

I don't understand what's going on but I can feel something bad. I try to breathe.

"Look at me. This will hurt."

I swallow and find the courage to look at her.

"You're my favorite person in the world. And we're both okay. Everything's okay, I promise. But I can't be your wife anymore."

I blink. "I don't ... wait, what?"

She's so calm. "I'm not capable of it. I'm different now."

"What? *Why?*"

"It's not important."

"Are you insane? Of course it's important!"

"I can't talk about it yet."

"What's going on? Please, you have to tell me what's going on."

"Just listen to me." She covers my mouth with her hand and stares into my eyes. "*Listen*. I adored you. My whole heart was yours. But the thing we shared isn't inside me anymore. I don't love you."

I pull away from her and shake my head. This is nonsense. "It's like last time, that's all. I'm an asshole but we both know that and I'll spend the rest of our lives making it up to you—"

"It's not about that. I don't care that you lied. Truly. It's so unbelievably small to me now."

"Bullshit."

"I'm not angry. I don't feel anything close to anger."

"How?"

"You can't see it now but there's peace deep inside and it has nothing to do with anger or sadness or even love. It's just … quiet. It's about wilderness."

"What? I don't understand. You don't sound anything like yourself. You sound like a fucking drone."

She doesn't say anything.

"I need you to talk to me, darling. Tell me what's wrong. What did they do to you?" My voice breaks and my heart breaks and— "*What did they do to you?*"

"Nothing. Nothing, I swear. I'm fine."

"Was it Shay?"

"No, it wasn't Shay."

"I don't believe you." I start crying as I run my hands over her arms and shoulders and face and neck. The burns on her, and the scars, my god. "You don't feel right, baby. I can't feel you. I can't feel you."

"I'm fine," she says. "I'm fine."

"Where are you?"

She closes her eyes as though in pain. "I'm right here but I can't do this anymore. I can't be with you. I'm not … the same."

"Open your eyes. Look at me."

She doesn't.

"*Look at me.*"

Reluctantly Josephine opens her eyes.

"Look at me and tell me you don't love me."

She licks her lips, just a darting of her tongue. Holds my eyes and calmly says, "I don't love you, Luke. I'm so sorry. I wish I could. I hate hurting you. I'm so sorry."

I feel sick because I believe her. I actually believe her. I'm falling into the gaping fucking darkness and I can't catch hold of anything. She reaches to touch my face. Her fingers slip on the tears there. I wrench away from her, my nerve endings too raw to be touched.

This isn't happening. I shake my head again. Take a deep breath. Stop the tears, stop the panic, stop everything. I allow my certainty reign. There are things I know and then there are things I *know*.

"Josi," I say softly. "Listen to me now. I don't understand what's going on and I don't know what's happened to you. But I'll look after you, and if you don't want that then I'll just wait. For as long as it takes, forever. I love you beyond life, beyond death."

There is a long, slow moment. We look at each other quietly. I remember so many moments, so much love. We have an embarrassment of love between us.

Only she says, "I never thought it possible but there are things bigger than love, and life, and even death. I'm sorry."

Chapter 11

There was once a girl who lived in a snow-covered forest. She was the only girl in this forest, indeed she was the only girl in any forest, or so it seemed to her. She wandered alone, day after day. She was the loneliest creature to ever exist. Once she saw a bird of prey and fearing it, fled. But the bird sat in the branches of a fir tree and sang sweetly to her. She heard the truth in its song and knew there had never been a girl in the forest to begin with, only one bird of prey and now a second, come to share its voice with her. They might be the last two in the world, but they were two, and that mattered.

*

December 20th, 2067

Josephine

If I could wish for anything it wouldn't be for the return of love. It would be for Luke's escape from the pain it causes.

"Love?"

We sit in the silence created by Dave's words.

"*Love?*" Claire repeats.

The dining tunnel is quiet tonight. The kids have all been sent to bed and the adults have gathered to discuss what is to become of life, our first meeting since Luke and I returned. I'm at the end of the long narrow table, in my usual spot. Luke is at the opposite end, in his usual spot. Between us sit Dave, Claire, Tobias, Will, Pace, Eric, Blue, Zachariah, Shadow and last of all is Guillaume, whom I belatedly recognize as the man whose foot I chopped off. I haven't seen him or the other members of his family since I got back, and I look at him now with faint relief that he survived that brutal day.

"If he was planning this when I was there, he never told me," Zach says of his father.

"Do we know when?" Luke asks but Dave shakes his head.

"If the drug has been successfully tested on Dave then they'll administer it soon and they won't make the mistake of giving any warning like they did with the sadness cure," Shadow says.

"It's not a drug," Dave says. He clears his throat. "I mean, it's not just a drug."

"So what is it?"

"They use a system of shocks to different parts of the brain and then inject you with neural pathway stimulants that trigger small seizures every time your brain fills with love chemicals like dopamine, so it immediately trains itself out of creating those chemicals. It's pretty genius, actually."

There is a horrified silence.

"Good god," Claire whispers.

"Doctor Frankenstein, eat your heart out," Zach mutters.

"Did they do this to you?" Luke demands.

Dave nods.

"Did it ... hurt?"

It seems like a stupid question to me – of course it hurt. My eyes dart up to the roof of the tunnel. Rationally I know it's not getting any lower but I could have sworn there was more space in here a minute ago.

"We need more information," Eric says.

"We always need more information," Pace mutters.

"What do we want here?" Luke asks. "In plain terms."

The discussion takes off and I listen quietly. They want the cures abolished. They want the current government removed from power. They want to find a way to reverse the cures already administered. They want action taken to start regenerating the land outside the wall, and they want the wall taken down. What they all agree on most strongly is that they want the Bloods either disempowered or turned to our cause and the Furies eradicated so that all of this can be made possible.

Three months ago I would have agreed with them.

Now it all sounds foolish beyond belief.

"There's no reversing the cures," I tell them. Their chatter ceases and all eyes move to me. "There's no 'eradicating' the Furies unless we make ourselves responsible for genocide. And there's no overthrowing the government unless you're all willing to spill an ocean of blood."

They stare. I keep my eyes on Luke because he's the one who will make these decisions, as much as our "democracy" would like to believe otherwise.

"We have an antidote for the cure," Pace argues.

"That was an antidote to the symptoms a Fury experiences, and it was made by a dead scientist and destroyed in Dodge's lab.

If we ever want to come up with a way to reverse the effects of the cure it will take many years, a team of scientists and a huge funding budget. So that stays out of the current discussion." I don't say that I think it's hopeless anyway – scans of a cured brain look fundamentally different in a way I can't imagine will ever be reversible.

Pace shakes her head angrily. She's not looking at me anymore. I've pissed her off but I can't find the energy to care – it's going instead into ignoring the walls of this tiny space and reminding myself to breathe.

"What are you doing?" Luke asks me softly. I realize belatedly that what I've said has let the air out of the room, like a pin to a balloon full of hope.

"Managing expectations." I look around at each of them. "If you think we're taking over a government without massive casualties then your heads are in the sand. Are you prepared to commit these kinds of crimes? Which one of you can murder? Who is prepared for slaughter?"

None of them answer because none of them are.

Except Dave. He says, "You are, Josephine."

"No she isn't," Luke snaps.

But Dave holds my eyes and we both know I am.

"What, then?" Blue demands of me, jumping at any chance to argue. "You want us to rot down here? Give up and carry on the way we are forever?"

I shake my head and take a moment to think about my next words. "Aside from Luke, there are no soldiers in these tunnels. Not real ones. We survive down here, we endure. Most of us have never taken a life. If we've fought, it's a fist fight with each other or a skirmish with unarmed Furies. We haven't faced an army of Blood soldiers. But that's what will need to happen. They have to be neutralized before we even get close to the ministers, and let me tell you right now – killing anyone at all, friend or enemy, is a different beast to surviving. Killing a Blood asks for a piece of your soul."

The silence deepens.

"It's gonna feel impossible, and it almost will be," I say softly. "So you must know how much you have to give. I can't be the only one who knows."

"You're not," Pace says, offended at the very idea.

"What makes you the expert on killing all of a sudden?" Blue snaps.

I don't answer. They think I don't know what I'm talking about. I can't bring myself to enlighten them.

"We know," Shadow assures me. They all say the same but I realize as they voice their certainties how childish it feels. Sitting around a table pontificating about how tough we are, how far we're willing to go. None of it means anything; it's air and words into silent, deaf earth. My fault for bringing it up.

I stand and my chair scrapes on the concrete. My hands are shaking slightly so I crack my knuckles to make them stop. "I've thought a lot over the last few months about the best way to do this, and I have plans, but they don't include getting rid of the Furies. Anyone tries to kill them, they go through me."

There it is.

I let them chew over their shock and stride from the dining room.

*

I'm heading for the northern tunnel when someone grabs my arm and wrenches me around. I react badly, shoving the person up against the wall and pinning my arm over her throat. It's Pace.

"What the hell is wrong with you?" she asks, purplish eyes wide.

I release her. "Sorry."

"You're not acting like you. You've never been cold but you're really goddamn cold, Dual."

"My name's Josephine."

She frowns as though I've spoken another language. "Okay, *Josephine*. What happened to you out there?"

"Nothing."

"Why do you have a burned-off face and a missing finger and a cut throat?"

I brush past her because all she's doing is tempting us both with a thing we once had but is now gone. All she's doing is pointing out physicalities when nothing that happened to me was done to my body. Nothing real.

I make my way quickly down the tunnel. I have to get out of here right now – I need the sky.

But there's someone waiting for me at the base of the ladder.

*

Dave

Josephine Luquet. What an anomaly. I stop her at the ladder. She doesn't display any anger though I know she's desperate to get out of here.

"A piece of advice?" I offer.

She smiles crookedly and motions for me to go ahead.

"The best way to fit in when you don't fit in is to mimic."

She tilts her beautiful head to the side and the look in her eyes is enough to make me feel as though she can see right through to my bones. "I've got no interest in mimicry. But thanks, Dave."

"Josephine."

She stops and I can see her impatience now.

"I agree with you, for what it's worth."

"About what?"

"About not killing the Furies."

This sparks her attention. "Why?"

"It's the kind of thing that destroys the people who carry out the action just as brutally as it destroys the targets. Mutually assured destruction."

"So it's a self-preservation thing for you?"

"It's a humanity-preservation thing for me."

She turns for the ladder. I watch her disappear lithely up into the darkness.

My brother finds me soon after. "Have you seen Josi?"

Something makes me hesitate. "No," I answer. Because I may not feel a whole lot but I know how to recognize emotion, and that girl was full to the brim with it. All she wanted was quiet, and alone, and above. And as part of the humanity-preservation thing, Josephine Luquet needs to be allowed at least part of what she wants. Otherwise I have the peculiar feeling she'll disappear once more, and this time she won't come back.

*

Luke

I can't find Josi – she's been disappearing every night since she got back and I have no idea to where. Instead I find her father.

Phillipe Luquet is in the training room lifting weights despite the fact that it's the middle of the night and he broke his wrist last week. He's one tough bloke. The first time he and I met was as he tortured me for my identity, but I never found the desire to hold it against him.

I go to a punching bag and start belting the crap out of it, but I give up after a few minutes. "What's wrong with her? This is bad, man."

Phillipe puts his weights down and glances at me reluctantly. "What she's saying makes sense."

"She hates the Furies more than anyone. They destroyed the Inferno and killed hundreds – including Hal. Now she wants to give them all a big cuddle?"

He doesn't say anything, just lifts a weight into a curl. His long, lean limbs are more wiry and muscular than any I've seen.

"And with me? Apparently she wants nothing more to do with me. And you can say whatever you want about that, man, but the last thing I remember between us was love. Whatever happened to her made it go away."

Horrifyingly, there are tears in my eyes. I dash them away impatiently.

"Whatever happened to her," Shadow says softly, "is her own experience, and traumatic or not, you can't erase it, boy. We are fluid – always changing, always learning. You can't make someone un-know something, or forget what they've been through. You can't control who she becomes."

"So what? I just give up? Put up with her not loving me? Fuck you."

He doesn't say anything.

"Fuck you," I repeat.

And then Shadow says, "Be brave."

I turn and get the hell out of there. He's asking me to be braver than I could ever be; getting over Josi would take more courage than I'm capable of.

I barrel into someone in the dark. It takes me a moment to realize that it's Dave.

"You okay?"

I swallow, wipe my eyes again and ask, "Want to come somewhere with me?"

*

We go to the beach where I proposed to Josi nine months ago. It's not like it was that night – there is something very unquiet about the sea under this particular moon. Dave and I walk onto the sand and watch the rough waves. I have no idea why I brought him here. I haven't got any security measures in place. If the Furies come, they come.

"How are you feeling?" he asks.

"Me? I should be asking you."

"Why? I wasn't tortured in a lab for three months."

I blink. I guess that's true. Except … "You've been tortured in your body for eleven years."

He shakes his head. "Nah. It wasn't like that."

"What was it like?"

Dave folds his arms. *Crash* goes a particularly large wave. *Crash, crash, crash* go three smaller ones. "It was just … quiet."

"Was it lonely?"

"For the first couple of years. Then I got used to it and loneliness seemed arbitrary."

I shake my head. "I wish I could have kept you from that."

"Lukey, it wasn't your job. It's not your burden to bear, as much as you might wish it were. I was your older brother.

I should have protected you. And I didn't. But that's the way of it, right? There's a whole lot of 'shoulds' and if you waste time thinking about them they make a trap of you."

I swallow. "Not 'was'. You're still my big brother."

He nods slowly. "Of course, Lukey."

I think of his shoulds and my shoulds and then abruptly I think of Anthony Harwood's shoulds. He'd certainly been trapped in the heart of them: they'd hollowed him out and chained him to his empty body. For a second I'm back in that asylum lab on that horrible night he died, listening to him tell us of his wife and daughter, the daughter he'd left to perish alone in their home.

"Do you have any of the side effects?" I ask Dave, suddenly afraid that this kind of soullessness will come over my brother. Anthony used to space out, like a robot whose hardwiring held a glitch. He used to draw birds all over everything, his memory rooted in that happiest of days so it wouldn't have to face the horror of what came after. I wonder if Dave has gone through anything like this, any glitches or lost time or dementia.

"Nope. I'm the successful case study they pin all their data on."

"So you're clearheaded?"

"Very."

"What about stress? Does that have an effect on you?"

"I don't feel stress. I problem-solve."

He glances at me and smiles crookedly – I realize my nose has crinkled with something similar to distaste. "Do you *remember* feeling things?" I press.

He shrugs. "Not really. I mean, do you? Or do you just tie the theory of emotion to particular memories?"

I try to think back to big moments and I suppose he's right – I know how I felt during them, I know the words, but I can't just turn a switch and feel the same things again. I wonder if Josi's eidetic memory allows her to. "I guess ... Do you still feel fear?"

Dave nods.

"When?"

"I don't know, Luke."

"Tell me."

"I felt pretty scared when you first brought me down here."

"Why?"

"Because I don't want to die."

"I'm not gonna let you die, bro."

There's a silence. I keep imagining him as a ghost already, I can't help it. Or perhaps he's not the ghost. Perhaps Dave's ghost – my old Dave – stands between us, reminding me of all that he was and all that this version isn't. He used to make me laugh so much. There was such animation in his face, such feeling in his voice. I would look at him and feel a closeness between us that couldn't be expressed or even identified – it just was. Intrinsic and infinite.

Now he's gone the way my wife has. Away.

"How would you feel if I died?" I ask. Why do I ask him this? Sick self-punishment, I guess. Vain hope. I'm trying to push and prod him, like Josi used to do to me when she thought I was cured.

"I don't know. How am I meant to know that?"

"Imagine. You can still imagine. That's still a capability of yours, right?"

"Don't get upset, we're just talking," he counsels, and the calm condescension of this pisses me off further.

"Then answer."

He breathes out, almost like a sigh but not quite. "I'd feel regret."

"And that's it?"

He shrugs helplessly. "Do you want me to lie?"

I believe I said exactly this when once upon a time Josi screamed at me to get angry. The air deflates from my chest.

"Just like I regret that they hurt you."

"I'm not hurt," I promise, like a vow. "They tried. Those fuckers tried. But they don't have the power to hurt me."

That power belongs to you, big brother. How could he not know that? He would have – he was kinder and more sensitive than any soul I've ever met. Which means that this isn't the same man. This isn't my brother standing next to me with a million miles of distance in his empty gaze, this is not Dave Townsend. It's someone else, some pale imitation.

I miss him now with such potency that for a second I can't breathe. I let out a groan, sink onto the sand and rest my head in my hands. Dave doesn't say anything, and he doesn't touch me. We just stay this way while the sea's hungry teeth creep toward our waiting feet.

I think of the other versions of us somewhere out there. I think of all the infinite universes and imagine that something has gone desperately wrong, lines have been crossed, a glitch in the hardwiring of existence has occurred. Somehow versions of Dave and Josi meant for other loveless worlds have crossed over and arrived in this one.

You can't control who she becomes. Shadow was right about that. And it must also be true of my brother.

But I was never as good at love as Dave and Josi were.

I loved them both as well as I could, as vast as the breadth of my soul, as unfathomable as the depth of this sea, and it still wasn't enough to keep them here. There are much bigger, stronger forces in the world than my will.

So what if this version of me isn't capable of loving these versions of them?

Chapter 12

April 1st, 2067

Josephine

After everyone fled the stormy wedding and arrived back in our dining tunnel drenched to the bone we realized there was only one way to warm up: don't stop moving. To that effect we've been dancing for five hours straight. And I mean everyone. Will's breakdancing as usual, which is endlessly impressive, and he's finally managed to get the incredibly sexy Henrietta to look at him with a certain light in her eyes. Blue is violently jumping around like he's in a mosh pit, heedless of whoever he might land on and royally pissing everyone off. Pace is killing it with some crump, Claire is swaying and waving her fists out of time to the music and Tobias is shuffling in an excellent albeit awkward Charleston. Even Shadow is dancing, although his interpretation of that is to stand to the side and nod his head minutely to the beat.

It's neither the time nor the place for me to play Elgar to Luke. At least that's what I tell myself. I'm so nervous at the thought that I could throw up. What a nutcase.

When we're all finally dry and warm we start feasting on the delicious wedding food Luke's spent the last three days overseeing. The ingenious morsels are laid out on the long table, which we've shoved to the side so everyone can wander over and grab handfuls while chatting. I'm grateful it didn't turn into a sit-down formal dinner, or whatever appropriation of that we could muster. Instead it feels completely relaxed. Fairy-lights have been strung up along the walls (I'm not worrying about where the power is being rerouted from – I'm *not*) and Will stayed up all of last night to paint a new mural. It's the most beautiful piece of art I've ever seen: I *cried* when we arrived panting and soaked through to see it.

I have no idea what time it is when Eric clinks his glass for a speech. No one hears him, of course, so he ends up jumping onto the table and hollering at the top of his lungs for everyone to shut up. "It's time for the speeches, heathens!"

"No," I groan. I'm perched behind Luke on an overturned milk crate, my arms draped around his shoulders and clasped over his chest.

"Our fearless leaders have made it official!" Eric announces. A cheer goes up and I can't help laughing. "And it's just as well because everyone knows the best societies are run by monarchs. Just don't go all Lord and Lady Macbeth on us, please." Now everyone is laughing.

"You'd be the first to go," Luke warns him.

"Yeah, yeah. But seriously. To see you both happy makes life sweeter for the rest of us, and that's an honest fact. To the bride and groom!"

"To the bride and groom!"

We all raise our cups and drink. It's not champagne, but we managed to pinch some wine for the occasion, which is a nice treat.

"I also just want to add to the end of that, that the whole reason Josi and I met was because she was hitting on me to make Luke jealous."

"I told you that in *confidence*, you jerk!" I snap.

Luke is laughing so much he bends over and I'm lifted off my feet.

Next to give a speech is Pace, and I brace myself. "Yo," she greets us, taking her place on the tabletop.

"Can we not stomp on the Madeleines, please?" Luke asks her, pained.

"We can shut up," she replies pointedly. "So Dual and I were forced to be friends. By which I mean that I was forced to be her friend. And let's be honest – those of us who knew her then know how much of a depressing cow she was."

My mouth falls open.

"So it was a real trial, having to spend time with her. She whined day and night and was basically the most sarcastic person you could ever meet. But I took it upon myself to show her the ropes and, being the endlessly talented teacher that I am, she eventually managed to become halfway useful for the occasional task or two."

"*Aww*," I mutter. Luke is laughing again so I squeeze him tighter in warning.

Pace grins. "So, being that she's useless, and not the sharpest tool in the shed and let's face it, she's not great to look at either—"

Hilarious. She's really got them rolling in the aisles now.

"—it's a lucky thing that our girl happens to have a heart too big for her body." Pace looks at me properly. "This heart of hers is big enough to protect the rest of her body. It makes her tough as nails but it also protects other people's bodies and makes them tough too. It's a heart that really,

really *loves*. God, she loves so much and so well it's like she made up the ability and showed it to the rest of us mere mortals, and it's actually kinda sickening when you put it that way but no less true. Her friendship changed my life. And Luke's not too bad either."

Pace immediately skulls her wine cup and applause erupts. I'm getting misty-eyed. "*Thank you*," I mouth to her but she just rolls her eyes and jumps down.

Dodge stands up wearing his thick glasses and squinting because they're meant to be for reading. I'm surprised he emerged from his dark little lab for the occasion. "Josi really likes books," he says. "One of the first conversations we ever had was when she quoted *Brave New World* to me, and said she wanted to live nasty. Well, Josi – I think you've done it. Getting married in the sewers is about as nasty as you can get! Cheers to that!"

"*Cheers!*"

"We got married on a *sea cliff*," Luke points out peevishly. "It was romantic."

Blue stands up and my eyebrows arch in surprise. He's such a jerk I never thought he'd have anything nice to say about anyone. "My toast is to Luke," he says. "I mean, it's for you too, Dual, I guess, but yeah, mainly to Luke."

I can't help grinning. At least he's consistent with his dislike for me.

"Luke, man. You're just the best." Everyone laughs, and Blue spreads his hands. "Seriously, though. Who here could say otherwise? The guy beat me to a pulp and I still think he's the best! For the record, I deserved it that day—"

"And every day!" someone shouts.

"But like, yeah," he goes on, rubbing the back of his neck. "Shit hits the fan and you deal with it, man. You know what to do. You save the day. You're the one we all want around. We'd be up shit creek without you."

"How eloquent." Luke grins. "Thanks, man!"

Next is Tobias, and since he can't climb up onto the table he stands before it, the cup in his hand shaking only slightly. He doesn't say anything for a while, perhaps gathering his thoughts, and we all wait quietly. I try to prepare myself but I'm starting to feel alarmingly emotional.

"My boy was born during a storm," Tobias says. His voice is soft so we all shuffle in closer, holding our breaths to hear. "One of the worst in recent history. Trees came down and roads were flooded. The power went out in the hospital right as Claire was giving birth. This still, silent little baby came out in the dark, with only the sound of the rain lashing against the windows for company. He didn't make a sound, and he didn't move, and I remember the moment I had the thought: that my little fella had died."

Luke goes stiff in my arms and I know he's never heard this story before.

"And then something astonishing happened. The storm ended abruptly. The raging winds and rain stopped as though a switch had been flicked. And this tiny baby took a huge lungful of air and screamed with bright, brilliant life."

There are goosebumps all over my skin.

"I knew what had happened, clear as day. The storm had found its way into the spirit of my son," Tobias says. "It never left him, that storm. It has given him courage and strength and passion. It gave him a mind with more curiosity than any I know. So it's more fitting than I can say that it found its way back into the sky tonight, that it might be shared with the woman he loves. You, Josephine, have earned that storm, because where it taught Luke to be brave and strong and passionate, you have taught him to be sweet and humble and generous. You have taught him to be a man. I won't say welcome to the family because you're already part of it. I will just say to you, my precious storm-boy, and you, my darling daughter, be kind to each other and you will share an extraordinary life."

I close my eyes and turn my mouth to Luke's cheek. I hold him so tight. The salt of his tears smudges my lips. Tobias makes his way to us and we both hug him.

"Thank you," I say. "*So* much."

We need a recovery break but there's no respite. Next to jump up onto the table is Will, and I'm not sure I can take any more.

"You okay?" I whisper in Luke's ear.

"Better than. You?"

"Much better."

"I don't have an amazing speech like that or anything," Will says shyly. "I just wanted to explain the painting."

We all turn to the picture behind him. He has painted the ocean again, but this time it is specked through with gold and silver, and instead of depicting a red throbbing heart at its center, Will has painted two ethereal figures whose edges dissolve into the wild waters and into each other. Fingers scatter apart and together in the other's hand. The girl's long hair twists into the man's head. Their feet burst into water and form once more inside each other. The couple *is* the sea, they have come from it and go back to it together. Lit by the fairy-lights, it's glorious and mesmerizing and it might be my favorite thing in the world.

"So Josi watches the sea any chance she can get," Will says. "And when she can't watch the sea she watches my paintings of it. I asked her a while ago what she likes so much about it and she said she had no idea. So I just kinda kept watching her and one day when she didn't know I could hear her she said something, and no doubt it's a quote from something."

My face goes beet red with embarrassment as I realize what he's about to say.

"Under her breath she said, *'It seems big enough to contain everything anyone could ever feel'*."

Everyone turns to me. I clear my throat and nod. "Yep, it's Anthony Doerr."

Will grins. "Anyway it made so much sense, why she'd love it. 'Cause that's who she is. She fights for our right to know our hearts. For our right to be like the sea: full of feeling."

As the people in the tunnel applaud I smile and meet Will's blue eyes. He smiles back at me and I feel a rope tied between us, connecting me to my dear friend.

"One more quick thing," he adds apologetically. Into the hush he says, more softly, "My best friend Hal used to say that we all have a wilderness inside us, and some of us live more deeply within it than others. He said we have animal hearts and that these animals need to be tamed. When I met the two of you I knew you both lived very deep within your wilds, while your animals dwelled close to the surface. It's not an obvious thing, but an innate one. I'd never seen two people more the same in that way. And I've watched time and again how when either one of you goes too deep and gets lost, the other will go in after you. You'll find each other in the deep wild, no matter what. I don't know much about love, but I think that must be what it means."

I go to the table so I can hug Will. I hug him so tight and forget not to cry. He laughs and hugs me back, and then he hugs Luke too.

"I thought you said you didn't have an amazing speech, you filthy little liar!" Luke says gruffly, tucking the boy under his arm.

"Okay, no more," I laugh. "I'm mortifyingly vulnerable."

"One more!" Henrietta says, waltzing her way onto the table. "I've been given the job of speaking on behalf of all us kids. None of us have any family anymore, not really, anyway. But the two of you, and everyone else in these tunnels, you've given us a family and a home and we won't ever have a way to say thank you for that. It's, like, bigger than words. You make us feel safe and that's sort of a miracle in this messed up world. Also you're both crazy hot so this makes sense, the getting married and all, it's only weird that it took you so long."

Luke and I laugh. "Thanks, Hen," I grin, giving her a kiss. "Thank you all," I tell the group of kids gathered to the side. They salute us. I look for Zach but he's not here, which makes me feel a little bad. I haven't spoken to him much in the time he's been here – in fact I don't think anyone has spoken to him much. We've been waiting for his father to demand his return but Shay's shown no such desire.

"Okay, now we *must* be finished," I announce, pulling my thoughts back to where they should be. "Right?"

"Actually …" Luke says. He climbs onto the table, surveys the crowd and shakes his head. "I feel way too high up here."

"That's because you're about eight feet tall," Eric tells him.

Luke jumps onto the ground and looks at me. Oh dear. Were we supposed to make up speeches? Because I can't do speeches. Claire arrives at my side and links arms with me, perhaps knowing I might need someone close for this. I glance at Shadow, but he's not looking at me. I can't even tell if he's listening, his eyes cast off somewhere distant.

I turn back to my husband (*husband*!). He takes a deep breath and tilts his head a little.

"You don't have to!" I blurt. "It's all been enough—"

"Be quiet and listen," he orders. "I promise I'll be quick because I know how uncomfortable sentiment makes you."

I sigh and wave for him to go ahead.

"First, thank you all so much. You've been incredibly generous tonight, and we're very lucky to have every one of you. If any of you are thinking about getting married, I highly recommend it, 'cause it's a great excuse to have everyone say really nice things about you. Actually, maybe we should make it a weekly occurrence. Hell, everyone should get married – even to themselves – and we'll all just gather around and sing their praises."

The laughter picks up. God, they love him. Something in the air just vibrates when Luke is in the spotlight. Something in everyone expands a little.

He waits for the laughter to die down, something difficult coming over his face. "When we lost my brother," Luke says, "I gave up on life. My heart felt brittle and ugly. I'd spent my childhood searching for things, trying to understand things, and adoring my older brother. I was frightened he'd leave me and then one day he did. I stopped searching and questioning. I stopped pulling things apart just to see how they worked. I stopped looking for any kind of answers because the world no longer held any beauty for me to discover."

He pauses and I see him swallow.

My heart is beating so fast and I want him in my arms, I want to touch him, I hate this five-meter distance between us and I'm a bit scared of his next words.

"And then you," he says so softly, eyes on me. "*You*, my darling." He lifts a hand to his heart as though it hurts. "You appeared, and the world surprised me with its grace."

Claire squeezes me and Luke goes blurry because I'm crying again. I dash the tears away so I can keep hold of his green gaze.

He smiles. "Life had never seemed more curious to me, or more beautiful. So this is what I want to say to you, Josephine Luquet. Thank you. Thank you for being my best friend, my family, my inspiration and my guide. Thank you for offering me the privilege of loving you."

I drop my face into my hands and weep. I can't help it, I have no control of myself anymore. Everyone's crying – I can hear sobs and sniffles and sweet murmurs. And then Luke is here and he's lifting my face so he can kiss me and wrap his arms around me. I was so, so foolish to think I needed more than what I have. I have an embarrassment of riches. I have more than any one person deserves. I have Luke Townsend, and that is the miracle to end all miracles.

*

After that we dance again. The music is slower now, and I dance with Luke like couples used to dance once upon a time. I think of Elgar again, but now I know I can do it. I can't make speeches, I can't put into words what I feel for him, but I can play it. I can give him the song that means the most to me.

I'm thinking that when Shadow appears. He clears his throat and we both look at him. "About time," Luke says, then hands me over to my father.

Shadow still has his crutch to lean on, and we awkwardly come together to dance in a slow shuffle barely more than a sway. "Congratulations," he says.

"Thanks. How are you feeling?"

He grunts, which I guess means okay.

Feeling emotionally overwrought is the only excuse I can think of for what I say next. "I understand about life's wounds. So whatever you are and aren't capable of, it's okay. You're my father and I love you regardless."

I look up into his face but I can't read his expression. Something tenses in him, something pained and broken. I have no idea what happened when I was born, or how it came to be that I was left on my own. I don't know why I never had him, or any parent, but it doesn't matter.

Phillipe closes his eyes. He pulls me into his embrace and I rest my head on his shoulder. "My girl," he murmurs into my hair.

It's enough to give me the courage to find my cello.

But I don't get the chance.

"Help!"

We whirl at the sound of the voice. It's Alo. He is pale faced and terrified. "Help!" he screams again.

I sprint to him. "What?"

"The others – we were messing around and something – ah shit, something happened – just *come*!"

We launch after the boy as he sprints through the tunnels.

"What happened, mate?" Luke asks him as we run.

"We snuck back to the cliff," Alo pants. "We just wanted to see it again, and we were messing around and Malia *fell*."

Oh god. We start running much faster. Luke takes off ahead. I find the presence of mind to tell Will to go to the storeroom for climbing gear and first aid equipment. He and Pace dash off together.

"Is she alive, Alo?" I ask.

"She was but Lawrence was trying to hold her and I dunno how long he could last … You have to hurry, *please*."

"We'll get her," I promise, but in my head I'm thinking it's a very high cliff and it's probably taken him at least thirty minutes to get back to us.

When I arrive Luke is kneeling at the edge of the tunnel. I pull up beside him and look down. The rain is still falling heavily and at first I can't see anything in the dark. But then I spot her. About halfway down on a small ledge, a crumpled body. And the ledge is unstable, moving inch by inch, ready to crumble from the cliff-face and drop Malia to her death. If she isn't already dead.

"I had her," Lawrence babbles. "I had her hand but it's so wet and I couldn't hold her and she slipped."

"It's okay," I tell him quickly. "It's okay. It's not that far, I'm sure she's still alive."

"The fucking cliff is crumbling!" Henrietta sobs.

Teddy has his hands over his face, unable to look, shoulders heaving.

"I'll climb down," Coin is saying. Malia is his girlfriend, after all. There's a ferocious determination in him, one I can see will get him killed. "I can do it. I'll get her."

"Don't you move," Luke orders him.

I share a look with my husband. "I'll go," I say. His hand is too damaged to be reliable. Plus I'm much lighter than he is, and if someone has to get onto that ledge beside the girl it can't be anyone as heavy as Luke.

"Wait for the gear."

"No time." The ledge lurches under Malia's weight, tipping her perilously close to the edge. I don't think anymore. I go.

I can hear a crowd of people behind me shouting and crying but I shut it out and disappear over the drop. I've never done this climb without ropes, I've never done it in the rain. The surfaces are slippery and moving as I make my way inch by inch down the cliff-face. I put my foot there and the earth disappears beneath it. I grab for a rock and my fingers slip straight off it. Breathing deeply, I pause and close my eyes. I can't see shit anyway, so I start moving again with only my hands and feet to feel the way. I concentrate on the shapes and lines of the cliff, placing weight carefully and waiting a moment to make sure each step is solid.

With the rain lashing painfully at my face I reach the space directly above the ledge. "Malia," I call.

She doesn't move. I edge down, placing one foot on the crumbling rock surface. It takes my weight and then shudders down a few meters. My heart lurches but the earth stops, thankfully. I move very slowly to where she's lying.

"Malia, wake up, sweetheart." My fingers on her neck manage to find a strong pulse. I'm hoping she was just knocked out from the fall and there's nothing broken in her spine. "Malia." I slap her cheek lightly and she stirs. "Shhh, don't move."

She moans and turns her head and starts to rise.

"*Don't move*, Malia."

She freezes as my words reach her.

"Good girl. You're okay."

"Where am I?" she whimpers.

"You fell down the cliff and you're fine, but we need to move very, very slowly now. I want you to roll onto your side. Keep your weight spread out – don't lift your head or feet. Okay?"

"I can't."

"Why? Are you hurt?"

"No, I just can't."

"Yes, you can. Keep your eyes closed and roll very slowly toward me."

With a sob she starts to roll.

"*Slower.*"

Malia whimpers but manages to do as I say. When she's close I turn and find the best hand and feet holds I can. I need rope but a glance up tells me the gear hasn't arrived yet. I search for something to hold onto and feel a smooth, raised thing in the earth. Quickly I dig into its edges and discover the tree root. I manage to jam my hand painfully beneath it until I'm pinned to the cliff. Next I dig in the toes of my boots until they feel deep enough to hold me.

"How you going, sweetheart?"

"I'm beneath you, what now?"

The ledge sinks with a rumble. Malia shrieks in terror and lunges for me before I'm prepared. She grabs the back of my leg and nearly wrenches me off the cliff, but I clutch on desperately.

"Climb up, climb up," I pant.

The ledge breaks off completely. Malia is wailing and hanging on to nothing but my leg now.

"Climb up to my shoulders!"

"I can't!" she sobs.

Okay. Okay. Either she doesn't have the arm strength or she's too panicked to use it.

Leaving my right hand clutching the tree root, I remove my left from the cliff and drop it down. My sense of balance sways and a moment of true fear grips me but I force it away and reach toward Malia.

"Take my hand," I tell her, even though it could easily pull us both from my hold.

"No, no, no, I can't, I'll fall—"

"I will not let you fall. Do you hear me, Malia? *I will not let you fall.* Reach for my hand."

She does. I feel her grip in mine, a slippery thing that yanks on my shoulder with enough force to dislocate it. Pain swells but I move the joint enough to know that it's still in its socket, thank god.

So now Malia is holding onto one of my legs and one of my hands, while I'm still facing the cliff and barely managing to keep my grip. I have to get her up before my muscles give out.

With a scream that comes from somewhere deep in my guts, I bend my elbow as though doing a bicep curl with the entire weight of another human. Her body rises. Her feet scramble at the earth and she manages to lunge for my shoulder.

"Okay, let go," she tells me. "Josi, let go."

I have to force myself to let go of her hand so she can grab onto my other shoulder. Her knees clench at my hips, her legs trembling with the effort.

"Okay, climb," she tells me.

I let out a hysterical laugh. "I'm flattered and all, but honey, I am not strong enough to climb with you on my back. We wait for the ropes."

"When are they coming? Why aren't they coming?"

"They are. Take a breath and stay calm."

A bolt of lightning strikes out at sea. My head is tilted far enough to the side to see a glimpse of its light. Things get really simple when you're clutching the edge of a cliff in a storm. Things get anatomically simple. Don't let go. That's it.

"Gear incoming!" a distant voice bellows from above and the ropes arrive. Attached to the end of one is a harness. I have to figure out how to get Malia into it.

"Okay, Malia. We'll get you into the harness and you'll be lifted up."

"What about you?"

"I'll wait here and they'll send it back for me."

"Oh god, Josi. *Thank you.*"

"Shhh. Let's just get ourselves safe before we start that." I look at the harness. "See those loops? Your legs need to go through them."

"I'll never be able to do that!"

"Okay, it's alright." I consider our options. "Can you reach your hands through them? Your weight will be lifted from beneath your arms, so it'll hurt. Plus the harness won't fit properly so you're gonna slip around in it, but if you hang onto the rope with your hands you won't fall."

"I'm scared."

I turn my face as far toward her as I can. "I know you are. But listen to me. You are much more than this cliff. You are a strong woman, and you're not falling, okay? Find all the courage you have. Find it now."

I feel her nod and then reach for the harness. She gets one arm through but a spray of earth falls on us and Malia yelps.

"Don't come down!" I roar to the people above.

But it's too late. She slips, loses her hold on both my body and the harness. I twist and grab for her. I get her forearm and grip on, digging my nails into her flesh.

"Hold on, hold on," I breathe.

"Josi!" she screams.

"Reach for me!"

Her arm is slippery and my strength is failing. Lightning strikes and in it I see her eyes, her wide, terrified eyes, and then as though in a dream she falls.

*

Luke

I watch Josi climb step by step to Malia. I watch her wake the girl and then I see their bodies move a little, just a little, to the edge of the cliff. It's hard to make out what's going on down there – two bodies look like one now – but I can tell they haven't fallen.

There is chaos up here. People keep shouting as though their words will make a difference. But it's down to Josi, and it's down to Will hurrying the fuck up with those ropes.

When he finally arrives I set up the harness and we fasten the end of the rope to every body we have here. It's dangerous, because technically every one of us could be pulled over the edge.

Anchored at the end is Blue, the most solid guy I know. Then Eric, Zachariah, Lawrence, Henrietta, Pace, Will and me, at the very edge. I didn't let Coin attach himself – he's trembling like a leaf. Instead I told him to watch exactly what was happening below.

"Everyone ready? Brace yourselves."

I throw the harness and rope over. Ideally we could have thrown two but it's much safer to get them up one at a time, so long as Josi can hold on. "Gear incoming!" I shout.

We wait for any sign that the ropes are being used but nothing happens.

Coin is lying on his stomach, peering down at his girlfriend. "They can't get it on!" he exclaims. "I'm going down to help."

"*No!*" I roar. "You'll disrupt the earth!"

But it's too late. He's over the edge, scampering down like a monkey.

"*Don't come down!*" Josi screams up at us, and then there's a different kind of scream. A blood-chilling scream.

I hear Coin moan in horror. Profound terror strikes my guts so hard I almost vomit. I inch to the edge and peer down. I can't see anything at first, but then I make out a single body clinging to the cliff and then a second, much smaller body on the rocks far below.

Oh god.

I close my eyes.

"What happened?" someone is asking.

"Luke? What is it?"

"Are they okay?"

"What happened?"

I don't know which body is which and I feel rotten to the core to be thinking of this now but I am, I'm thinking of which body fell and which is still clinging to the edge.

Focus.

I exhale slowly. Garner the things in my mind and body that were trained for moments like these. Gather what makes me, me.

"Everything's okay," I tell the others. Then I call for Coin to climb back up. The boy does so, very slowly. When he reaches the lip of the tunnel I haul him in and he collapses, sobbing, onto the ground.

"What happened?" Pace asks again, but this time she's whispering and she sounds scared witless.

I look at them all. "Someone's fallen. I'm not sure who."

The grief is palpable but I can't get lost in it.

I peer down at the surviving figure. "Grab the harness!" I shout to her, but there's no sign she's heard me or maybe she's in shock.

"Whoever is still on the cliff isn't moving," I report. "I have to go down and help her."

Will gets me a second rope and I tie it around my waist. "I need half of you on my rope, half of you on the other. Everyone up the back there, grab onto someone and help anchor the weight."

A whole bunch of people waiting in the tunnel come forward to help. I climb over and they lower me down. I can't climb because of my useless fucking hand. It's so stiff as I grab the fissures in the earth. In the dark I peer down. She isn't moving. I can't make out who it is. *Please*, my heart says. And what a cruel thing to beg for. What a terrible hope.

Finally she looks up and I see Josephine's face. Great suffocating relief bursts in my chest. I make it to her side. She's clinging on, shivering in the cold and the wet, and there's a ghost in her eyes.

"Josi," I say. "Take hold of the harness."

"I said I wouldn't let her fall."

"Take hold of the harness."

I reach over her for the harness and move it to her, helping her to thread it through her left arm first. She won't move her right, though.

"It's caught," she says. "It was the only way I could hold her weight." There's something awful in her voice.

I dig at the earth around the tree root and manage to pry her hand free. Her balance shifts and she tugs on the rope. I pray they can hold us both up there, and they do, they hold firm while I get her right arm through the harness.

"Start climbing," I tell her.

But she doesn't. She lets out a deep moan of grief and presses her face into the mud. My heart breaks. I don't let her hear it. "Don't. Get to the top, Josi. Just get to the top."

With an aching sob she starts climbing. I let her go ahead and then I follow her, staying below in case she falls. We can't climb the whole way – we have to be pulled the last few meters because the cliff has crumbled too badly. It is an immense relief to my agonized hand. But they pull us both up and we slump onto the cold concrete.

Nobody says it. Nobody even says her name. They just help Josi to her feet and shepherd her back home. There are hands and arms and people to help all the children; Coin can't walk and has to be carried home. I wait until they've all left, until I know they're safe, and then I turn back to the cliff.

I peer down to the beach, to the child's broken body there. She was fourteen and she was beautiful and she was ours and for a moment I hoped she was dead.

I sink to my knees and whisper to her. *I'm sorry. We were supposed to protect you. I'm so sorry.*

*

Josephine

Claire makes me drink something hot and full of sugar. I sit and stare blindly at the wall of the infirmary for what must be a good half hour. And then all of a sudden something occurs to me and I throw off the blanket and start running.

I can hardly breathe as I careen through the tunnels and into the boys' barracks. A huge cluster of kids is down the end and I push through to find Coin at the center. He's not making a sound, not speaking or crying. He's staring at the wall and smoothing his hands through his long blond ponytail, over and over, locked in it. His friends are crowded around, weeping and trying to comfort him but he's just blank.

He spots me coming for him and flinches. It breaks something inside me.

Instead of whatever he thinks I'm here to do, I reach for his hands and force them to cease their frenzied obsession. "This was not your fault."

"It was," he whispers. "I killed her."

"*No.*" I pull him against me and he clutches at me and I hold him so tight while he cries. "No, *no*, Coin. It wasn't your fault. It wasn't."

"I saw her body. I saw it fall."

"It's not your fault."

*

In the end our wedding night is a terrible, terrible night. When I finally leave Coin it's only because he's fallen asleep and his friends promise to stay with him all night. They're grieving too – Malia was everyone's friend. She was sweet to all and everyone loved her.

I make my way, bleary-eyed and near catatonic with exhaustion, back to my bed. Luke's sitting on the edge of it, waiting.

I almost can't cross to him. I am ashamed of how much better it will make me feel to be in his arms; I don't deserve that kind of comfort. But I do cross, my body hardly my own, and I sink onto his lap and he kisses me and undresses me and I need him so badly that I can hardly breathe, hardly think. The pain in my chest wells until I'm crying as he makes love to me. And afterwards I sleep more deeply than I have in a long time – since the last bout of depression, probably. I dream of wings and scales and fur. I dream of her body taking flight at the last moment and soaring into the sky with wild joy instead of scattering to sad pieces on the rocks.

Chapter 13

April 22nd, 2067

Josephine

The mats beneath me are soft and I can pretend the scattered pinpricks above are stars, instead of holes in the silo roof. Around me are dozens of young bodies lying close together, "star" gazing the only way we can. Trips to the sea have been banned. Trips outside our gated tunnels are forbidden. My throat closes a little each day as our home begins to feel more and more like a prison. Instead of releasing my fist I have started clenching it tighter. Fear of loss tightens my grip. If I could forbid them from doing anything that might hurt them I would, and even though I can see the irrational nature of such thoughts, I can't stop them.

We buried Malia at sundown. Collecting her body from the rocks was terrible. She was so absent from the broken thing she became that it made me think for the first time that perhaps we do have souls. Her funeral was on the cliff-top, where her body now rests. Her death was a brutal reminder of how swiftly life changes. The guard can't come down, nothing can be taken for granted. Coin didn't go to the funeral – he stayed in bed for a week straight. I know the feeling. It's one of sifting through quicksand, of weighing a thousand tons, of being too tired to open your eyes, too tired to even breathe.

He's here now beside me, his feet entwined with mine. I have someone else's head resting on my tummy, someone's arm wrapped beneath my neck, a bony knee poking into my rib. We are bodies entangled for comfort and warmth. It's cold in the tunnels. Too cold to be alone. Too lonely to be alone.

"That's Onomatopoeia," Lawrence says, pointing at a group of holes. He's been creating constellations in our ceiling and giving them silly names. He, Alo, Teddy, Henrietta and Coin have grown inseparable since the accident, the five of them having been with Malia when she fell. I still don't really know what happened that night, but I know it bound them together with iron.

"Why Onomatopoeia?" Hen asks.

"He's the god of *pfft* and *shhhhh* and *swish* and *ahhh*. Those three stars there are his harp *twanging* and that cluster is his butt *farting*."

Amid the giggles Teddy mutters, "Only one of those is an onomatopoeia, genius."

"What's that group there called?" Alo asks.

"That's Gluteus Maximus, the Queen of Donkeys. She has a giant ass beneath her."

They erupt into laughter. He's got a theme going tonight, clearly.

With a peek over my shoulder I see the entrance is still empty. Where is he?

"Who are you looking for?" Georgie asks me. It used to unnerve me how closely she watches me, and how many inane questions she asks, but I've grown used to it. I think she's just a super curious kid. Thankfully she was nowhere near the cliff when Malia fell, and like most of the other kids, missed seeing the horror of it.

"No one."

"Who do you think?" Lawrence sneers, then makes orgasmic noises not appropriate for children.

"Sometimes I swear you're five years old," Hen tells him with a sigh of long suffering. His noises only get louder.

Someone shoves him and the effect is knock-on – a knee connects and sends an elbow into a shoulder into a foot and soon everyone is grumbling in irritation and snapping at Lawrence to shut up. He laughs, unperturbed, and pulls Alo into a rough tumble that has absolutely no concern for the many other people nearby, including me. They land on my stomach and I give a mighty *oof*.

"Now that's an onomatopoeia," Teddy announces.

Alo and Lawrence scramble off me with hasty apologies. I regain my breath and get to my feet. There must be murderous rage in my eyes because both the boys shrink. The other kids are laughing at their expressions.

"Haven't had enough training for one day, huh?" I ask. "You wanna fight?"

"Not with you."

"Well, too bad, you little thugs."

They're not exactly little, actually. They're sixteen years old and happen to be the biggest of all the teenage boys, meaning they're bigger than me. I point at the others to make a circle and then I dart in at Lawrence, stepping behind his foot and throwing my shoulder into his chest. He hits the mats hard but I'm already sweeping my leg around to take Alo's feet from beneath him. Within a few seconds they're both flat on their backs, winded.

As the kids cheer a voice asks, "Attacking the children again, are we, dear?"

I whirl to see that Luke has finally arrived.

"We're not children!" Lawrence is outraged but all Alo can do is giggle as he manages to get his breath back. "Besides, she's a chick. I'm not about to smash a chick."

I roll my eyes and don't bother with that one, since he obviously knows it's untrue. The girls launch into a tirade about how sexist and asinine he is, while I go help Luke pin up the large white sheet.

"All sorted?" I ask.

He grins and nods.

"Sweet. Little bastard doesn't deserve it though."

"He may be a little bastard but he keeps morale up. They'll all love it, anyway." Luke spins around and clears his throat.

They continue chatting and laughing. He's too polite.

"Quiet, losers," I say.

The kids fall silent with curiosity.

"Life's been rough lately," Luke says, "so we thought you deserved a treat. Tonight's screening is the 1960 classic Hitchcockian film *Psycho*. Just don't sue us for showing inappropriate content to minors."

There is a moment of silence as they realize what he means and then a gasp of delight runs through the crowd, followed by ear-splitting squeals and booming cheers of ecstasy. Lawrence jumps into the air with fists pumping, crowing at the top of his lungs, while the noise level could wake the dead.

I burst out laughing at the scene, and Luke throws his arm around my shoulder with a grin. "I don't think they're keen."

Most of the adults come to join us and we sprawl once again on the mats, entangled and enjoying the first moment of shared happiness in weeks.

"Will, my man, roll it!"

Will starts the old projector, which he and Luke sneakily set up this afternoon, and we watch the fantastic black and white film unfold on the sheet before us. Despite it lacking color or effects or even 3D let alone holo tech, it scares the crap out of just about everyone. Most deal with this by giggling hysterically, and for once Lawrence doesn't say a word except to *shhhh* everyone. He takes his cinema very seriously, apparently.

When it's over I have to be the bad guy who tells them to go to bed. They bitch and moan about it but eventually acquiesce, since I threaten no more films unless they earn them. I spend a few hours walking the tunnels, on the look out for danger. I come across one of the boys sneaking into the girls' barracks and punish him with extra chores. I feel like a warden but I can't stop. I'm terrified of all the bad things that can happen to them, terrified of my own responsibility. When the hell did I agree to parent dozens of unruly teenagers? I'm barely more than a teenager myself.

Eventually Luke finds me at one of the Fury gates, where he mostly knows to find me these days. I've been standing here thinking about that awful journey from the Inferno, hunted and on the run. We lost so many in those brutal days, fighting to keep the Furies back long enough for the others to keep going.

"Baby, come to bed." Luke yawns now, bringing me back to the present.

"I'm just—"

"Patrolling, I know. But it's Blue's shift, not yours."

I don't move. For some reason I can't. There's a male Fury and from what I can see of him, he might once have been a very young man. Younger than me, maybe. His mouth opens and closes with a snap. He keeps sniffing through his nose like a dog. His fingers clutch at the metal bars of the cage keeping him out. Several of them are broken and twisted but he hasn't noticed. Old blood stains his mouth and neck.

I hold the creature's eyes and say softly, "I hate them."

And it's so true it eclipses everything else. I draw the knife from my boot and stab it straight into his eye, his red, burst eye.

"*Josi.*"

I watch the dying Fury before me. He grunts and flails and then sinks oddly to his side. The others of his kind don't turn to him until he's completely dead, but the second he is they tear into his body. I reach through and stab as many as I can, gouge my knife into as much flesh as I can find.

Strong arms pull me away and my knife clatters to the ground on the other side of the cage. Luke lets me go and we watch the feeding frenzy. My eyes rest on the fallen blade, unnoticed among the fray. It was a good knife; I'll be sad to lose it.

"I want them gone."

"I know that. We're trying to work out how."

I breathe out and shake my head.

"You're reckless, Josi. It's starting to scare me."

I frown and look at him. To my ears it sounds like he's describing someone else. "Am I?"

He frowns right back at me. For the first time in our lives I think it's an uncertain look, a searching look, one that might not necessarily yield any answers. It unsettles me, as I think it does him.

I try to explain. "I feel … wary. Nervous."

His eyebrows arch. "You hide it well."

I swallow and look again at the Furies. Was that reckless? Yeah, maybe, I suppose. Guess I could have lost a hand. But it seems worth it to me, to kill a few of the fuckers.

"The cliff with Malia. Climbing down there before the gear had arrived …"

"I had to. You knew that."

"If it was my op I would have waited."

I stare at him. "It was your op. It was *our* op and we decided together."

"No, you launched yourself down that cliff before I could weigh in."

"We take calculated risks. You taught me that."

"And the risk in that situation was too high. You lose the coin toss and you both would've died."

"I win it, and we both would've lived."

"Did you both live?"

I recoil as if he's slapped me and touch the cage for balance.

"I'm not trying to hurt you," he says. "It wasn't anywhere close to your fault. The point I'm making is that you're too willing to risk your life."

"For our people? I can't see that as a negative."

"You're a leader now. You have to start thinking about yourself as an asset."

"Luke, Jesus. You sound like a fucking Blood."

"I am a Blood."

"What?"

"I don't think it goes away, as neat and tidy as that would be for us. I understand risk and reward and the value of lives—"

"Woah, stop." I stride away.

He follows me to our room and even though there's no door and no sound-proofing and half the resisters are within a stone's throw, he says loudly, "Don't walk away from me."

"Keep your voice down."

"We're talking about this, finally, so let's talk about it. You think it's your job to save everyone, and you'll die to do it.

But that's not good leadership – that's immaturity. It's an inability to make tough choices."

"*I'm* not in charge of this place," I hiss. "If anyone is, you are!"

"Avoiding the topic."

"I don't need you to attack me about character flaws, alright? I don't need that from you."

"It's not a character flaw!" he snaps, exasperated.

"Immaturity? Inability to make tough choices?"

"It's a learning curve, Josi. I've got a shit ton to learn too. What I do understand is how to remove myself from my emotions and my personal attachments in order to do what's better for the community as a whole."

"Well, great, aren't you just perfect."

He rolls his eyes and it only infuriates me more.

"No, seriously – you are, aren't you? You're good at everything, everyone loves you, you seem to have all your shit together, you don't hesitate, you don't question, you just act and it's always right, *right*?"

He shakes his head impatiently.

"Sometimes you're so perfect, Luke, that it's impossible to even reach the stratosphere you inhabit. You can build fucking cellos with your hands and create perfect boundaries. I'm an emotional ugly mess around you. I'm imperfect and it gets to you, doesn't it?"

Luke's eyes widen. He stalks toward me. "Come *off* it. That person you're describing has nothing to do with me."

"Liar."

"I'm so far from perfect it's not even funny."

"True. A girl dies and you want to criticize me about it."

He grunts and is suddenly upon me, forcing me back against the tunnel wall. "*No*, Josi. I'm scared!"

I pause, surprised.

"You're so brave it terrifies me." My breath is coming quickly and his hands pin me to the wall. "You're fragile," he says and his face is so close to mine, his words against my lips.

I breathe out. My edges have scattered like in Will's painting. I lift my chin. "You came down that cliff too. With a broken hand and an unfastened harness."

"For *you*," he snarls. "And maybe that's the problem. You make it all blurry. You make everything blurry, when it used to be so damn clear. Now I'd climb down any cliff for you. But you – you climb down cliffs for everyone because you don't value yourself."

"Fuck off," I breathe, and shove his chest.

He moves closer.

"Sometimes I could just throttle your stupid, perfect neck."

"I just want you to hear me, for once in your stubborn life. You're precious, Josephine Luquet. You're *fragile*. We both are."

One of his large hands lifts to my jaw and holds it firmly. My teeth clench and I wrench my face from his. He follows my mouth, grazing it but not kissing me.

"We're fragile," he repeats, and then his lips take mine.

I lift my hands to his neck and clench it tightly as though I might just squeeze. My mouth opens so our tongues can trace. His damaged hand has found its way beneath my shirt to my breast, his warm finger to my nipple. I bite his lip, angry at the simplicity of desire and the ease with which I'm consumed by it. For a second I hate it and I hate him, and then the second after that I don't hate him at all. I know something very well.

I say, "You're wrong, Luke Townsend. We're not fragile."

*

September 16th, 2067

Josephine

I abseil down the sheer face of the wall. My hands grip and release as I control the tension of the rope and the velocity of my descent. Wind whips up and my stomach bottoms out continuously, but I love the feel of sliding down through the air; I love the thought that I could be falling and it might feel almost the same. On either side of me are half a dozen kids all managing with varying degrees of fear – I'm pretty sure none of them feel as inclined as I do to drop eight hundred feet to the ground.

"That's it," I call over the sound of the wind at such altitude. "Nice and smooth. Relax your muscles."

No matter what I say it's a gut-wrenching activity. The earth is so far distant that were there people down there I'm not sure I'd see anything but dots. We wouldn't be doing this if there were any other way to get the kids out. This happens to be a blind spot in the city's surveillance. There are no blind spots inside the wall, but there are a couple outside it, which makes it relatively safe to escape this way with our freshly rescued teenagers. *Relatively* being the key word.

One of the boys – Patty – is weeping continuously and Ziyi, who is a grown woman, lets out a scream every time she has to let go of her tension rope to swing a couple of meters. Which is often. But she's doing it. She's damn well doing it. Pace and Will are way ahead of us, moving with lightning speed in order to reach and check the bottom, while above us Blue and Eric keep an eye on the top of the wall as they descend.

My focus is keeping the kids calm, while wondering what's taking Luke so long to get here. My earpiece delivers Teddy's message as though he's inside my head, and sometimes it really feels that way. *"Still all clear. But hurry it along, would you? This whole thing is nerve-wracking."*

"Says the kid fifty meters safely below the ground."

"I can't do this!" Patty announces at that point. He's to my left, with a girl called Ange in between us.

"Yes, you can, you already are," I tell him. "Take it one second at a time and just keep moving."

He stops altogether and I do the same, shouting for the other kids to keep going. "What are you afraid of?"

"Are you insane? *Falling!*"

"You're afraid of dying," I supply.

He nods and I can see him reconsidering the wisdom of leaving with a group of strange rebels he knows nothing about, most of whom aren't much older than him, and who point out very obvious facts.

"You fall, you die, right?" I say. "But here's another equation. You stay where you are, you die. You try to climb back up, you die, guaranteed. The only way not to die is to keep descending and reach the bottom."

"Oh my god," he whimpers.

"Toughen up, get moving."

I hate telling him to toughen up, and in any other situation I wouldn't, but when being tough saves your life you gotta be tough. He starts moving, more slowly. Blue and Eric have nearly caught up to us. Right down there on the ground is the opening to a tunnel that will eventually lead us to our tunnels. Abseiling down the wall means not having to cross the highly regulated city with a bunch of stolen teenagers in tow. It does, however, suck when said teenagers are afraid of heights.

As I wait for Patty to catch up I take a look out at the world behind me. I've told the kids not to do this under any circumstances, but heights don't bother me. In fact being up here is kind of like coming home. The air smells different, feels different against my face. Far out on the horizon sinks the golden sun. The enormity of the world reaches something inside me: it is the hugeness I find comforting, my tininess within it reassuring. Despite the general anxiety and the not-wanting-anyone-to-fall part of all this, I'm happy. That slowly rising red moon has no hold over me. I'm free, and I'd do this for *fun*.

Which is why, of course, the universe decides to give me a great big middle finger.

We've made it to within about fifty meters of the ground and we're in the home stretch when it happens. Along the wall, at its base, is an old gate that has long since been out of use. A wall doesn't need a gate if no one's ever supposed to go through it, after all. It's been barricaded and guarded from the inside, so I'm somewhat surprised to see a car explode through it into the barren beyond with us.

"What the hell?" Blue exclaims.

I squint to see that part of the metal gate has been ripped off and entangled with the car, which has rolled several times and now rests on its roof not all that far from where we're descending. Who the bloody hell would be driving a beat-up old car out through the Blood-guarded wall into a wasteland of nothing? At sunset, no less. How did they get through? And *why*?

I don't stop to think. Because in my appraisal of the strange occurrence I've spotted further cause for concern. In the distance something approaches. Many things – human figures, in fact. And in the world as we know it human figures in the beyond means one thing: Furies. I am abseiling to the bottom with more speed than I've ever descended with – I am basically falling. I leave Patty with Blue and Eric and I high-tail it to the ground, my hands burning on the ropes, my guts in my mouth. The ground rears up to connect heavily with my boots, causing my knees to buckle. Pace is wrenching me upright and unclipping me from my harness before I have a chance to blink. I can see the lid to the tunnel is open and kids are already being shepherded down the ladder. We'll make it with time to spare, we'll be fine.

But whoever is in that car will not.

I take a long, deep breath and make a decision.

"Get everyone into the tunnels," I order Pace.

"Duh."

"I'll meet you at home."

"What? Why?"

"The car."

"Dual, *no*!"

"I can make it. There's time."

"They don't matter! They're not ours!"

But they all matter. And anyway, Luke's on his way. When Luke's around, Furies die. I can't take them on my own, not that many, but we can definitely take them together. He's probably already started his descent behind us.

I take off at a sprint, barking over my shoulder for Pace to get below. She'll do as I say. That's how it works on ops: you obey whoever's in charge or people get killed. To Teddy I say, "Send Luke after me but make sure everyone else gets below."

"*Aye aye. For the record this makes me even more nervous than the abseiling.*"

"For the record that's not high in my priorities right now, Teddy boy."

My feet pound over the hard earth. I don't draw the two pistols from my thigh holsters, not yet. I pass the opening that was once a gate and see a crowd of Bloods working like an army to get it blocked up. They don't give a shit about who's gone through because whoever's gone through is toast. They certainly don't care about one girl sprinting across their line of sight – she won't last long. Their concern is the horde of snarling cannibals headed their way.

Sometimes Furies get inside the walls. I don't know how, but I suspect it has to do with the tunnels. When I first encountered them a few years ago Luke and I were in an abandoned building right in the middle of the city. They were myths to us then, a story with which to scare children. Then I saw them again the night I carried him unconscious from the asylum – in fact, they saved our lives that night, interrupting the Blood hunt for us and turning it into a violent battle. However they do get inside, it usually isn't long before the Bloods vaporize them, but I've never seen them try to deal with a group this big.

I reach the smoking car. It looks less like a car than an artfully abstract metal sculpture at this point. Rusted red curls amorously with shining silver; steel hands rear up from the earth and clasp together. Inside this mess are seven people, I think. *Seven*, all crammed into a tiny vehicle, even tinier since it got squished by the gate. My heart thumps wildly as I make out body parts belonging to children in the mix. The body parts move, though, so they're still alive. I have to use my boot for leverage to wrench open one of the dented doors.

"Help," an adult voice pleads.

"I'm here, it's alright," I assure the voice, still trying to work out who is where and how to get everyone out since nobody seems to be doing it themselves. I should have brought Pace with me, dammit – I could have used the help but I can't stand the thought of endangering any of the others. And let's face it: this is one hell of a risk.

You're reckless, he told me. *You're fragile.*

"*No response from Luke's comm., Josi,*" Teddy warns me.

"What? What do you mean *no response?*"

"*I mean he's not responding! What the hell else do you think I mean?*" Teddy's voice sounds mildly hysterical but I'm currently dealing with the child I've managed to pull from the wreck. She coughs and blinks awake so I leave her to drag her brother free.

On the other side an adult woman has climbed out the window and is trying to get the seatbelt from a third child.

"Hurry," I tell her calmly, because I don't want to freak her out completely but she really needs to hurry.

There's a man upside down in the front seat. I check his pulse and find him still alive but he doesn't wake when I shake him. The knife in my boot saws through his seatbelt and he falls on his head, which sucks but is unavoidable. I drag him inch by slow inch out of the mess, but something gets caught and stalls me. Shit. I crawl over his fleshy body and into the car to try and see what the problem is. Part of the gate has completely mangled one of his feet. Both feet are now twisted into the body of the car, trapping a fourth child who is wailing in terror.

"Shhh, it's alright," I tell the girl. "You're safe. Can you climb over your daddy to me?"

"Is he dead?" she asks, and then asks again.

"No, but I need to get you out, okay? Crawl to me now."

I can see the woman – presumably the mother – now helping a very old person out of the back, a second woman who's at least eighty. She is trembling with the effort of dragging the poor woman free but I don't have time to help. The child wriggles over her father.

"Is he dead?" she asks. "Is he dead?"

"No, he's alive," I grunt. I have her in my grasp now, but getting us both out is a feat. I have to use her father's body as an anchor and drag us both under the hot, sharp metal of the vehicle using only one arm. I manage to dump the girl on the ground outside the car and then turn back for the dad.

The earth is trembling. I can feel the vibrations of many, many feet drawing near. Where the hell is Luke. Where the hell is Luke. Where the hell is Luke. It's in my head like a mantra because I don't want to consciously think about what I'm about to do. About how I'm drawing my knife, but this time it's not to cut through the tough material of a seatbelt, it's to cut through the flesh and bone of a man's ankle.

At first it's harder than I thought it would be, but I think that's because I'm timid. I try to imagine this as a piece of dead meat, one I must chop to survive, and as I think of the flesh like that – like flesh and not a person – I'm able to hack through the ruined leg until I reach the bone that has already sheared in half upon impact. A hideous image enters my mind without warning or explanation. An image of me ducking my head and biting through his leg, tasting his blood and skin and tissue and fat in my mouth.

What the fuck?

I shudder in revulsion.

"What are you doing?" the mother screams at me through the macabre thought. I ignore her and get back to cutting.

That's when the man wakes up.

He gives a mighty roar of pain and lurches upright only to bash his skull on the park brake. Blood trickles into his eyes but it's the least of his worries. His jerking has lodged my knife deep into the fractured bone of his ankle and I can't get it out, and I'm sure he's doing way more damage to the amputation than I am.

"Stop," I try. "It's okay, try to stay calm—"

"Get off me!" he yells. His fist comes out and takes me in the cheek. It's a hell of a blow and I feel my head spin nauseatingly.

"*Stop*!" I growl through the pain. I meet his agonized, panicked eyes and hold them fiercely. "My knife's in your ankle. I'm cutting your foot off to get you out of this car because if I don't you'll die. Take a deep breath and let me finish." And then I add, even though it feels awkward to say it, "For your family, let me finish."

His jaw clenches and he rallies more courage than I thought possible. With a sharp nod he lets out a mighty sob of pain but he doesn't move again. He braces himself on the bits of metal he can find and he roars as I cut through the last of his leg. His wife speaks to him in French, a steady stream of words I don't understand. He comes free weighing less than he did; he comes away smaller than he was.

The ground is shaking.

We crawl out of the car into the waiting arms of his family. "Get to the tunnel!" I shout, pointing. "Help your grandmother," I order the children. They all swarm on the older lady and help her over the distance. Meanwhile the mother has managed to get her husband upright and supports him as he hops his way heroically after the rest of his family.

It's time to draw my guns now. I lower myself behind the wreckage and line up the Furies in my sights, using the rubber wheel of the car as a rest. I fire and hit a skull, then a chest. I have finite ammunition, but I just need to slow them until the family reaches the tunnel. Then I can run.

"Where's Luke?" I snap.

"*I don't know, I don't know,*" Teddy wails. "*Josi, get out of there! There's way too many!*"

I shoot again and again, firing through the magazines of both guns.

"Are the others all clear?"

"*Yes, they're safe. Get below, Josi.*"

I glance back to see that the father has lost consciousness. Too much lost blood, I guess. The mother and her four children are dragging him over the ground.

I keep firing. I run out of bullets. I turn and sprint. Blood rushes in my ears. I make it to the family and push a child out of the way so I can haul the man to the tunnel.

But the Furies are arriving.

With both my knives I turn to meet the first of the fray, slashing fast and clean. I go for throats and eyes, not bothering with chests, as that won't slow them enough. I've said it before: in moments like these a badass sword would really come in handy. I try to cover the angles, try to block any from getting through. All together there must be a hundred of them. Too many for me. Too many for Luke and me. I don't know why I thought he'd make the difference. This was always a suicide mission, as it turns out. I'm suddenly very glad he didn't appear in time to help. At least the Furies haven't arrived in a group, but in drips and drabs. Some were faster than others and so they come in a steady stream, a couple at a time instead of all at once. It might make the difference between living and dying. It might.

A single glance tells me that most of the family is in the tunnel now, a glance is all I have time for. And then something terrible happens. Something so terrible that it breaks my heart and mends it and teaches me of the courage of children. Of girls. Of *humans*.

The girl I dragged over her father's body hasn't climbed into the tunnel with the rest of her family. I can hear her mother screaming her name – *Sienn*. She has a blade. It's small. She's at my side and she means to use it on the Furies. She's only eleven, maybe twelve, maybe ten.

I twist and dive. The Fury lunging at her takes my boot in his head. I hit the ground and scrape my side badly but I'm moving, rolling over and shoving the girl at the tunnel. She tumbles toward it but I'm already raising my knife into the thigh of a Fury, wrenching it through its artery. I'm drenched in a waterfall of blood. The creature slips and falls straight onto me. The air leaves me but I can't stop yet, not yet, because the girl is still above ground, she's still trying to fight with her little knife and it's so so brave but I have to get her below.

I shove the body off me and slash quickly through its neck. There's a very brief respite in the attacks but there are more Furies coming and coming. *Josi*, my flickering earpiece weeps, *Josi*. I drag myself to my feet in time to see Sienn stab her blade into the arm of a Fury I thought I'd already killed. She gives a wild scream of rage as she does it. The monster snarls in pain, bats the weapon away and grabs hold of Sienn's shoulders. It lunges at her, but I smash my shoulder into its side and send its weight off the girl. Pinning the creature by the balls, I cut its throat, then turn quickly to shove the girl to the tunnel, to where her mother's waiting hands grab desperately at her.

"Go!" I scream, meaning to follow, but they're already upon me. All I have time to do is lunge for the grate and slam it shut over the tunnel mouth before I feel my legs pulled out from under me. I am dragged over the earth and completely overcome. I manage to twist upwards in time to stab through the eye of one Fury and slash another's cheek, but they have me now. They have me and I can no longer move. They're all here, blocking out the sky, all of it but for a single scrap of twilight violet blue. Stars have appeared, a veil for the halo of gold sitting atop the earth.

The voice in my ear fades until I can no longer hear it.

I stare up at the beauty above and I imagine rising from beneath these hands and mouths and teeth and bodies pressing me down down down. I rise and fly away from it all. From here, from way up here, I think of many things. I think of the people in the tunnels. I think of my father. I think of how I'm dying the same way Hal died, feasted upon by monsters. I think I like that I die fighting. But these thoughts come in snippets, too fast and scattered to hold to.

The one thing that doesn't come in a snippet, the thing I grasp easily and will never let go of, is the thought of Luke. Wherever I go now, I will think always of him. Wherever my spirit travels, whatever is made of my soul. Even if nothing happens, even if my life is extinguished and my body turns to dust, that dust will think of him, and love him. Let my body give life to this earth, let it give rebirth.

Let my heart love him beyond that life, beyond my death.

This is the last thought I have before the monsters crowd out the sky.

Actually, there is one more. It is this:

Fragile indeed.

Chapter 14

December 23rd, 2067

Josephine

"Volunteers for the crapper?" Luke hollers into the dining hall as we eat breakfast.

To dead silence.

I roll my eyes and raise my hand. I've had a three-month sabbatical from toilet duty so it's probably my turn.

Luke's eyebrows arch as if to make sure I actually mean it. Then he throws me the matches with a quick shrug. "Your funeral."

"It's a Christmas miracle!" Pace announces amid the hesitant laughter. "Someone has actually volunteered for the crapper."

"She needs a second," Luke says. "One of you kids can get off your asses and help her." He's in a bad mood.

"Sure as shit isn't gonna be me," I hear Lawrence mutter. "No pun intended."

"You've never done it," Henrietta points out. "I've done it three times already."

"I've done it five," Alo is quick to add.

"I vote the king of the crapper goes with her," Teddy says and they all look at Coin.

"I can't. It's too gross and I have OCD."

"Conveniently."

"I'll go on my own," I interrupt, not in the mood for their bickering.

The kids all protest and start to say they'll go with me but I'm already striding from the room.

"I'll help her," I hear a voice offer. "Since you're all too piss weak. Pun intended."

I glance back to see Zach following. I also see the expressions of the other kids – boy, do they hate him. He rubs everyone the wrong way, and what's worse is he does it on purpose.

"Don't fall in," Lawrence reminds him sardonically.

Zach and I head for the stairs in silence. I light the lamp to guide our way, and in the flickering light his scar makes his perpetual snarl even more pronounced.

"So what are we feeling guilty about, Josephine Luquet?" he asks. He always calls me by my full name and I don't particularly like it.

"Nothing, Zachariah Shay."

"Bullshit. No pun intended."

"Enough with the shit puns, alright? They're barely even puns."

We stop in at the supply room to get the gasoline, then head for the lavatories.

"Nobody volunteers for the worst job down here unless they're feeling guilty about something."

"You did," I point out.

"I'm an anomaly. Too far evolved to feel guilt."

My lip quirks. "Oh yeah? What evolutionary purpose would a lack of guilt serve?"

"Do you know how much time and energy people waste on guilt? Particularly for things they weren't responsible for?"

"Sure, but it exists as a way to regulate our behavior and maintain social skills. No guilt, and we'd all just go around doing whatever we want."

"Sounds good to me."

"Yeah, until any one of the hundred people who hates you decides they've had enough of your sneering superiority and offs you with a hatchet in the back."

"Oh, shut up already, Josephine Luquet. You're boring me."

I smile properly now, but that disappears as the smell hits. We've come to the edge of the upper tunnel. Before us sit the pit toilets in all their foul glory.

I step out and open them one by one. The stench hits me and I groan, quickly pulling my shirt up over my nose and mouth. I start spraying the gasoline down the holes.

"Jesus, this is grim," Zach says.

"Help me out, would you? Light a match and throw one into each toilet."

He looks appalled at the idea of moving any closer, but delicately does as I've instructed. He gags badly enough to heave the contents of his stomach up, which thankfully is just a bit of bile.

"Get a move on."

Once the pits are all lit we move to open the smoke flutes and lower them down over the toilets.

"Whose idea was this, anyway?" Zach asks once we're standing to the side to monitor the burn-off. He sounds impressed.

"Your favorite person. One Mr. Luke Townsend. Right after he figured out how to get us clean drinking water, cooking fires and power."

Zach rolls his eyes but I can't help remembering those first awful days in this place, after having blocked off the Furies with a dislodged train carriage. Luke turned that brain of his to understanding how everything down here worked, and to figuring out how we could remain alive in the most unlivable conditions. He explored for weeks on end and discovered an old, closed off coalmine, which he used to build hot, low smoke emission fires. He designed the smoke flutes, and then he set himself to finding a clean source of water. One of the tunnels, he found, was blocking off a running stream, and so he needed an enormous industrial drill. Steal such a thing we did, on a desperate mission that got two people killed, and then Luke used it to crack through the earth until he reached the underground spring. His mother said she probably shouldn't have spent his childhood stopping him from digging holes because it had turned out to be quite a useful skill.

"We're alive because of him," I tell Zach.

But he's not buying it. "No one's that perfect unless they're hiding something ugly."

"Who says he isn't?"

Zach's eyes alight on me, hungry for ammunition, but I shake my head. Luke's not perfect, as much as I used to needle him about it. He's a pathological liar, but then again so am I. Once upon a time we were perfect for each other.

"Are you really going to stop him from killing the Furies?"

I nod.

"Why?"

This is the question no one else has asked me. Most people have avoided talking to me since my bewildering declaration to protect the Furies, but not Zach. "Would you slaughter a pack of wolves because they aren't human?"

"*I* wouldn't, but many would."

I shake my head. "Not people I want to be around."

"Then what are you doing down here?"

I think it's meant to be a joke, but it falls flat. The toilets are really burning now, and the smell of the excrement has mixed with the scents of gas and smoke to make up a particularly god-awful stench. My eyes are watering with it.

"The Furies aren't wolves," Zach says.

"No, they're more human."

"What's so good about being human?" he asks flatly.

I look at him properly, feeling a gust of elation. "I have no idea," I tell him honestly. Our eyes meet; I can see the flicker of my lamp flame reflected in the darkness of his. That sneer of his never goes away, it will be plastered on his face until his flesh turns to dust.

"Why do you have that scar?" I ask. "Surely Daddy dearest could have managed a proper surgeon for you? I can't imagine he'd want his work on display."

Zach's lips quirk humorlessly. "You serious? Course he would."

This is unnerving. I'm about to let it go when Zach speaks again.

"He wasn't happy with my progress. I'd been suturing pig carcasses for months and they weren't up to scratch. So to teach me a lesson he carved open my face and made me stitch it up myself. I was ten."

I stare at him, my arm hairs standing on end.

"Luke thinks he's going to kill my father, doesn't he?" Zach asks.

I clear my throat. "He'd like to. I think he'd like to very much."

Zach's gaze is bleak as he searches my face. "He can try. Just let him try, Josephine Luquet. But you and I both know what really has to happen."

I nod once and a silent pact is made between us.

He says, "It was really bad here with you gone."

*

At one of the punching bags I spot a very small girl. It takes me a second to place her face, and then all at once I feel a rush of heat inside my mouth, as if I might vomit. I freeze in the middle of the training session – there are people moving all around me, tackling and grappling with each other, doing push-ups and sit-ups and any number of exercises, lifting weights and generally flurrying with movement. In the corners of my vision they start to seem very wild, very savage, like creatures moving in for an attack. But I can't look at them straight because my eyes are captured and held by this one little girl who is far too little to be punching a bag but is trying anyway.

"You okay?" a voice asks at my side.

I blink and nod.

"You're pale," Luke murmurs, and touches my arm to help. I wrench it away from him and duck from the menagerie of limbs and mouths and eyes. I'm breathing very fast as I rush through this tiny shrinking tunnel, desperate for air, for quiet, for sky. My feet stumble on the rails of the ladder and I nearly fall, but manage to burst up through our covered tunnel hatch and into the grassy hills. I suck a huge breath into my lungs, then another, locking my eyes to the twilight sky.

I don't care if there are Blood patrols out here. I don't care if I'm spotted. I'm too overwhelmed to care, and even though it's unforgivably reckless I don't duck for cover. I just stand here, trying not to look at the mighty wall in the distance.

I haven't seen Sienn since the day she raised a knife to help me face the monsters. Not since the day her courage made me fall to them.

I suppose I owe her my life. Or at least the rebirth of it.

*

December 24th, 2067

Luke

I'm not sure I've ever approached a more miserable Christmas. It seems like we should be happy but there's this heaviness draped over us all. Having returned to the tunnels after my three-month vacation has made it clear how unbearable the walls have become to those who live within them. The kids are desperate to get out. The adults are run ragged trying to keep things from falling apart. Food is scarce and not varied enough – I can see how badly malnourished everyone is growing. Living on bread and water isn't enough. Mom says just about everyone has come to her with symptoms of vitamin deficiency. A brutal stomach flu recently ripped through them and left them even worse off. Without Josi or me here to run the supply operations, they wind up returning with a few measly tins and some very close calls to report. Nobody's said a word about Christmas tomorrow – it's too depressing.

Something has to change. Either we leave these tunnels and this city, or we find a way to drastically improve what we have.

Josi and I haven't spoken since the meeting, unless you can count yesterday's brief interaction in which I managed to make her sprint from the arena with nothing but a few talented words. I seek her out now, and find her repairing one of the wood fire smoke flutes, which has clogged, rendering an entire cooking fire useless. I can see the coals getting cold already and curse whoever stopped watching it long enough to let that happen. Josi's head is right up in the flute and she's banging a wrench at something within.

"Josi?"

Her head pops out and I can't help laughing at how covered in coal she is. Her face is blackened with soot and her hair is sticking up at odd angles. Without thinking I reach to wipe her face and show her how dirty it is, but before my skin connects she jerks out of reach.

My hand drops, a pit forming in my stomach. "Sorry."

"No worries. What's up?"

"You noticed how bad things have got?"

Josi nods grimly. "We need proper food."

"I'm gonna do a run for supplies but we need to start thinking bigger."

I watch her hesitate, wiping her sweaty brow with the back of her filthy hand. "I found something," she says. "Get armed up and I'll show you."

"Now?"

"Tonight, after dark. Don't tell anyone."

"How very clandestine."

She doesn't smile, just shoves her head back up the flute.

*

"Is this where you've been coming every night?" I whisper several hours later. We are flat on our stomachs, crawling through the reeds of a riverbank, both dressed entirely in black and armed to the teeth.

Josi doesn't reply, just commando crawls up an incline. There she stops, waiting for me. As I crest the rise, shapes appear below us. Several lights, from both a large house and what looks like a factory.

"What is it?" I ask. We're a long way from the city – this entire rural area was abandoned, as far as I knew. Nobody could grow anything out here anymore.

"A farm."

My eyes widen. True enough, there are no trees on the other side of the house, not for miles, implying paddocks or fields. "What kind?"

"Poultry and pork, and a whole lot of vegetables."

"*Poultry*? Holy shit." We've found dozens of abandoned farms out here, not a single one working or occupied. None of them had been set up to raise poultry – since captive chickens were the only birds to survive the plague, they have become a rare delicacy. This is a strange little miracle indeed. But …

I shake my head. "We can't hit it. It's too close to us."

"I don't want to rob it. I want to make it ours."

My mouth falls open. "And how exactly do you imagine that working? The Bloods would be on us in minutes." Same reason we haven't started farming any of the other land we found – there's plenty of it, just no protection from surveillance.

"We use the people who work it as our cover."

"And the produce? City's gonna notice if a huge farm like this stops providing."

"We'll only siphon off a tiny portion for ourselves."

"The owners, then? Why would they agree to that?"

"Because we'll make them."

I don't like the sound of that. But frankly I'm thrilled at the prospect of fresh meat and vegetables. I'm playing devil's advocate, but if she hadn't said it I would have: at this point I'll do anything to make this work.

*

December 25th, 2067

Luke

Pace, Will, Zach and Dave are with us this time. Christmas day has come and gone without much fuss. A few people tried to set up a bit of a games night but no one's heart was in it. There are more pressing things to deal with, so we put on a movie everyone's seen a thousand times and snuck away to do another recon trip.

"Wowzers," Will says.

"It's between 800 and 900 acres," Josi says, looking out over the farmland.

"*Wowzers.*"

"How the hell do you know that?" Pace demands.

"I've been mapping it."

"On your own. At night. Without telling anybody. Like a full creeper."

Nobody responds to that. Pace is struggling with the new Josi almost as much as I am. The only person who hasn't seemed to find her changes concerning is Will, who is the same as he always was with her, whether he notices her detachment or not. Perhaps unsurprisingly she is more relaxed with him than with anyone else.

Josi checks the time and points. Almost simultaneously the lights in the warehouse shut off.

"Neat trick," Zach comments.

We wait another thirty minutes and then creep down through the dark. Josi's worked out where to enter the building – there's an unlocked ventilation window two stories up, which we have to climb to in order to squeeze inside. My shoulders and then head get stuck and for one awkward moment my legs dangle from the window as Zach and Dave whack my skull painfully through. Zach definitely whacks way harder than he needs to, and mutters *fatass* loudly under his breath. Inside we hang from the window ledge by our hands (mine hurt like a motherfucker but I try not to make a sound) and shimmy our way across to where there's a large metal drum we can swing onto. Josi is lithe as a cat as she drops down, leaping off the drum and landing in a smooth roll.

"Show-off," Pace mutters, then does the same but with much less grace and a lot more cursing.

Dave jumps down last and because there's no chance of him landing without breaking something I try to catch him but end up getting flattened painfully on my butt. Will and Pace do their best not to piss themselves laughing, fail, and Zach politely reminds them to shut up. He's jittery as hell, always the first to kindly point out how many ways there are to be killed, though when you stick him over an open body he's a freaking superhero. As much as I hate to admit it. To be honest I don't know why he's with us tonight – Josi brought him without explanation. She seems to be the only one in the tunnels who can abide his presence, since he spends most of his time casually insulting everyone else.

Josi's way ahead of us by the time we hurry after her. The building is full of farming machinery – giant sleeping metal beasts we pass in the dark. The smell of oil and dust permeates, followed by the undeniable scent of livestock.

Through a door lies a huge pen within which are hundreds of pigs. Most are sleeping, some snort and sniff and rifle through the dirt in their pens. It smells intense in here, that animal scent of shit and piss and life. We walk through the pens and as I look at the beasts I wonder how they get them in and out of this building.

The answer becomes brutally clear as we go through a vacuum-sealed exit and into a much cooler space. Meat hooks and conveyor belts line the walls, above which are hung swinging, gutted pig corpses. It's an abattoir.

"Oh god," Pace whispers.

They don't leave that pen. They don't go outside into the fresh air to roam on the grass and feel the sunshine. They are born there and raised there and when they're fat enough they're taken next door to be slaughtered.

Josi leads us silently through this nightmare place. I can't see her face but her spine is rod straight as her footsteps pound over the metal grating. We leave this building and break into a second, only a few meters away. The smells and noises are different here, but just as overpowering. Soft clucking and the rustle of feathers. As my eyes adjust to the darkness a terrible thing reveals itself and a wave of horror descends upon me.

There are thousands and thousands of chickens in tiny metal cages barely big enough to hold them. Their talons curl over the grating, growing out of shape, and their wings have never been stretched.

Josi walks through them and we follow unwillingly. I have to close my eyes at one point. The conclusion I come to as we reach the end of the enormous battery farm is that humans are evil.

"We're coming back for them," I say.

"Let's let them out now," Will begs.

Our fingers are itching communally for the cage doors, but I shake my head. Josi isn't listening to us so I answer. "Soon, when we have a way to care for them."

It's then that I see tears glistening on her cheeks as she stares in at one of the little white chickens. I reach for her and promise, "We'll come back." But she pulls away from my touch and rests her head on the metal. It reminds me of the way I caught her looking through the Fury cage the other night.

We all start for the door, silently knowing it's time to get back. But Josi murmurs for us to go ahead, she'll meet us at home, and when I reach the door I see her sinking to the floor beside the cage, clutching at it as though to offer some sort of wordless comfort. I grit my teeth as I leave because she is so much braver than I am – me who's desperate to get out of here so I don't have to look at this monstrosity any longer, me who just wants to pretend I never saw such a thing.

*

January 1st, 2068

Luke

We make our move on the first day of the new year. Fifty of us, fully armed, descend upon the farm. We seize every worker and tie them up. We cut off the power supply and the communications line. Teddy moves in to blanket the farm in firewalls and new code that will make our presence invisible to the Bloods. He runs all surveillance on a past loop and disables any alarms. We take the owners separately.

Two sisters and their husbands share joint ownership, and we keep all four apart. We have their five respective children corralled in the living room of their house, surrounded by the kindest of us to reassure them of their safety. And then we sit down with the oldest of the sisters, Frida McDonaugh.

We're in her office at the end of the factory. She is tied to a chair and Blue's gun is trained at her head. I sit down in the desk chair she probably works in every day and place my gun on the table between us. Josi stands behind me, fury exuding from every pore.

"Your farm no longer belongs to you," I tell her.

"Deed says otherwise."

I eye her shrewdly. She's an earnest woman with calloused and dirty hands and sun-bleached hair that tells me she doesn't just sit in here – she works her farm.

"Where are my children?"

"Safe and well. They'll remain that way if you cooperate. Actually they'll remain that way even if you don't cooperate. We don't harm children."

Frida's shoulders relax infinitesimally, so she must believe me. "You're resistance, aren't you?"

"Correct."

"The ones on TV last year."

I nod.

"What do you want with the farm?"

"We want everything to stay the same, except we want a portion to live off."

"Not the same," Josi says softly.

"True," I agree. "We'll be making drastic changes to the treatment of animals."

Frida sighs listlessly. Her eyes move to the window and the sky beyond. "You can try. We'll all be dead within the week."

"Why?"

"You think my family wanted it like this? Farm's been with us for generations. Bloods come along and break the fair treatment laws and force us to farm more than we can. You think I like seeing those creatures caged like that? But you change it, the productivity goes down and they'll know something's wrong." Then she says, meeting my eyes and shocking me, "I'd give you anything you asked if it didn't mean the end of my children. I would, sir."

"Why?"

"Don't need anger to know something isn't right. Don't need fury to resist."

That's how the plan changes. We realize that instead of threatening or blackmailing the McDonaughs into doing our bidding, we can include them in the plan and ask them for help. As the evening wears on we get the same response from each of the farmers separately, and finally return them to their children. In their living room we sit and discuss our plan with the four of them, and as they serve us tea it all becomes very civilized.

Here's the simple fact. If you increase the workers on a farm instead of having machines and cages deal with the animals, then you get happy, healthy livestock that will breed and produce substantially more. Plus we can increase the amount of vegetables with extra workers, and we certainly have them – we have over a hundred in the tunnels. Our people get food, exercise, work in the sun and a change of scenery, their farm gets inundated with new life, new energy, unpaid hands and bent backs. The farm will make more money and it'll be helping to fund the resistance, which, as it turns out, is a bonus for the McDonaughs. We'll have to vet the workers they already have to make sure they can be trusted, and Teddy explains about the technical aspects of dealing with security.

It all sounds peachy but I can see the rage hasn't left Josi's eyes. Halfway through the meeting she vanishes back to the animals.

I, for one, am immensely relieved that we haven't just caused another disaster. It's about time something ran smoothly for a change. We haven't been doing much resisting lately, so now that I no longer have to worry about our people dying of scurvy – or cabin fever – I can get back to business.

Although Teddy's done a thorough job amping up our security, we still stagger our return home so we don't move in one enormous, incongruous group. I wait until everyone else has made their way through the dark before I set off. I take a deep breath of the cool, night air. There's something peaceful about walking through nature in the dark, not having to worry for once about being seen. I'm enjoying the rare moments of being alone, listening to my footfall on the grass. There was no sound in the lab, for three months no sound but my own thoughts growing louder and madder. No fresh air, no stars and no moon.

I catch a glimpse of two figures emerging from the animal factory. It only takes me a moment to recognize their walks. I change course and meander down the hill to catch up with Josi and Dave, but before I reach them they stop and look up at the stars and I find myself unwilling to interrupt their silence. I don't think either of them would particularly welcome me, anyway. Things with Dave are strained for some reason I can't interpret and things with Josi are ... Well.

So I pause a way back and tilt my head up to the crescent moon. I don't look at the moon very much anymore. She and I have a complicated relationship. I used to love looking at all her shapes, and then one day I no longer admired her – I became a slave to her. Under her red gaze I did something I can't remember and whatever it is, it's completely destroyed our lives.

Their voices drift over to me.

"Do you feel anything?"

"In general?"

"When you look at the animals."

My brother considers. "Pity. Concern. I don't want to see any creature being harmed or caged."

"But you don't feel love."

"No. Not like I once did."

"But any kind? Even an approximation of it?"

"Not really. I mean, I'm not entirely sure. It's not like I have a way to test it."

"When you look at your brother, what do you feel?"

Dave doesn't answer and my heart twists.

"Did they hurt you, when they took you?" she asks him next.

"Not too much." He pauses. "Why, Josephine?"

She shakes her head.

"Did they hurt *you*?"

"The Bloods didn't take me," she replies.

"I know that."

After a while she says, "Not too much."

But her mutilated body says otherwise.

"Happy new year," he tells her gently.

"Happy new year," she replies gently.

Something about the quiet, shared compassion I can hear feels sweet.

But who is *they*? I can't stand not knowing, and since neither of them will tell me the answer, I decide to look elsewhere. Leaving them in the dark, I walk home to our tunnels and seek out Pace. She's feeding Hal in a high chair we pinched for her and immediately orders me to remain quiet.

"I don't want him getting all worked up again."

I nod and sit, watching the little boy munch on his mashed potatoes. "Ba," he says, reaching for me, then "Woowoo."

"What's that in baby language?" I ask.

"Beats me. Tonight went well, huh?"

"Yeah, really well."

"Thank Christ. I swear my hair's falling out from lack of vitamin D."

"Hey, Pace …"

"Mm?"

"Were you with Josi when …?"

She sighs. "Yes. But don't ask me because she's already told me not to talk about it."

"Why?"

"She thinks if you know what happened you'll worry more."

"Nope, I'm maxed right out on the worry front."

"It's not like it's a secret or anything. I mean, you must have assumed what happened. You were meant to be there."

I was? Heart pounding, I try to stretch my mind but there's nothing there, no memories whatsoever. "Where was I meant to be?"

Pace looks at me like I'm a lunatic. "On the wall. For the holding facility evacuation."

I don't remember the wall or an evac. But I'm vaguely remembering a mission now, just snippets to retrieve a group of kids scheduled for the cure. We've done a few of those, though, so I'm not sure if I'm remembering old missions or the one Pace's talking about.

Goddamnit. "What happened, Pace? Just fucking tell me!"

"Woah, chill. Take your temper elsewhere."

Sure enough, Hal spits up his food and starts shouting loudly like he does when anyone raises their voice around him.

"Just go away, will you, Luke?" Pace snaps, so I do, mumbling an apology.

Okay, so it was a mission to free the new kids. Presumably we took them down the outside of the wall, as Josi and I talked about a few times. And I know everyone thought she'd been killed, I just don't know how.

I make my way to the tech room. Teddy's asleep with his face pressed to one of the tablets, his squished cheek projected up onto the wall behind him. I sit at another table and start going through our old surveillance footage from the cams in Josi's contact lenses but everything from the sixteenth of September has been wiped. She's about ten steps ahead of me and it's infuriating.

She hasn't wiped the radio feeds though. I pull up Teddy's from that day and listen to it with headphones. I hear him giving information to our operatives in the field, talking about normal banal stuff. My voice is on there – which is unnerving because I don't remember speaking the words – and there's lots of Josi giving instructions. From what I can tell she's getting the kids out and yes, taking them over the wall.

Then I hear Blue say, "What the hell?" And the whole thing changes. Voices grow quick and urgent. Things like *hurry* and *go* and *get them under*.

I hear a conversation between Josi and Pace.

Get them home.

Duh.

I'll meet you there.

What? Why?
The car.
Dual, no!
There's time. I can make it.
They don't matter! They're not ours!
Get everyone safe, Pace. Don't argue.

Then I listen to Teddy's hysterical urging for her to hurry, to leave it, that this isn't safe, there are too many, it's a suicide mission.

I hear Josi asking *where's Luke*, over and over, I hear Teddy saying he can't get any response from me, I hear him sobbing her name and then suddenly the feed goes dead.

When I take the headphones off I feel dizzy. Teddy is awake and watching me worriedly.

"What happened?" I ask him, but it doesn't sound like a question.

He doesn't try to avoid it like everyone else has been doing. He says, "They took her."

"Who did?"

When he tells me the answer it feels like I've known it all along. It feels like it was always going to happen, like it's the most obvious thing in the world.

"The Furies."

Chapter 15

September 17th, 2067

Josephine

It's hot. I don't know where I am. Pain holds my head captive and I'm not sure I can open my eyes. In fact, I think they're swollen shut. The sound of footsteps is all around me. I can't see so I concentrate on what I can hear. Breathing. Lots and lots of breathing. There is a huge group of people surrounding me. A chill runs down my spine as I feel myself being lifted off the cold ground. I'm carried and the hands that hold me have fingernails that puncture my flesh. I know they're not my people because they're not talking. There are no voices being raised to give orders or ask questions. It's too silent with only the rustle of limbs and the thump thump of my blaring pulse.

Where's Luke? My head's too fuzzy and I can't remember what happened or how I got here—

The wall. I remember the wall. And Luke didn't come. He wasn't answering Teddy's radio pleas, which means something went wrong on his end and god what if he's hurt *what if he's dead*?

I'm carried a long way with this terrible fear in my heart. I can taste blood and bile in my mouth. I count the seconds so I can work out how far I'm being taken but it's a stupid endeavor because I have no idea where I started. I know the scent and feel of the tunnels, and I know that this isn't them. I'm above ground somewhere, but I can't think of how that's possible. It lasts a long time. I move in and out of consciousness. I vomit from the nausea of being carried and the pain in my head. The mess goes all over me but my carriers don't stop or comment.

Finally the air outside grows cool enough for night and we stop.

There's a crack and a sting on my face. Someone has slapped me.

"Wake," a deep female voice commands.

I manage to open one of my eyes just a crack. Enough to let the dim inky light of twilight fill my head. Enough to see the moon high above, just a wink of it. It hangs red, tinged with blood, and I understand all at once, like a blow, how this has happened. It all comes back to the blood moon. Somehow, it's what has kept Luke away.

And instead of devouring me outside the wall like I assumed they would, the Furies have bewilderingly kept me alive and carried me god only knows where, and now as I peer up at them I see just how many there are and know that even though I may still be alive right now, it can't possibly last long.

*

September 22nd, 2067

Josephine

My veins are empty. The percentage of fluid that is meant to make up a human body is on average sixty. I think I have dropped well below that. I think I might be steadily drying out and very soon I will be at zero percent. I will be a shriveled husk of a creature preparing to become dust, the very same as what she is lying upon. I will dissolve into the ground and the sky. Into a world of endless endless dust. When my eyes worked better I saw dust in every direction. When I could taste I tasted it in my mouth and nose. When I could hear more than the sluggish thump of my slow heart I heard it swirling on currents of wind. My skin, now too raw to distinguish sensations, felt the dust flick and press and coat it. There's no water left in this world. There is certainly none left in me. My mindless mind takes up residence in the ocean but I don't have the imagination to even keep it filled. Instead it turns swiftly to a dry bed of salt.

I am done. Turned inside out and wrung dry. I'm at my end and I have no power to forestall it any longer.

The hands that appear above me are unfathomable miracles. They trickle fresh cool water into my parched mouth and somehow I am returning to the edge of life once more. I can't make sense of it until I see the eyes above and recognize that every blood vessel in them has burst. The red of them is the brightest thing in this yellow gray world.

The red is how I remember where I am.

And I wish simply that I'd been left to die after all.

*

September 23rd, 2067

Josephine

I sleep feverishly and dream of the beach.

In this dream I walk on the sand, my bare feet sinking in the coarse dunes. But beneath me the earth begins to tremble. The sand vibrates with swaying patterns until from beneath it rise hundreds of adders, their scales coiling out and out and out. I gaze at the roiling, slithering ground beneath me and—

I wake from the nightmare to something far worse.

*

When I finally lurch into consciousness it's with the undeniable knowledge of not having eaten anything for days. I've hardly had anything to drink, either, except that trickle of water that kept me from the very brink of death yesterday. I feel wretched, worse than wretched. Some of my bones are broken. My head screams and screams and screams. The skin on my body is so raw that the air itself burns upon it. I stink of vomit and shit and urine, so that my guts churn and I nearly lose what precious little fluid I still have. But the swelling of my eyes has finally gone down so for the first time I look at the enormous world around me.

What I see makes my heart freeze in my chest cavity.

Yellow, windswept plains stretch in every direction. I'm no longer in the hot barren dust bowl that sucked every drop of moisture from my body, but in quite a different landscape. The sky is a pale gray and the air feels cooler than I expected it to. There is a crispness to the world. An edge of frigidity. It's not the air, though, that makes me cold deep inside.

It's the pit of snakes I've woken within. Only they are worse than snakes because once upon a time they were human.

There are hundreds of them and they sit in clusters. They're quiet, unnervingly still. If every instinct in my body weren't telling me otherwise, I might make the mistake of thinking them normal humans. But they're pale and filthy, their clothing tattered to within an inch of its existence, and their eyes – their eyes are the bleeding red eyes I've come to loathe.

A sound leaves me before I can stop it.

Hundreds and hundreds of those crimson eyes turn to me. Panic explodes like a tidal wave and it doesn't matter that I'm starved and dehydrated and severely wounded. It doesn't matter that I'm surrounded by hundreds of them or that I patently have no way out. This panic turns me wild and desperate and before I even make the decision I'm on my feet and I'm running.

They reach for me and I feel their cold, sharp nails bite into my flesh. They're quick and I'm laughably slow. I scream and sob and try to struggle but weakness has caught up to me and I find myself abruptly on my knees. "No," I sob. There's no strength or courage in me now. No calm. I wanted to die bravely for that family but instead I've survived to become a seething mass of fear. Pissing, shitting, puking, trembling fear.

One of them takes my hands and wrenches them behind my back. I feel rope binding my wrists painfully. I scream again, struggling and falling, but without my hands I land flat on my face. A booted foot prods my shoulder and shoves me over; pain sears through my collarbone and I know it's one of the broken ones. My ankle might be broken too, and several of my ribs on both sides. I give a pitiful sob of pain and then allow myself to weep uncontrollably. Dignity is lost – I think it was long gone already.

One of them is closer than the rest. A woman. I know her face. I've seen it before. I haven't thought once about it since that moment but she was at the Inferno attack, watching me. She was the one who uttered those low, crawling words. *Pure flesh.*

I flinch and try to wriggle away from her. Dirt mixes with my tears and saliva and smears my face. I can hardly see through it but it doesn't matter, I don't want to, I want to curl up and disappear, I want the pain to end, the unbearable potency of terror, the humiliation of such terror, I want it all gone and to not have to look at this woman's disturbing face. I don't get what I want – I'm sure it won't be the last time.

She kneels and peers at me. The blood vessels in her eyes have burst like in all those of her kind, but I can also see the veins beneath her pale skin and they look horribly bruised. That face, it's one of nightmare. She bares her teeth not in an angry way but in a feral way. I've never seen anything so terrible.

The woman lifts me to my feet – she's remarkably strong – but my knees buckle. It takes two of them to drag me over the brittle grassy hill. I don't know where we're going but I don't have the energy to do anything except weep. We move through the entire crowd of Furies, who look at me but make no sound, and up an incline. On the way down I'm dropped and crash to the ground. With no way to stop myself, I roll. Pain again, much worse now as all my wounds are impacted simultaneously. I wonder as I tumble over and over if you can die from pain. Luke told me you couldn't, once. He said pain was only pain, it wasn't even real, but right now if I were in any position to, the thought would make me laugh. Pain's more real than anything.

Sudden cold strikes me. And wet. I stop rolling and realize I've fallen into water of some kind. I gasp and try to find my bearings so I can plunge my face in and drink greedily. It's amazing how quickly I feel it inside me, how much of a difference it makes to my body. I have to use my elbows to make sure I don't drown face first in the foot of water, but soon I've guzzled enough to fill my belly to bursting.

Someone pulls my hair to jerk me upright. On my knees, I see a small stream winding its way through the low hills. I have no idea where we are, except to guess that the cooler climate must mean we're north of the city and inland away from any view of the sea. But if I follow this stream it will take me to the ocean. Follow the ocean and I'll find my way home.

I'm wrenched to my feet and pulled away from the stream. Only half a dozen Furies are with me, but who am I kidding? I wouldn't be able to beat one in this condition.

"What do you want?" I ask.

No one replies. I didn't expect them to. They just shove and pull me back up the hill to where I see that the rest of them are on the move. Together like a swarm of locusts they run. The earth rumbles with their footfall. The woman and her group of five men press in around me and start to follow. I have no choice but to hobble along with them as fast as I can. My battered body groans in protest; I can hardly bear the agony of my left ankle. But there's no way out of it. When I fall they prop me up. When I slow they prod me faster. After hours of this I vomit again, nicely dirtying my recently rinsed clothing. I don't know how I keep going, aside from the Furies. I don't know how I manage to stay conscious. I'm not sure where my thoughts go, but they're far from my body.

When night falls the group stops and I collapse.

I must sleep because I wake with the moon high. It's losing its red tinge as we move away from the blood moon – it must be late September. I watch it instead of facing my surrounds. The temperature has dropped drastically with night. I'm shivering and there's a hollow hunger pain in my stomach. But as I lie here I feel marginally more myself than I have in many days, and I start to formulate a plan. It's not anything, really, but it's going to keep me alive. The simple necessity of it will be my survival: I will live long enough for my body to heal and strengthen enough to escape. I won't allow myself to starve to death. I won't let my mind drift away and give up. I'll simply bide my time and look for an opening. I just have to hope that opening comes before the Furies find a use for me.

*

September 28th, 2067

Josephine

If my calculations are correct, I have been with the Furies for ten to twelve days. I drink water regularly from the stream we've been following north, and I eat strips of some kind of meat that they silently offer me. It's raw so I cook it on the fires they build for warmth. I have no idea what the meat is, but the fact that they're not eating it makes it safe to assume it's not human. Josephine and human meat do not go together. It will not be happening.

I'm kept in the center of the huge group at all times, unless I'm being escorted to drink. My ribs hurt less, as does my collarbone, but my ankle is getting worse the more I have to trot along on it. It has swollen to the size of an apple, and has a concerning purple tinge. Each night when we stop I lift it high and wish I had an ice pack.

Hell if I know where we're going in such a rush. It feels more urgent every day.

The Furies eat less than I do, because there is no live meat anywhere, except me, of course, who they ignore. They are starving faster than I am, but only once have I seen the result of that. Yesterday one of them dropped dead and the others finally had a feast. They've been running faster today since devouring the body of their fallen comrade. And hey, who wouldn't be on top of the world after that?

I've decided that to keep my spirits up I will sing, or tell stories, or crack jokes, and I'll do all of this out loud so the Furies can hear me and know they haven't broken me. I'll do it out loud so that I can at least pretend I'm not talking to myself.

I start with true stories, anecdotes not from my life but from Luke's. I tell the Furies, not because I like them but because I like my husband, about all the things Luke used to break and repair, break and repair. I tell them about how he once dug a hole so deep it unearthed the water pipes and the Townsend family had no water for a week. I tell them how he decided to disconnect the fridge to see if he could use it to power their toaster more efficiently and promptly exploded the kitchen. I explain how he shaved their cat to see what its skin looked like and how they never had another pet after that. And even though I laugh as I tell these stories they start to make me sad, so I begin to make up my own.

I tell of sea creatures and winged people and ships riding the clouds through the sky. I tell of a girl with a moon for a heart and a boy with wires and cogs beneath his skin. This girl and boy set off on a journey to find the last birds together, to follow the world to its end, and along the way they meet all kinds of extraordinary friends. A hare with violet paws that lead a path for them to follow. A hot air balloon driver who can only speak in verse. A pair of conjoined trapeze artists and their lovers, the ghost-hunting twins. Best of all they discover, after a seemingly endless mission, a flock of swallows who dive in such joy that their bodies make painted patterns in the sky.

I talk and talk and talk. I don't care that it costs me energy or breath. I don't stop.

*

Miracle of all miracles, this afternoon I spot something on the horizon.

"Look!" I exclaim, jumping up so I can see over the dim-witted heads of my companions. "What is that?"

It turns out to be a road, and on this road sits a pub and a petrol station. Unfortunately and unsurprisingly neither is functioning. The Furies stop outside and a handful go into both buildings. I follow and am immediately flanked by my guard – the same five men and one woman who've been with me since the start. I go into the petrol station first, seeking food of some kind, although what could have survived the last twenty-five years or so is a mystery to me. There's nothing left on any of the shelves but a thick layer of dust. I kick through it, finding my way behind the empty counter and into the staff office. This is filled with old, disused tech and a few photos of people who are long since dead. I do manage to find some tins of tomatoes, chickpeas and lentils, amazingly, but I have no idea how I'm going to get them open. I hand the tins to my guards, wanting to test what they'll do, and amazingly they hold them. Huh. They obviously don't want me dead because they always cooperate when it comes to feeding me.

Then I discover a toilet. "I'm using this," I announce. "I don't care if it doesn't work. Don't follow me in here."

Apparently I'm not all powerful because they do follow me in and watch me while I'm peeing. It's totally weird.

Next we check out the Sitting Ducks Pub. With its beer-stained red carpet and sporting trophies all over the walls, I feel like I've stepped back in time.

"Wanna hear a joke? A neutron walks into a bar and orders a beer. 'How much will that be?' he asks once he's finished and the barman says 'for you, no charge'."

I look around at their faces. "Get it? No? Nothing? Jeez, I give you science humor *and* bar humor mixed into one and still nothing. Lighten up."

There are packets of peanuts and crisps and pretzels behind the bar, which I lunge upon greedily. I stuff a whole packet of cheese and onion chips in my face and then force myself to stop and ration the rest. The pack-horses will carry them for me.

The kitchen stinks with rotten food and I decide I don't want to eat anything that's been sitting in here for years with this stench. On the floor is a layer of dust, but strangely this time I can see tracks in it. Footsteps, but also evidence of things being dragged. It occurs to me what the tracks must mean: the Furies have already been to this pub, and must have been thrilled to discover a bunch of dead bodies. A shudder moves through me and I wonder *again* why they haven't eaten me.

One of the Furies shouts from outside. This is rare enough that it piques my interest. There are only a few of them who ever speak, and when they do it's either with very brief, simple sentences or with wordless sounds that convey meaning. My bestie is one of them – I think she's pretty high up in the pack hierarchy, though I can't work out how it functions. They don't give each other orders, but there is a definite feeding dynamic. When one of them dies the others basically go feral and start fighting each other for the meat, but when the speakers approach the rest make way for them, unquestioningly. It's not age, as far as I can tell (although I could be wrong there because it's damn near impossible to guess how old they are) so it must have something to do with strength. Or it could be the length of time they've been with the pack. Maybe those who came first or were turned first are in charge.

In any case, we rush outside and I'm carried along in the sudden urgency to get on the move again. I try to look for what could be causing this panic but I can't see anything. Pain shoots through my ankle and I swear loudly – there's potent delight to be taken from loud swearing, trust me. We run a lot faster than we normally do. It feels like we're being chased and I keep craning my neck to check and consequently stumbling into the backs of the Furies in front of me. Boy, they must find me annoying.

It's getting colder by the day. Soon I'll have a greater worry than starving to death, and that will be freezing. I'm still wearing my combat gear – a long-sleeved black skivvy, a black vest and black cargo pants, all filthy and ripped. The outfit is lightweight for maneuverability, and not particularly warm. It's also getting really difficult to pull my left boot on after rewrapping my ankle.

I spot something again, this time a much larger smudge in the distance ahead. I'm astonished to realize it's a forest. We're definitely a long way north then, as there's nothing but a huge radius of barren planes around the city. Over the next hours we follow the road to the trees. They are unlike anything I've seen. Taller and wider than any within the city's walls, these are magnificent, their bark holding a deep ochre tint. They can only be redwoods – I recognize them from old photography and never in a million years thought I'd witness the real things. They must be ancient, and so much taller than I can see. I read once that the tallest living tree was a redwood called Hyperion, at 379 feet high. I start to imagine him here somewhere, that I might unknowingly brush my hand along his trunk.

My throat is thick as we plunge into their midst. I feel tiny and surrounded by warm, throbbing life. Their immensity touches something inside me and the world feels abruptly more bearable.

It's dark now, under the shelter of the forest. But I glimpse the sky sometimes, and I can't help thinking it looks much more gray than it did. Much angrier. The air has a frigid bite to it and I can't quell the thought that something is coming.

The Furies stop before nightfall for the first time. They make fires, lots more than usual, with all the fallen kindling and debris. I'm grateful to stand near one while they stoke and build them to be as hot as possible. Someone shouts wordlessly and they all hunker down around the fires and against the bases of the trees, huddled together. I am pulled against the woman's body and the repulsion it causes me is impossible to ignore. I lurch back up and try to get free, escape the touch, but several sets of hands force me back down and refuse to let me move.

Very soon I understand why.

The blizzard hits.

*

September 29th, 2067

Josephine

It's shockingly cold. And so much louder than I expected. The wind howls ferociously through the trees, sweeping the snow hard against our shivering bodies. It lasts all night and I don't get a wink of sleep, my teeth chattering so loudly I think they must surely be about to shatter. The *pain* of the cold is alarming and then it's numbing.

By morning the blizzard has ended and I can no longer feel my extremities. The world is white and bright and dazzling. It's actually very beautiful. But I could pretty much see it all swallowed into a massive hole for the agony it put me through last night.

Some of the Furies are up, moving through the snow to stoke the fires. The heat they managed to create before the snow fell was enough to keep the deepest coals hot and if I weren't so frozen I might marvel at this. As it is, my heart rate has dropped very low and my breathing has slowed. I recognize the signs of slipping into hypothermia and know I must get up, must move, but I can't seem to make my muscles obey me.

That's when the men from my guard lift me to my feet and force me to follow them, force me to start running, slow and ungainly at first and then faster as my temperature rises. The relief is so much that I nearly burst into tears, but since my initial blubbering mess I have refused to cry again. Instead I laugh. I laugh as my muscles remember how to move and burn in doing so. The sound of my voice trickles through the still, snow-covered forest and up into the ancient branches. My feet sink in the deep white but the more effort it takes to move, the warmer I get.

Back at the camp one of them passes me a packet of chips, which I scoff with shivering fingers. This Fury watches me eat and doesn't try to take any for himself. I suppose barbecue chips don't seem so appealing when you've developed a taste for chowing down on human flesh. It's weird, though, the way he watches me. I catch them all doing it. Perhaps weirder still is that I never see any malice in their eyes, no anger or hunger or savagery. Only curiosity. The more time passes, the clearer it becomes that they don't consider me a source of food. What they do think of me is still a whopping mystery.

I study the one watching me now. I don't normally do this – it's easier to hate them when they're all the same, all ugly and torn and hungry. But now I look at this particular Fury. I can't really guess his age because his skin is papery and the bruising around his features makes him look older than he is, but maybe between 20 and 40. He has blond hair, he's very tall – even taller than Luke, which is unusual – and he'd be taller if he didn't stand so hunched over. He has a rough beard – most of the men do, which tells me they're still growing and living like humans do. His irises, within the ghoulish sea of red, are a pale blue. This disturbs me, for some reason. Thinking of their eyes as red is easier than seeing the real colors within the burst blood vessels. His clothing was once a pair of jeans and a t-shirt that says something. I have to peer hard to make it out: *Schrodinger's cat walks into a bar ... and doesn't.*

A breath leaves me, almost like a laugh. It's a shocked breath. A breath of I-can't-believe-I-just-told-a-science/bar-joke-of-my-own-and-he-has-one-on-his-shirt. And let's face it, it's a much better one. It abruptly, undeniably humanizes him. I try not to imagine who he was before this but I can't help it. Suddenly I can't stop imagining.

And just like that, my stories change.

Instead of telling stories about Luke, or making up stories about alternate mes and Lukes, I start telling the stories of the Furies around me. I make up adventures for them to have lived, I invent the lives and loves that made them exceptional before they were ruined.

This man, this science nerd man, I call Astro Boy. I decide that he's not a psychologist, but a paleontologist, and wearing this particular shirt is like a treacherous act to his profession, one that his colleagues give him shit for. I imagine he has seven older sisters, all of whom are in equal adoration and exasperation with him. They ask him why he hasn't met anyone yet, over and over, like it's his decision, like he has any choice in the matter. One of them tells him he'll be alone forever at this rate but he just can't work out what she wants him to do differently. He doesn't mind, anyway. He's more interested in bones and fossils. He has a trilobite collection larger than any of his college friends. He wanted to be the first to find a new species in fifty-three years. And actually he quite likes psychology experiments, the ones from the twentieth century that pushed the boundaries of professional conduct. He thinks privately that he might just as easily have gone into this field, but would never admit it.

I start giving them all stories. And with these silly made-up lives now existing in the spaces between us it is much, much more difficult to hate them. I don't actually know why I've just done this to myself.

*

Today we don't go anywhere. We stoke the fires and rest. Some of the Furies disappear, presumably to hunt for food.

I take the opportunity to keep my swollen ankle elevated, and to watch the monsters.

They're capable of every physical task, have perfect balance and movement, which means their cerebellum is intact. Their logic centers are too, their ability to reason and infer, they have incredible threat instincts and more energy than a normal person, presumably from the adrenalin coursing through them. Their language capabilities are low. Some of them may have lost those capabilities altogether, or may simply see no further need for them. Their social behavior has deteriorated, but not to anywhere near the degree I thought. They only grow savage and aggressive when it comes to food. In normal circumstances they're very calm with each other, very unthreatening.

For the first time in a while I think about Doctor Meredith Shaw, and of course my very own doctor Ben Collingsworth. They'd know the answer to this – it was they who were responsible for these transformations in the first place. Trying desperately to cure anger, they instead created human after human who suffered terrible, murderous side effects. The two of them alone would know exactly which parts of the brain are functioning in the Furies and which have been disconnected. I'd give anything to understand – my curiosity comes alive with the thought.

Night is falling when I see the thing that changes it.

One of the men from my guard – not Astro Boy, but Washington, named thus because of his gray beard and hair shaped like a top hat – sinks to the ground in what I can only deduce is severe hunger. He's grossly emaciated and on his last legs. The other Furies in my group look at him but don't move to help. How can they?

Not long after this the hunting party returns with five dead bodies. They have been gruesomely killed – who the hell are these dead people? Furies who died while on the hunt? A different gang? Surely not humans – there aren't any alive except in the city. The corpses are dragged into the center for the leaders – two males and a female (my female). The three of them go to it and remarkably the rest wait.

The female, who I've decided to call Medusa, turns away first. She has hardly eaten anything, but tears away an entire leg and carries it to us.

I am mortified but some scientific part of me must be fascinated because I keep watching, curious about what's going on.

Medusa carries the severed leg (delish!) and drops it on the ground before Washington's prone form. One of the others goes for it but she snarls at him and he backs off. Washington attacks the leg and manages to eat the whole thing on his own – remarkable given the amount of Furies those bodies have to feed. We watch as he demolishes his meal and as he does so I realize something.

He was dying. She could have let him die. I would have assumed they'd be happy when bodies dropped, as it meant sustenance for the rest. But she literally took the food from her own mouth to keep him alive.

And I don't know what that means, but something about it scares me more than anything else about the monsters. Something about it makes them seem very, very human.

Chapter 16

January 5th, 2068

Luke

The paddocks have been set up. The coops are built. We take the pigs first. The exchange for them is less traumatic. A group of us herds them slowly and gently *not* toward the slaughter room but out the other way, through the warehouse and into their very own five acres of grass. They don't want to go at first, snorting and squealing and terrified of any human interaction, but once they explode outside into the comparatively enormous space they acclimatize beautifully. A great cheer goes up from our crew, a distant one since those in the pens don't want to frighten the pigs. But almost all of us have come above to the farm and now wait at the fence in the distance to cheer on the liberation. I join the pigs in their pen and show them the food and water troughs. Then I sit with them, in the corner where I won't get in the way, and watch their saddlebacks wiggling. There's so much more intelligence in their dark eyes than I expected.

The chickens are a more difficult task.

We've built them nests and roosts so they won't be overwhelmed by the space, but they have clear access to the outside paddocks for when they're ready and capable of venturing out. Some of them will never be able to walk, most will never fly.

We carry them now, one by one, into the outdoor coop. The McDonaugh's vet is on hand, helping to treat any wounds on their feet or wings, gently rubbing soothing balm into their raw skin.

We are halfway through moving the birds when I pass by Josi for the first time in a while. We both have a chicken cradled in our arms. Mine is a golden beauty with missing feathers on her head and rump. She's smaller than most and I feel fiercely protective of her; she is fragile in my arms.

Josi's bird is black and red and unruly. She wants free. I walk along the grate in time to see Josi pulling her out of her tiny cage. The chicken squawks and flaps its mangled wings and Josi struggles to hold her.

"You okay?" I ask, moving closer. My goldie is quiet and perfectly behaved and for a second I love her.

Josi doesn't respond, too focused on her chicken. She gathers the broken creature into a firm embrace, keeping its wings in tight, and she leans down and soothes it with gentle murmurs. It's almost like a song, and for the first time her singing voice isn't so bad. Like this – soft and cooing – it is suddenly sweeter than anything I've heard.

I stop and stare – I can't help it. My heart thumps against Goldie's chest and the moment is profound.

Josi's chicken gentles in her arms. "Lovely girl," I hear her murmuring.

And it's so obvious: the love she feels and is capable of. Whatever she may think, whatever damage she's undergone, she hasn't lost the ability, as she told me she had. Perhaps she no longer loves me, but in this moment the potent tenderness in her hands and voice tells me everything I could ever have wished for: she isn't gone. Not by a long shot.

I make a decision. I won't look for the answer anymore. I won't ask her or anyone else what happened. I'll let it go, I'll let *her* go, let her have or be whatever she needs. I only want for her what she wants for herself, even if it doesn't include me.

I walk past her and smile a real smile, the first in months.

"What are you so happy about?" she asks.

I shrug and laugh. "The chickens have changed everything."

*

January 10th, 2068

Dave

I can no longer handle Mom and Dad's pleading stares so I've started helping out at the farm more than anyone else. I spend time with the animals when the others have left – all except Josi, of course. She has almost become one of them, sleeping in the pens with them at night.

This evening she brushes herself off earlier than usual, heading for the paddock gate.

"Where are you going?" I call. Luke's favorite chicken, Goldie, is in my arms, quiet as always. I gently deliver her to the nest and shut the coop latch.

"I gotta teach a history class," she tells me. I must express surprise, because her eyes roll and she says, "I know, I know. I'm terrible at it, but I'm trying to make an effort."

"Can I come?"

She shrugs and nods for me to follow.

We make our way over the grassy hills and along the creek. We don't talk – Josi rarely talks unless she's asked a direct question – but I find myself, oddly, wanting to. Not with anyone else, but with her, at least. The overtness of their feelings make me retreat, but Josephine is almost as detached as I sometimes feel. I guess that makes her safer.

"When did you get married?" I ask.

She sighs audibly. "April Fools' Day."

"Was it as much a joke to him as it was to you?"

Her eyebrows arch. "That was a surprisingly nasty question from someone who isn't meant to feel anything."

"I don't feel nothing. I feel plenty of things."

She doesn't respond to that.

"I didn't mean to be nasty. I was trying ... to make a joke, I suppose. In very poor taste."

"My marriage isn't a joke."

I feel flushed at the expression in her eyes. I think I'm embarrassed, actually. "Sorry."

She doesn't contradict my need to apologize so obviously she thinks I should have. "Oh dear. This is going poorly."

Josephine Luquet snorts. "Everything these days goes quite poorly for me. I can't seem to have a conversation with anyone that doesn't result in me wounding them."

We walk in silence for a while. The moon is almost full.

"Oh, Dave Townsend," she sighs. "How extraordinary you are. How infuriating." Then she adds, "Your poor family."

"I'll try not to take offense to that."

Unfazed, she replies, "You can't take offense. You're cured."

"I could pretend."

"Who would that benefit?"

"A great deal of people." I stop and she stops. "You mimic. You make them think you're the same as you used to be."

"Why?"

"Because it's hurtful to them if we're not, and it doesn't cost us anything to pretend."

She starts walking and I hurry to keep up. We reach the tunnel entrance – a covered knoll you have to be very perceptive to find. Before I climb down she says, "For the record, no one thinks you're the same as you used to be."

"For the record, they have no idea how different I really am."

*

Josi's class is interesting. It's obviously her first since she returned. Her kids are jittery with nervous excitement. They pepper her with questions, none of which she answers. After about ten minutes of unceasing demands she stops them with a hand and says, "This is a history class. I don't have time to waste on personal stuff."

"Then we want to know about the love cure," Henrietta announces, to much agreement.

"Yeah, what the hell is that about?"

"They can't actually do it, can they?"

"Of course they can't."

"Well, they managed the others, so why not this?"

Josi waits for the hubbub to die down. "Yes, the government is planning to administer a cure for love."

There's an eruption of horror. A lot of *bullshits* and *hows* and *no ways*.

"Romantic love, or all love?"

"All, I assume."

"Why?" a beautiful boy with the face of an angel asks. I'm still learning their names and I can't remember his.

Josi's eyes go to him. She folds her arms and settles deeper into her chair. "There's a long history of diagnosing love and its symptoms as a disease, Alo. Particularly the limerence of love."

"What's that?"

"Limerence is romantic love. Desperate, aching, shivering, can't think, can't eat, can't sleep love. It's the obsessive demanding part of love that turns us into slaves."

"That's not real," a boy called Lawrence says.

"Of course it is!" a tiny girl named Georgie hisses, who looks no older than about eight.

"Why?" Josi asks Lawrence.

"It fades."

"Is that your experience of it?"

He colors and a few of the kids snigger.

"I'm not criticizing you, I'm genuinely asking for your experience."

Lawrence shakes his head. "I haven't had one – I'm a dude."

There is a chorus of groans at that.

Josephine frowns and I see the ghost of irritation in her face. "I don't have time for gender stereotypes or sexism. You know better."

His smirk is wiped clear. "Sorry."

"Why is the ability to last indefinitely the only determinate of truth?" Josi asks them. "If I felt angry yesterday but I don't today, does that mean that yesterday's anger wasn't real?"

"Love is different," Henrietta says.

"How?"

"It's bigger then anger. It's a state of being, not a feeling."

Josi looks intrigued by the general noises of agreement. "So what about people who fall out of love?"

"Well, maybe it wasn't real to begin with," Henrietta replies confidently. "Maybe that was limerence."

The kids agree.

Josi considers it. Her eyes look so strange in this light. One is almost lost in shadow, the other glittering like no eye I've seen. I have a sudden image of her and my brother meeting, and I think I could understand how the unflappable, unreachable Luke Townsend might fall under her spell.

She says, "Even stars die. The brightest stars burn for millions of years. They burn with unfathomable energy, and then one day they turn supernova. They throb and swell and they claim energy from everything around them. When they explode they let off a burst of energy so catastrophic that they suck in everything in their radius. We can see this energy from earth with our naked eyes even though it's billions of light years away. And then they're gone." She pauses, licks her lips absently. Her eyes go up to the roof of the silo, where dozens of holes look like stars. "A life is finite," she says softly. "We burn very brightly and then we die, just like stars do, only much more quickly. Just because something ends doesn't mean it's any less real, or any less important." She stands and adds, "Everything ends. Even love."

The worst part is that on her way out she walks straight past Luke, who has been leaning against the door and has heard the whole thing.

Once I would have known exactly what to do to make him feel better. Now I can't think of a thing. I can only stand here looking at his destroyed eyes and hearing the upset voices of the teenagers behind me.

*

Tonight I see the guitar.

I'm helping Dad build a new door for the food pantry (which is gratifyingly un-empty) when I see it sitting in the corner. It's just the handle poking out from behind a mess of plastic tarp. But I know it. This wooden thing made up the most significant portion of my life, after all.

I cross to it and unearth it from the chaos. It's a lightweight creature from a long while ago, battered and not well shaped. But it's a guitar. I perch myself on the side of a bench and start tuning it, my fingers knowing what to do without my mind having to help.

After I have it as close to tuned as possible I look up to see Dad staring at me. There are tears in his eyes and I immediately regret touching the instrument.

"Sorry," I say.

He shakes his head quickly. "Please. Can you play?"

I consider it. This might hurt them more than it helps, implying I feel more than I do. Music has a way of doing that. I don't want them to expect things from me that I can't deliver, not for myself, but because it will inevitably result in their pain. But in the end Dad's face is so desperately hopeful that I figure music can never be harmful, not as I know it. So I nod.

*

Luke

I return from a full shift on the farm to the never-ending task of kneading dough for bread. Even with meat and vegetables coming in, mouths are hungry and there's never, ever enough bread. Most days I feel pretty pleased with myself over the industrial-sized cooking area we managed to build and ventilate.

The kids corner me in the kitchen as I'm kneading. Six of them. Lawrence, Alo, Henrietta, Georgie, Coin and Teddy. There's something tense between them and none of them seem to want to speak first.

"If you won't talk, get kneading."

None of them move to help.

"What's wrong?" I direct my question at Lawrence because he's always the talker.

He hesitates. "Josi. We had a class earlier."

My stomach tightens. I was there.

"She's not herself," Henrietta says.

"What's wrong with her?" Georgie asks. "Where did she go?"

"And how'd she get all those wounds and stuff?" Alo asks. "Was she on a mission?"

"Was she with you in the Blood lab?" Coin asks.

"Nobody's telling us anything!" Lawrence bursts. "She's our friend and we deserve to know."

I knead and think, knead and think. Their concern makes my chest ache. "She wasn't with me. And she wasn't on a mission. Something happened to her and she can't talk about it."

"But you can!"

"I don't know what it is." That quiets them. I don't think they ever imagined I might not have the answer. "She can't speak about what happened," I repeat. Knead, knead, knead. Put your whole body into it. Don't think, that's your problem. More kneading, less thinking. "Something hurt her. Or someone. And when you get hurt badly enough you have to change or you get broken. So whatever she is now, however she is, that's how she's survived. Be glad of it."

I see Teddy duck his head and in the flash of candlelight tears glisten in his eyes. Frustrated, he storms out. I know he thinks it's his fault, or maybe just feels more closely connected to it because he was there in her ear when she got taken.

"Will she get better?" Georgie asks in a whisper.

"How should *he* know?" Henrietta snaps. "Nobody knows." She's angry, they all are. And frightened.

It startles me when Lawrence steps forward and puts his arms gruffly around me. It startles me so much that I cry a little. Just a few tears, one sobbing breath. Then I push him away and impatiently dash at my eyes. Return to kneading.

"She's alright," I promise. "She loves you."

"She said love ends," Georgie says through her own tears.

"She didn't mean it."

"She's strong," Coin agrees pleadingly. "She changed but she didn't get broken, right?"

I nod but I'm not sure it's so simple. I used to think it was, but now I don't think being broken is the only way to perish. I think surviving can sometimes cause it too. I think enduring can.

"I want to kill whoever hurt her," Alo says in that painfully intense way of his.

I meet his blue eyes. "If I ever find out who it was," I tell him, "you won't get the chance."

That's when we all hear it. The solitary notes of a guitar.

Coin makes a sound of pain, as though someone has stabbed him in the guts. He spins toward the sound. The last person to play that guitar was his girlfriend before she died.

And as we all listen I know. I know exactly who's playing the plaintively plucked notes through the tunnels with so much talent.

Something ruptures inside me and I sink to my knees.

I feel Alo and Henrietta reach for me. I feel their hands on my shoulders but I'm listening to a sound I never thought I'd hear again, not until I died.

I lurch to my feet and follow the sound into the dining room. Other people are gathering. Mom and Dad are there. Listening as my brother plays the guitar.

It's a folk song, one he wrote when he was eighteen. A bluesy raw thing. He lifts his voice and sings. A voice I know, one I've heard in my dreams. That scratchy soulful *beautiful* voice.

I waved to you,
I called to you,
I sang to you,
but you were facing
the glory of the sunset
and didn't know.

I cover my face. It's found something inside me I didn't think was there. Something old, from long ago. A part of me I forgot. How is he able to do it? Play like he used to, with the same heart, the same feeling?

When I open my eyes it's to see Josi listening from the other side of the room. To see that Dave is singing to her. And to realize that he did this for her. She smiles a little, a painful sort of smile, and then she leaves.

I wished you'd go,
I wished you small,
I hoped you silent
I watched you fall.
Now I wait,
I'll wait, my love,
Oh I'll wait for your true night.

He sings to her departing form, and then he finds me in the crowd and shrugs and smiles as though he did his best, and then he sings the rest of his song to me. And anything that was missing between us has returned. Even if he doesn't yet know it.

*

Dave reaches the end of the song but before he can play another Coin storms over and wrenches the instrument from his hands. "*This isn't yours!*"

Dave immediately raises his hands in supplication.

"Coin—" Lawrence tries, but something has unsettled deep within Coin. The boy sends a fist hard into Dave's mouth.

I'm moving by the time it lands, dashing across the space to help Lawrence pull his friend off my brother.

"Easy, easy," I tell the struggling boy. Tears flood his eyes and the guitar has fallen to the floor. Coin wrestles himself out of my hands to crouch over it and gather it to his chest.

"Don't you fucking touch it," he snarls at Dave, then sprints away with the instrument.

Dave is still sitting exactly where he was, only now he has a hand lifted to his bleeding lip. Into the remaining silence he says, "Sorry."

It seems so absurd for him to be apologizing that none of us know what to say in return.

*

Josephine

I hear it happen because I'm listening from within the next tunnel. There's a scuffle and Coin's upset voice and then he goes running past with the guitar and instead of following I let him go. I would have followed, once. But now I can't be under the ground that long. I've reached my limit and have to head for the ladders.

On a whim I change direction and wind my way to the cliff opening. There lies the sea, unchanged. As beautiful as it was four billion years ago.

I haven't been here since Malia's burial. Before that, my wedding. Those days seem very long ago. A different lifetime, a different version of me.

I suppose I got what I wanted, didn't I? Parallel universes, alternate Josephines. For some childish, greedy reason I dreamed of those other lives running alongside mine and I wanted to know what they were, I wanted to be in those alternate lives, little knowing the one I had was perfect. What kind of monster lives a life of deep wealth and longs for something else? What kind of person knows a profound, life-shaping love, and would risk desiring a universe in which that might not exist?

A sociopath, that's who.

Regardless, I opened Pandora's box. I can't go back.

So I lift my fingers to my mouth and I let out a long, piercing whistle.

*

October 1st, 2067

Josephine

We walk the snow-covered forest silently. Well, they do. I walk it quite loudly.

"Medusa, I've decided you used to be married to Washington. You're childhood sweethearts. Your families took holidays in exotic places and you spent the whole time sneaking off to make out. But then you, Medusa, had a scholarship to veterinary school and a quick path to becoming the world's most famous snake charmer. You even took up playing the bansuri, and snake charmers from the farthest reaches of the world came to see you work your magic, astonished when you turned even the most steely-eyed of fans into stone. But Washington, starlet that he was, had become rather successful in his own right: winning George Washington lookalike competitions, of course."

I look at my audience to see if they're appreciating the genius of their backstories, but no such luck. Washington and Medusa walk with their usual animal grace, eyes and ears peeled for threats or food, utterly ignoring their chatty prisoner.

"So Washington started touring the world with his act, and you didn't see each other for years. But one day you wound up at an international fair in India, for the biggest celebs in the world. You were seducing your snakes, Medusa, and Washington was walking around looking leaderly, and your eyes caught across the tacky conference room and you knew. Damn the reporters and the fans. Damn the paparazzi. Damn all those who said a mythical snake charmer and an impersonator of sixteenth-century founding fathers couldn't be together. Damn them!"

They walk on. At least I'm amusing myself.

That stops being the case very soon.

Normally I'm tied by a rope and tugged along when my pace falls. But since the blizzard they've stopped tying me up and allowed me to walk without bindings. This means, however, that as I unwittingly slow, Astro Boy pushes me from behind. And it isn't a hard poke, or a violent shove. It's hardly a push at all. He places his hand on my spine and ushers me forward in a way that seems almost, *almost* gentle.

It startles something inside me, something deep and feral. I turn and smash my fist into his face, then thrust my knee into his guts. He hits the ground hard but the others are already on me like a great big pileup, throwing their bodies on mine and pinning me to the ground.

"Get off!" I snarl. "You fuckers! Don't you dare touch me! *I've had enough*!"

I don't want their hands on me – I can't stand it. I struggle wildly until something connects so hard with my cheek that the world spins.

When next I become aware, they're no longer on top of me but staring down from above, all six of them. The sky inside the circle of their heads is a gray white; the tall trees reach so high. As I lie here looking at this spectacle, light, tender snow begins to fall.

A sound leaves me. "What's going *on*?" I beg. "What do you want with me?"

Instead of answering they lift me to my feet and gently bid me to follow the rest of their kind.

*

October 13th, 2067

Josephine

My crisps have run out. If I dare to touch my abdomen I can feel my ribcage jutting out much farther than it used to.

My body is more like it was in the last years of the blood moon, when it was being fed upon from the inside. It's eating itself, and I'm not sure how much longer I'll last without proper food.

We travel more slowly now, because I'm not the only one starving to death. The forest keeps us sheltered from the worst of the blizzards. But I don't know where we're going, or if there's even a destination planned. I hope like hell that we're not just walking for the sake of walking. But then again a destination is equally scary.

My ankle is slowly starting to heal. It's taking the longest and causing me the most pain, and there was a point where I thought it would just get worse until it killed me, but finally it's started to shrink and lose its violent colors.

I've tried to escape three times and each time I've been caught within minutes. There are too many of them, and no way through. Not when I'm unarmed and slowly starving to death. Medusa has a knife in her belt but she hasn't raised it to me, not once. Their fists and feet and teeth do enough damage without it.

After nearly a month with the Furies life has become about my stories. I try to keep them up, day and night, but it's getting so hard. I hardly have the energy to summon my voice, let alone cajole my imagination into working. But when I don't tell them I feel myself slip toward depression, and that is a gaping dark more frightening than anything they can do to me. Depression, for me, means my whole body shutting down, my entire self becoming too heavy to move, which results in sleep. And right now I can't afford even a single second of feeling like that. I can't sleep: it would kill me.

It seems funny sometimes that I'm staving off the illness that has plagued me since I was a child and I'm doing it here, for the first time, during the worst days of my life, purely out of necessity. Maybe everyone who suffers depression ought to be captured by monsters and taught the value of optimism in the most brutal way possible. Asylums could offer it as a health package: *Feeling blue? Holiday with zombies – it works a treat!*

We've left the snow-covered ground and now walk through green and brown forest. Sometimes we find roads to follow, and a few times we've found abandoned buildings with nothing much inside them. Old ranger huts, I guess. I wondered for ages why the Furies didn't take shelter in the pub and gas station we found – they knew the blizzard was coming at that point. But it became clear to me when we found a block of public toilets (yee gods, the smell) and they didn't take shelter from a rain storm. It's because they couldn't all fit within. Back at the pub, there wouldn't have been room for everyone, so they stayed together and ran for the forest.

Which is actually mind-boggling if you think about it, and I do. The more time I spend in their midst, watching them, the more like a family they seem. Or at least a pack of humanoid animals who care for each other.

But that's way too difficult to deal with, so I try to keep thinking of them as soulless cannibals. I hold the appalling clarity of Hal's death in the forefront of my mind. I remember everyone who died in the tunnels as we fled, too old or too young or too feeble to escape. I relive Georgie's parents getting caught and devoured and Luke lifting the tiny girl with his broken hand and carrying her the entire way across the country.

Luke.

Oh, I think of Luke.

He's the worst thing about all of this. He is the only reason it sometimes slips into being unbearable. I try so hard not to let him into my heart because with him there the rest is so much uglier, but sometimes, like in this moment tonight, he slips in and takes very firm purchase.

They'll assume I'm dead, and I hate to think what that will do to him.

My words are love letters to him. When we stop I write them in the snow or the dirt. I tell him even the things I didn't say aloud when we were together. It seems strange that those things exist, even after a marriage, but they do. I've never told him of my childhood. My life in the foster care system. There were abuses I suffered that I would never have burdened him with, that I barely even burdened myself with remembering, but I say them out loud now and astonishingly it's quite cathartic. I feel ashamed even to be bringing such things into consciousness, but a part of me craves being able to share them with someone or something. Even just to say them aloud once and let them scatter in the wind. The reality I draw closer to each day is that this terrible journey will probably be my last chance.

I haven't given up, but if I do die out here I want the universe to know I tried to share what I couldn't share, I tried to offer as much truth as I was capable of. I tried to *feel* as much, in the end, even if those feelings hurt.

*

Medusa and her gang take me to wash. This is another mystery of the way they live: why are the same six always designated to me? How do they know that? Was there an order given when I was taken? That these five men and

Medusa herself would watch over me, no matter what? Or do they feel it, somehow? Also, why do they know I need to wash when they don't bother with it themselves? Unless they're only taking me to drink, and letting me do as I wish?

The river is wide where we reach it, wide and fast moving. As we descend to its edge I imagine flinging myself in and being swept away. From this vantage I see my body plunge in and sink beneath the surface, bobbing back up and tumbling downstream. A piece of driftwood, as easily flung about. Even as I imagine this I can see that it's too cold and too fast; I'd die before I got anywhere near the other bank.

I sink to my haunches and dash the freezing water onto my face and neck. I don't wash anywhere else because I'd lose too much body heat. But cleaning my face and taking a long drink is the thing I look forward to most in my life now. These moments are my favorite, even more so than when I eat what measly food I find. I feel alive, truly alive.

The others have all taken a drink and now watch me enjoying the water. Medusa is crouched beside me, her awful eyes so shrewd. Something strikes me, some impulse, and I turn to her and offer a handful of water. When she doesn't move I edge closer. Holding her gaze, I trickle the water over her crown. It slides down her dirty face and she recoils.

I remain still, posing no threat. After her initial concern she stops fidgeting and holds as still as I do. Curiosity drives my hand to reach out and touch her cheek. She flinches but doesn't move away, so I carefully, slowly try to wash her face clean.

She responds by lifting her hand to my cheek and rubbing it the same way I'm rubbing hers. When I move my hand to rinse her dirty hair, she moves hers to mine. Her brown eyes, which have always seemed so utterly devoid of life, are suddenly filled with something I don't know how to name, something deeply confronting and aching and too much. My hand drops and I turn away. I don't know why I did that or what I thought it would prove, but all I feel now is dirty.

One of the men grunts a loud warning signal and I react by swiveling to look up the hill. What I should have done was run. No, not even that would have helped.

Something moves in the corner of my eye. A fluid thing. A dream thing. It's under my foot – I've stepped on it. There's a sharp pain in my little finger and I look down to see the smooth coils of a snake slithering away into the brush. Just like the ones I dreamed of.

A gasp leaves my mouth. There are definite puncture wounds on my finger, which is already swelling. Without thinking I turn, reach for the knife at Medusa's belt and chop it straight through my finger.

There is a moment of dead silence. Nothing makes a sound, not the river or the wind or the trees or my own breathing. The world has frozen and within this picture I see my pinkie lying in the mud, unattached to my hand.

A low moan erupts from me, a long broken thing.

Pain.

I cry in confusion. I can't work out what my finger is doing on the ground. There's so much blood, it saps from my whole body and gushes out of the missing piece.

The Furies – the men – lunge for the finger and I see one of them eat it. A scream erupts from me and I fall onto the bank. The sky above is so gray, it's always so gray and so huge and it's spinning and falling and I'm so sick that I retch. Someone is holding my hand and it *hurts*.

"Don't," I sob. "Please."

But the finger and the mouths and they're eating it, they're eating a piece of me over and over and over.

I'll never survive this, even if I survive it I'll never survive it.

*

Something happens now. Outside my control, impossible for me to deny, a place from which I will never return. The world as I know it tilts.

I always thought my memory was perfect, or near to it. But it wasn't: it may have been photographic but it was also selective. It was cleverly, carefully, *preservingly* selective.

*

No longer.

Chapter 17

February 12th, 2068

Josephine

Luke and I build fences together. I didn't mean for it to happen that way, and I'm not altogether sure he did either. But the animals need more space, so the farmland must be divided differently, which means new fences have to go up. I've been through physical training with a Blood, and this is still the most arduous physical task I've ever endured.

Well. No.

That's not true. But all the things that happened in the north, those are things outside this world. They're not counted in the normal measurements of a life.

Huge wooden posts go up at specific intervals. Holes are dug deep with enormous drills and the posts are lowered in, then bashed deeper and deeper until they can stand on their own. We layer wire between the posts, which requires pliers and immense arm strength to ensure the tension is taut.

Luke's faults have never been to do with physical tasks – he takes to this like a fish to water. I find myself watching him sometimes. I'm no longer a person who wants an intimate, lasting connection – or is capable of it – but I'm very much human, very much a woman. Nothing changes that part of our nature. So I watch him and I want him just as I've always done. But as much as I would like to have sex with him, I could never put him through that kind of emotional confusion. For him it would ask more than I have to offer.

So we fence. In silence under brilliant skies we hammer poles into the earth and I feel half alive for the first time in so long. It's where I belong – I've known it for months now. Working the land, using my body.

This afternoon is a hot one. We have water bottles on the back of the truck carrying our posts. I head over and take a long drink. As I do, I watch Luke carry the enormous plank of wood and lower it into the ground. His shoulders and back and arms tense with the effort.

I take him a water bottle. He drinks thirstily, wiping sweat and dirt from his brow.

"You're a lot stronger than you were," he tells me.

I return his bottle to the truck and head up to the next entry point.

"That sounded like a layered statement, but it wasn't meant to be." He smiles. The sun on his tanned face is a warm kiss; he lifts his eyes to it, closes them and shakes his head a little. "It's just nice to see, is all."

He's weaker than I remember him – his time in the lab has affected his muscles and stamina – but I don't tell him that. He's already working his way back to normal, and capable of more than most, evidenced by the hulking posts he lumbers around.

"The sun." He sighs ardently.

My instinct is to keep working, but I'm torn by this unexpected desire for him so I stay where I am, paused at the next point a few meters away.

"The lab was even worse than the tunnels," he admits. "I think perpetual dark is much better than perpetual light. Fake light, anyway."

He goes to the truck and lifts another wooden slab over his shoulders. He carries it to me and heaves it into the ground with a grunt. I steady it, using the pliers to attach the wire and bind it in place. Then Luke hammers it lower and lower into the ground.

"Through the crust we go," he murmurs. "Here it might be about ten miles deep."

I frown and look at his face.

Without returning the look he keeps talking. "Now through the mantle. One thousand, eight hundred miles deep we go. Down and down, through the silicate rocky shell. Next into the liquid layer of the outer core. It's getting really hot here, and thick. This layer is iron and nickel, it's hard to move through, like a heavy fog but more dense. It takes us about fifteen thousand miles to pass through. And at last we've made it to the inner core. It's really, really hot here, trust me. As hot as the sun."

He looks at me now. His eyes in the glare are colorless.

I can feel myself slipping through the earth's layers. "How do you know?"

"I used to dig."

"What were you looking for?"

"Anything. Everything."

And even though it's cruel to be pulling him on this lead, I find myself asking, "What did you find?"

"A whole lot of dirt," Luke says. "Dry soil and moist soil, depending where I dug. Sometimes pipes. Sometimes I found tree roots and water and then I found buried dog toys and once even a wrapped up dead rabbit skeleton.

My favorite was when I found a beautiful tin box full of treasures."

"What was in it?"

"Toy soldiers and drawings of robots and a Hardy Boys novel. A letter to the other side of the world. And a wish bone." He stops and sounds so wistful as he remembers it. "Dave wanted to snap it and make a wish 'cause he thought it would be a thousand times more powerful than a normal one, but I knew we couldn't snap it. I put it back in the box and buried it again and I thought about it some nights and I made wishes on it anyway. It might still be there now."

I don't ask him what his wishes were – that would be taking this even beyond the intimacy we've already impeached upon.

"So, in answer to your question, I found nothing," Luke says, and then he winks. "And everything." With a smile, he heads back for the next pole and we return to work.

But I can't help sinking through the earth, through bones and treasures, to all the places I never thought to imagine, too lost in the sky and on the surface levels for it to occur to me.

*

March 1st, 2068

Josephine

I'm on a kitchen shift when Luke enters. He doesn't greet me personally, but he says a big hello to everyone and then starts pulling things from the pantry.

"Woah, easy there," Pace chides him. "We barely have enough for these loaves."

"Then let them eat cake!" he announces. "Seriously though, I'm gonna make a cake."

"And how do you imagine you'll do that?"

"Watch the master, my pretty," he tells her and explodes into work.

I'm a terrible cook so I'm on vegetable peeling duty, but I gotta say I don't mind because it's pretty great to have vegetables to peel. Luke sings while he works. I don't look at him, but the others sing along or giggle. It's Henrietta's seventeenth birthday and it occurs to me that maybe her strong and persistent feelings for Luke are starting to be reciprocated.

I try to work out how that makes me feel. I really imagine it, the two of them getting together, first physically and then falling in love. It doesn't feel good, but then again I don't really have the energy to acknowledge it feeling bad, either. However jealous it makes me, it pales in comparison to the repulsion I feel when I imagine doing anything about it. That kind of intimacy – even the intimacy of conflict – would be a nightmare.

"We've got another birthday girl coming up soon," Will announces.

It takes me a minute to realize he's talking about me. Jesus, birthdays – who cares.

"*And* a wedding anniversary!"

Oh no.

My eyes go unwillingly to Luke. He has flour on his face and shrugs flamboyantly. "One year doesn't count when you've been separated for so much of it. We'll do it later."

There are a few vocal disagreements to this, but he brings them around.

I finish up on my vegetables and head out, needing to get the hell away from there.

"Hey." He catches up to me in the tunnel. "I know we're not doing an anniversary. I just said that to get them off our backs."

I nod.

All I can think about is his body in this small, dark tunnel. He takes up so much space, he always has. And his smell is doing something I'm unprepared for.

"Maybe we should tell them properly."

I blink, not following.

"That we've split up," he clarifies.

"Oh. Yeah, if you want."

"At least then we won't get hassled about stuff like this."

I nod again.

Without warning he reaches up to pluck something from my hair. "Potato skin?" He laughs, then brushes my hair behind my ear. It's so casual, like it always used to be, and yet so, so not. "Maybe you should get someone to take over my job," he murmurs. His hand is so hot on my skin. "Or you'll have dreadlocks to contend with."

Does he think I care about my hair? "I should shave it off."

"Yeah, probably." He smiles flippantly and then bounds back to the kitchen.

I watch him the whole way.

*

March 3rd, 2068

Josephine

"So, happy birthday."

This lukewarm salutation is proffered by my even more emotionally inept father.

"Thanks."

I don't have a room anymore, since I stopped going back to the one I shared with Luke, so mostly I sleep above ground. This also helps to make sure nobody can find me. Alas, Shadow has managed it.

I was sitting quietly on a hill overlooking the farm, minding my own business and not bothering anyone when he appeared in the dark. It must be about 1 a.m., meaning I've been twenty-three years old for an hour. The moon is very bright, but it always feels bright out here.

We don't say anything. I used to be pretty chatty, but even then I found myself lapsing into silences with Shadow. Now we're at terrible risk of never speaking to each other again.

Eventually, as the sun begins to rise faintly over the horizon and turns everything an inky gray blue, he speaks. "When you were little and I thought I'd lost you I was shocked into numbness. Every word I could think of speaking or being spoken was an offense to your memory. There was no me without you. I was lost. It was a profundity of grief that was never again rivaled, even when Shay took me and did his worst."

I know what he's trying to say, and I agree. No matter what's done to your body, it doesn't rival losing the ones you love.

I clasp my hands and try to work out how best to convey that this is the last conversation we'll be having on the subject.

"You were my father a very long time ago," I say, "but that ended when I was left to people who hated me and decided to experiment on me. Whatever you think happened to me over the last few months is not what you imagine or went through, and it's not your responsibility. I'm not saying this to hurt you, I'm just trying to be clear about my expectations." I stand and brush myself off. "Goodnight."

There is a pause and then he murmurs, "Goodnight."

*

When I get back to the tunnels for my breakfast shift in the kitchen it's to find that I'm the first person here. And sitting on the bench is a wrapped present. I pause to look at it. It's flat and rectangular, like an A4 sheet of brown paper with a red ribbon tied around it. I'm disappointed to see it – I've been praying that no one would do this. I dread the attention this birthday will bring, and the thanks I'll have to give for whatever gestures they think will draw me back to the woman I once was. I don't deserve presents and I wish I could find a way to make them see that.

I consider not unwrapping it, but leaving it there. But that's cruel, and I can't stand the thought of being cruel. Uncomfortably I untie the ribbon and look at the card.

Josi. From all of us. We love you however you are.

My pulse picks up inexplicably. Why do I feel nervous? My fingers pull back the brown paper to reveal scores of music.

A sound leaves me. The Bach suites are all here. There is Benjamin Britton, who I once loved because he wrote all his music beside and about the sea. There is Beethoven and Debussy, and last there is the Elgar cello concerto I once tuned my heart to.

I can't fathom where they got any of them. So much physical music was lost when the world ended and paper became so much harder to come by. Instruments are rare enough, music even more so. These scores look very old, some of them worn at the edges, some smudged or faded. They must have been stored somewhere or perhaps maintained in the old library. I am overcome with their beauty and the sweetness of the gesture, and I am overcome with a sad sort of guilt that I will never be able to use them.

*

March 24th, 2068

Josephine

"Tell me again?"

"Sally Higgs, 23 Swan Avenue, Mica Powell, 2/12 Port Lane, Eli Fjordsson, 44 Markham Street and Ray Burns at 1 Brockwell Street."

Luke nods. "Let's start with Ray and work our way east."

We set off, keeping out of the glow of the streetlights and following the quietest route. We're dressed in normal clothes and any weapons we carry are concealed so that if we're spotted we look like a couple of drones out for a stroll, and not resistance fighters on a mission to steal the medicine of the recently deceased.

Tonight it's just Luke and me. I've made a point of not being alone with him too much over the last couple of months, but this had to happen tonight and we were the only two not already occupied with other tasks. So up we've come, to the suburb in which he and I used to live together.

In fact, there it is. Our very own apartment block.

We walk past in silence, neither of us saying a word about the things that lived and died in that penthouse. It's sort of insane to me in this moment that we could walk past it without a word, but we do and that's that.

A woman pulls her garbage bins onto the gutter in front of us and we immediately take hands as we pass her. She glances at us, smiles and heads back in. Our hands drop.

We cross the bridge of a canal and I see all the houseboats moored, the ones I used to peer into and wish I owned.

Some are offensively fancy – floating piles of money – while others pretend to be less crass with their wealth by hiding it inside. I unwittingly search out my favorite and spot it moored a few meters up the river. It has a garden of flowers on its roof, a burst of color within the surrounding grays and timbers of the more expensive boats. It's smaller too, and through the windows you can see that one of its walls is completely lined with books. I always wondered who owned that one, and why they never spent any time in it.

Then we're across the river and the boats are gone. We cut through a small park with, not grass, but wood chips for children to play on. Past the primary school and our local shopping center. All these places we used to walk by together. Up ahead is a metal sculpture of none other than Minister Falon Shay's first beloved wife. I've been dreading it, but didn't say a word to change our course, and neither did Luke. I saw it a million times when I lived here but I had no idea then that this woman was my mother.

As we draw near I can't help but stop.

She's been vandalized, and now no longer has a head or arms. She's a torso resembling the Venus de Milo, and I find myself smiling.

"Love the new look," Luke says. "Must drive the locals nuts."

He's got a point. Everyone walks around here with giant sticks shoved up their asses and if you don't scrub your windows daily or trim the hedge to regulation height you get passive-aggressive notes dropped in your mailbox.

"Maybe we have a Renaissance vigilante," I suggest.

"And he calls himself Pythokritos."

I blink. "Huh?"

Luke smiles and shrugs. "It looks like the Winged Victory, don't you reckon?"

I tilt my head and study it. "I was just thinking the Venus de Milo."

"But she has a head. The Winged Victory has no arms and no head."

"But it also has wings."

We peer at it and despite that, I think he's right – it does look like a wingless Winged Victory.

"I can't believe you know who made that statue."

"There you go, after all these years, still thinking me just a pretty face."

Our footsteps sound softly as we turn the corner onto Brockwell Street and head toward Ray Burns' house at the very end. We case the place but Ray only died two days ago so there shouldn't be anyone occupying it yet. Security is hackable so once the alarm is down we break in a back window and creep through the dark floors of the large townhouse, searching for bathrooms. I find a guest toilet with a marble toilet brush, then a shared bathroom with nothing but strange paintings of pugs and little hotel toiletries. I leave the former and grab the latter, despite a fleeting amusement at the idea of giving Pace a picture of her least favorite type of dog. In the upstairs bathroom is where we hit the jackpot: medication. Ray Burns died of Parkinson's in St Mary's Memorial, and just as we hoped, his bathroom is chockfull of the pills Tobias desperately needs. We haul it all into a backpack and head for the kitchen.

It doesn't feel good ransacking the houses of the newly departed. It's a bit like robbing graves, I imagine. But I've never had too much of a problem with it because I figure if I died, I'd want people to take all the stuff I couldn't use anymore. And it's better than robbing them *before* they die, when they actually need their medicine.

Ray has a few tins of tomatoes, some flour, sugar, oats, pasta, honey, just the usual crap you have in your pantry. We take it all and get out of there, headed for the next house on the list.

We burgle all night, not talking much. If we do say anything it's light – a joke or two, a few comments about how the other half live. Luke whistles softly and the sound of it calms me without me realizing it. Once our hands accidentally touch and I pull away so quickly he asks if he hurt me. There's an awkward moment when I say no and he realizes how badly his touch affects me, and then we go to opposite ends of the house. The next time we pass I can *feel* the tension in the air between us. The hairs on my arms stand on end, for Christ's sake.

We're in the last house on our list when the cops show up. Of course we haven't turned on any lights – we can work in any depth of darkness – so I have no idea how we've been spotted by a neighbor, but there you go. The second you start thinking you're on an easy op is the second it goes wrong. The car pulls up out the front, its red and blue lights shutting off with the engine. The cops don't say anything, they just peer in the front windows, shine their torches and then press the doorbell.

Luke and I are watching from the upstairs bedroom. We look at each other for ideas. There are only two of them so it's hardly a big deal, we just need to make sure they don't find a reason to call for backup.

A man comes out of the house next door. He talks to one of the officers and points to the side gate, where we entered. The cop approaches it, meaning he'll spot the broken window out the back soon enough.

Luke points to the manhole in the roof.

Despite not wanting to be confined in a small space with him, I shrug and nod. We climb up onto the dressing table and into the dusty roof. I cough and then swallow the discomfort in the back of my throat. For a while we just lie in the dark and listen for what's going on in the rest of the house.

"You ever wonder why so many of these massive houses only have one person living in them?" Luke whispers so quietly I barely hear him.

I don't reply, because I haven't ever wondered.

"It's like the richer you get, the lonelier you get."

"Their spouses have all died, it's why we pick them."

"But no kids or relatives?"

"You don't live with your kids or relatives," I point out. "Not once they've grown up."

"I guess. But still. One person tinkering around in this huge place … it's depressing."

It sounds pretty sweet to me. Better than being crammed into a too-small, windowless tunnel with a hundred other people. I wouldn't take this suburb, though. I wouldn't even take this city anymore.

This thought reminds me of the ceiling and the walls. It makes me very aware of them. I try to imagine floating up through the ceiling and into the sky, but more and more these days this imagining is difficult to hold onto. It slips through the fingers of my mind and I can't ignore the shrinking walls or the approaching roof or the steadily dissipating oxygen. It's too small in here, way too small.

Without warning I'm panicking.

"Josi?"

I hate this. I *hate* it. I have to get out. I need the sky. I need earth under my feet. I need to breathe, I can't breathe.

There's blood in my mouth I can taste it, it's choking me, I'm drowning in the heavy rank iron of it—

Hands take my face and then Luke's mouth is on mine. He's done this before – in an air-conditioning vent while I freaked out about wanting to kill Falon Shay. That time it calmed me, distracted me. This time it doesn't. Instead of getting lost in the kiss I'm nauseated with alarm and shove his face roughly away. I'm *so* angry with him for touching me without my permission. My skin is flushed and raw with it; it's repulsed. I'm so angry, in fact, that for a second I hate him.

My fist snakes into the first part of him I find, which happens to be his bad shoulder, the one that dislocates under a gust of wind. He grunts in pain and rolls onto his back. "*Fuuuuuuck*," he hisses, clutching it.

Something in my guts is churning, clenching, tightening. Something because of the smell of him or his pain or the rupturing claustrophobia inside my skull. I don't know what the hell I'm doing as I slide on top of him in the small dusty space and I don't actually care. I'm throbbing. Vibrating. I hate him and I hate myself but some nasty compulsion makes it impossible for me to stop. Someone walks through the room directly below us as I hold Luke's jaw with one hand and undo his jeans with the other. His eyes widen and he groans but I can feel his erection getting harder as I press myself against it. He tries to kiss me; I push his face away and he moves his hand instead to grab my hip and all of a sudden he's deep inside me and I can't breathe but I can and the hungry thing in me is clawing at him, needing him. We fuck fast and hard, in silence except for our breathing and our raging heartbeats, listening to the sounds of the police in the room beneath us. "They musta gone already," one of the cops says right as Luke thrusts so hard that I come. He shoves his hand over my mouth but I hardly notice because the roof explodes off the house and I'm in the sky after all, in the stars, rushing steadily away from the vile black shame that has become the ruler of my soul.

*

When we're alone we climb out of the roof and I carefully rotate Luke's dislocated shoulder back into its socket. I give him two aspirin but he's pale with pain as we leave the house. I carry both the backpacks filled with medicine and food and he doesn't argue – as well as dealing with his shoulder I can see he's also lost in melancholy. He doesn't mention what happened in the roof or my temporary madness. I feel a moment of gratitude that he doesn't use it to demand more of me.

Back at the safe house, we sit at the kitchen table so I can place his arm in a sling. He winces as I maneuver his wrist through the bandage. "Okay?"

Luke nods.

I notice his other hand clenched on his thigh, his bad hand. He must have used it too much tonight because it's swollen and inflamed. I hesitate, then remind myself that in no part of my self-reevaluation did I decide to become ungenerous. So I take the hand and gently massage the joints like I used to. He makes a sound, one of both pain and relief as I work the tight knots from the muscles.

"Thank you," he says.

Broken bones heal by calcifying and becoming stronger. All the bones in the human body do this except for those in the hand, which heal a little weaker, a little more painful. And when you break every single bone in a hand, it might heal but it will never be the same. It will always remind you of that pain, each time you move it, each time it makes a fist, each time the temperature drops. It will tell you in a million tiny ways how much less it is than it once was. You'll be reminded, Luke once told me, of your fragility, day after day after day.

"I never believed you when you said it," I murmur.

"What?"

"How fragile we are. I get it now. Did the Bloods teach you that?"

"They tried to teach me the opposite. It was Dad who taught me about fragility because I kept forgetting mine."

There is a long silence as I finish massaging his poor hand.

Then he says, "I know what happened to you."

My hand drops his. I frown.

"I think I do." Luke leans forward and looks into my eyes. "You remembered."

I stand abruptly and take several clumsy steps back.

He raises that hand in a gesture of peace, promising silence with it. He won't ask me anymore.

My shock trickles away, my heart slows. It's not so surprising that he figured it out. He doesn't know the reality though, or any of the dizzying details. He thinks he knows the girl with a moon for a heart but he doesn't.

I turn and walk to my bedroom, muttering, "Night."

It isn't until I'm closing the door behind me that I hear him murmur, "Goodnight, darling."

Chapter 18

Inside a stone prison lived a little girl with a moon for a heart. Most days the moon made her lonely, but once a year it hollowed out the inside of her so severely that it left a great gaping hole the likes of which nothing could fill. No matter how she tried, no matter how ravenously she consumed, no food or drink could sate the wild emptiness. One day she couldn't stand it any longer and, with everything she could lay her hands on too cold or dead to be of any sustenance, she caught the scent, instead, of a small rodent. This she captured and devoured, tearing into its warm flesh with sharp teeth and a hungry soul. Upon waking the next morning she remembered nothing of what she'd done, but saw her reflection covered in sticky, steely blood.

*

A year later the hunger was worse. A rat wouldn't do. She needed something larger, warmer, wilder. She needed something she could hunt and kill, something whose life force would fill the hole within. She bit into the furry body of a hissing cat but this wasn't enough. She was so hungry. Desperately, maddeningly hungry. Her wandering feet took her far from her home until she found a girl her own age playing in her backyard. The girl didn't run, but offered to play with her. She died with the moon girl's teeth in her neck and an unnatural strength squeezing the air from her windpipe.

*

The year after that there were two victims. Both of them adult, neither suspecting until too late that the gangly teenage girl could be capable of ending their lives. She ate all the pieces of them, starting with the fatty flesh and finishing with the organs. The heart tasted best: it held the most blood, and if she could be quick enough to bite into it while it still beat, the more the better.

*

Much to the moon girl's agony, the hunting and the feeding did nothing to ease her starvation. She was wasting away from the inside and the more she ate the hungrier she grew. Each time the moon overcame her she wandered farther, alone beneath the red hewn sky. Her frenzied feet searched and searched for a nameless, impossible thing. An end to the creature she'd become. Her senses heightened along with her strength. She smelled more than she ever had; could catch the scent of life from a long way away. Even the clothes on her back became too much sensation to bear and so she took to wandering naked and primitive as the first humans once did, though their hunger was natural and hers was something entirely other. It fell to a pattern. Her monstrosities grew as she learned tricks for survival. She ate and ate and ate and ate.

*

But the loneliness.

*

It was worse than the hunger. It was transfixing. No creature, she understood – even a monstrous one – was meant to be alone.

*

One day the world as she knew it changed.

*

Once there was a girl with a moon for a heart who escaped a stone prison to live in a snow-covered forest. She was the only girl in this forest, indeed she was the only girl in any forest, or so it seemed to her. She wandered alone, day after day. She was the loneliest creature to ever exist. Until a different kind of day came. A day in which she saw a bird of prey and, fearing it, fled. But the bird sat in the branches of a fir tree and sang sweetly to her. She heard the truth in its song: there had never been a girl in the forest to begin with, only one bird of prey and now a second, come to share its voice with her. They might be the last two in the world, but they were two, and that mattered. That was the thing that mattered more than her moon heart, because it was the thing that made a final, profound end to her hunger.

Chapter 19

October 15th, 2067

Josephine

I don't know how many days have passed. I have vague recollections of a moon rising maybe twice. But I haven't been occupied by the passing of the days or nights, or by the pain in my hand or the presence of monsters. I've been existing in the perfect clarity of my memory, which has at last decided to take me back to the beginning.

It doesn't hit me in chronological order, but all at once. Part of my delirium is due to sifting through the madness of so much information, so many new memories, and putting them into a semblance of order. The rest of my delirium is due to the content of such memories. The stars could fall and I wouldn't know it; the earth, I think, must be burning. I used to dream of vague pieces of these memories, but now they are whole.

It began in Ben Collingsworth's lab, with needles and electric shocks and pills. With the kind words of a mad scientist as he tortured children for the greater good.

It began with rodents and cats and it progressed to people. There was so much death. It was brutal beyond belief.

But all of this I knew.

What I didn't know was why I killed, or how. I thought it a cold, psychopathic desire for death. I thought it was madness. I was so wrong.

It was a desire for *life*. A hunger for it.

It was base, instinctive, primitive, feral.

It was *animal*.

I fed on my prey like a predator is designed to. Like it evolves to. Like the Furies do. With no cruelty, only survival. If hunger becomes too great we eat. If we are carnivores we eat meat. If there are no animals we eat humans. If we are no longer humans we eat humans without it being cannibalism. Those are the things I remember in absolute, throbbing detail.

When I wake from the fever to find myself still among them, my amputated finger having been heavily wrapped and clumsily cauterized, the threads to my own humanity and the woman I've been untie and slip steadily away. Because the most important thing I remember is not that I fed on people, it's that I knew exactly what I was doing as I did so.

*

March 25th, 2068

Josephine

I watch the clouds forming into the shape of a bear. It's one of those sad circus bears balancing on a ball. The sky behind him is so blue it's almost mocking. He soon moves wistfully out of his shape and away into the air. Another cloud twists into an S and I think of Medusa and her snakes.

"Yeah, it's only those four," Luke says.

I roll onto my stomach and peer into the building opposite. We're on the roof of a skyscraper, lying atop two hundred stories of financial advisors and lawyers and accountants. Nobody comes up here because they're too busy working like machines. I reach for the second pair of binoculars and lift them to my eyes. I adjust the focus and the kids come into view. Four of them, as Luke said, held in a secure hotel, awaiting the cure for anger.

The kids are the children of two of the ministers. According to Zach these two ministers in question are best friends, their wives close, their children the same age. Two sets of twins, which is eerily strange and no doubt to do with genetic tinkering. They're the first four children from within the Gates to ever undergo the cure. It's been made public as a response to the ongoing attacks of the rebels in freeing children. When we found out last week, Zach explained begrudgingly that it was a genius stroke of strategy on his father's part. The more we attack with messages of oppression and liberation – the more teenagers we free – the more concerned the drones have been getting with the state of things. We've been hacking their television feeds to show videos stating how hypocritical and fascist it is for the regime to cure all children but their own. So goddamn Falon Shay has come up with this.

"It's a dare," I say. "He's begging us to attempt it. Keeping them in a public building outside the security of the Gates. It's a trap."

"Even so," Luke replies, unfazed.

"Don't you think we have a million other things to be worrying about?"

"You were the one who always said the children came first. They're our priority."

I let out a breath. It was only last night that we did the medicine run and Luke's arm dislocated – he's in no shape to attempt anything, so we're on reconnaissance only. A surveillance trip to establish the reality of whether or not we can actually do this. I realize now that it was never up for debate. No matter how dangerous I argue it is, Luke will make it happen.

"Okay, aside from the risk," I say, "Is it right?"

"Huh?"

"Stealing children from their parents and holding them captive in underground tunnels."

He looks at me like I've just murdered a baby. "*Freeing* children from an oppressive regime that will promptly rape them of their emotions."

"Taking them from their parents, their homes, their whole lives. From everything they've known and offering them something frightening and dangerous."

"We give them the choice for a better life."

"By whose standard?"

He shakes his head. "You sound like Shay in his propaganda videos."

I don't take offense to that because I know he's only trying to wound me as much as I've wounded him in the last twenty-four hours.

"What exactly are you trying to say, Josi?"

"I'm not saying anything, I'm just asking questions."

"You want to add more kids to the list of casualties in this war? You want them to have their feelings stolen like all the other poor men and women who live with altered brains and mood swings and constant numb confusion?"

Tiredly I murmur, "Feelings are overrated."

He glances at me and then shakes his head. "Some pretty thick blinkers you've got on there."

"Or maybe I'm seeing clearly for the first time."

"We'll have to agree to disagree."

"There's a lot we're agreeing to disagree on lately." *Like the Furies.*

He turns to me. "Do we agree on the one thing that counts?"

I look at him, waiting for his take on what that is.

"That Falon Shay has to die and the ministers must be disempowered?" I don't answer straight away and he adds, "They're trying to cure *love*, Josephine. That's just batshit."

I choose my words carefully. "First I want to know what you imagine will take the regime's place."

"We've talked about this. A council."

"Of whose choosing?"

"Ours."

"And who would we choose?"

"Those of us from the tunnels, first. Then we'd add people from different communities. Hold elections for more members. We'll make it as varied and inclusive as possible."

"And who gets the final say on things?"

"We vote."

I sit up and raise my knees in a loose cross. "Luke. You know none of this will happen without a leader people can believe in. Councils are good in theory but we're rebels. Shay's been telling them about all the supposed innocents we slaughter. They won't want a council of faceless insurgents running the city. They need a real person who can inspire them to hope. Someone who will be just, intelligent and trustworthy. Someone who will offer them all the things that have been missing from their lives." I pause and search his face. "You know it's you, don't you? Tell me you understand that."

"I don't want it. I never wanted it."

"But it was always going to be yours."

He sits up and we're closer than I'd like. His green eyes flash in the sun. "Only according to you."

"And everyone in the tunnels. People *love* you. Plus you're more qualified than the rest of us put together – you've seen the way things function on the highest levels. It'll only work if it's you, Luke."

"Josi, listen to me. The only thing I've ever wanted – like, literally since all of this began – is you. I only went looking for the resistance because you wanted me to. I can't be a leader because if push comes to shove I'd prioritize you over everything – over this whole damn city. And I'm not saying that to get you back or anything, it's just fact."

I lace my fingers over my knees. "That's not a problem anymore because I'm not part of the equation. I'm not an option you can choose."

He's a very good actor so he hides it well – how much this hurts him. Calmly he says, "I don't buy it. Not after last night."

"That was biology."

He snorts.

"I know that sounds dumb. But there's a lot of things I can't control about my behavior and it comes down to biology. I had to come to terms with that or it would have driven me insane. Some part of me wanted you last night but I'm really sorry it happened because the last thing I want is for you to be hurt."

"Well, too bad. I'm hurt. A lot. All the time. That's what happens when your wife wakes up one morning and decides she doesn't love you anymore."

"It wasn't a decision. It was just … a truth."

"Did you, or did you not, love me the day we got married?"

"Of course I did—"

"So the truth revealed itself as a response to whatever happened to you, which means it wasn't an organic truth, it was a means of dealing with trauma, which means it can be overcome."

I sigh. This is not going well. "Look, shit happens, things change. It is possible to fall out of love."

He shakes his head stubbornly and turns back to the kids.

I do the same, wondering when we will stop having this conversation. I suppose the answer is when I find a way to convince him of what I'm saying. And to do that I will need to engage something drastic.

"There's one thing I believe in as much as I believe in us," he admits softly, eyes trained on the other building. "I *will* kill Falon Shay, no matter what it costs me. For the damage he's done and the things he's taken. For the monsters he's created."

I reach to finger the gun at my belt and reply absently, "If only you could see me for one of them, you'd know as well as I do how over we are."

*

Luke

I'm thinking about last night as we walk back through the tunnels. It was such a brutal blow, to have the love between us turn rough and animal. To have her feel a million miles away even as I was inside her. Her detachment in those moments frightened and humiliated me, the lack of intimacy she forged in an act that used to be our most intimate. But even having pain between us is better than nothing, and if letting her control what happens between our bodies helps her to return to me, then I'll do anything she wants.

Because it was during those swift, aggressive moments that I realized the truth. She's not dealing with what was done to her. She's dealing with the things she did to others. And that, for Josi, is much worse. Whatever horrors she committed has made her believe she doesn't deserve anything gentle or intimate; it made her believe she doesn't deserve love.

We reach the outer gate and I scan my prints to open it. I walk through in time to see two bodies in the dark, parting swiftly.

Josi and I stop, staring at the lovers.

"Hey," Eric greets us. His partner is in the shadows behind him and I can't make out who it is.

"Really, Eric?" Josi asks. "This is the second time I've caught you sneaking out to some lover's tryst. You don't have to hide it."

"We're not sneaking around," he protests. "There's just limited privacy unless you go into the dark."

"Who's with you?" I ask. "You're not in trouble."

"Really?"

I shrug. "What do we care if you make out with someone?"

The figure moves into the light from our torch and my heart sinks. "Oh. Maybe you are in trouble."

It's Alo, beautiful Adonis Alo. Sixteen-year-old Alo.

"We weren't doing anything," he says.

Josi snorts.

"Jesus, Eric," I snap. "Both of you are coming with me."

"We haven't done anything wrong!" Alo says.

We take them to the tech room because it's the most private and usually sheds the most light. Josi trails behind because I give her a look that says she better bloody well help me with this, even though it looks like the last thing she'd choose to be doing.

"Out, Teddy," I order.

Teddy looks up from whatever computer crap he's doing. "I'm in the middle of rerouting the—"

"Out."

He sighs and leaves, and I sit Eric and Alo on the two chairs. Josi leans against the door while I pace, trying to think what to do.

"Luke—"

"Shh." I stop and fold my arms. "You're thirty." I point to Eric. "And you're sixteen."

"So?" Alo demands.

"So this is not happening. I can't let it."

"Luke—"

"It'd be negligible of me! We didn't bring you down here so you could get preyed on by older men who should know better!"

"Hey!" Eric protests. "I didn't *prey* on him."

"He didn't. I pursued him, I swear."

"It doesn't matter, you're a child."

"Is this because we're gay?"

I roll my eyes. "Please."

"Luke, I swear, nothing's happened," Eric promises. "That was the first time we ever kissed."

"It won't happen again," I say. "Not until he's eighteen."

"Why?" Alo snaps. "It's such an arbitrary number! I'm not a fucking child – you bring us down here and demand we grow up so damn fast, you make us adults in every way and then expect us not to know our own hearts?"

I rub my eyes and look at Josi for help.

She is studying Alo and Eric with an unreadable expression. When it's clear she's not going to weigh in, I turn back to them. "We trust you to be more responsible than this," I tell Eric. "It's not just their physical health we're trying to protect, but their mental and emotional, too."

"You sound a hundred years old," he snaps, but I can see shame color his cheeks in the blue light.

"Well, someone ought to, since even the adults are acting like children."

"Do I get a say in my own life?" Alo demands angrily.

I meet his huge dark eyes. "Maybe we do ask you to grow up fast in every other way, but not in this. This is the one part of your innocence we have to protect. I'm determined to. Fall in love, fine, but no contact between you until you're eighteen, or there'll be serious trouble. And I'm not talking about extra chores."

I stride from the tech room before they can argue further.

Josi is so silent in the dark I don't even realize she's with me until I reach the ladder to the sleeping tunnels.

"You agree, don't you?"

She nods.

"But we let Malia and Coin kiss as much as they wanted."

"They were the same age."

The tension in my chest eases slightly. "It is different, isn't it?"

She nods again.

"So why didn't you help me then?"

"I don't have anything to do with it."

My mouth falls open. I think, if possible, I feel more betrayed than ever. "Can you at least come make a plan with me? For the twins?"

Since I've made no move to climb she overtakes me and starts gracefully up the ladder. "Go after them if you want. I've got bigger things to plan for." Then she's gone, up through the opening.

I stare after her.

My feet take me slowly to the storage work space. Dad's sitting on a stool, shaking badly and instructing Dave on the task of refilling the generator's fuel since he can't do it himself. Dave's not doing a very good job of it, by the looks of the mess.

"Hi, boyo," Dad greets me. "All smooth?"

"Hunky dory." I swing my backpack onto the bench and rifle through the contents for Dad's medicine. "I've got Levodopa and Apomorphine."

"Both."

That means it's been a bad day. He won't be able to open the bottle himself so I pop the lids and pass him two tablets. Then I reach for the generator from Dave, who surrenders it gratefully. I ignore the itchy sensation in my fingers that wishes to take the engine apart and instead finish refueling it.

"Can I ask you a favor?"

Dave is busy trying to clean the grease off his hands, which is a futile mission down here without any proper sinks. "Sure."

"Can you play some classical stuff to Josi?"

He frowns. "*To* her? Like a serenade?"

"No, like … just … around her."

This doesn't seem to clarify anything for him.

"She's a cellist." I sigh. "But she hasn't played since she got back, and I thought if she could hear you play some of her favorites it might …"

"Seduce her." He smiles gently and rests a hand on my shoulder. "I can try."

There it is again, his kindness. It gives me pause. "Do you really feel nothing?" I'm like a broken bloody record today.

"Not nothing. Just not … much."

"Why are you down here helping Dad with something you don't know how to do if not because you love him? Why do you spend so much time with Mom when she nags you constantly? Why do me favors?"

Dave glances at Dad and then back at me. His gaze flickers, hiding distant discomfort or maybe confusion. "I don't know," he replies. "There are things that drive us besides love."

"But not to be kind or generous, surely." I frown. "Unless it's self-serving, but I don't believe that. Not about you."

He shrugs and pats me on the head like a dog, then heads for the door. "I dunno, bro. Maybe it's habit."

When Dad and I are alone my old man says, "Give it time."

I don't know what he thinks time will change, but I nod anyway.

*

After I've unpacked all the new supplies and had Mom check my shoulder and hand, I head for bed but go past the arena like I always do. Inside Josi is already training at the bag, punching it with the lean, coiled strength she's developed. I watch her train sometimes and marvel at the change in her body, once so weak and now filled with power.

Zach is there with her, holding the bag and discussing something while she punches away. I watch their body language without being able to hear their voices, and I can see the seriousness in the tension of his face. She lands a mighty cross and he stumbles backwards with a groan. Offers her a rueful smile, says something short and then to my astonishment I hear the trickle of her laughter.

I'm ashamed of the hot, bitter jealousy it spikes. I haven't heard her laugh in six months, that reality like torture for me, and yet she offers it up so easily to this strange son of our enemy.

I love her laugh. Once upon a time I lived off it. If I tried to do that now I'd starve to death.

"Luke?"

I lurch in fear and clutch at my heart. "Jesus!"

"Sorry!" Dodge splutters. "You were a million miles away."

Josi and Zach have heard us and walk over. She's sweaty and sexy as hell. I swallow and move my eyes forcibly to our scientist. "What's up, man?"

Dodge looks between all three of us and then grins. "I made something that will help."

"With what?"

"Our pest problem." I sense Josi stiffen beside me as Dodge explains, "I've made a gas that will kill them. We just have to evacuate for the day and set off the bombs."

"Like a bug bomb," Zach points out sardonically.

"Exactly!" Dodge agrees, oblivious to his tone.

I look at my wife and see a cold fury descend upon her. She doesn't say a word, just turns and walks back to the bag. She punches it once, twice and then lands a brutally heavy spinning kick; it's enough to make the seam split, and sand pours all over her feet.

*

October 20th, 2067

Josephine

I've hardly moved in days. It isn't the pain – the pain is nothing. It's my body filled with lead. It's sinking to the bottom of the ocean and not being able to swim back up. Not being able to breathe.

I can taste blood in my mouth. They've been feeding me raw human meat to keep me alive. Some part of me must still be trying to survive because in a daze I eat it. I eat it and think *why not?* At this point, why the fuck not. I haven't washed, so I stink of my own waste again. And my head is filled with endless endless horror.

I thought I knew about monstrosity. I didn't.

I thought I'd barred the door against the wolves but the wolf was me all along.

Now I want out of this prison of flesh.

*

I manage to sit up and the simple movement makes my head spin. The day is cold but I can't feel it. I peer bleary-eyed around at my surrounds. Another part of the forest, as unremarkable and beautiful as the last. I can hear the river but the last time I went to drink it didn't turn out so well. I don't need water. What I need must be stolen. It's back in its place on Medusa's belt.

She's chewing on a bone and has never looked so feral. I sidle closer; the movement causes all of my crew to look at me. I haven't moved in days and perhaps they're relieved they won't have to keep carrying me.

I gaze at each of them and then Medusa. Her eyes are light brown inside the red. The bone (I think it was someone's arm, once) pauses in her mouth as she peers back at me.

I make my next move slowly and deliberately, and I give her everything I have left with this unbroken look. *Please*, the look says. *I'm done.* And while we hold it I reach for her knife.

She lets me, watching closely. She knows I won't hurt her: she can smell it.

Astro Boy makes an agitated whining sound. A warning. Someone shuffles nervously. But the others don't move to stop me, they only watch.

I lift the blade to my wrist and press hard enough to break the skin. A bead of blood blooms and slips down my skin. Two quick incisions along the artery will do it, one on the left and then one on the right while I still have the strength.

I don't mean to hesitate, but my eyes go up to the white sky through the trees. My whole soul goes up there, such that it is.

I don't spare Luke a thought. I don't care about him anymore. I don't care about a single thing or person left in this ugly world. It's devoid of anything worth saving, and I am the worst thing of all, the ugliest by far.

Thick, suffocating hatred fills me and I press the knife—

*

Something moves in the sky.

*

A gasp leaves me and the knife falls from my trembling fingers and there are tears of shock filling my eyes because—

Because far above in the empty white flies a bird.

I sink onto my back and watch the glorious beauty of its solitary flight, and I weep for the sudden reminder of the world's sweetness.

Chapter 20

October 20th, 2067

Josephine

I follow it, ducking between trees and craning my neck to see where it flies. Medusa and the boys run after me but don't try to stop me – instead they seem curious about my sudden burst of energy. All I know is that I can't lose sight of the bird.

We plunge into a valley, the floor of which is a long narrow clearing. The bird is circling above, not moving on but watching something below, I think. It swoops lower and I make out the shape of it. Small in body, but with incredibly long wings and a prominent hooked beak. It's a bird of prey, I have no doubt, but I'm not sure what kind.

The bird lands on a tree branch about twenty meters high. I walk closer, making sure to keep as silent as possible. The Furies are eerily still at the edge of the clearing. So much about them is unknowable and really creepy. I ignore them and keep my eyes trained on the bird.

As I draw near I'm surprised at how close it's letting me get. From here I can see better. It's several shades of brown and tan, with a deep chestnut in its wings and flecks of white throughout. The beak is more hooked than I thought, and there's a ring of yellow around its liquid black eyes.

I think it's a falcon.

My heart. It's beating out of my body.

"Where did you come from?" I whisper.

The falcon's head turns and beholds me. A very long, swollen moment stretches between us.

Without warning it launches into the air.

Don't leave.

I watch it rise high and angle itself north. It disappears behind the trees and my heart breaks at the thought of never seeing it again.

But if ever I wanted to take meaning from life, if ever I decided to believe in signs, it would be now. It would be in the unbelievable timing of that bird's appearance in my life.

I turn back to the Furies, those monsters I nearly killed myself to escape, those who have revealed how perfectly I belong with them.

And I smile.

*

The Fury army angles east this afternoon. I walk as fast as I can with the endless throbbing pain in my hand, searching the sky for distraction. It isn't until late that I see the falcon again, flying above us, circling back and keeping pace with the group.

I laugh aloud in astonishment. I wonder if it has any idea it just saved my life.

*

October 21st, 2067

Josephine

We come upon a village this afternoon. The bird has been following us as we take the winding road through the forest in the direction of the sea. I spot it high above or perched in a branch, always watching. I wonder if it's looking for food, trying to interpret whether or not we're to be eaten. It doesn't seem particularly bothered by our proximity, more curious than anything. An idea has been percolating and I want to see if I can find it something to eat.

As we walk through the center of town, the Furies fan out to search the abandoned buildings for god knows what – stray people, I suppose – and I catch sight of a building farther down that is completely blackened. It's been burned in a fire. So has the one next to it, and actually the whole rest of the street has been scorched away. An enormous arched building that I assume must have been a church at one point is now blackened char, but still holds curiosity for the Furies, who kick in the crumbling door and enter in a flood.

Something feels wrong about it. There's a prickling sensation on my arms as I follow them, driven by a powerful curiosity I should know better than to obey.

I walk into what's left of the sooty church and find a graveyard. There is a sea of blackened, burned bodies and the smell hits so pungently that I gag. They're not laid out, but scattered and twisted, making me sure they weren't laid to rest here but burned alive.

Oh god. It was the smell of flesh they were following, and I watch the Furies lunge at the charred remains, apparently not caring that surely most of what they're eating is ash. They tear and snarl and chew, fighting each other with wild hunger.

I am about to vomit as I stumble back outside and suck in a gasp of clean air. The world spins dizzily around me. There must be more bodies in other buildings because as I walk through the town I can hear the feeding frenzies on both sides.

There's only one answer for what happened here. The plague hit. But burning the infected did nothing to stop the spread and eventually they were all dead, this entire village, just like this entire cursed country and maybe even the world.

It occurs to me like a blow that I'm alone. For the first time since I was taken I'm not being watched. My feet quicken and I duck into one of the houses that wasn't burned down. It smells of mold and rot and I'm almost certain there are dead bodies hiding in here somewhere. I go straight to the kitchen in search of food, but I only find tins I can't open and oats filled with weevils. I devour the oats, heedless of the wriggling creatures I can feel sliding down my throat. In moments like these the hunger is too great to ignore, and I can't even think about escaping. Not until I've fed.

Although, really, where would I go? I can't go home, not now that I've remembered what I am. I doubt I'd even make it that far on my own, without the warmth of other bodies to stave off the cold, without beasts to bring dead flesh for me to eat. There's survival in numbers, even if those numbers are captors. Each day that passes, however, feels less like I'm a prisoner and more like I belong.

Still, I move around the house hurriedly, looking for anything I might use. Even if I don't plan to escape, there is something I want more than anything, and I'll need to be alone to have a shot at it.

I find a backpack upstairs, but as I fill it with warm clothes from the cupboard I catch sight of a body in the next room, a child's body. My hands stall to stare at it. It isn't plague ridden and it isn't old. In fact, it might only be days dead. What does that mean? Are there other people out here somewhere? But why leave a dead child in this house? Why not bury him?

My hands shake as a new idea occurs to me. I was right when I told the kids in the tunnels that I had no line to cross anymore. I just had no idea how right.

I drag the child down the stairs and out the front of the house. It's easy – he's so little. I don't apologize or beg forgiveness. He's gone. He's flesh. He's food. And I need the Furies to trust me.

"Hey!" I shout. "Medusa!"

I've been saying her name every day, addressing her with it as much as I can because I want to see if they're capable of learning cognitive behavioral patterns or language recognition. I know she can speak, I just don't know if she can learn new words.

Turns out she can. Upon hearing her name Medusa bounds out of a building about a hundred meters down the street, spots me and sprints my way. I feel a moment of fear as she thunders toward me, but after a loud cry she simply lunges onto the child and starts devouring him. Her group of five arrives and she lets them have at it for a few minutes. The sound is always the worst. The crunch and slurp and chew and swallow of it all. The wetness of it, the *meat* of it.

Medusa growls and they pull back from the mess that was a child.

To me she says, "Feed."

It makes the hairs on my neck stand on end. She so rarely speaks that it chills me to the core. Steeling myself, I do as I know I have to. I've got to be brought into the fold, made one of them in every way. So I kneel and lean my face to the gray flesh of the child's thigh and I bite. It's not like the other times, when I've been given meat I never saw beforehand. This is actually a corpse that I'm biting into with my too-blunt human teeth. This is real human blood spilling into my mouth and coating my throat. The blood moon envelops me and I flash between all the memories of myself until I'm so disoriented I lose all sense of where and when I am. All I know is that I'm eating as I have done too many times before, and that I am no longer Josephine Luquet, but something much, much less.

*

October 22nd, 2067

Josephine

We've set up camp nearby the village to take advantage of the several hundred dead bodies. I spend the time making my way through the wasteland of a village and scavenging. In the houses that haven't burned down I look for food and supplies. I manage to come up with quite a good haul, plenty of rations, weapons and best of all: clean, warm clothes. I spend this morning looking for something I can use as bait. There's an old, slightly moldy packet of dried apricots that will do nicely, and I place these under dusty jars propped with the ends of chopsticks. They're pretty good little traps, if I do say so myself, though it takes *ages* to get them balanced right.

*

October 25th, 2067

Josephine

For the last three days I've sat apart from the group. Close enough to be visible but far enough that it's quiet and still. I have in my pocket a treasure. One I finally found in the trap I placed in the church, taking its fill like the rest of us scavengers. Now I hold its small, wriggling body in my hand and sit quietly between the great oaks of the forest.

I'm not sure if this will help, but I whistle like I have for the last couple of days. One long bending note. An arching note. I don't know about animal calls, but I know about the sound of a note, and in this one I put all my sweetness, all my yearning.

I do this for the next hour or so, send this gentle call into the woods.

And eventually it comes, just as it has been doing every day. Curiosity, I'm sure. The sound is an unusual one. It lands on the outstretched branch of an oak, partially hidden behind leaves. I can feel it staring at me.

Out of my stolen coat pocket I produce the mouse. I hold it by the tail and let it squirm visibly.

The falcon's eyes narrow in on it.

The mouse makes small noises of fear and lurches helplessly.

I think the falcon is female. She has wider wings than I would have thought, but quite a large body, which makes me think she must be a young female. In Will's book it said that males are about a third smaller than females, and that as youths a falcon's wings are wider so it can learn flight skills, then taper down to become faster and more agile in high-speed maneuvers. This little girl looks like she's in the process of growing up. She is fine and delicate, more fragile than anything I've ever seen. More precious to me than anything in this world. And I think she's been following me.

"Here you go, girl," I murmur.

I give a sharp whistle and throw the mouse to the ground. It scampers out of my sight but the falcon is already moving. She dives with impossible speed, extending her piercing talons. As she ducks out of the dive her wings spread and her talons pluck the mouse from the long grass. A thrill fills me, prickles my skin, electrocutes the tips of my hair. It's primal and powerful and intimate, somehow, watching her hunt and kill her prey so close to me. She doesn't fly off with the mouse, as I thought she might, but tears into it on the ground there, pulling pieces free and tossing them back into her throat to swallow.

Something happens to me as I watch her feeding on the mouse I trapped with apricots. Something I'm not prepared for.

The shame of what I've done goes numb.

My edges ripple and solidify once more into a new shape, and I feel myself sink into my proper place in this enormous wild savage *beautiful* world.

The falcon looks at me then, right into my eyes.

And it all becomes so clear, what the Furies are, the reason they took me, and everything I must now do. Hal spoke of taming the animal within. But I think he was wrong. I think we're meant to let it free.

Chapter 21

March 30th, 2068

Luke

I've never seen Josi train so hard. Beyond her usual strength exercises, she's been focusing on flexibility and agility – she's preparing herself for something but she hasn't said a word about what. Not to me, anyway. She talks a whole lot with Zach, the two of them constantly scurrying off to have their private little meetings. It's really starting to get under my skin.

This evening I catch them talking in hushed tones as they shovel muck out of the pig pen.

"... not like he actually cares, he just wouldn't be able to stand the idea of someone taking something that belongs to him."

"Except you don't, Zach."

"I know that but he doesn't."

"Works for us."

That's when they see me leaning on the fence in the setting sun. "Hey. What's up?"

"Just shootin' the shit," Zach grins, holding high a shovel covered in literal shit.

"You doing any actual work or are you just grumbling about old daddy again?"

He stiffens and I see the wall go up. "I guess you'd know a thing or two about that, huh? Given the state of yours."

I'm about to thump him when Josi sighs and interrupts. "Alright, enough."

"Boss invited us in to have a shower," I tell her brightly, ignoring the sniveling cretin she keeps company with.

"Yessssss!" Zach exclaims. "Even my dirt's getting dirty."

"Not you, shit-boy," I say with a satisfied grin. "Shower's for grownups. You get to stay here and keep shoveling."

He shoots me a filthy look. "Probably just as well. You stink worse than the rest of us combined, Townsend."

I laugh boisterously and head for the house. Showers, when they come, are blissful, priceless things. I close my eyes and let the warm water sluice over my face. The dirt that comes off my body is altogether too much for comfort as it trickles down the drain. I scrub every inch of me and wash my hair twice. When I can't put it off any longer I turn the taps off and climb out to dry myself. There's a bath in the corner. I smile, knowing how much Josi would love to have one.

It feels gross putting less than clean clothing on my extremely clean body but it has to be done. I pad into the living room, towel drying my hair. Josi's sitting on the couch next to ten-year-old Buck, who is reading something on a tablet. She's watching the other child, Birdie, who's only three and playing with lego on the carpet. Her face shows no expression.

"There's a bath!" I announce.

She stands and brushes past me for the bathroom. "Nah. Quick shower'll do."

Frida's in the kitchen cooking so I wander over and perch myself on a stool behind the bench.

"You two are staying for dinner," she tells me.

"Yes, ma'am. Can I help?"

"I'm just doing a veggie pie, but you can make the salad."

I round the bench and start chopping vegetables.

"Maybe you can settle a bet we've got going, sir."

"Frida, god, for the last time please don't call me sir."

"I'll call you what I see fit, sir, and nothing less."

I sigh. "What's the bet?"

"What on earth it is between the two of you."

"Who? Me and Josi?"

"Some of us reckon you're exes. Some reckon you haven't got together yet. One of the workers said you were brother and sister but he got laughed out of town."

"Christ, does everyone need to weigh in?"

"Just about. So which is it?"

I shrug and chop the carrot faster. "Well, we're not brother and sister, but that's about all I can confirm. If you ever settle that bet, be sure to let me know."

I catch her eyeing my wedding band but don't offer an explanation. Frankly, it's none of their damn business.

*

Dinner is a strange affair. They're kind people but Josi doesn't talk much so it's down to me to ask all the right questions and be the grateful guest. She watches Birdie a lot and I feel that same old ache in my chest, wondering how different our lives would be if we'd been able to get pregnant. Maybe a child would have saved her from becoming this distant loveless person. Afterwards we thank our hosts and head out into the starlit paddocks. We have to jump over a couple of fences to reach the creek, then balance over a thin beam we put down as a makeshift bridge.

"See you tomorrow," she says abruptly and then melts off into the dark.

I walk a few more steps, then on a whim I follow her.

She's quick and silent but I made a career out of being quicker and more silent than anyone. I track her footsteps in the grass and find her heading up a hill in the opposite direction of our tunnels. She cuts over the hill and through a patch of forest before emerging on the lip of a high ridge. From the bottom I peer up at her, but she doesn't do anything, just stands in the dark and watches the sky.

Where has she been sleeping? Is this all she does at night? Just waits out here alone, unable to be inside?

I feel a pang of sadness for how lonely that seems. Then I feel a pang of my own sadness, because I'm constantly surrounded by people and feel just as lonely as the woman on this hill looks.

A sound pierces the night and I'm surprised to realize it's come from Josi. A long, musical whistle.

I frown. Weird.

Then I lurch forward with a warning cry on my lips as I see Josi attacked.

*

October 30th, 2067

Josephine

Once the Furies have had their fill of the village corpses we head toward the sea. I still have no fucking clue what we're doing, but I've started to get the sense that maybe they don't know either. They just stay together and look for food, keeping within the relative shelter of the forest. I think I can use this to my advantage, but I have to be clever about it.

I feed the falcon every day and she stays close. In my pack are a dozen mouse corpses and one live mouse in a jar, so I have nearly a fortnight of her presence to look forward to. I don't know what I'll do when I run out; I can't bear the idea of her leaving. It's occurred to me to capture her and train her – I have ideas about how I might do that, it's why I found the twine and sewed the little hood – but I can't bring myself to. It would be a tragedy of sorts, to tame such a creature. So I just feed her and watch her and hope each day that it won't be the day she goes.

Medusa trusts me now. Since offering her the boy's body and showing my allegiance by feeding on him I've felt a shift in the dynamic. They don't stare at me the way they once did, with caution and curiosity. They don't follow me to the river or watch my every move. They simply include me in the feeding, and if they come to the river it's to share in the drinking. I don't speak to them anymore, or tell stories. I've lost my appetite for fantasy. But even I feel the difference: I'm comfortable, even grateful to have them around me.

And I'm no longer disturbed by this notion. I'm the same as them, after all. It would be arrogance to be disturbed.

So, with this newfound trust, I start carefully working us to the front of the army. I've worked out that there are roughly five hundred of us. My gang of seven is nothing to the size of the whole, but we have a big advantage: we have Medusa. There's no doubt she's one of the strongest; the others defer to her. She doesn't take a leadership role except in our little gang, but I'm convinced I can use her to turn us south.

Day by day, with the falcon flying above, I've brought us forward and started prompting our movements. Medusa moves with me, always, as though we are strange silent companions, so if I gently push south, she thinks nothing of doing the same. It's my scent, I know. Scents don't lie, and mine tells her she can trust me. Mine tells her we're the same.

The problem will be when we get to the plains, the grassy hills that stretch for countless miles and hold no food. I can't imagine they'll be keen to head back through them for no conceivable reason. I have an idea about this too, though.

It's twilight when I wave the mouse and wait for the falcon to land in a nearby tree. My eyesight's worse at this time of day but hers is much better. It's magic hour. The horde is still moving – we don't stop until deep dark, and even then we only stop for a few hours of sleep. So I decide to see if the falcon will feed while we're on the move, while I'm surrounded by others.

Out of the corner of my eye I see her swoop low and land in a tree I'm walking toward. I hold the mouse up, letting her see it dangling. But before I can throw it to the ground, she moves. I'm startled into keeping hold of the creature and that's when something astonishing happens.

She lands heavily on my arm and snatches the mouse from my fingers. I take her weight with a yelp of surprise and then immediately go still. She gobbles the mouse and then remains on my arm. Her claws gouge holes in my skin but I don't care, I am glad of them. Tears prick my eyes as I look at her, so close. She is glorious, her plumage more speckled than I thought, much richer in color. She's so pretty, her dark eyes looking at me and then away as though I'm hardly of interest. She's playing hard to get and I laugh a little through my tears. Carefully I reach up with my left hand to stroke her chest feathers. She lets me. She's so silky.

I'm jostled from behind by the many moving bodies so I decide to start walking. And the falcon stays where she is, catching a free ride. I didn't need to catch and tame her after all: she came of her own choosing.

My chest swells and aches with love.

I decide to name her.

*

October 31st, 2067

Josephine

Tonight she brings *me* the mouse and drops it at my feet.
And I know we belong to one another.

*

March 30th, 2068

Luke

It's the shape that confused me. And the complete bewilderment of the *type* of approach. Things don't fly anymore. They don't come from the sky.

Which is why my feet start sprinting up the hill and my voice shouts her name as something drops from the sky toward her head.

But what I'm seeing in the dark confuses me. Part of the shape detaches and falls to the ground while the other lands on Josi's arm with the distinct sound and shape of *wings*.

I stop. My heart is beating with too much power, too much fear. For one second I think I've gone mad again – I've returned to the blood moon's prison and my imaginary birds have returned to plague me.

But then Josi turns and looks down at me, and she smiles because there's a falcon perched on her arm. A real one.

My legs give out and I sink to my knees.

Josi walks down the hill to me. "Shh," she says. "Be easy. She's brave but you need to be calm."

I don't understand, but something about the extraordinary beauty of the moment doesn't surprise me in the least. Of course Josephine Luquet would find the last bird. Of course it would be hers.

"How …?" I clear my throat and climb slowly to my feet. "What …"

"Luke, this is Intirri. She's a Barbary falcon, about a year old. I think, anyway."

I let out a breath and it turns into a soft laugh. "Oh my god. Hello, Intirri. It's a pleasure to meet you."

"Do you want to touch her?"

I nod and reach very carefully for her chest plumage. She feels soft and lovely, and doesn't seem to mind my touch. "Where did you find her?"

"She found me. Forest up north."

"What was she doing?"

"Hunting."

"But ... how?"

Josi shakes her head and in the moonlight I see her smile soften. "I don't know. There's so much more out there than we know. The wall of this city makes the world feel very small, but it's not – it's enormous and full of mysteries."

I quickly wipe the tear that has spilled onto my cheek. It's so obvious now, how Josi survived what she did.

"What did she bring?"

"A rabbit. Want to make a stew for dinner tomorrow?"

"Won't she want to eat it?"

"She's already eaten. She brought that one for me."

I smile and stroke her wing feathers. I'm so unprepared for how easy it is to fall in love with an animal. It happens as simply as the body's next heartbeat, as though we were made for it as much as we were made to pump blood through our veins.

"Thanks, Intirri. I love rabbit stew."

We're quiet for a while. I stroke Intirri and think of nothing but how lovely she is.

"So this is why you don't sleep inside anymore?" I ask eventually.

"Neither of us particularly likes walls."

"What was it like out there?"

Josi considers this, making a soft clicking sound with her tongue to Intirri. She is so much more alive than I've seen her in the last months. "It was difficult," she admits finally, "and good."

"Why was it good? Because of Intirri?"

"Yes. And because I learned who I am."

"Someone who doesn't love her husband anymore?"

I expect her to sigh or move away or end the conversation. I shouldn't keep pushing the point over and over again, only

I just want to understand and she won't explain it to me. I've fixated, locked on like Coin does in his mania, and I know it but have no way to unlock.

Josi surprises me though. The bird softens her. "I found something simpler. I had to, because loving you nearly killed me. But if you think it means I wouldn't still die for you, you're wrong. That's what happens up there – you learn the things you'll live for and the things you'll die for. I'd die for any one of you, just as I'd die for Intirri. That's how simple it is in the north."

My throat aches and my chest aches and my whole life aches. "But what would you live for?"

This time she does turn away. She carries her bird back up the hill and says over her shoulder, "Something else." And I see a glimpse of what she's trying to keep hidden: a predator on the hunt for its prey.

*

April 1st, 2068

Josephine

"Happy anniversary!"

I stifle a groan and smile instead. I've put up with this for most of the day. My thoughts are with Malia, and I wish the rest of them would have enough respect to realize.

I run through my training exercises, pushing myself harder and harder. Luke's training the others with the usual comedy routine. I cross to him and mutter, "Push them harder. Blood hard."

He frowns and eyes me. "They're young."

"No, they're not."

I see him warring with that but he obviously understands because he nods and starts leading them through the drills he used on us last year in the lead-up to the sadness cure.

Things are simple. If you start a war then you'd better be willing to win it.

In the unspoken lead-up to this war we cancel all classes and focus on the mental and physical toughening of all. It's time to move.

*

I place a city map on the table. We're in the middle of dinner and everyone looks at it in puzzlement, some moving food and drink out of the way. Luke, Pace, Eric, Will and Dave are at this particular table, but I feel the curious eyes of others looking our way.

I prod the outlined buildings. "Blood compound. They don't sleep here but it's where they train, and where their weapons, armor and tech are kept."

Luke nods, flashing me a look that he says he already knows what I mean.

"This is where we hit," I say. "I want it under our control. Every Blood accounted for. Then, and only then, we take the Gates."

"That's insane!" Eric protests. "Aren't there like hundreds of Bloods there at any one time?"

"They come and go, but yeah," Luke says. "It's highly secure. No way in or out unless you have Blood ID, and that's not something we can fake."

"Doesn't matter. As for the coming and going, I want all heads thinking of a way to get every single Blood into that compound at the same time."

"Not gonna happen," Luke says. "Specific security measures interchange agent presence."

"That's why I said start thinking." I look around at the people who've come to peer at the map over our shoulders. My eyes go to where Teddy is sitting on the side of a table. "Everyone." The boy nods and hurries out.

"I thought the idea was to stay as far away from that place as humanly possible, Josi," Dave says.

I meet his eyes and smile as gently as I can manage. "It'll be okay, trust me."

He studies me expressionlessly and I wonder what he sees. After a moment he shrugs. He's worried about his brother, that much is obvious.

To Luke I say, "Start deciding on a team of about fifty for this."

He doesn't respond, just stares at the map. When he belatedly looks up there's a light in his eyes. A hunger. I knew as soon as the idea was presented to him he'd have to do it. To Luke there's no bigger challenge.

What he doesn't know – what none of them know – is that no matter what we do, most of the Bloods of the city will be missing when he attacks the compound. But I don't tell them that. It'd defeat the purpose of this mission, which is actually not at all to do with taking down the biggest stronghold of our enemies, but something else entirely.

I leave the dining hall to find Zach waiting for me in the tunnel. I gesture for him to be silent as we make our way down a ladder and away from listening ears.

"Will he go for it?" Zach asks softly when we're alone in the dark.

"Of course. He can't resist a challenge."

"Arrogant prick."

"Don't," I warn and he immediately looks contrite. "Have you been doing your exercises?"

"Yes."

"Six times a day?"

"Yes, Mom."

"If you think you can, start doing them more."

"I'm gonna be fine, Josi."

I refrain from voicing my doubts about that – it's the one part of my plan I'm not entirely sure of, and I hate having to rely on someone else to pull this off.

We walk together to Dodge's lab. I use the word "lab" very loosely. He's commandeered the junction where several tunnels intersect because it has slightly better ventilation. All his work's on a piss-poor little table. Luke's rerouted some of the power for him to have refrigeration, and he keeps a fire going at all times, but all his tools are old or broken enough to have been scavenged from the junkyard. His workspace in the Inferno may as well have been a NASA lab compared to this shit hole. But he doesn't complain, just ferrets away down here night and day, making do with what he has.

"How's the gas going, Dodge?"

He looks up from a very burned Petri dish, waving a handheld blowtorch toward us.

"Woah!" We jump backwards and he immediately points it down.

"Sorry!" Once he's turned it off and raised his goggles he shrugs. "Gas is coming along. I have several canisters already, and I've been working with Teddy to come up with a time-release for it."

"When do you think it'll be ready to go?"

He scratches his chin, getting soot all over it. "A week, maybe?"

I nod. "Great. We gotta head but you're doing brilliant work, Dodge."

When Zach and I are moving quickly down the tunnel once more I say under my breath, "We have a week to get everything set up and to destroy that gas."

*

I take the time to visit Coin tonight. I'm not sure why. The thing about not wanting to be ungenerous, I guess. He's lying on his bed, staring at the ceiling, and he barely acknowledges me when I sit beside him. This is a very 'past Josephine' thing to do, not a very 'current Josephine', but I set aside the different versions of me for the night.

"Do you want to come for a walk with me?" I ask him.

"I'm pretty tired …" Stroke, stroke, stroke that hair.

"Please, Coin."

It surprises him, so he nods.

When he realizes where I'm leading him he stops. "I don't think I …"

I take his hand and lead him gently on. It doesn't take us long to reach the cliff opening where Malia died a year ago. We sit with our legs dangling over the edge and watch the ocean.

"Some animals eat their dead," I say.

"That's awful."

"Yeah, I thought that too but now I'm not so sure."

He glances at me like I've lost my mind. Sometimes I'm not entirely sure I haven't.

"It's kinda like taking their life force and living off it. It's like having them inside you even after they're gone."

He doesn't say anything for a long while. Then, "Well, I'm not saying I want to eat her or anything, but I wouldn't mind having some of Malia in me."

I smile.

But then he says, "It hurts all the time. I thought it was meant to get better but it doesn't. I feel so alone."

I put my arm around him and pull him against me. "I know."

"I don't know what the point of all this is. It feels like we live in hell. We're all alone in hell."

With a breath I decide to tell him the thing I learned on the day I tried to kill myself, but instead saw a bird.

"You and Malia were both born fourteen billion years ago," I murmur. "All the things that make up your heart have existed since the start of time. Your bones were once comets streaking through the sky. Your muscles might once have been ocean. All of you is made of all of this." I gesture to the world laid out before us, the sky and the sea and the infinite horizon. "Malia didn't disappear when she died, she went back to all of this, just like you and I will. So when you feel alone, think of how unbelievably connected we are. We're part of an enormous, beautiful, miraculous family. That's the point."

He buries his face on his raised knees and I feel him trembling as I stroke his hair. I do it for him because some compulsion makes him need it.

I think it again, I think it like a mantra: We are all the same. The cured and the uncured, the Bloods and the Furies. We are all made of the same atoms that make up the last living bird, and the disease that wiped the rest of them out. The only sense I can gather from that is that no one thing is worth more than another, no person or creature of more value. And if someone tries to make the world otherwise, make us believe otherwise, then he can't be allowed to remain. When I fight – and fight I will – it will be in the name of that.

Coin says, strangled, "It's my fault she died."

I hesitate, then say the thing I never would have admitted before the Furies, before Intirri. "Yes."

He sucks in a breath. "So how does being connected with the universe make that better?"

"It makes you strong enough to own it and carry it. That's yours now, and it'll be yours until the day you die. But so will the grace of the world."

"Shame and grace. That's what we get?"

I look at him, at how young he appears in the moonlight. But that treacherous moon plays tricks on us all. Coin's not young. None of them are.

"Yes."

Chapter 22

April 5th, 2068

Dave

The tunnels are in a flurry of activity. Plans are being made left, right and center. I've been keeping close to my brother so I know what's going on, but it's becoming clear not just to me, but to everybody, that Josi isn't being transparent about her plans. Luke and I are on the way to the arena when we catch sight of her and Zach disappearing down a ladder to somewhere I thought was out of bounds.

I glance at my brother to gauge his reaction, but his jaw tightening is the only indication I have that he's bothered.

"What's going on with you two?"

He shakes his head. We go over to the bag so he can make me punch even though it's obvious I'm not improving. I just don't care about fighting. Of all the things that have changed, considering myself a pacifist isn't one of them.

"She's stopped talking to me," he says abruptly. "She only talks to Zach."

"You don't trust him?"

"Fuck no. He's a suspicious creep and I have no idea why she can't see that. Or won't."

"What – do you actually think he's still working for his father?"

Luke doesn't respond either way, but he doesn't dismiss the idea. "Josi's lost her center. She's soft about the things she should be hard about, and hard about the things she should be soft."

I consider this. "You're the leader of the resistance."

"No, I'm—"

"You are, Luke. So start making some tough decisions. It's your responsibility to keep your people safe."

"What are you saying? That Josi's a *threat*?" He sounds incredulous.

"No, I'm just saying watch her. Get her talking. You need to know what's going on down here. And you need to be in control."

He doesn't like this, I can see, but he doesn't argue. I punch the bag and he scoffs impatiently. "Stop fucking around and give me a real punch."

I try to punch harder but I don't have much strength to begin with. "I'm coming with you, right?"

"No, mate. You're not in any shape."

I let the bag go and it swings to him. "Luke. I'm coming with you."

"Why?"

Because I can't be in these tunnels when you go, that's why. "Because I want to help."

"But why?"

"Why shouldn't I?"

"I dunno. What's motivating you to risk your life?"

He's always pushing me to admit I feel more than I do and I wish he'd stop hoping. I say, very clearly, "Justice, and a peaceful world. Whatever you may think about me, I don't wish for the deaths of others. So if I can help to ensure the safety and prosperity of our city, I deserve the right to, don't I?"

Luke tilts his handsome face. It was so startling to see him grown up into this unknowable man. I still catch myself peering at him in wonderment. His hair is quite short – about the same length as his beard, now – and beneath his dark brows the set of brilliant green eyes look at me the way they always used to. With admiration. It makes me uncomfortable.

"Of course," my brother says.

Something in my stomach falls. My whole life is rushing to a point from which I can't turn back.

"I've been practicing the pieces," I tell him.

His smile is so delighted that for a moment I imagine slipping into his skin and feeling what he must feel. Because that's the thing about Luke. I think he feels more than anyone down here, more than most of them combined. How must it be, to be so wrapped up in emotion? So driven by it? It's been so long for me that I can hardly remember.

"Can I stay in your room tonight?" I ask him. "Mom's driving me nuts. She's made me eighteen cups of tea today and keeps trying to make me put on more layers."

"Sure." He laughs. "Got plenty of room now that it's just me."

"What was it like between you ... before she changed?" We're not talking about Mom now, obviously.

He rests his head on the bag and his smile changes, turns sad. "It was ... big. Sometimes I got scared by how big. I thought I'd never be able to handle the size, and how much she always seemed to need from me."

"So why'd you keep on?"

"'Cause it costs nothing to give someone what they need, mate. In fact it feeds you. I learned that from her, 'cause of how much she was always giving me."

This stirs something in me, but I'm not sure what. I keep prodding, wanting to inventory what's going on in my brain. "So why … what happened to her?"

He meets my eyes. "She got wounded too deeply, so she built herself a new skin, a much tougher one, thinking it'd protect her from enduring the same again."

"But you think it won't?"

He shakes his head. "It may do. She's got the strongest will you'll ever come across and she's made it tough enough to keep me out. Maybe it will protect her. But I'm more worried about that first wound. It's still under there, eating away at her, 'cause she never let the saltwater get inside to heal it."

I breathe out in a rush. The back of my neck is prickling inexplicably. "I'll follow her tonight. Come, but stay back where she can't see you."

*

"Following her" is much easier said than done, especially when you're carrying a guitar *and* a massive cello and she moves like a wraith in the night.

I catch up to her, panting and dizzy, at the chicken coop of the farm. "Josi," I gasp.

"Relax."

I realize she stopped to wait for me and thank god for small mercies. "How'd you know I was following?"

"You're no spy, Dave Townsend, let's just say that."

There's a silence.

Limerence

"Come on then. Are you gonna try and convince me to play or will I send you back before you can bother?"

"I'll bother." I hand her the cello and bow and she takes them reluctantly. "I still can't believe my brother built something so beautiful."

"Why can't you believe that?"

"He was only ever good at pulling things apart."

"That was a long time ago. You should give him more credit." There's definitely a bristle of protectiveness in her voice.

"I'll reserve judgment until you show me how it sounds. I'd bet money he cut corners somewhere."

She laughs softly at my poor attempt at manipulation.

I spread my hands. "Listen. Here's the truth. I play, and stuff happens inside me that I thought would never happen again. I need help to explore that. You said once that we all need to *know*. Well, this is what I need to know."

It's not the truth, as it happens. But Luke needs this. And I'm better at manipulation than I've let on.

She searches my face and sees only honesty, so with a sigh she strides up the hill and plonks herself on a stray log. She tunes her cello and plays a few practice notes. I can already hear in them her skill.

"What do you want to play?"

"Anything."

"No, not anything," Josi corrects impatiently. She's pissed off – I can feel it in waves. "Tell me which pieces you like and I'll tell you which I know."

"We could just make something up?"

"You want to *jam*?" she snorts. "Fine, go ahead."

I start plucking at my guitar, slow and gentle. I'm not sure what's about to come out but I was always better at letting my fingers do what they want. Luke told me about Elgar, and I remember it perfectly, having played it just about every day for a year, but I'm not going to bring that out too soon. She'll spook if I don't ease her in gently.

As I pluck the melody Josi lifts her bow and plays long, simple notes beneath it, filling out the sound until it swells over the quiet hills.

We play like this for the next few hours. Somewhere behind us Luke is probably listening. And I'd even go as far as to say Josi's enjoying it.

Eventually weariness hits and I stop. "Thank you."

She doesn't reply and I realize she's struggling with words. "Don't … tell Luke about this."

"Why not?"

"Because he'll think it means something it doesn't."

"Like what?"

"Really, Dave? You're cured, not obtuse."

I smile. "Just wondered if you'd say it."

"Will you take this back for me?"

I take the cello from her.

"He thinks it makes me vulnerable," she admits suddenly.

"And doesn't it?"

"It used to." What goes unsaid is obvious: it used to, but now nothing does.

I am more determined than ever to keep an eye on her. Luke's got love blinkers on, but I'm entirely free of those. I'm smooth, round wood without a single blemish, and as such I might be the one person who can truly see what a threat Josephine Luquet has become.

*

Luke

In the end I don't follow Dave and Josi. She needs her own space, and listening to her play without being invited seems like a betrayal. Instead I go to sleep and dream of Josi's most brutal words – *the thing we shared isn't inside me anymore.* The dream shifts, abstractly, to Jean Gueye's face through the kitchen window, interviewing Mom about fifteen-year-old me. And then moves finally into something else entirely, something sticky with remembered violence, with the cold clinical deaths I've long since compartmentalized.

I wake in a cold sweat to my brother's face. "Easy," he says. "It's alright. You were dreaming."

I sit up and wipe my brow. "Jesus." My heart won't slow. I can't stop my thoughts and suddenly I can't keep lying here without an answer to a question I've never been brave enough to ask.

I fling myself off the crappy mattress and walk over the freezing concrete to where my parents sleep.

"Mom," I whisper in the dark. "Mom."

She wakes with a lurch and grabs onto me. "Luke?"

"Why did you let them take me?" My voice cracks.

"What?"

"You okay, Lukey?" Dad asks, waking too.

Dave has followed me and stands in the opening.

"*Why did you let them take me?*"

"Who?"

"The Bloods! Jean fucking Gueye! Why would you give your child to those monsters and let them turn him into one?"

"Luke, it was better for you—" Mom tries.

"You have no idea, do you? What they made me do? The only way you can become a full Blood is by murdering people!

They make you *kill*, Mom. And they make you do it until it means nothing to you."

She lifts a hand to cover her mouth but there's a vacant look in her eyes. At least she's not laughing, I guess. I stand and pace away from them.

"Luke—" Dad starts but I shake my head.

"No, don't. I just need to know why. Because when you sent me into that cold prison you took me away from my brother, and I wasn't there to protect him. And maybe if I had been I wouldn't wake in the dark to a stranger I hardly recognize!"

Nobody says anything, they all just stare at me. The silence is unbearable. They never would have watched me suffer like this without either scolding me for the fuss or comforting me for the pain. This silence is a reminder of the flesh missing from the skeleton.

"Somebody answer me, please," I beg. I spin to face Dave. "Say something!"

He remains silent and expressionless.

I stride to him and shove him hard in the chest. "Say something, you goddamn robot!"

"Enough," Dad pleads. "Take a breath, boy."

I slam my eyes shut in fury but try to breathe, try to calm down. They don't speak, just wait for me to become more like them, more contained. As the anger trickles away it leaves space for a terrible sadness that is so much worse.

"I can't stand this emptiness," I whisper. "You're all ghosts. I have a family of ghosts."

I leave and they don't try to stop me.

I search the tunnels for something. I know Josi won't be down here, but I keep searching anyway, not sure what the hell I'm looking for. Someone. Something. *Anything*.

What I find is Shadow.

He's alone in the arena, watching something on the projector. I move closer in the dark to see that it's an old news report. He's done this a lot lately, but I've never joined him. The reporter's soothing voice drifts into the silo.

The Prime Minister himself has issued a statement saying the best doctors in the city could do nothing to stem the onslaught of the particularly bad strain that took the life of his beloved wife. Olivia Shay, only nineteen when she married the minister, was taken far too young by the violence of this unidentifiable disease. Only compounding the senseless tragedy is the death of her infant child. Prime Minister Shay begs his citizens to vote yes on Proposition 42, the mandatory vaccination of all children under the age of twelve. He also promises further scientific progress on the matter of all infection, stating there may be a future in which disease doesn't exist. The leader of the opposition has spoken out to hail this as science fiction, and by no means something the public should hope for.

Shadow looks at me in the eerie light from the projector. "The days when there was an opposition party at all."

"Before they were all assassinated by Bloods."

A picture flashes up on the sheet, a photo of Shay's young wife. She is beautiful and strikingly like Josephine, when you look for the similarities. One part of the news report is true: Olivia was far too young to have died. The rest seems to be a completely bastardized version of events.

"How do you know Josi's yours?" I ask.

"Olivia and I had been together for years before she got pregnant. She was unable to leave Shay but they were estranged."

"Why couldn't she leave?"

"He's a violent monster with an army to protect him." Shadow hesitates, then admits, "I did plan to get her out. It consumed me for years but before I got the chance she was dead. Along with our daughter." He looks me full in the face now. "There's no way Olivia died of the plague. Shay killed her when he discovered her plan to leave him."

"Have you spoken to Josi about this?"

He doesn't reply.

"Have you spoken to her about anything since she got back?"

"She doesn't want to talk."

"Shadow, what the fuck?" I snap, losing patience. "All she cared about was getting you back. She didn't sleep, she hardly ate, she was desperate at the thought of you suffering. And what have you fucking done? Huh? Ignored her?"

"I was out there every day, searching the plains for her."

"And yet you can't even talk to her now. Grow a spine, mate. She's your daughter and she's drowning and you're doing nothing to help her."

He doesn't reply, surprise surprise.

"We don't get much anymore, but we get each other," I say. I look him up and down and can't help the disgust that fills my voice. "You're not even cured."

I turn and walk across the big silo.

"You're all twisted up, kid," he says, not bothering to raise his voice. "Come and have a spar. Settle down."

"I don't have the stomach for it tonight," I reply. "I don't have the stomach for you."

I don't know where to go after that. I can't face my bed without Josephine, and everywhere else down here seems suddenly so oppressive I might suffocate in my sleep. So I walk to the cliff, and I climb down even though it's dangerous with a hand I can't rely on, one that hurts so bad by the time I get to the bottom that I think I might pass out. I walk onto the sand and straight to the water, wading out and out in the dark. There's a moon above, but it's a baby and hardly sheds any light.

I don't know what I'm fighting for anymore. Ghosts who'll never come back to life. People who don't care that they're able to feel. A loveless, childless future.

I suppose there's one thing I can rely on. Killing the man who's responsible for all of this will feel good.

*

April 5th, 2068

Dave

I'm in a group returning from the farm when it happens. We've just climbed down into the first tunnel. Josi and Zach are up ahead with a group of kids. Luke and Will are bringing up the rear, and not one of them is paying attention. They've spent too much time in these tunnels without anything happening and they've forgotten. Not intellectually, but physically. They've forgotten inside their guts how dangerous the belly of the world is. But I haven't – I can't seem to think about much else.

So it's me who's uncomfortable when Lawrence plays his usual game of "poke the sleeping bear". Except he's not poking sleeping bears, he's poking very much awake cannibals. The rest of us pass the Fury gate with nothing more than a few loathsome glances their way, but Lawrence hangs back to tease them. He lives deep in the delusion of his own invincibility: the privilege and curse of the young.

I pause, watching him. I'm nervous, so I catalog it. There seem to be a lot of Furies today, and they grow more and more savage the longer he stands there, prodding at them with his knife.

Luke reaches me and follows my gaze. "Lawrence," he barks. "Get moving, idiot."

"Coming," Lawrence assures him cheerfully, but doesn't come anywhere, and to my consternation Luke continues on without waiting for the kid.

I hesitate, unsure what to do. My hands are vibrating.

"Leave the loser," Henrietta tells me as she walks past, flashing me a beaming smile that could rival a floodlight for intensity. "Lawrence, you muppet," she shouts.

He laughs and gives a last stab.

But it seems today is the day he learns what comes after pride.

The gate gives a lurching creak. I freeze.

The world *slooo o o o o o o o o o o o o o o o o o o o o-o ows*.

Dreamlike, I watch.

As the volume of bodies behind the iron gate becomes too much for the hinges, even fortified as they are. As the gate slams down on top of Lawrence and the Furies flood over him, trying to reach him through the metal. I listen as the boy screams under the crushing hungry weight.

I'm closer than the others, but I don't move.

It's Henrietta who flashes past me, her blond hair streaking out like a horse's tail. It glitters, almost. She has a knife but it's too small for the number of opponents. Still she attacks them, trying to force them off the gate. Luke and Will blaze past, weapons raised. The others barrel into the fray too, hacking and slashing at Furies in a throbbing bleeding mess.

I see Josi cleave a machete through a head, despite her pact, despite everything. I watch Luke drag Lawrence out from under the gate and fling the smaller boy over his shoulder. He is a ragdoll to my brother's mighty form, the one forcing its way out through the hungry snarling bodies as the others try to make a path for them. But Henrietta is too deep. I can see her in there, a flash of her face here, a flicker of her hair there, obstructed by the pale veined shapes of monsters. A sound is drawn from my mouth – do the others know she can't get free? They're all falling back now, unaware.

All except Will. I watch the boy plunge through, teeth and nails tearing at him as he fights his way to the girl. I lose sight of him in the madness – Luke is sprinting past with an unconscious Lawrence and shouts at me to run – but after a few seconds I see Will surge back into view, this time dragging Hen beneath his body so the Furies won't reach her. I don't hear it but I can see his blood-drenched face cry out in pain and fury and the fight of it all and he isn't stopping, he won't stop, I can see it in his body as he *drags* her through.

I slam my eyes shut.

I don't feel stress. I solve problems.

So where is the solution to this problem? Why am I not finding it? Or even *searching* for it? Why am I standing here, stolen away by the sudden alarming existence of beauty within this horror?

Around me the noise is a screech of violent music. Voices raised in fear and pain and hunger and rage rage *rage*. Metal grating on concrete. The thunder of footsteps and heartbeats and blood in my ears. The throbbing swell of it all, like the crescendo of a movement, like all the instruments in the world have come to join the trembling rise.

Open your eyes. Open them.

I open my eyes. Josi is there now, fighting to reach Will, and I give a choked gasp of relief (swiftly cataloged) before I see the ocean of limbs crash upon her and force her under.

Gunshots ring out, cutting through the cacophony as nothing else can. They are so swift they must be coming from an automatic weapon. Which means … Yes, there's Shadow – he's the only one who carries a machine gun. He's on the other side of it all, having just come in from the farm, and he's hailing bullets into the mess. Bodies drop, reduced to the meat they are. Josi surges free – she's lost her machete but now carries dual knives. They twirl and slice with a life of their own, a dance of their own, and oh, how she moves, how she moves through it all to reach Will and help him drag Henrietta free.

"Shadow! Go back up!" Josi shouts, but I see the older man remain where he is, firing and reloading and firing and reloading. How many of the creatures are there? From which bowel of hell have they crawled?

"Dave! Get moving!" Will roars as he tears past. Henrietta is lolling woozily between him and Josi, who grabs me by the wrist and wrenches me along with them. My feet kick slowly into action, moving as if underwater. I'm humiliated by whatever it is that I am; the feel and stench of it is hot.

I'm unable to keep up but Josi turns back often, cutting down any of the beasts that get too close and then tugging me along. We make it to another gate and slam it shut behind us, blocking off any access to the farm. The Furies surge at the gate and I think for a terrifying moment that they will break through this one too, I'm sure of it. The hinges will creak the same, the metal will fall the same, the monsters will flood the same.

"Dave!" Josi shouts near my ear. The suddenness of the sound catches hold of my attention and I remember to run.

I'm not sure how long it takes us to get home. I've stopped marking the passing of time in this dream, this nightmare. Gates shut behind us, all of them seeming so flimsy to me now, so pitiable. What is metal and fusion when faced with the unquenchable rage of humanity?

The infirmary appears suddenly: I've forgotten where we're running, or why.

I watch Josi and Will place Henrietta gently on a bed. Luke is already here with Lawrence, bidding Zach to hurry. All look wan with fatigue but in my eyes there is a glow to their skin, a glow made entirely of the spirits inside them, the wailing courage of the impossible battle they fight against mortality.

I move toward them and see that Zachariah is fitting a drip into Lawrence's vein. The boy's chest looks ... caved in. I reel back in shock, involuntarily lifting a hand to cover my mouth. Somehow he's still awake through the mess of his body.

"You better bloody well fix this," he says to Zach.

"Shut your mouth," Zach snaps. "It's what got you into this mess in the first place, idiot."

"I'm not ready to go," Lawrence says, looking at Luke now.

Luke reaches for his hand. "You're not going anywhere, mate."

"Good, because I'm not ready. Is Hen okay?"

"She's fine."

We see the moment the morphine or whatever it is hits him because he goes droopy and delirious. "Do you want to know a secret?"

"Sure, mate."

"I love it down here. Everyone hates it but I love it because a place isn't home unless it's filled with people to love and that's us, you know? I really fucking love you all.

There's a roof to the world and you found a way to break it open and now we're all flying ... We're flying ..." He loses consciousness.

"That shut him up," Zach mutters, but I can hear the tremor in his voice, see the sheen in my brother's eyes. I, too, feel something at the boy's carelessly generous words. I feel ... something. But as I try to catalog it I realize I haven't the faintest hope of identifying it. Josi is here now and I think she might feel it too. She's watching Lawrence very closely. As though she has recognized the words, or the opening in the sky described by a delirious boy.

"What have you gotta do, man?" Luke asks Zach.

"I can't see anything without an X-ray or a CT so I have to open him up and repair any of the organs that got crushed and reset the broken bones. This level of bruising has to mean internal bleeding."

"Yeah, plus his chest is, like, angling the wrong way."

"Yeah, plus that."

"Well, get to it then."

"I *am*!" Zach hisses. "Back off, Townsend!"

Luke raises his hands and quickly moves back.

"Take a breath," Josi orders Zach and I watch him do so.

"I can do this," he says to himself. "This is something that I can do." He takes another breath and then uses a scalpel to open Lawrence's chest. Blood spurts and trickles. What remains of the chest plate must be pulled open so he can reach inside and feel through the gruesome meat to find what's wrong. The sight makes me lightheaded.

That's when we hear, "Help!" and spin to see that Henrietta is pointing at Will's unconscious body on the ground.

"Will!" Josi flings herself to the floor beside him. She shakes him but he doesn't wake.

Luke scoops him up and places him on a third bed. "He's not breathing and I can't feel a pulse."

"Start CPR," Zach orders with his hands wrist deep in another boy's chest cavity. "I'm tied up here."

"Where the fuck is Claire?" Josi roars. "Dave – get your mother!"

I am disoriented as I watch Luke pump Will's chest. Josi leans to breathe air into his blue lips. He looks like a wax figure. A doll made to resemble a boy. Something has gone from him. But still they work.

Luke's putting his whole body into pumping. I realize with a start that he's looking straight at me as he does so. His eyes are calm and I think: this is his superpower. Being able to find true calm, not the manufactured kind. Facing disaster with his steel green eyes and shaping it to his will.

"Dave," he says. "Pinch the inside of your wrist as hard as you can."

I don't understand but I do as he says. It's all so dreamlike. Who am I to deny him anything?

The pain is sudden and sharpens everything in my mind to a knife-edge.

"Go get Mom."

And I'm running.

*

Josephine

I breathe all of my will into his lips, all of my fury and determination and I think to him, to the universe, *I will not let this happen.* You are not dying, Will.

To Luke I say, "Not Will."

He nods once, still pumping hard and fast and calm. "We're not getting anything from him, Zach."

"Whack him on the chest."

"I thought you weren't meant to do that because of the ribs—"

"Broken ribs are better than being dead. *Whack him hard*!"

Luke balls his fist and slams it into Will's heart.

"Again!"

He does it again, and as I hold my breath Will takes one.

I clutch at my heart.

"He's not out of the woods," Zach warns us. "Monitor his breathing and pulse. He could slip away at any moment. How are you doing, Henrietta?"

"Fine," she says through the tears that are making steady tracks down her face. "Help them."

Dave careens back in with Claire in tow. She takes in the scene and comes to help us with Will. "Step back now, love," she tells me. "It's alright, he'll be alright."

But I have a terrible feeling as I step back and let her take over. I have this sick dread in my guts that someone is dying tonight. That Will is dying. And I'm not sure I'll survive it.

*

Claire's assistants arrive to help and Luke and I are sent outside to wait. We pace the tunnel for a few minutes and then I've had enough. I stride away from him with my mind awhirl at the realization that I can't get out of here – I can't leave through any of the safe tunnels, as they're now filled with Furies and if I open them I don't know if I'll be able to get them closed again. I don't know where to go. I can't handle the walls as I careen down the steps to the south

Fury gate. I fling myself at the metal, clutching at it as though I can press myself through it and into them. It occurs to me that I can, really, and so I unlock the gate, open it a crack and step through into their midst. They're not my Furies, but they know me just as the others did. They smell me; I smell as they do. Their bodies brush mine and I feel their warmth and it helps a little with the squeezing roof. It helps with the broken heart, as it's always done.

I stay with them a long time, listening to the sounds of their breathing and pleading with my pulse to calm and pleading with whatever forces choose our death to leave Will and Lawrence a little longer, just leave them to our care a little longer. We'll protect them better, I promise.

It's Dave who finds me in the end. The Furies smell him and surge hungrily for the cage. I am pressed in with them and at first he doesn't see. But when his eyes alight on me in their midst I see a look of vindication flood him.

He doesn't say anything about the Furies. He says, "Zach wanted me to come and tell you. He slipped away."

*

Dave

I knew there was something wrong with her but I never imagined this. I follow her again, unsure what else to do. I can't get the image of her standing among their bloody eyes and bloody teeth from my mind. Her beauty within their ugliness is a haunting thing seared into my eyelids; I'm not sure I'll ever leave the sight behind.

She moves as though looking for something, tearing through the tunnels in a haze of grief. She goes to her old bedroom but finds nothing there, and that's when I realize what she's looking for.

She finds him in the dining hall, looking at Will's wedding painting. I stop at the door and peer in, something sick forcing me to stay. I've become a voyeur of other people's lives. She makes a sound and he turns from the mural to see her. Then they're crossing the space and connecting fiercely. Their bodies melt and fuse; they unfurl like time-lapse footage of flowers blooming and vines twining intrinsically together. They are glorious and destructive: I can see the evidence of it in the way they clutch at each other, trembling and desperate and fearful of what this will reap. They are the figures in the painting, dissolving into one another, dissolving from two people into one.

I watch for far too long, my body and thoughts on pause. I search their seeking bodies as I search my own heart. And what I find makes me turn from their love, ashen.

My feet take me to my father. He is alone in the workshop, even so late at night. He's whittling something small, his hands having found a rare moment of peace from the tremors. He looks up at me. Rises to his feet.

I am blank. Everything about me is blank.

"I'm a useless human being," I say with perfect clarity.

"Dave—"

"Maybe if I'd helped he might not have died but I didn't. There's no purpose for me. I have no ability to do anything. I have no skills that will benefit anyone. My brain doesn't even function with clarity – not when it's supposed to. I can't offer anyone love or affection, I can't grieve what's lost. I can't feel the beauty I see everywhere. So why am I here, Dad? Why did they make me into this?"

There are tears in his eyes but he doesn't know what to say.

"What will be left if they do this to us all?"

"I don't know, my boy." His voice cracks. "That's why we fight, to make sure we never know."

But it's too late for fighting. It's too late for any of that. They don't understand and it's not their fault, but they are ants beneath Shay's foot and when he decides to take a single step they will be ground into the earth and this time there will be no crawling free of it.

Chapter 23

April 5th, 2068

Josephine

Luke and I put our clothes back on slowly. There's a persistent tugging at the base of my heart. I don't have space for it, I need to be focused, I can't be falling apart. So I think of the north. I think of Medusa and Astro Boy and Washington. I think of Intirri and know I have to get to her.

"Don't go," Luke pleads softly.

"I have to find a way out," I explain as gently as I'm able. The long dining tunnel has been getting smaller and smaller since we untangled our bodies.

He sits on the edge of the table, feet on a chair. Rubs his face wearily and then silently watches me buttoning my shirt.

"Sorry," I say. Sorry I let this happen again, sorry I have to leave you again.

"Will you come and see him with me first?"

I shake my head.

"You won't even say goodbye."

"He's gone. He wouldn't hear it."

I turn with the feel of Luke still on my lips, the taste of him on my tongue. I have a long run ahead of me if I'm to make it out of these tunnels tonight.

*

Luke

I watch her leave me with nothing but the tingle of her ghost fingers on my body. Each time I think she's circling back in to me she reveals how very far away she really is. So I go to the infirmary by myself. And find Zachariah sitting with his head in his hands.

I feel no pity for him. Instead there is only cruel resentment. It isn't his fault. I know that, of course. He's a boy. Barely more than a child, and yes, he's capable of amazing things but no, he's not a doctor, not a real one. He can't be blamed for this, because in this he was more than anyone else could have been, more even than anyone could have asked him to be. And still I hate him a little for not saving this life.

I cross to the corpse and sit beside it. It still looks like him, only now something catastrophic has been lost. Henrietta's crying is the only sound I can hear as I sink into the chair and take the boy's hand and bring it to my cheek.

I'm not ready to go.

I wasn't ready for you to go either, Lawrence. I could never be ready for that.

A spark has gone out, I will say in the morning when they all come to hear an explanation for this unforgivable loss. His laughter held us together. His unquenchable spirit kept our hopes alive. He was one of a kind and we will be so much less for the loss of him. That's what I'll say.

For now I sit with him until I can't stand the sight of his broken chest and then I go to the lab and tell Dodge that I want the gas ready to be dispersed tomorrow night. I don't care anymore that Josi wants them alive, because she left me here to deal with this and so I'll deal with it the only way I know how. Rage swells in my heart, eclipsing all else. I'll kill the fuckers and not lose a wink of sleep over it.

*

April 6th, 2068

Josephine

I wake to discover that a heavy gray fog has blanketed the world. The grass I've slept on is moist and my body trembles with cold. I give a quick whistle and wait for Intirri to emerge from the gray world, wings spread to land on my arm. She holds me with a gentle grip so her talons don't gouge my skin.

I stroke her gently, soothing her unease in the fog. We're a long way from the farm or the resistance tunnels – this was my only way free of the ground, and it's a little too close to the wall for comfort. The fog, at least, protects us from being seen.

"What do you think?" I ask her. "Time to go back?"

Her wings rustle.

"I know. I don't want to go either." I close my eyes and rest my forehead gently against her soft chest plumage. "It'll go quickly now. Luke will want to set the gas. I might not make it back out tonight."

I look at her dark eyes. "Will you wait for me?"

We hear it at the same time. Footfall nearby.

I turn to face it and wait, wondering who managed to follow me from the tunnels without being detected. But what I see in the fog are the shapes of two people I don't know. Hikers traipsing through the hills with walking poles and wind jackets. A young man and woman, likely a couple.

They stop the second they see me, standing in the fog with my falcon. Their mouths fall open and fear strikes. It must be how I look – wild and dirty and gruesomely scarred.

I throw Intirri into the air and she explodes up and away into the fog.

"Run," the man tells his partner softly.

"There's no need to run," I say.

But the girl is already running.

"How do you have a bird?" he asks me.

The wound on my throat throbs as I watch her run and I know. I know.

"Tell her to come back," I instruct him, "Or you both die."

"How do you have a bird?" he asks again, blank.

"Come back or your boyfriend dies," I call. I wait a few minutes and then hear the sounds of her return. They stand together, awaiting my decision. It's a strange feeling of power. I didn't think I looked scary enough to illicit this much obedience. Maybe it's not just how I look, but how I sound and smell. Whatever scent they've unconsciously picked up from me has triggered their amygdalae and their bodies are screaming at the approaching threat.

"I'm sorry," I say.

And I really, truly am, much more than I can say. It's a brutal world. And the animal is free.

*

Luke finds me dragging them into the marshes. I don't realize he's there until the girl's face has sunk below and I turn to see the horrified expression of my husband. He doesn't say anything. His eyes are doing something to me that I shouldn't have to endure.

"They saw Intirri."

"You chose a bird over the lives of two humans?"

"Yes."

The set of his jaw turns rigid. We walk silently back over the hills toward the tunnel opening. It will take hours to follow the massive detour around the Furies; I'm not sure how much of this screaming silence I can endure.

"They would have sent the Bloods here. The hills would be crawling and soon they'd work out that they have to look underground."

He doesn't reply so I stop trying to explain myself. Heavy hatred hangs in me, but it's been there a long time now.

Just get through this. Get through the end of this fight and then you can leave or die or whatever you need to do to make the shame end.

*

Luke makes an announcement about Lawrence. It breaks something in everyone, destroys something in the kids. Angry and fearful, they demand something be done and Luke being Luke – the solver of every problem, the winner of hearts – he offers them the perfect answer: an end to the monsters who did this.

He announces our evacuation from the tunnels tonight. We have nowhere to go but up to the hills and marshes I slept in last night, the ones that would now be crawling with

Bloods had I not made the choice I did. He asks them to pack warm clothes and blankets and drinking water only. It'll be safe to return in the morning, when we'll have the service for Lawrence, and then move into preparation for the attack on the Blood base tomorrow night.

There's a lot of commotion when they hear that – they don't understand why it needs to be so soon, so rushed, but they don't realize we've been preparing for this for months.

When they've dispersed to grieve and pack, Luke gives a terse nod for me to follow him. Dave comes with us, offering me a hesitant smile I'm sure is meant to be comforting but isn't. It isn't anything.

In the tech room I almost have a heart attack. Waiting for us there is Lawrence, laughing and giving us the finger.

It takes me far too long to realize it's a holo, and Teddy is under the desk drinking stolen whisky and weeping over the sight of it.

Luke crawls under, drags Teddy out and wraps his arms around the boy. The four of us watch the holo footage together. Lawrence is acting out the scene from *Psycho* we've now all seen a million times. He gets completely undressed and we have to watch his bare ass as he pretends to shower in a very feminine way and then shrieks to feel an invisible knife stabbing him. We're all laughing as he gets entangled in the invisible shower curtain, crashes to the invisible bath and lies still for a ridiculously long time. He finally explodes into a bow, sending kisses to his audience.

"You are such a loser," Alo's voice tells him from off-screen.

"Au contraire, amigo. I'm a winner."

"Can we see less of the winner, please?" Hen asks, arriving with a towel to wrap around his waist.

"You're right," he grins. "The goods are all yours, Hen. Wouldn't want to share 'em with the undeserving masses."

The holo ends. There is a long, empty silence.

"What a fucking joke," Teddy mumbles into the dark tech room. "Sixteen years old. Sixteen fucking years."

Luke takes the whisky away from the boy and indulges in a mighty swig himself. He passes it to Dave, who passes it to me. I put it down without bothering. No time to be dulling the edges of this nightmare, time only to sink so deep we might yet make it out the other side.

"I need you to pull it together, Teddy boy. We need you more than ever."

Teddy looks not back at Luke but at me. His glasses are askew, his eyes dull. "My friends keep dying. I'd rather they stopped."

I nod.

It seems to be enough for him because he pulls himself up, with help from Luke, and turns to the screen. "I have something for you. Was gonna show you this morning but then everything went to shit. Yet again."

"Good boy. What have you got?"

"I can send out a signal that will disrupt all the Blood comms simultaneously. Protocol when one goes down is for that agent to immediately return to base so they can be fitted with a new device. If it happens to all of them at once, they'll automatically go back to base without knowing that the others are, too. See what I mean?"

"It's nice, kid," Luke says appreciatively. "Simple and straightforward. And shaking up their comms won't hurt us for the attack, either. When can you do this?"

He slumps in his chair listlessly. "I dunno."

"We'll get you some coffee and sober you up. We need it ready by this evening, before we evac."

Teddy sighs. Nods.

"What if they just switch the frequencies over?" I ask.

"This'll disrupt all of them. I forgot to say that bit, didn't I? Probably gonna be a problem for us too."

"It'll shut ours off as well?" Luke asks. "How?"

"It's a bit like an EMP but instead of taking out all power it'll hit all the radio frequencies, even the protected ones we use."

"So we'll have complete radio silence. For how long?"

"Depends how fast they can get it back up." He shrugs. "Couple of hours. Maybe less."

"Think you can work with that?" I ask Luke.

He frowns and walks straight out, lost in thought and too angry with me to answer.

Something's bothering Dave. "You'll be with us, right?" he asks me.

I make sure to meet his eyes as I nod. That's how you lie.

*

Dave

I'm making a habit of following Josephine Luquet. At first, yes, it was my own rather pathetic curiosity but now I intend to make sure she doesn't stuff anything up or get in Luke's way. *Surely* this is something I can be capable of. Surely in this small way I can help my brother.

I keep as silent as humanly possible. I half expect her to hear me anyway – she seems to have a supernatural set of ears on her – but she keeps moving and doesn't look my way once. I'm uncomfortable; after all, I really like the girl, and it's no secret how much my brother loves her. But sure enough, she leads me to Dodge's little makeshift laboratory. In silence I watch her pile the gas canisters into her pack and climb out of the tunnel.

Caught redhanded.

My stomach sinks. I was really hoping to be wrong.

*

My brother, of course, doesn't believe me. I mean, I'm sure he does believe me, but he goes through the motions of arguing, defending, denying and then checking the lab himself, where Dodge miserably admits to having left the canisters unguarded.

Luke doesn't say a word, but I follow him around like a little puppy as he searches for his wife. We find Zach in the infirmary tending to a recovering Will and they both deny having seen her. Shadow is cleaning guns in the armory and hasn't seen her. Pace is changing Hal and hasn't seen her. And all the while we search I can feel my brother's anger rising. It's like a physical sensation on my skin, a palpable prickling. He's about to lose it.

"I'm here," her voice eventually sounds from up ahead. She's sitting on the middle rung of the ladder that goes down to the water treatment tunnel.

Luke and I stop before her.

"Tell me you didn't," he says.

She doesn't look happy or smug, she just looks calm. "I did. I'm sorry."

"How did you get rid of it?" I ask.

"Water stops gas from diffusing into air particles, so I dropped them straight into the run-off stream. It's toast."

"Do you have any idea …?" I ask, then realize that of course she does.

Luke hasn't said anything, but that bristling prickling sensation is getting worse.

"How are we meant to get out of here to make the attack?" I ask, since by the looks of him my brother is gearing up to something pretty high on the Richter scale.

"I'll program the train. You can take it straight to the subway beneath the base."

My eyebrows arch – I didn't even know we had a train.

We wait for Luke to respond to this, but he doesn't. He just stares at her, looking lost. "I don't know who you are anymore. You're out of control."

She jumps to the ground and nods. "Fair enough. Do what you have to."

I'm lost. I follow them both back to the arena, wondering what's going on. Luke retrieves something from the armory along the way. When Josi sees what it is she goes apeshit.

A set of handcuffs.

"Are you kidding me?" she snaps. "There's no way you're getting those on me. I have stuff to do."

He approaches her. I watch in astonishment as she moves into a fighting stance. "Punish me however else you want but you're not locking me in here. *You can't.*"

"Don't fight me. I'm not in the mood."

"Like hell I won't fight you, condescending asshole."

He rushes her at the same time she dives. I scramble out of the way of the fight erupting. Josi's fist swings by Luke's head as he ducks sideways and goes for her guts with a jab. She curls inwards to take the weight from the hit and then twists away.

There are people trickling into the silo now, assuming this is a training spar.

"Nice, haven't seen this in a while," Blue exclaims happily.

"Block the door!" Luke grunts.

Those watching are confused, but do as he says.

He kicks her feet out from under her and she hits the ground hard. Luke's weight comes down on top of her but she manages to get a knee into his groin and roll free. Their fists are a blur now, hitting and blocking with incredible speed. Josi has only one advantage and that's the fact that Luke isn't trying to hurt her, simply contain her long enough to get the cuffs on. She sprints for the door but he dives for her arm and tightens his iron grip. The momentum carries her back around and she uses it to send a heavy kick into Luke's shoulder. He grunts in pain but keeps hold of her and starts dragging her to the side. There's an exercise bar soldered to the wall – that's what he'll be going for, as it'll be impossible for her to escape.

"What's going on?" I hear someone ask worriedly.

"Ease up, Luke!"

"They're not training, dumbass."

Josi struggles wildly but he's so much stronger than she is. He has his arms completely around her middle, binding her arms to her body while he drags her.

So she does the only thing she can – she turns her face and bites down on his shoulder so hard that I see blood spurt.

Jesus Christ.

"Chill out, Josi!" I hear him snarl. "This is happening no matter how badly you hurt me."

Her elbow finds enough room to hit him hard in the ribs and then she uses the slight loss in pressure to wriggle down and out of his hold, sending the same elbow into his solar plexus. With a spinning twist she dashes for the door but he catches up and flattens her.

"Someone wanna give me a hand here?" he roars, using his whole body weight to keep her flattened.

"How could you?" she gasps.

"How could *you*?" he yells into her face. "How could you not see the danger you've put us in? It's unforgivable!"

By this point Blue and Eric are there to help contain and drag her over to the bar. Luke cuffs her hand to it and they all step back.

She flashes such a filthy look at Eric that I see him shrink into the ground. "What's going on?" he asks guiltily. They're obviously friends.

"Let her go!" Pace has arrived. She storms over in a fury, metal glinting in her face. "Take those things off her *now*, Luke."

There are a lot of calls of agreement.

Josi sinks to the floor, crossing her legs and letting her cuffed wrist dangle against the metal.

Luke turns to the crowd that has formed. He opens his mouth and closes it again, has absolutely no idea what to say. I'm sure he'd much rather keep them from thinking the worst about her.

So I do it for him. "I caught Josi destroying the gas. There's no longer a way to kill the Furies."

"Bullshit," Pace snaps amid the panicked chatter. "No way we're believing a drone over Dual."

"It's true," Josi says softly. "I did."

There's a horrified silence.

"*Why?*" Pace whispers.

"I told you I would. I'll say it again: you want to kill them, you go through me."

A wall of sound hits. This is clearly the last thing they ever expected her to say, not Josi, the one who's fought the hardest to get them free of the monsters and kept them held at bay so long. It doesn't make any sense. I can hear a girl crying somewhere. The anger is rising to shouts and arguments.

A scuffle has broken out and Luke pushes through to reveal the rough wrestling of several boys. No, not wrestling. There are two of them trying to hurt a third.

Luke wrenches Coin and Alo off their quarry and I see that it's Zach. He rises, angrily rubbing his split lip. His eyebrow is bleeding too. He's older and bigger than the other two boys, but untrained in combat. He's copped a face full of fist, by the looks of it.

"What the fuck is wrong with you two?" Luke demands.

"Get off!" Alo snarls, struggling wildly.

"He did it on purpose! He hated him!" Coin exclaims.

"Did *what* on purpose?"

"Let Lawrence die!"

Zach doesn't say anything, simply looks pale as the accusation lands.

"He's probably in on this crazy shit with Josi," Alo adds. "She didn't lose it until he got here. Cuff him too."

"Zach hasn't done anything wrong," Luke says, though it seems to pain him to do so. "No more fighting. Go cool off."

He releases Coin and Alo, who both spit on Zach before striding out of the silo.

"You can go cool off too," Luke tells Zach.

"I'm plenty cool."

"*Go.*"

The boy looks ready to argue bloody murder, but catches sight of someone in the crowd. I follow his gaze to see that Josi has swung up onto the bar and sits there now, shaking her head at Zach.

He holds his tongue and heads for the exit.

I am stunned to see people spitting on him as he passes, so many people, more than I ever would have imagined. Sane, smart, kind people. *Adults*. Their hatred of him is so unfounded. Not one of them witnessed his heroic efforts to save Lawrence last night, none of them saw the way he fought tooth and nail for the boy's life, on and on and on for hours. They have no idea. They just spit because it feels better to hate the prime minister's son.

"Don't," Luke tells them. "Don't start acting like savages now. He's a boy."

When Zach is gone I watch my brother look around. I can see a million thoughts chasing their way through his green, broken eyes. This is a lot to deal with for one person. I wish I could help him somehow, even just to bear the brunt of the betrayal of the person he loves most. But I can't, I don't know how.

"Obviously we won't be evacuating anymore," he says. "Therefore I'll be moving the operation to tomorrow morning. Anyone I've previously spoken to will report at six a.m. in the dining hall where I'll give you your orders. Everyone else is to go about your normal routines. I'll have a new roster made up to cover the shifts of the thirty who'll be above ground. I'm leaving Josi here for the moment until we work out what to do about her actions. This will happen together, after proper discussion, and not before. No one will come here during her incarceration, except to deliver food and clothing and anything else she needs. I'll be posting guards to ensure this. Understood?"

He's trying to protect her from their anger, obviously. But I think he's also probably trying to ensure she doesn't elicit help to escape.

"Clear out."

They all trickle out with varying degrees of reluctance. I can still hear crying – it must be frightening to think their two leaders have turned on each other. And with such terrible timing, too.

When they've gone it's just Luke, Pace and me. And Josi.

"Pace," Luke warns.

"You can shove your orders up your ass. I'm not leaving her."

"That's exactly why you have to go – I can't risk you letting her free."

"How?" she demands. "With my superpower strength? I don't have the key, Einstein."

"Pace, it's fine, just go," Josi tells her.

"Like hell—"

"I don't want you here."

Pace looks as though she's been hit. Her mouth opens but nothing comes out. Her shoulders sag a little and she spins on her heel, leaves without another word.

The three of us remaining are quiet. I have no idea what to say, and think I should probably leave too, but before I get the chance Luke is speaking.

"Until we get back," he tells Josi softly. "'Cause I got no clue how you're planning to stuff things up next, kid. When I get back we'll talk about what's going on with you, but right now I don't have time for it. You're fine here, so sit tight."

"I'm not fine," she says, very calmly. "You can't leave me inside. The roof."

He is ice cold as he leans in to her face. "You wanted me to be the leader of the new world? Make a new life for our people? For *all* people? Okay. I will. That means keeping threats to our safety detained. So you stay where you are or things are gonna get very ugly."

And he goes, he leaves her there to stare after him in shock.

I stand awkwardly. My eyes catch on the terrible scar around her neck, still sewn through with black, ugly stitches. Why she won't let Claire or Zach remove the stitches is beyond me, but right now I see a drop of blood slide from the wound's very edge.

"You're bleeding," I point out stupidly.

She lifts a hand to carelessly brush the blood away. Then sighs. "Dave. You were right, you got what you wanted, so go."

"I didn't want this."

"You wanted to protect your brother. And for that I'm glad. So keep doing what you're doing."

As our eyes meet I realize this is why she never made any plans to come with us: she knew she would destroy the gas and knew that Luke would have to jail her. Maybe she thought she could get away, but she knew she wouldn't be coming with us to take down the Bloods.

And as I realize the same I can't help feeling a wash of true fear.

I leave and wander the halls. It is quiet as a tomb down here, buried beneath earth and cement. It's a crypt for all those living here, their heartbeats thumping together as one living organism. But organisms aren't meant to live so far beneath the earth, so close to the warm heart of the planet, so far from air and sky. I think it must be turning them a little mad. I saw it tonight in their hatred of a blameless boy. They are meant to be righteous and loving and fighting for what's right, but they're just people, as capable of hatred as any. Probably more so.

*

Here's a secret:
 I am too.

Chapter 24

November 3rd, 2067

Josephine

I'm looking for a vehicle when it happens. We're in another plague-destroyed town, this one along the coast. My plan to turn the Furies south has run into a brick wall. They don't want to go back over that long stretch of dusty plane. Understandably. But my plan isn't done yet – there's another part to it. One that requires a vehicle of some sort. So I'm rooting through garages to find vehicles that a) still run and b) have fuel.

It's late afternoon when I discover the truck. It has an open bed, which is perfect. It also has a full tank of petrol and several extra drums, which is too damn perfect. It has no battery power, but I already have a generator ready for that. I connect the car battery to it and wait for it to recharge itself, and as I'm sitting here in the dusty garage, lost in thought, I'm grabbed from behind.

"Don't move," a voice says. A very human voice.

"Woah, careful," I say quickly. "I'm no threat to you."

He has a knife at my throat. I can feel the blade already breaking the skin of my neck.

"We've been watching you, girl. You're with the zombies."

There are probably many smart things to say in this situation, and none of them are: "They're not zombies." But say this I do. Like a moron.

He snarls something unintelligible. He smells terrible – there's something chemical all over him and I recognize it belatedly as gas. He must be trying to disguise his human smell from the Furies. Smart, I suppose, but it seems like a dangerous game to play, in a world where open flame is now the only heat and light we have. Hey, it's his body.

"You're coming with us."

"How many of you are there? How have you survived out here? Where do you live?"

He tightens the knife and I fall quiet.

Someone else enters the garage by ducking beneath the half-closed roller door. I hear the footsteps, then the female voice. "Hurry up! Bring her!"

But. I have a plan. And even though, yes, a couple of months ago I would have jumped at the thought of being taken captive by humans instead of Furies – at least humans can be reasoned with – I've moved well beyond that point. I don't belong with the humans, after all. And I have a plan.

"I'm not going anywhere with you," I tell them, fingering the small item in my pocket.

"Struggle and we'll kill you. Got no real use for another. Just wanna know how you're surviving the zombies. Happy to use this knife, little girl. So no struggling."

I smile.

My elbow, which he has left disastrously free, goes straight back into his testicles. He yowls in pain and in a moment of pure outrage he carves his knife through my throat.

"Don't!" the woman yells.

But it's done. My throat is slit.

Warm blood spills down the front of me and I choke. My hands scrabble for my neck, seeking to close the gaping hole there. I can't swallow, can hardly breathe, but I don't stop. On the ground now, I pull the lighter from my pocket. With trembling, blood-soaked hands I fumble to roll it, and then hold it to the asshole's body.

He goes up like a bonfire.

The woman shrieks – she's too close to him and alights just as easily.

Gasoline has gotten on me too – I feel flame bite at my cheek and ear, catching in my hair. I crawl away from the burning, wailing, running bodies and try to bat the agonizing fire out while also keep my throat closed. I'm not dead, which means something is still intact. But I'm losing a lot of blood.

And my head ... it's not so straight anymore. It feels melted. Warped.

Sound goes and all I'm left with is the silent flailing of burning limbs. And through the flames and smoke come more figures, a couple of them I recognize.

The sight of her red eyes is the most immense relief I've ever known. Oh, Medusa, I do love you.

*

April 7th, 2068

Josephine

It's very difficult to find a way to sit that doesn't send my arm to sleep. I've worked out that basically when it starts to tingle I have to climb up onto the bar and let the blood flow back down again, before returning my bum to the much more comfortable mats on the floor. It's rather horrid, but not really too bad compared to some of the debacles I've been in.

The main concern, obviously, is my claustrophobia. But I'm trying to develop a means of shutting that out. Such as meditation. Once upon a time it was Luke who taught me how to meditate. Just as he has taught me so many of my skills. It feels like a very long time ago, but wasn't, really. I take a deep breath through my nose and hold it for eight seconds, then let it out through my mouth. I think of nothing but a single object, I hold it in my mind's eye as I count my seconds and breathe as slowly and calmly as I can. Only problem is it's tough to meditate when your arm starts burning from lack of blood every few minutes. Eventually I perch myself on top to try the next round – my bum will probably go dead but I can ignore it more easily.

The image I hold in my mind is Intirri, the shape of her as she soars through the sky. I hope she's alright.

"Hi."

I open my eyes to see Shadow standing below. The guards obviously didn't manage to stop him from getting inside. Good luck to them.

I swing down onto the mats and cross my legs once more. I'd rather he wasn't here, but maybe he'll distract me from the roof.

"Hi."
"Got yourself in a pickle, huh?"
"Guess so."
"Want me to let you out?"
"Nah."
"Got something planned?"
"Yeah."

"Thought as much." He hesitates, then asks, "Can I help?"

I can't keep the smile from the edges of my lips. "You already are."

Shadow sits with his back to the wall. It's the first time I've ever seen him look slightly ill at ease in his body. All the wounds are really stacking up, and there's a stiffness to his movement that was never there before. I realize abruptly that he's in his late fifties, and he's been fighting for his life for the last quarter century. He needs a break from all this madness.

"When this is over," I say warmly, "you're retiring."

But he says, "This will never be over."

It takes all the warmth from my heart. "What are we bothering about then?"

"We're just keeping afloat. That's all there is."

"So why are you here if you don't think we're gonna make an end to it?"

"You."

I rest my head on the corrugated plastic of the silo behind me. I don't know what to say to that.

We sit in silence for a long time. It reminds me of the nights we used to spend together at the Inferno, sitting quietly on the wall or walking the dead forest in silence.

"I think it's time we spoke of your mother."

"No. I don't want to."

"Why?"

"I just don't."

He shakes his head. "Bad luck. We're doing this. She … your mother …" He clears his throat. "She loved you very much."

"Okay. Thank you. That's enough."

"Don't you have questions?"

"I used to. Not anymore."

"She and I met at university. I was her professor."

"Oh, Jesus."

"We fell in love immediately. But she wanted to work in politics, and she'd caught the eye of the leader of the opposition party. He married her within a month of having met her."

"Why? I mean why did she?"

"To this day I can't tell you. In any case I didn't see her for a few years, and then we crossed paths at an art exhibit."

I snort, even though it's not funny.

"She was a sculptor. She called it a hobby, I thought it a calling. Her work was on display and it was beautiful. Transcendent. And sad. I worried for her safety. We reunited."

"What a way with words you have."

"She couldn't leave Shay."

"Why?"

"Fear. We carried on in secret, and then she got pregnant. I knew if I didn't get her free of him he'd have a hold on you, too, and I'd never get either of you free. So we escaped. She finally found the courage to do it, because of you. The plague began wiping out the world. Shay put the wall up. You were born. And a year later Shay found us. Took you both back. The next I heard you were dead. I left."

I don't say anything but I'm thinking very loudly: *I was born outside the wall?*

Shadow says, "It's a funny thing, realizing he probably saved your life. If we'd still been out there when the plague hit we would have been the first to go."

"Instead she was."

He shakes his head a little. Then he says, even more softly, "I sometimes think I was born for her, and whatever purpose my life held failed in her death."

I don't speak for the sadness of this. To speak would be to let it in, even if I told him I've had enough, I can't bear any more, please, no more.

But he says, "Shay killed her."

Of course he did. It's part of why I came back.

Eventually Shadow stands to leave. "Chin up, my girl. Whatever this mess is will sort itself out."

"And if it doesn't?"

"Then it doesn't."

Classic Shadow.

*

My next visitor is Claire Townsend. She brings me a fourth blanket, my toothbrush and toothpaste, a pillow, a cup of tea and my cello. It's so thoughtful I almost burst into tears. I can't play it. Not if I want to hold my nerve. Murderers don't deserve to play an instrument: it's too joyful. Plus I'm handcuffed to a bar.

"I already told you how I feel about you, darling girl. I won't say it again."

I nod, thinking this must be the end of it, but alas she goes on.

"We don't get to choose the terrors we survive, only that we do survive them. And you, Josephine, are better at this than anyone I know. But I will give you one tiny piece of advice, and you can ignore it as you wish, as I'm sure you will."

Claire's not laughing as she takes my hand. I want to snatch it away but force myself to remain still.

"Surviving is much easier if we don't have to do it alone."

She leaves and I think: *I know this. I already know.*

Limerence

*

They might be the last two in the world, but they were two, and that mattered. That was the thing that mattered more than her moon heart.

*

My next prison visitor should not be out of bed. He moves slowly and as the light from his lamp flickers I can see the bandage around his skull, hiding the holes Zach had to drill in his head to release the pressure of his swollen brain.

Will sags to the ground beside me. "Well, aren't you a dummy?"

"Guess so."

He opens his mouth to say something, then gives up and simply rests his head in my lap. "Love you," he mutters as he drifts off to sleep.

I rest my hand on his shoulder and try to meditate, try not to think, try to do anything but ponder how desperately ruined I would have been had he died.

*

April 8th, 2068

Josephine

I'm not sure what time it is when something wakes me. I think it must be very late. I blink and straighten, noting in the dark that a figure has crouched before us. A figure I know very well.

Luke touches Will gently. "Hey, mate." Will looks up and Luke smiles the warmest, loveliest smile. The smile I once adored. God it's sweet, that smile. "Sorry to wake you, pal. Mind if I have a word with Josi?"

"Sure thing, boss." Will starts to rise and Luke practically lifts him to his feet.

"I'll help you to bed."

"Nah, I'm good. Stay here and salvage something."

Luke hesitates, then hugs the smaller boy. Will whispers something in his ear that I can't hear, then makes his way slowly out of the big silo.

When we're alone Luke sits beside me. I'm so tired. I wish he hadn't come. At least he doesn't try to touch me.

"You okay? You need anything?"

I don't reply.

"You really socked me one in the nads, Jose."

"Good." There's a short silence. "You all prepped for tomorrow?"

"For in an hour, you mean? Yep. I'll need your help with the train."

I nod. It's much later than I thought it was.

"Talk to me. It might be our last chance and if I die I want to do it understanding what compelled you to do this."

"I don't know how to explain. It will sound too meaningless. Too small to encompass any kind of understanding."

"I'm not quite as stupid as I look. You could try."

"You're not stupid at all. You're the smartest person I know." My words are starting to run out. "I'm just like them," I try. "The Furies. They're not … what we thought." My fingers stray to the stitches in my neck. How many times did they save my life out there?

"I love you so much. But what you've done ... it feels like you don't want me to love you anymore."

The arrogance of men, always. "It's not about you."

"I know, but what?"

Silence. I tried to tell him but he didn't listen.

"Whatever end you're angling for, I can't understand it unless you explain it to me, and you won't. Which doesn't leave us with anywhere to go."

He is correct. Sadly correct. I lift my eyes to the holes in the silo and can't help remembering the silly names Lawrence gave their constellations. There isn't much light in them now, which means the moon is just a sliver beyond. Soon they will start to twinkle with the rising sunlight, but by then it will be time to move.

I thought it when we were above ground in the safe house, and I think it again now. The only way Luke is going to let me go is if I take drastic measures. And I don't want him going up there clinging to some memory of what we had, thinking it will return. So I will arm myself with the one thing he and I have always struggled with: the truth.

"This love you have for me," I say softly, "I don't think you know its true face."

"What does that mean?"

"You say it over and over. All these words. You tell me things like how you loved me the first moment you saw me but I *hate* that, I've always hated it because it's such bullshit. Love isn't sight. It isn't attraction. It isn't what you can see in someone's skin or bones. Your love, whatever it was made of, wasn't about me – it was about you and what you needed to happen at that point in your life."

He doesn't speak, so I draw a breath and go on. "Do you know when I first loved you, Luke Townsend? It wasn't when we met, or when we first kissed, or even when we first made love. I loved a version of you then, and there were real pieces of you in that version, beautiful pieces, but I didn't love you honestly until you were honest with me. The first time I loved you properly was the first moment I truly hated you. When you told me you were a Blood and broke my heart. That was when love became real."

I close my mouth and determine not to say any more. I can't: I have no words left. Something hurts in my chest that I thought had died, and I think I'd rather it had. Luke stands and paces away from me. He is a shadow in the silo, a giant lumbering mass of muscle and pain. When he turns to me he sinks to his knees like he can't help it.

"Shall I tell you a secret?"

I stiffen with sudden concern. It's his tone.

"I didn't love you the first time I saw you. I told you that as a mercy. The truth is much uglier."

*

September 16th, 2064

Luke

She's had more night terrors than usual in the last couple of nights. She's started sleeping during the day and screaming then, too. Her body has grown so weak I think she must surely be dying, so I've decided to break into her house and get her to a hospital, regardless of my mission objectives to stay out of contact at all times. This is what I'm thinking as I watch from the roof opposite hers, what I'm thinking as I follow her from her apartment and into the street. She is barefoot and in some sort of fugue state – I think she must be sleepwalking. She gets on a train in this state, somehow, and I follow from the next carriage down, keeping her in my sight at all times. People are staring at her in concern – she looks like some sort of street urchin, hair tangled, feet bare.

She gets off in the outer suburbs and starts walking through the tree-lined streets. She's heading for bushland, I think, though why I have no clue. Every minute I think *now, I'll stop her now*, but instead I just keep following and watching.

Until I see what she's searching for. She wants trees and nature and wildlife, she wants away from the city, from its noisy soulless buildings and its metal glass steel trappings. She wants out.

There is a tent beside the hiking track. I see it much later than she does. And I see her circling it, smelling it, listening to the sounds of the people within it.

I watch my charge, an eighteen-year-old girl, unzip the tent with slow deliberateness and climb in. There are sounds – voices and then shouts and then screams. At first I'm not sure what's happening, but then there is blood and I know. I don't move to help the people. I just watch.

Two of my colleagues arrive. They are armed, but don't draw their guns, opting for their knives at such close range. They approach the tent from the opposite direction and still I remain hidden and silent. The thought of what they will do to her makes my heart thump painfully but some dark thing inside me has vowed not to interfere with anything, it has vowed to watch it all, every minute of whatever this is.

The first Blood – he's a red – cuts the side of the tent open but before he's even finished his arm has been snapped.

The rest of his shoulder and collarbone is broken with the force she's applied and he hits the ground, unconscious from the pain. The second Blood – this one a blue – orders her to come out immediately, drawing his gun and aiming at her silhouette. She lunges, mindless of the fabric of the tent dividing them, and tackles him to the ground. Through the plastic she goes for his neck, her teeth mauling him violently open. He tries to shoot – a bullet is fired but it whizzes past her head and by then he's dead, his throat torn open with such savagery that she didn't even need to emerge from the tent.

When she does, I see her face is covered in blood. She is ravenous as she bends to keep at the agent's neck, chewing and sucking and devouring.

I move backwards very slowly until I'm far enough away to puke my guts into the bushes.

Then I straighten and return to the scene of the nightmare. She's not human, I know that much. She's not what I thought she was, not even close. She's something very *other* under the light of this crimson moon. She is animal, plain and simple. And I can't stop the adrenalin pouring itself through my body, flooding it, making me shake and curse and want a dozen things I can't name. If she smells me, she doesn't act on it. Instead, once she's finished with all four of the corpses she turns and continues on through the trees. Continues her hunt, perhaps. A whining frenzied noise comes from her mouth, like a cry or a moan or a baying. Agitated, she removes her bloodstained clothes as though they cause her skin pain. Whatever has become of her mind is primitive and primal. I've never seen anything like it.

After she's gone from my sight, I make a swift decision that will change my life forever. I hide the bodies somewhere until I can return and dispose of them properly, and I vow never to tell anyone what I've seen here tonight. Not even Josephine Luquet. Because one thing is for certain: for this she would be exterminated from the world, and for some unfathomably depraved reason I think I would die before I let that happen.

*

April 8th, 2068

Josephine

"You think I don't know you," Luke says. "You think I don't know the darkest, ugliest, most monstrous parts of you, but I knew them before you did. I saw them."

I don't move; I can't.

"Did you not think about that night? Before I found you in the bar? Didn't you wonder what I'd seen?"

I didn't because I couldn't afford to.

"I saw the worst. Before that night I thought I knew you. I'd been watching you. You were sweet and sad and innocent and then without warning you were none of those things. You were so violent I had no way to take it in. I watched and watched – I made myself watch – and then you woke to a new day. You were small and vulnerable again. I watched you find your way home, steal clothes off a clothesline. I saw you collapse and rise and collapse and rise. I saw all that you were in that night and that morning, both sides of the truth, a bigger truth than even you knew. And that was when I loved you. For the endurance of the unendurable."

I squeeze my eyes shut. My mouth is filled with saliva and I might be about to vomit but still he doesn't understand, *he doesn't understand.* He thinks me an innocent vulnerable girl trapped in the body of a monster but I'm nothing like that. I *am* the monster, and the blood moon simply set me free.

I am drenched in humiliation – I can't stand his eyes on me, and never want to be looked at again.

Then he goes on, and I feel everything drop away.

He says, "That's not even it. That's not true. Christ, I can hardly say it, even now."

I open my eyes and look at him.

"I told myself that's how it was afterwards," Luke murmurs, holding my gaze in the dark. "But the truth … I saw you turn animal and I wanted to join you. Not the killing, obviously, but the freedom. I wanted to be the same as you, as wild and simple. So if it's your monstrousness that you think I can't handle, you're wrong. If it's the shame you think I don't understand, you're wrong. *I see you.*"

There is an endless, endless night between his words and mine. There is an infinite life. There is death.

I say aloud the thing I understood in the north, when all else fell away. I say aloud the thing I now realize he already knows, knew long before I did.

"This is a kingdom of wolves."

We must be wolves to survive it.

Luke crouches before me and reaches to touch my cheek. "And I hope I'll see you on the other side of it."

Then he's gone.

Chapter 25

April 8th, 2068

Dave

As I'm saying goodbye to Mom I notice there's a rash all over my hands. She sees it and makes a concerned noise, retrieving some lotion and massaging it in for me.

"Just stress," she consoles.

But it's no consolation. It is a terror. My body is turning against me. I can be attacked from every side, even from within.

"Why do you stay here?" I ask her. "It's a place of death."

She holds my eyes and frowns. "I look around these tunnels and see only life."

Oh, my mother. How I used to love her. She was the strongest of us. I think she still is. I wonder what she sees when she looks at what I've become.

"I think you should leave," I whisper. "I think you should get out of here while you still can."

"We'll go when it's time, and not without everyone else." She finishes rubbing the moisturizer into my hands and gives them a squeeze. "Help your brother. Do the best you can."

I nod but I'm not sure my best is worth much.

*

Luke

From the silo I go straight to the barracks, but the kid I'm looking for isn't in his bed. I find him instead in the infirmary, dozing on one of the gurneys. Probably to avoid being shivved while he sleeps by his bunk mates.

"Zach," I whisper, not wanting to wake Will in the next bed.

Zach lurches awake in a panic. I press my hand to his mouth and then drop something into his hand.

The key to Josi's handcuffs.

He looks down at them expressionlessly, then nods.

*

I have Shadow, Blue, Eric and Coin help me carry the drill onto the train. Next, I set Teddy up with the train programming instructions Josi left scrawled beside her open cuffs. She and Zach are long gone by this point, though I have no idea to where.

"Get us here," I tell Teddy, pointing to a spot on the map directly beneath the Blood base.

"This is fifty feet underground," he points out, looking green from his hangover. "And there's no tunnel exit points anywhere near here."

"That's why we're bringing the drill, kid." I clap him on the shoulder and then start jogging home. When I get to the dining tunnel, Will is waiting with the rest of my soldiers.

"No," I tell him. "You're not coming anywhere near us."

"You'll have to cuff me, then."

"Will, you were dead two nights ago."

"Yeah, and now I'm alive."

"Your head—"

"Is bandaged and well."

"It's got *holes* in it, for Christ's sake."

"How's that different from normal?" He grins.

I can't help it – I snort. Rub my eyes wearily. It's only six a.m. and I'm already exhausted at the thought of what we're about to do. "Fine, kid, but don't you dare die again."

"I'm not gonna make a habit of it, trust me."

"Right, you lot, all armed and fitted with tested comms?"

"Yes, sir!" they answer, sounding like good little soldiers. I keep remembering the words Josi spoke about how they aren't real fighters, they've never faced an army of Bloods. But I'm hoping they won't have to. Not if the plan goes smoothly.

"Then we have a train to catch, amigos. All aboard."

"We're coming," Coin tells me, sidling up with Alo and Henrietta, all three of them heavily armed and dressed in Kevlar vests.

I hadn't chosen them for the op. I can't stand the thought of them in danger – losing more of them would take us beyond repair. But something in their eyes is undeniable. So I nod and let them pass.

Before I leave I find my parents. They're in the kitchen, frying eggs and talking swiftly under their breaths.

"You run a tight ship, chef," I tell Dad.

He turns and bursts into tears.

"Woah, god, why are you *crying*?"

"Because you're doing something inconceivably stupid," Mom answers for him.

"I've got this, alright? I know what I'm doing."

"Can't you stop your brother from going with you?"

So that's what Dad's crying about. The thought of losing his oldest twice.

"I don't have a right to," I say. "He wants to help."

"He isn't trained like you are."

"I'm not gonna let him out of my sight, I promise. If anyone's safe on this mission, it's Dave."

I give them each a long hug. As I pat my Dad's back I can't help laughing. "You old softy. I go on ops all the time."

"Not like this. Just do me a favor and remember where the line is. You don't cross it, not for anything."

"What if I have to cross it to get back to you?"

"You wouldn't be you anymore."

I search his face, wondering if he really believes this. Because I don't. It's easy to say that from one side of the line, but what he doesn't realize is that I've already crossed it a thousand times. And from this side of it the view is much better. I kiss his cheek and say nothing: those of us on this side keep the secret. Cross the line enough times and it disappears.

*

On the train Teddy is sweating up a storm. He smells of whisky. And he's got Will, Pace, Alo and Coin chattering over his shoulder, telling him what to do and pointing out any errors he makes.

I stride into the driver's cabin. "Everyone out. Leave the poor kid alone."

They file out grumpily and Teddy sighs in relief. "I think it's ready. I can't guarantee the speed you'll travel, though – I think that only gets programmed once you're moving – so I have no idea of your arrival time. Also I can't be entirely sure the train will stop where it's supposed to."

"Okay, well, good enough is good enough, mate. You head back to base and we'll be in touch from there. I'll let you know when I want you to set off the comms virus and recall all the agents."

"Aye aye, boss. Can I tell Josi what's going on?"

"She escaped."

His face splits into a grin.

I laugh. "Try not to look too concerned about it."

"Oh, come on, you and I both know she'd never do anything to hurt us."

I nod but I'm not so sure, since technically she already did a massive thing to hurt us. I can't stop thinking about how easily that gate broke, letting the Furies flood much, much closer to where the rest of my people are sleeping. And with all the best fighters away on this op, there'll be no one there to protect the seventy odd left behind. If another breach happens, they're all dead.

"Stay safe, Teddy. Keep an eye on the watch rosters and make sure every single gate is being guarded at all times."

"You're leaving *me* in charge of that? *Why?*"

"'Cause I know I can trust you with it. Go on, hop to it. See you on the other side."

He starts the train and then hurries to jump off. As the giant metal contraption whirs quietly to life after a year and a half of slumber I walk back through its carriages, remembering each and every mission this train carried us to from the west. This journey will be much shorter. In no time at all we'll be beneath the heart of the Blood stronghold.

*

Josephine

It is decidedly *not* fun to ride a speeding motorbike through a narrow, pitch-black tunnel without a helmet and with a terrified teenager clinging painfully to your back and screaming in your ear. Just saying.

We don't dismount and take any of the number of exhaust hatches into the streets above. Instead we careen into a different set of tunnels – the subway tunnels – launch off the platform into the air and land heavily on the concrete between the tracks with a wild skid. I give a whoop of exhilaration while Zach screams bloody murder. Actually, maybe it is kinda fun.

I gun the engine down the tunnel and pray like crazy that we don't encounter a train. This is, after all, the working section of the city's subway. I probably could have looked up the train timetables, but that would have been far too intelligent.

We zoom past platforms filled with astonished passengers waiting for their train. I'm looking for a particular station – Ensfield – and when I see it approaching I gun the engine even harder.

"What are you doing, you maniac?" Zach shouts hysterically. "Slow down!"

But we'll need speed if I'm to hop us up onto the concrete gutters running alongside.

"Hold tight!" I shout.

"Oh fuck you—"

I rear us up on one wheel and angle my front to land on the gutter, using the engine's momentum to carry us up and onto the platform. Terrified people launch out of the way as I gun the bike straight for the stairs. Zach has one consistent scream exploding from his mouth – his lung capacity is quite impressive. We hit the stairs and the bike bounces around, smashing our spines into pieces and nearly flinging us off. I manage to keep my hold on the handlebars and Zach manages to keep his hold on me as we clatter up and out of the subway.

I turn us left and fly straight up the main street, whizz onto the highway and take that down a few miles before the exit to the supply depo.

This is where it gets tricky.

As it turns out, even soulless bloodsucking demons need food. Who knew? So if we can't use the sewage tunnels or the prostitute route in, we use the food route. At the supply depo, trucks are filled, under heavy security, and then driven inside the Gates for delivery. I've done my homework (and by that I mean Teddy did my homework for me) and know that our best shot at not being detected at any of the security points along the way is to stow away on a freezer truck. We can't cling to the bottom, as the Bloods use mirrors to look beneath the cabin. We can't hide in the freezer, as they search that three times along the way. And we can't just commandeer the truck for the obvious reasons: eyes and fingerprint scans.

Which leaves us one rather squishy option, for which I thank the food gods – they nearly starved me to death in the north and gave me this skeletal-chic figure, while consistently filling the guts of the poor rich ministers. Zach'll be fine – he's a weedy little creep already. So we just have to get inside the depo without being spotted. I've got the guard shifts memorized, as well as the loading schedule. Over the wall we go, shimmying over the barbed wire and avoiding the swinging cameras. That makes it sound rather simple, but with Zach in tow, it is not. He's as ungainly and uncoordinated as a baby elephant, and has a pain tolerance of minus five. You just have to touch him and the poor peach bruises. Which is curious to me, as he's no stranger to pain. His father has made sure of that.

We wait behind the building and I count the minutes. This is a dance. Know where the cameras are, know how they move and when. Know where the guards are, know how they move and when. Find a path between the two and dance it like crazy. While running left we duck low, pause three seconds and then twist out of view of the oncoming guard as the camera sweeps the other way. It takes a good ten minutes to reach the back of the parked truck. Zach keeps watch while I unpick the lock on the back – skill à la Luke – then scurry away to await the next guard sweep. We now have a thirty-second window to climb into the back with all our gear, not inside the freezer, but on top of it, squeezing into the very narrow space between the roof of the fridge and the top of the truck's interior.

It's immediately hot from the freezer's exhaust. I was hoping it wouldn't be this hot because boarding the truck here means waiting for them to load, which will probably take at least another forty minutes, then the journey on top of that. But trying to board anywhere else was too time-tight.

I'm already sweating by the time they start loading the frozen food into the freezer below us. They won't spot us at this angle, and hopefully they won't think to look up here. They sure take their sweet time about it.

"Lazy bums," Zach mutters.

They won't hear us over the exhaust engine but I tell him to shut up anyway.

The truck finally takes off and we have to endure the tension of several security sweeps. They don't find us, but it's getting mighty hot up here, and this is one hell of a small space.

Panic threatens the back of my mind but I focus on counting seconds and listening to the progress of the truck. As we stop for the third security point I know we must have reached the security gate. I can hear the guards checking the driver's prints and doing yet another sweep of the truck. We take off and I breathe a sigh of relief, until there's a shout and the truck slams to a sudden stop.

The force sends me sliding along the top of the freezer straight into the exhaust pipes. My arm connects with it and the cold is so severe that it burns straight through my shirt. I slam my mouth shut so as not to scream. Zach slides to my side and tries to wrench my arm away, but the cold has fused both my skin and the shirt to the pipe, like a tongue getting stuck to the ice in winter. I grit my teeth and rip myself away, leaving material and a chunk of skin behind. I'm flooded with nausea as the pain does its work.

There's a guard inside the freezer, searching right up the back of it. He's directly beneath us. Woozily, my mind goes to the last time I was hidden in a tiny space while guards searched below. The thought of mounting Zach and having my way with him like I did to Luke makes me nearly burst out laughing maniacally.

Thankfully the overzealous guard deems the truck clean and lets us go through. We make our way to the back of the food storage building and are backed into the unloading bay. Zach and I then have to wait until all the food is unloaded. There'll be a short window here, maybe. We slide to the edge and heave ourselves down from the cramped space. I land and peer around the storage hangar. I can hear footsteps returning to lock up the empty truck, and pull Zach around the truck just in time. We scurry into a space between looming boxes and hunker down. It's immensely relieving not to be simultaneously burning, freezing and suffocating to death.

The burn on my arm is bad – I can see down through the layers of my skin, and all of them are pink and shiny. Ugh. Another burn.

The truck leaves and we're locked in. But that's fine. I have a lot of experience crawling around in air vents. They really should start building them too small to fit inside. We climb up into the nearest and follow it through the kitchen building. Great thing about the Gates community is that apart from all the individual mansions, the rest of the buildings are all attached to each other. This is supposed to lower possible infiltration points, but it pretty much means that once you're in one section, you're in all.

Soon, however, the vents run out.

I'm prepared for this. Zach should be too. He doesn't look any stronger than he did a month ago, though.

"Did you do your exercises?"

"Yes! You've asked me like fifty times."

"'Cause I don't believe you."

"Guess we'll see now, won't we?"

"Guess we will. When you fall and die I'll make sure to say I told you so."

We make a childish face at each other and then start donning the climbing gloves and shoes. They have grip pads on each finger and palm, and all over the feet. But they're not magic – the only way to keep from falling is to have excellent upper and core body strength. Which Zach, the liar, does not.

The building we're in right now is the antechamber of the "Great Hall". They call it this to denote some fucking medieval power apex, no doubt. It is pretty "great" in size, I have to admit. And its roof is made of a spectacularly carved glass walkway. Beautiful, artistic glass. Glass that is going to pose the greatest challenge on this mission.

This glass atrium is suspended over the lush gardens that line the hall's interior. It's meant to let the sun in, while casting glorious beams of light on the various flowers, and giving the people in the Gates a spectacular view as they cross the hall. It is truly a beautiful piece of design, but we have to follow it somehow in order to reach the parliamentary rooms – there's no other point of access to them. Can't just walk through it, as cameras cover every inch of it and motion sensors line the floor, alerting security any time someone is crossing it. But the cameras don't point upwards, to the glass ceiling.

I go first, lying flat and spreading my weight as wide as I can. I feel a bit like a spider as I extend my arms and legs right out, crawling along at a painstakingly slow pace. I have to keep my weight spread so as not to crack the glass. It's tough work – the muscles in my arms and shoulders and all through my core scream for mercy. My knees and toes and palms hurt against the glass, and the blood has all rushed to my face. God, I think I've really bitten off more than I can chew here.

I pick up the pace, wanting it to be over, trying to get some speed. Scurry goes my spider body, stretched and trembling. I can hear Zach behind me, cursing a storm. If someone happens to walk beneath us we're fucked, but it's unlikely, as the glass bridge is only used on special occasions.

Unless you're the Prime Minister, apparently.

I freeze in absolute horror as none other than Falon Shay walks along the glass tunnel directly below us. *Don't look up, don't look up, don't you dare look up, you son of a bitch.* He's going to – he'll cross beneath our shadows and that'll be it. But he's reading on his tablet, head down, striding along without a thought for the outside world. He notices nothing and soon is gone back the way we came.

I sag in relief.

Only to hear the glass give a soft, sinister crack.

My head whips around to see that Zach has collapsed from his spread eagle position, too weak to hold it.

"You lazy bastard," I hiss. "You didn't do them, did you?"

"They were too hard!"

"I'm leaving you behind. You deserve to be found."

"Josi! Don't!"

Another crack snakes out from under his hip.

"Relax, idiot. Spread your weight right now. Move off that crack."

He starts to do so but the glass splinters in every direction. I think quickly. The glass will support far more weight if we're hanging from beneath it. I inch back to Zach, making sure to remain on a different pane. His is about to go. He reaches for my hand but I'll never get him off in time. So I brace myself to catch him, thinking with mild concern that every time I've had to do a mission that involves climbing in recent months it has turned out very poorly. The glass goes and I swing Zach to the edge of my pane, which he grabs hold of with his sticky gloves. It should hold him for a minute or two. I just hope nobody was watching the security cameras at that exact moment.

"You're gonna climb along the underside of the glass, upside down like a lizard, okay?"

"Are you out of your damn mind? There's no way in hell I can do that!"

"It won't crack from beneath, trust me."

"What kind of physics is that?" he hisses. "The fantasy kind?"

"The glass is set into the underside of the frame which means that from that side, the frame will take more of the force of weight than the glass will, so—"

"I don't actually care! It was a rhetorical question! How am *I* going to stay attached?"

"Was that another rhetorical question?"

"NO!"

"You hold on, dumbass."

"I will curse your name until my dying breath, Josephine Luquet."

"Then do it while you climb. The suction in your gloves and shoes will keep you on the glass, but your body will have to do a lot of work to move you along."

I realize pretty quickly that I'm going to have to do it too. The glass beneath me has started to crack, not to mention Zach requires examples of everything before he can even attempt to do it himself. I swing down and feel my pads suck onto the glass. Upside down, the blood is *really* rushing to my head.

"How do I get the pads off again?"

"Like we practiced. You roll your wrist and ankle to release the suction – slowly!"

We make our slow way along the underside of the glass ceiling. It's not even a little bit fun. By the time I've made it to the edge and swing down onto safe, uncensored floor, my body is jelly. Weak, trembling jelly. Zach is still halfway across, moving much more slowly.

"The quicker you get here the quicker this is over," I hiss.

"I can't do it," I hear him mutter. "This is beyond me. I'm done."

"No you're not, Zach," I tell him fiercely. "If you fall the censor is triggered, camera picks you up and the alarm sounds. Plan is done. We're dead. So just keep going. Ask of yourself more than what you've given before. You *are* capable of it."

He moans and keeps going. Inch by inch. Hand by hand until he gets to my side and falls straight to the ground. He hits hard on his back and the breath leaves his lungs in a whoosh. I drag him around the corner to where I'm hoping the cameras won't spot us.

"Get up. Come on. We haven't even got to the hard bit yet."

"Oh for the love of god."

*

Luke

Drilling *up* is much harder than it sounds. The drill's weight and gravitational pull want it to drop down constantly, so you need a very strong force to keep it moving up through the matter. A force stronger than five men standing at its base, trying to shove it up through sweat, tears and curses.

I stand apart, watching, thinking how desperately I want to help them, knowing how much stronger I am than any one of them and also knowing how simply unable I am. My hand can't hold the too-wide edge of the drill. Not with weight from above. It physically won't grip on. So here I stand, thoroughly useless.

I've got Teddy in my comms, letting me know the virus is ready to go. The rest of the team are lined up behind me, armed and ready. They know the instructions: fan out, ten of them to a level, infiltrate and shoot to wound every agent in sight. Legs, arms, shoulders, keep shooting until they're down and they stay down. Ziplock their hands, keep moving.

There should be very few here at this time of day, so I'm not predicting large casualties on either side. It'll be when the Bloods are recalled all at once that things will start getting interesting.

We're a little behind schedule because the train dropped us a couple of miles too far and we had to lug the huge drill back with us. But soon we break through the cement block of the basement floor, thankfully without bursting any pipes. The drill is switched off and discarded as we flow up into the building.

"*Basement clear, over.*"

"*Approaching floor one now, over.*"

I hear gunshots as I mount the stairs to floor three.

"*Casualties on floor one, count three so far. East wing is cleared, over.*"

Shit. I should have known they wouldn't be calm or skilled enough to shoot to wound. Their panic makes them shoot to kill.

"*Approaching second floor, over.*"

"*Ah shit, targets on second floor in west corridor, four I think. Cover me.*"

More gunshots, a rain of them.

"*Targets down in west corridor, moving north, over.*"

I listen as the team's stream of reports comes in. So far so good. I reach the third floor with my team in tow. Only Will, Shadow and Dave are with me – I've left the less experienced in much larger groups – but I figure the four of us can take a floor to ourselves. Well, three, really, since I'm basically just keeping Dave hidden behind the rest of us. The Bloods are ready for us by now, but there aren't enough of them and they aren't armed for combat. They go down quickly, one after another. I wound and ziplock mine but there are plenty of dead here too, far too many. It feels like a massacre, and it is, it's a terrible thing.

You have to know how far you're willing to go.

One of the teams reports a successful seizure of the armory, which pretty much means we've won the game. The first part of it, anyway.

We clear all floors, check every room, every corridor and elevator, every cupboard and locker and nook and cranny that could hold a person. The tech team and any other staff are immediately zip-tied. They're not combat soldiers so they don't fight back. On this I'm strict – none of the staff die.

Finally I radio home. "Teddy, my man. It's total recall time."

Chapter 26

April 8th, 2068

Luke

Five minutes after the comms go down there is an alert in the mainframe of the Blood security database declaring that no less than six-hundred-and-twelve individual agents are currently being recalled to the base. That's a shit ton of Bloods.

This does not turn out to be true. Less than half show up. In fact it's only about a hundred and fifty.

We're ready for them: I've already overridden the security system and everything that once turned this building into an impenetrable fortress now makes it a prison. The Bloods are shepherded – not by people but by locked doors and overridden elevators – onto one floor where they are locked and monitored. The trick is never to get close enough to let them do any damage. None of their prints or retinas will work to override the new security. They don't have high enough clearances – they're all reds and blues. Had a gray been here, he or she would have been capable of the override, but since I'm the only one in existence … bad luck, losers.

I have no intention of killing these people. The first wave of casualties was a necessary regret so that we could take the building, but the rest don't need to die. They're loyal to the government, so we just need to become the government.

What's really freaking me out is the whereabouts of the other four hundred agents.

The only Bloods that should be left free are the forty or so currently guarding the Gates, but since they can't call for backup and we now have their ammunitions and supplies stores, we should be able to take them out.

But where the fuck are the rest? I have no comms to contact Teddy, not until he gets them back up again.

"My math skills aren't very good, I'll admit, but these numbers aren't adding up," Will points out.

"We're missing 76 percent of them," Shadow says.

"Wow, Rain Man, on the other hand, is apparently very good at math."

"It's actually 75.6 percent, if we're being technical."

"Jeez, what other hidden talents do you have?"

"Quiet," I snap unkindly. They both fall silent. "Teddy, you there?"

No answer.

"I don't like this. It's against protocol and they don't do anything against protocol. The only person who can override it is Shay. But since the comms are all down I don't see how he could have."

"Is there some way to override the security from where he is?" Dave asks.

"No, it's manual – why we had to get inside this building to do it."

"Could he have diverted the agents elsewhere?"

"He can't – the comms are down," I reiterate impatiently.

"But what if he just told them," Dave insists. "Like, face to face. The old fashioned way."

"Why would he have access to four hundred agents at once?"

"At precisely the moment we make our attack?" Will agrees.

"How would he have known?"

Dave spreads his hands. "You don't want to see it but it's right in front of your eyes."

I stare at my brother, unease uncurling in my guts.

"We have a mole," Shadow says aloud.

"We've suspected him all along!" Dave exclaims. "I fail to see how this could be a surprise to you."

"Zach's not a mole!" Will says. "He's just ... a bit of a douche."

"Wake up," Dave orders. "He's Shay's son. And you haven't seen the insidious hold Shay has over everything he touches, but I have. Zach's a slave to it – they all are. Whatever he's been cooking up with Josi either means she's in on it with him, or he's leading her into a trap."

"Well, then I guess it's a bloody good thing she's handcuffed to our silo," Will points out.

Except ...

"Except she's not," I say softly.

*

Josephine

I'm alone now. I've found my way into the parliamentary room. There is a long table down the center, a trickling water feature on the back wall and a glass skylight in the roof. The walls are covered in faint, almost invisible DNA strands. It reminds me of the DNA molecule sculpture in Shay's front yard. If the freak thinks he can change our DNA then he's got another thing coming.

I climb onto the table and wind the skylight open. Air rushes in and soothes my overheated face. I could wriggle my way out of it right now, I could be standing in the sky.

But I don't. I climb off the table and take my seat at the head of it.

I tap on my earpiece and ask softly, "Are you in place?"

No response.

I ask again and wait.

But still no response comes from Zach. The only person I have chosen to rely on for this suicide mission. And he should definitely be responding right now. Unless something has gone wrong.

Too late, the door opens.

*

Luke

"We've got eyes on security cams from here, right?" Will asks, taking his seat at one of the tech consoles. He's a whizz with it – not like Teddy is, unfortunately, but still damn good. Before we know it we're looking at footage from within the Gates. "If Shay knows what we're doing then maybe he'll give himself away somehow."

"What, by miming his thoughts to the camera?"

Will shrugs and starts scrolling through the four trillion cameras that monitor the quiet little community. Since we have no way to contact Teddy, or anyone else for that matter, and we have no idea where the missing four hundred Bloods are, there's not much to do but peer through the holo visuals and hope for a clue to what the hell is going on here.

I'm caught in a very difficult place. I chose to believe in Josi – against all my better judgment I chose to believe in her trust in Zach. But maybe I was wrong to do that. Maybe Dave's right and the sniveling little bastard has betrayed her.

Why did I give him the key?

The footage of the grand hall and the parliamentary rooms flashes up. We see, together, the six fully armed and armored Blood agents marching for the door to the room where waits a single, lonely girl.

"Let's go," I say, even though if we enter that compound we're likely never getting back out.

Not one of them argues.

*

Josephine

"Josephine Luquet. What a nice surprise."

I don't stand up. He looks just as I remember him, with that hooked nose and cold, cruel eyes. He's flanked by half a dozen Bloods in full swat gear – helmets and machine guns and all. Which is a real bummer.

I smile. "Gosh, is all this for me? I'm flattered."

"You're to be my most prized possession, dear. I can't help a little excitement at having you here, laid out on a platter for me."

"I suppose not. We're all human, after all."

He smiles. "Now there I might have to disagree. I've seen you, you know. Blood agents often wear cameras as well as earpieces and that footage gets sent back to base. Human, I am afraid, you are not."

"Maybe not, but whose definition should we go by?" I ask. "Because I've seen things too. I've seen children in labs and bodies in cages and people demented by rage and lack of rage. I've seen a statue of your first wife, the one you claim died of plague. I've seen a birdless sky after you shot them all dead. And I've seen the broken nose and the sliced mouth and the scarred body of your only son."

His mouth hardens at the mention of Zach. "You're a brain-damaged child," he says simply. And then he shoots me.

It's a shorn-off *shotgun*, of all things. I have a millisecond to think *where the hell did he get that* and then the force to my chest sends my chair rolling on its wheels and slamming into the wall. I've had a lot of injuries in my life, but I've never been shot in the chest before. It's a wrecking ball to my ribs. It's all the air gone in a great whooshing vacuum. It's pain exploding out from the core of me to all the furthest points. I blink my sightless eyes as I scramble for breath.

I wasn't expecting it. I'm certainly not expecting him to shoot me again.

He does.

This time the force slams my head back against the wall and the pain is lower, in my guts, making them churn and roil and oh god I'm about to puke. My hands are tingling and I can't feel my feet. I have a gun but I can't reach for it, I can't move, I can barely work out if I'm still conscious. Things have broken, things have definitely broken.

He's too close. Not even the vest will stop the force of his next bullet from skipping my heart if he does it again. I can feel it now, stuttering in my chest, flailing wildly against the impact.

I manage to drag my eyelids open. I'm coughing badly and can't stop. Through my streaming eyes I see Shay watching me. He's so smug I want to scream but I can't stop coughing.

"What did you think was going to happen?" he asks me. "I'd let you sit there and reveal whatever plot you've set up?"

He moves closer, his finger on the trigger, double-barrel still aimed at my heart. "That's not how the world I built works. In *my* world, I win."

Jesus, why did I think he wouldn't kill me? I thought he would want me alive to cut open and study, I thought it would buy me time. I forgot about his ruthless decisiveness.

I ignored how dangerous he is, thinking I could be more so.

"Your men aren't yours anymore," I wheeze clumsily. I wanted to do this well, to see the look on his face when he realized he hasn't won at all, but I'm ruining it, rushing to the end, wanting the pain in my chest gone. Every time you think you've grown used to pain, that it can't possibly bother you any more, it does. It really, really does.

Where the fuck is Zach? Why hasn't he come? A terrible thought refuses to be denied: he's left me here. Or lured me here. And that will be the end of me.

"We took the Blood base," I gasp. Clumsy, clumsy, clumsy.

That's when he smiles and I feel cold inside. "You think I didn't know what you were planning? *You think I didn't know where you've been hiding?*"

Inside my bruised chest my heart thumps. It hurts, it hurts so much.

He moves closer, right up close to my face. It's an insult, getting this close to me: he knows I can't move to hurt him. But just to land his point home, he cracks me over the skull with the butt of his shotgun.

The world flashes with a bright light and then spins and spins and spins. I can taste metal and I think my neck has disappeared. Instead there is a head lolling on something that can no longer hold it up.

"You're rats in those tunnels, scurrying around in filth and waste, bringing disease and unrest to society," I hear Shay tell me. I hear it above all else. "So I did the only thing I could. I sent exterminators to clean you out. Four hundred of them."

He looks at his watch. Into my blurry eyes. "They should be about done by now."

*

Luke

We're close. The Blood compound is near the Gates, for obvious reasons. We don their combat gear, take one of their vehicles and bluff our way inside. They're undermanned, it seems, which means the four hundred missing Bloods aren't here. I take one of them hostage and use his eyes and prints to get access to the main building, and then through several doors. The security is lax beyond belief – there's something big going on. Some reason Shay thought he'd be safe from attack.

It's too easy to reach them. Way too easy. I'm nervous as we cross the glass corridor and approach the parliamentary room, unhindered.

The doors are wide open. They're waiting for us.

My eyes scan the room. Take in the sight of Josephine draped on a chair at the end of the room, blood streaming from her skull, a strange wheezing sound drifting from each of her breaths. It sounds like she's punctured a lung. And worse, more terrifyingly, one of her eyes – obviously the one that got impacted by whatever wound cut open her head – has ruptured. All the blood vessels around her black eye have burst. She looks almost grotesque, stranger even than the Furies appear, with her one blue eye remaining unscathed. It's like looking at two different faces at once.

My heart reaches wildly for her.

"Luke Townsend," Shay greets me. "Returned for more tests?"

I don't say anything.

"Or maybe," Shay goes on more softly, "you miss it."

My eyes move to his without my permission.

"The blood moon and its monstrous power," he says. "Doesn't it just kill you, Townsend? That the worst thing I ever did to you was take that power away from you? You tell yourself you wanted the blood moon's help in destroying me, but it was more than that. You liked it, didn't you?" He moves a little closer. "I know you. I *created* you." He looks now at the other people in the room, lingering on Shadow and then Josephine. "Each of you."

Fear flickers in and out of my heart like an old black and white movie. Not at his words. But because we got to him, at long last – five of us, armed and well trained, all of us wanting him dead – and yet I can feel in the room that he still holds the power. His Bloods have their weapons trained on us, for starters. His own gun hangs easily in his hand. But it's more than that.

"Door," I say softly to Shadow and Will, who fall back to watch the door. Dave stays by my side.

I could raise my weapon and take him through the skull, but I don't think I could do it before a dozen bullets riddled my body. I consider doing it anyway.

While I think, I ask, "Why'd you make it so easy to find you?"

"Because I don't need it to be difficult," Shay answers. "I only need it to be difficult for you to leave again."

If this turns into a gunfight, everyone in this room is dead. That's fact. But I have to kill him somehow. I have to change the dynamic.

I stop thinking about power and dynamics as soon as he starts talking, just, as I'm sure, he planned. This is all his design, I now see.

"The missing Blood agents," Shay says, and even clever as he is, there's still pride in his voice. Still a sick, childish arrogance. "I'll paint you a picture, shall I? Four hundred Bloods moving their way through the veins of the earth, destroying everything in their path like the deadliest virus of all. Made for this very purpose. To cleanse. You and yours, Townsend – your day is over. This is how I deal with disease: I wipe it from the world."

The floor disintegrates beneath my feet.

My mother and father. Pace and Hal, Teddy – all of them. More than seventy people, including children and elderly, all friends and family. All slaughtered.

I can't move. I've disintegrated with the floor.

"Oh god," I hear Will whisper.

Shay is so cold as he looks at me, watching for my reaction. I'm too empty to give him one.

No. Scratch that. I'm not empty.

I thought I knew rage.

I didn't.

I thought I knew violence.

I didn't.

But before tonight is through, Shay will know these things, even if I have to show them to him with a body full of lead.

*

"We all know it. It's been said by anyone with a modicum of intelligence throughout history. Love is weakness. It's a disease that ravages the mind and body and leaves you soft. I *will* forge a world cleansed of its mess, that I promise you."

We are listening to his tirade because he has left us no other choice, unless – the gun battle, unless all of us dead.

"Love was what lost you this fight," Shay goes on. It occurs to me that he's biding time, waiting for his four hundred soldiers to return from their slaughter and finish us off. Which means I have to get to him before that happens.

"Misplaced love, unfounded trust. It destroys everything, in the end."

He's talking about the mole. And he's right, I suppose. We trusted the wrong person and here we are, undone.

I trusted the wrong person, because I love her.

All the threads that tie me to my certainties are unraveling. My mother and father – *oh fuck* – no, don't think about them, not yet. Hold onto your control. Hold it with those steadfast hands of yours.

Except they aren't anymore, are they? They're useless, powerless hands, just as I have become, standing here waiting for the end to decide which of us to take, when once I would have made all the decisions myself.

I hear Shay say, "You'll be arrested first, condemned and then executed as terrorists by firing squad. My agents will be making their way through the compound now. You'd do best not to fight them."

I can't see a way out. I can't. My mind is full of black, poisonous rage. It's full of regret.

*

Then.

She says, through the gasping, scraping wheeze of her lungs: "No, they won't."

*

All eyes go to her. She can't move – that much is clear. She's taken two shotgun blows to the chest, by the looks of the mess of shirt and Kevlar. Her head rests on the wall, her body limp like a ragdoll's. That kind of punishment could easily have killed her, even with the vest. The force of the shots gets distributed more widely and is more than capable of smashing a person's abdomen to pieces. She's lucky to be alive.

But the expression in her ghoulish eyes speaks nothing of pain or luck. The expression in her eyes is one of deep certainty.

It's predatory.

"Your agents would have lived. But you sent them down into the bowels of the world. You ordered their deaths when you thought you were ordering ours."

"What are you talking about?" Shay demands.

"You think I didn't know about your mole?" she wheezes. With a coughing laugh she adds, "You heard and saw what I wanted you to."

The back of my neck is tingling.

"I'll paint you a picture," she offers, even though it sounds like each word and each breath must be agony. "Four hundred Bloods moving their way through the veins of the earth, intent on destroying everything in their path. Finding, instead, a force sent straight from hell. One made by you. A hungry one."

My poor, inadequate mind is only now catching up, only now allowing the pieces to shift into place. Why she wanted them alive. Why she said nothing of her plans.

There's true fear in the minister's eyes now. "Do you believe I'm that stupid? We knew of the Furies. There weren't enough to face the force I sent."

"There weren't," she agrees. "There are now. The tunnels are crawling with them. Do you think I would have returned without an army?"

She coughs and I see blood splatter her chin and shirt. But still she says, holding all the power in this room, all the power in the world, "No one's coming to save you, Shay. Your Bloods are all dead."

Then, without moving her arm, she fires the gun at her thigh and shoots my brother in the chest.

Something snaps with a rubbery twang inside me.

Chapter 27

November 13th, 2067

Josephine

This time when I go for the truck, I look both ways first.

Five days I lay on my back, in and out of consciousness. There is a pink shiny burn on my face and black, clumsy stitches in my throat. I felt these being sewn into my body; I remember very well the moment I opened my eyes to see Medusa leaning over me with a needle.

I don't have time to waste lying on my ass. Once the fever passed I rose and started hunting. There are people around here, and I don't know where they came from or how they survived, but I need them. For the plan. The plan. Don't ever forget the plan, don't ever let go of it. It's the only reason you're still here. It's everything.

So I find the hiding spot of the tiny group whose members cut my throat; I find them because I can move through the dark as though born to it; I can hear and smell them without need of my eyes. I wait until they're asleep and then I kill one of them with a silent twist of his neck. I drag his body over the earth, all the way back to the seaside town. He's heavy and I'm weak – it takes a long time. I make sure none of the

Furies are nearby as I load him into the back of the truck, now gassed and powered up.

Then I start the engine and drive out onto the road. I wait.

They come, curious and ravenous for meat.

And this is how I'm going to get us back. I don't want to do it on my own. Nothing's good on your own. You need people, even if they're barely people.

I drive and they follow the corpse on the back, Medusa and Washington and Astro Boy at the front of the horde. My bird flies above.

I think *I don't know who any of you were before this, and I'm so sorry this was done to you. I'm so sorry to be taking you back. But the world needs you yet.*

The plan. The plan. Nothing else matters.

*

April 3rd, 2068

Dave

I'm smooth and unblemished. I see clearly and without emotional bias. I am a pacifist. This is what I tell myself as I creep into the dark and make the call I was sent here to make.

It takes time to patch through. There are security measures so no one down in this hell hole will detect my call.

But when he comes online I say, "They're in the tunnels. They've been hiding underground among the Furies. I have coordinates. They plan to attack the Blood compound by taking out all the comms, including their own. Luquet is out – they don't trust her anymore so she won't be a problem. How should I proceed?"

Falon Shay says, "Good lad. You've just ended a war before it's begun and saved thousands of lives. I'm recommending you for the medal of honor."

"And my family? You said they'd be safe."

"They will be. Of course." He pauses and then murmurs down the phone line, "You're a strange creature. Why does it matter to you that they're safe?"

I would answer if I could but I don't know how. "What are my orders?"

"Place the router near their comms so we can listen in. And when you know it, relay the exact date and time of attack. Dave, I … You mean a lot to me. You know that by now. You're the most remarkable thing I've ever made."

As I end the call I think about being made, or created, and how that happens. I know I didn't make myself, not as I am now, so maybe he's right. Maybe I am as he made me. I suppose it doesn't matter as long as I know what I know and fight for what's right. Hurt the few to save the many. Stop a war. Surely they knew these concrete tunnels would be their tombs?

I'm a pacifist.

I am.

*

April 8th, 2068

Josephine

The trajectory of the bullet slows mid air and my mind stretches out beyond it in every direction, deep into the earth and high into the sky, back into the past and forward into the future.

Limerence

I live a single moment of knowing.

I thought love was what separated the humans from the animals, the innocent from the monstrous. I thought I had to be dangerous, I thought I had to be creaturely to survive and to win and that meant I couldn't also love.

I was wrong.

It was there all along, only I couldn't see it. It was there in the gentle touches of the Furies, in Medusa's finger on my face and the threads she sewed into my throat. It was in their simple generosity and the way they kept each other alive though it might mean their own deaths. I saw it in the eyes of my bird, in the flight of her wings, felt it in the weight of her on my arm. I saw it in every moment she came to find me, knowing somehow that I needed her. There is love in even the most beastly of creatures, in the care they offer each other; it lives in the atoms of their bodies, in the molecules of those giant trees and the shelter they provide, it lives in warm bodies huddled together against the cold and in someone carrying for you a tin of tomatoes over miles and miles even though you'll never be able to get it open. It lives in the worst parts of us as well as the best. It lives deepest of all, sometimes so deep you can't see it anymore, so deep you can forget it's even there.

This is what I think as my bullet cuts straight through Dave's chest and he hits the ground hard.

*

It's Shay who cries out. He lunges for Dave, cradling him and giving the game away in a single moment. Had I not known before, I would know now. But I did know before. I've known all along. It's Luke who couldn't hear it, who would never have believed it had I not just proven it.

He stands frozen, too shocked to move at all except to take a few dazed steps away from them. He looks like he could spit on his brother, there is so much hatred in him. He looks as though he wishes Dave dead.

That's what I'll mourn in all of this. That I doused the love between brothers.

The Bloods close in to protect Shay, too well trained to leave a gap through which to reach him. I can't get to him any more now than I could a moment ago. But I don't need to. I just need to keep breathing.

And I need to say the one thing that matters. The one thing he should die knowing.

"You're wrong," I tell Shay breathlessly. "Love is only a weakness to those who can't feel it. But to those who feel it deeper than all else, deeper than life or death – to them love is a weapon. Withhold it, and you arm your enemies. Offer it freely, you arm your friends."

"Bitch," he hisses. He is serpent-like: I see the forked tongue dart from his mouth. No. Calling him animal is too kind. In this moment of hatred he is all too human.

"You have a son," I remind him. I point with one finger at Dave's still body. "That's not him."

"My son," Shay snarls, "is a failure of feeling. A mess of human flaws. But David was pure. Scraped free of everything that sullied him. More my creation than any child of my body could ever be. You'll all burn for this."

And we would, too. There are six heavily armed Blood agents with automatic weapons aimed at our hearts. Turn this into a gun battle and we all die – that's been clear from the start.

But I have another ace up my sleeve, one who finally moves into play.

I warned Shay. I did. *Withhold love and you arm your enemies.*

One of the Bloods moves. He reaches down and takes Falon Shay by the throat, hauling him back against his body.

"Don't move," the Blood says.

"What are you doing?" Shay demands. "Stand down!"

But the Blood's gun is pressed hard against Shay's back, right over the heart, and he doesn't stand down. "I want you to know," the soldier says, "it isn't love that killed you. It's your cruelty."

He pulls the trigger and the Prime Minister drops, dead.

With them facing away from us, I fire and Shadow fires and Will fires, killing all five of the Bloods. Leaving the sixth to remove his helmet and reveal himself as the son of the minister.

I meet Zach's eyes. His are rapturous, fevered. I've never seen such elation or freedom. The curl of his twisted, scarred mouth makes him terrible. I had no idea how much he truly hated his father, but I should have. I didn't want him to do this, I wanted it to be me, it *would* have been me if I'd foreseen the shotgun to the chest. It couldn't be Luke, not if he's to lead the city. So instead a boy has killed his own father, and I'm frightened of what it's stolen from inside him.

"There are at least forty Bloods still inside this compound," Shadow says quickly.

"No time to worry about that," I say. "Get Dave moving, now."

Luke looks at me, confused and so ghostlike. I'm not sure he remembers his name at this point.

"He's not dying," I say as clearly as I can through my gasping lungs. "*Move.*"

Shadow and Will lift Dave's body between them, Zach comes to push my wheeling chair because I'm unable to move and Luke trails behind.

Through the glass atrium we hurry, through the kitchen and into the medical wing. Bloods we kill because they won't stop until we're dead. Anyone else we disarm. Shadow and Will haul Dave's body onto an operating table. The nurses cower in a supply room and we leave them be.

It's Will who remembers to take my mangled vest from me. I groan and sob with the pain of being moved; there is fire in my chest, all through the heart of me. I think I'll never move again. "Shhh," he whispers, easing me out of it and tenderly wiping the blood from my eyes.

I nod in thanks, slumping once more in my wheelchair.

Zach has removed his combat gear and washes his hands, pulling on plastic gloves. It's a very different atmosphere to our shitty infirmary underground. Here the lights are bright, the sterilization is thorough and the instruments are advanced. He cuts off Dave's shirt and then peers at the wound.

"Right where you said," he marvels. I nod. Straight between anything critical and out the other side.

Luke is standing at the door, unable to take in the shock of his brother's betrayal. He looks at me again, seeking an answer, condemning me with his eyes.

The truth is a heavy burden. It was there to be seen all along – why else put Dave in Luke's cell that first night?

*

February 1st, 2068

Josephine

He's knee deep in mud when I approach him.

"I need to speak with you."

"Hallelujah. What hell froze over?"

I nod my head and Luke follows me around behind the pig pen where we can't possibly be overheard. I take precautions anyway. "Where's your brother?"

"Helping Dad sort screws or some other stupid shit that doesn't need doing. Why?"

Again I look around to make sure we're alone. "We've got a mole."

Luke folds his arms and levels me with a look. "Finally you're catching on. Zachariah fucking Shay."

"It's not Zach. I think it's your brother."

The look turns into a *look*. "Come off it."

I step forward and take his face in mine even though I don't like to touch or be touched. I do it because this is more important than anything. This is everything. "Listen to me," I say, holding his green eyes with all the certainty I possess. "I might be wrong but I don't think I am. I'm going to set you up with a plan. This is the plan you'll share with your brother – with everyone. This is the information we'll feed through to Shay. But I'll be making other moves, ones I won't even tell you about. What I need from you is to keep your eyes open, and when the time comes you have to lock me up. Make sure it's public, make sure everyone knows I can't get free to make any moves of my own. Make it clear I'm out of the game. You'll know when the time comes – it'll be when you're about ready to kill me."

He doesn't say anything.

I hold him tight. "If I'm wrong, I'll bear it. You don't have to believe me, and he won't get hurt. But if I'm right we'll know. We have to know."

"You're not right," he says. "For the record. I know him."

"Okay, good. Will you help prove me wrong?"

There is a long silence and then he says, because he's Luke Townsend and he loves me, "Yes."

Love is a weapon. And I need every weapon there is in this fight.

*

April 7th, 2068

Luke

As her knee slams into my balls I can't help feeling as though I should have said no. I sure as shit did not agree to have my testicles ruptured.

With a wild roar of pain I manage to get her onto the mats and pinned beneath my body. "This is it, right?" I hiss in her ear so the crowd of onlookers won't hear. "I'm meant to be locking you up now? 'Cause you said I'd want to kill you, and I do. I'd quite, quite like to murder you."

"This is it," she agrees, before plunging her teeth into my shoulder.

*

April 8th, 2068

Josephine

I wish I had been wrong. I really do.

Zach starts repairing the damage. He's completely focused – you would never know that a short while ago he shot his father dead.

"Did you bring reinforcements?" I ask Luke, Will and Shadow. They all look at me blankly, which I take to mean no. "Nice job."

"We were a little too worried about you to be thinking straight!" Luke exclaims, semi-hysterical. I've never seen him like this, utterly out of his mind. He's lost his famous control. He's what he would term a liability. And I'm not exactly much help either, slumped here like a paraplegic.

"Easier to get in with fewer people," Shadow explains. "Didn't think far enough ahead."

"Can't call for backup, either," Will adds glumly. "No comms."

"Are the others okay?" Shadow asks. "In the tunnels?"

"I evacuated them after you guys left this morning," I answer. "They're safe. Teddy can't get the comms back up because he's not in the tech room. Did you lose any at the Blood base?"

"Not one," Will murmurs. "Lost an awful lot of them, though."

I swallow, trying to rid myself of the ache in my chest. A life is a life is a life, no matter which side it fights for.

The Bloods arrive. Outside the door, which we have barricaded but not well enough to last any extended amount of time. They order us to lower our weapons and come out with our hands up.

"How original of them," I wheeze.

"Uhh … we're kind of … stumped, aren't we?" Will asks.

"Can't fight forty," Shadow says placidly.

"You can at least stop them from getting in those doors before I stitch the traitor closed!" Zach snaps.

Will and Shadow move to block the door. There are no windows, only a skylight way up in the two-story ceiling, and that's too high to reach from the outside. Yet again I've found myself barricaded inside, with enemies battering down the doors to kill us.

Dave takes the moment to gasp violently into consciousness.

"Stay down!" Zach exclaims, trying to hold his bleeding shoulder in place.

Dave moans and struggles and Shadow crosses to hold him down. Luke doesn't move anywhere near them, only watches blankly. "Give me a hand, son," Shadow grunts.

"Not a chance," Luke replies with a repulsed curl of his lip.

"Luke," Dave pleads, crying in pain.

"Easy, kid, you're okay," Shadow tries to soothe as Zach hurriedly packs the hole in Dave's shoulder.

"Why are you comforting him?" Luke asks. "The pain's well and truly earned."

"Luke," Dave tries, more in control.

"Why'd you do this? How could you?"

"To stop a war," Dave pants. "You can see that, can't you? What—*owwww*—what happened to my shoulder?"

"Josi shot you."

He blinks and looks at me. "You did? Why? Because you hate me?"

If I could move any closer I would, but instead I just sit here and try to see his face from this angle. "I don't hate you, Dave. Believe it or not, I understand what you were trying to do. But if you'd helped us there would have been even less bloodshed."

"Stop it!" Luke snarls. "Don't even talk to him – he doesn't deserve it!" He whirls on his brother and I can see how badly he wants to hurt Dave in the tremble of his shoulders. "*Mom and Dad would have been down there!*"

"He said they'd be safe! He was going to pardon my family!"

"And you believed him? You're a fucking moron."

Dave shuts his mouth with a snap. I see a sort of quiet come over him. I recognize it – he's resigned to whatever fate has found him. The hatred of his little brother. The failure of his one objective.

Luke isn't done. Bluntly he says, "You're not my brother. You're nothing like him. He was brave."

I wonder if this has wounded Dave at all, but see no evidence of it. I think that makes it all the harder for Luke to stomach – that there's no regret, no pain at the making of this betrayal.

"This is getting harder to hold," Will warns from where he's got his back pressed to the locked door. Shadow returns to help him. The Bloods on the other side have something with which to ram and the lock won't hold against it forever.

I hear a strange noise then. A sort of *tap tap tap*; an avian cry.

My heart constricts with fear and my head whips up to see Intirri at the skylight, trying to get in to me. "Oh god."

"Is that a *bird*?" Will demands.

"Intirri, go!" I try to call. "Leave!"

If they see her they'll try to kill her – she's a plague threat. I search around for a ladder – they must have a way of reaching that window, but as though my thought has summoned the dark deed, distant shots sound. At first I don't know where they're coming from, but Luke has moved to a different angle to peer up at the bird.

"I think they're on the next roof along," he says. "Firing at her."

I lunge for the skylight, forgetting about my body, which roars in denial. A scream tears from my mouth and I slam my eyes shut against it.

When I open them again it's to see feathers exploding into the air and then her wing falling still against the glass.

A shocking sound erupts from me; it's the slicing of my spirit, the tumbling away of it, the desertion of it. The kind of baying a wolf offers to the moon with its most mournful of hearts.

I thought I knew pain.

Before my howl has even ended Luke is moving. Up onto the cabinets, monkeying his way up the rows of shelves to their highest, moving fast enough that his weight won't collapse anything underfoot and then without a second's hesitation he launches himself off the shelf, through the air toward the roof, his body stretching as far as it can, hands reaching right out to clutch at the sill around the glass. He grunts with sudden pain and his right loses its grip, swinging low. He's holding that tiny ledge with only his left fingers now, and I can see the pain in his paper-white lips.

He won't be able to hold on, not with one hand, and a drop from that height will break his legs.

Just as I'm preparing myself to watch him fall, I see him reach up with his broken hand and grip the edge of the window. The pain, it must ... I've seen him sweat and moan with the punishment of that hand after having done nothing more strenuous than simple tasks like gripping something too tightly or unclenching it too quickly, but this ...

With a trembling cry, he lets go with his left hand and takes all of his weight on the mangled right, the only way he can reach up to unlatch the window.

The glass opens inwards and gives him something to hold onto. I can't see Intirri anymore, and soon Luke has hauled himself up through the opening of the roof and he too is gone from my sight.

The guns continue to fire.

*

Luke

Muscle and bone and nerve endings have betrayed me. Something has come utterly undone in my hand; the things that hold it together have fled me.

But her bird ... I must.

So I force the hand to do what it's unable to do. I hold its pieces together with nothing but sheer force of will, because yes, I'm fragile but I'm also resilient, I'm also more than flesh and bone. I make it up onto the roof.

She's so small, lying there like that. Her blood and feathers have smudged the glass. I sweep her into my chest, holding her with my bad arm and angling my body over hers. She wakes, makes a sound, a soft call not unlike the sound Josi just made, the sound that will follow me to my grave and into my nightmares.

"Shhh," I whisper, cradling the beautiful little falcon.

They're still firing, the men who've been taught to see flight and think death. I draw my weapon and line them up, one at a time. In the silence that comes after the passing of their lives I look up into the cloudless, empty sky. She is a warm miracle in my hands. A good way to ease a wounded heart. A good way to start approaching the far distant concept of forgiveness for a betrayal too deep. A good way to remember what matters. This is how Josi survived – with sky and a bird. Maybe it's how I'll survive what my brother has done.

*

Once upon a time a sickness was brought to us by the birds, one that wiped out millions, and so we hunted any bird who survived that sickness and shot them from the sky. We obliterated them from the world, sent thousands of species extinct.

In my arms lies the last of her kind.

Or maybe, I think, she is the first.

Chapter 28

April 8th, 2068

Josephine

"She's alive!" he calls down. "They only got her wing!"

Tears spill from my eyes as I let them fall shut. I have sunk so deep into my chair that I'll never climb back out.

"There's a way out up here!" he shouts next.

A smile finds my lips. They're going to make it.

"Go," I tell the others.

Dave is packed and bandaged to within an inch of his life and is now sitting up. Zach peers up at the skylight. "How are those of us without superpowers meant to get up there?"

"There has to be a ladder somewhere," Will points out.

"Probably not *in* the operating room," Zach snaps.

Shadow starts lifting the operating table up onto the desk.

"Everything just had to be so damn majestic for you, didn't it, Dad?" Zach mutters as he helps try to broach the distance to the abnormally high ceiling.

"Hey, stop!" Luke shouts. "There's rope in the pack on your back, Shadow!"

Shadow unzips his regulation combat pack or whatever it is and sure enough, there's a coil of rope. He throws this up to Luke, who manages to fasten it to something up there, then shouts for us to hurry while the way is still clear.

Zach starts climbing without a single glance backwards.

"Come on, you," Will says, moving to help me.

"Don't."

Something passes his eyes, understanding and then blunt refusal. "No way."

"I'm not getting up there," I tell him softly. "My chest plate is broken, I think. All my ribs. My lung is punctured. I can't move. I can hardly breathe." *I think I'm dying. And I think I'm okay with it.*

"We'll carry you."

"Not possible."

"Bullshit. No."

Shadow arrives then. He doesn't say anything, he just lifts me from my chair and even though I scream in pain he doesn't put me back down or stop, he just drapes me like a baby over his body, like we are hugging, but I can't hold on, I can do nothing but lie here like dead, useless weight. "Just leave me," I wheeze, or I try to wheeze, but I don't think much makes it out of my mouth.

Will scampers up like it's the easiest thing in the world, then turns and offers encouragement. Which I don't think Shadow appreciates, because it mostly consists of needling him about how old he is.

I have my eyes and mouth clenched shut against the feel of sandpaper sawing at the edges of my bones. From this position every breath sends a needle straight through the center of me.

Shadow climbs hand over hand, which is no easy feat on your own, let alone with an extra lump of human draped over you. I can hear his breathing grow more and more ragged as he inches his way up. Will was joking but he was also more right than he realized. Shadow's too old for this. He's had too many debilitating injuries, has been brought back from the brink of death too many times. This is too much to ask of him.

Dave is still below. There's no way he can climb up, so we left him for last in order to pull him up from above. But there's no way Luke, Will and Zach can pull all three of us – Luke's only got one hand and the other two have rather limited upper body strength.

This isn't going to work. Some things just aren't logistically possible, and getting two severely injured people up a hanging rope is unfortunately one of them.

I make a swift decision, sending my heart up through the roof to where my husband waits, to where my bird waits. I'll leave it there with them. They'll look after it.

To my father I say, "It's alright. It's enough now. I love you."

And I let go of him.

I fall heavily onto the operating gurney and feel the last meager breaths of air flee my broken chest.

Dave launches himself onto the bottom of the rope and in the chaos of the door being battered in, they drag Shadow and Dave up as quickly as they can and even though they're shouting my name they know there's nothing left to do now, nothing but to get that rope up and save the ones they can.

As the Bloods surround me I tilt my face up to the square of clear blue sky.

It seems this is how I've faced all of my deaths.

*

Dave

I've always been very aware of my own cowardice, but even I'm surprised at the new depths of it. She drops to the bed right beside me. I could stay with her, or try to help her, but instead I scurry onto the rope and allow myself to be pulled to safety. I wonder if maybe love and sadness and anger are the things that allow you to be brave. Or if maybe I'm just a coward.

Luke's voice as he screams her name is a riot of sound. There's music in it, music for heartbreak. But I hear music everywhere.

I reach them and am in the process of being pulled onto the roof when I feel something attach itself to my foot. I give a gasp. Don't even have time to look down before I'm being wrenched back into the room.

Luke drops the bird and lunges for my arms – one hand can't quite keep hold of me, but the other's grip is made of iron. My shoulder shrieks.

"Hang on," he grunts.

Will and Shadow are trying to haul Luke back and me with him, but it's not enough, I'm being dragged down by the force of way too many men. I'm about to be split in half. Or else I'll simply drag Luke with me into the abyss. And I can't have that.

I look up and meet my brother's eyes.

"Don't let go," he tells me. "Don't you dare."

I'm meant to be smooth and perfect and pure. That's what Shay tried so hard to create when he turned me from a man into a drone. But I'm not. I'm far from pure, no longer smooth but blemished with mistakes, with treachery and lies. Take everything but fear and you create the worst kind of creature that exists. That is a creature incapable of anything true, anything real or selfless or brave. Act always in fear and you tear the world down around you.

But as I look at my brother I realize something simple.

It seems that maybe I can be brave after all. For him, for my little brother, I can be anything.

I say, "Turns out love doesn't live where they thought it did."

Not in the mind or the heart but everywhere, everywhere.

I pull free of his weak hand and draw the knife he armed me with. Awkwardly I slash it through his hand and as his muscles jerk he has no choice but to let go of me.

"No, no, no—"

I crash down in a tangle of Blood bodies and limbs. Elgar plays in my heart as I fall, a last wish, a last regret that I couldn't give it back to his wife, and then I hear my own skull hittin—

Chapter 29

April 8th, 2068

Luke

Please, not again.

Chapter 30

April 8th, 2068

Josephine

It's an accident. Nothing more than an accident. As he lands his head hits the floor at the wrong angle. And that's it.

That's how he dies, when the rest of them suffer no more than a few bruises and sprains.

That's how he dies.

My eyes are glued to where his body lies, awkwardly strewn in the position it landed. They don't move him. They don't straighten his twisted limbs or close his eyes or clean the blood pooling beneath his skull.

And it is profoundly unbearable to me.

So I will do it.

I drag myself off the bed and tumble to the ground, hitting hip and elbow and broken ribs so hard that my vision goes black. When the world blinks back into life I drag myself, hands still cuffed, over the cold tile floor to his side. My breathing is a horrendous rattling wheeze, louder and shorter with each.

"Stay where you are," a Blood orders me. He sounds oddly sad. Or maybe it's my imagination.

I ignore him and creak myself into a sitting position. It tears something within. Perhaps one of my broken ribs has punctured something else. I don't know. I don't know anything except that I have to spare him this indecency.

With painstakingly slow movements I pull Dave's leg into place, twisting it around and lying it straight. I do the same with his arms, one after the other, and the Bloods let me. For the first time since I met him he looks peaceful. It's true peace, not enforced emptiness. It's fullness. I'm crying and my tears are falling on his face as I reach to close his eyelids.

It's all I can do. My body gives up. I slump over him and rest my cheek on his chest, imagining that a heartbeat will stutter back to life.

It doesn't.

I close my eyes.

And as I drift off I hear the skull shattering sound of an alarm tone. Three bursts. And then a voice being broadcast over every speaker in the Gates.

Attention. This is acting Prime Minister Jane Folley, speaking on behalf of the Ministers United. All agents are to stand down. We wish to discuss the terms of our surrender to the resistance under the guidelines of the Treaty Act.

I repeat, we surrender.

Chapter 31

April 14th, 2068

Josephine

The world returns slowly. Or, more aptly, I return to it slowly. Some dark place filled with beasts has kept me captive but now I rise ephemerally to the white, blinking, beepingness of reality.

Medical machines hum softly on either side of me and the sheet covering my skin is the softest I've ever felt. I don't recognize where I am and the disorientation makes my heart rush in fright.

"Easy there, kiddo."

The second I hear his voice my pulse calms. I tilt my head and see him sitting at the window, reading a book. My father.

"Where am I?" My voice comes out sounding very weird. Rough and scrapey, which I assume must be from whatever tubes they shoved down there.

"In a hospital."

"What? How can—"

"Shhh. You're safe. City's ours. You could probably have this hospital named after you if you wanted."

"I do not want." I settle back on the bed, gingerly noticing the tingle of pain in my abdomen. I've never been admitted to a hospital before, not once in my life, but as I note the remarkably different state of my body now compared to when I was last awake, I think I'm rather grateful the timing of my first visit worked out so well.

"You've been in an induced coma for the last week," Shadow informs me. "Doctors wanted you to heal before you started flinging yourself from roofs again."

It hits me like a lightning bolt. Dave. Oh, Dave. "Where's Luke?"

"Keeping busy. Think he was a bit shocked at the amount of work it takes to overtake a government. Ministers have been cooperative, though. Turns out they were all terrified of Shay."

"Is he ... okay?"

"Not really."

I want to ask if he's come to see me but that feels selfish, given the circumstances. I wouldn't be surprised if he hated me, after that mess.

Shadow closes his book and peers out the window. I have no idea where we are or what his view holds, but he says, "All looks the same from here."

Which I suppose is the depressing fact of the world. You can change it all you want but it never really changes. Though maybe there's comfort in that, too, and beauty.

Someone waltzes into the room and I gasp with delight. It's Will, carrying Intirri on his arm. "Look who's been missing you."

Intirri's leg is tied by a thin cord to Will's gloved wrist, she's wearing a little leather hood over her eyes and there's a bandage around her wing. She looks alarmingly un-wild right now, but at least she's alive.

"Come here, darling," I sigh in relief as Will coaxes her onto my arm. Her wings spread a little and then settle back down. I remove her hood and let her peer around as I stroke her.

"Just needed to make sure she didn't try to fly before she could," Will explains the trappings.

"Thank you."

I untie the cord from her leg and then unwrap the bandage.

"Vet said she needs to keep that on another few days …"

"What does a vet know about birds?" I ask. I climb out of my bed and hobble for the window, ignoring their protests.

I push the window open and give a lilting whistle. Then I launch Intirri off my arm and into the air. Her wings spread and flap as she sinks toward the ground – she will either fly or fall.

She flies.

I laugh as she catches a pocket of air and bullets up and over the world. Her cry is joyous and free as she circles around, showing off her skills. She's exactly where she's meant to be.

*

Will stays all afternoon with me, even when I drift back to sleep. When I wake he reads to me from the bird book he gave me all that time ago and somehow managed to salvage from below, though don't ask me how.

"*Falcons have an astonishing ability to achieve what's known as 'wind-hovering', or 'standing flight', meaning they can hover in the air with almost zero wind.* Huh, cool."

"Are the kids all okay?"

"They're having a ball, running rampant," he replies, closing the book. "Claire and Tobias are in charge of disciplining them and they want it to be known that they should be given medals." His expression softens. "It's good for them to have kids to look after. Until they all go back to their families, anyway."

I feel sad for Will, that he doesn't have anyone to return to. I don't think he'll be straying too far from Pace and Eric, though.

"What are we going to do about your paintings?" I ask him. "How can we leave them down there?"

"I'll do you some new ones," he offers with a smile. Then blurts, "Me and Hen are together."

My eyes widen. "For real?"

He nods. "She came round in the end. Said it'd always been me, she just wasn't ready to admit it."

"You charming devil, you."

"That's me. Winning hearts left, right and center. Do you think it's my collection of moth wings or my love of poetry that gets 'em?"

We laugh.

"You never read me any poetry," I point out.

"I'm not a complete loser."

"Hey, I like poetry! I used to read it to Luke all the time, until I caught him snoring in the middle of one."

"Philistine."

"Tell me about it. What's your favorite?"

He shrugs and rubs the back of his neck.

"Go on, dork. Quote me something."

"I do like this one by Mary Oliver. She's my favorite. But just one line, that's all I can stand to say out loud."

"Okay."

Will smiles. "*Tell me, what is it you plan to do with your one wild and precious life?*"

*

April 15th, 2068

Josephine

I wake this morning to the sound of a baby crying. Groggily I roll over and sit up a little, peering at the unhappy child in Pace's arms.

"Poor little man."

Pace looks at me with arched eyebrows. "Poor Mom, more like. He's teething, apparently." Her expression narrows in on my face. "I was about to announce that Sleeping Beauty has awoken, but right now it looks more like Frankenstein's monster has risen from the dead."

"How kind."

"How are you feeling?"

"Pretty good."

"I find that hard to believe. You cracked every single rib, punctured your lung, broke both collarbones, fractured your sternum and dislocated your hip."

"Jesus."

"Yeah, but the upside is that apparently medicine has progressed beyond the Middle Ages and the world forgot to inform the tunnels. You'll be right as rain. Bones are all set and healing. Plastic surgeon even had a go at that mess on your neck, so the Frankenstein stitches are a little less dramatic. Only – fair warning – they did have to intubate your trachea to get you breathing again, and it damaged your vocal chords even more than they already were, which is why you sound like a chainsaw. That's permanent. I wanted to be the one to tell you." She sounds suspiciously pleased.

"You're a sociopath."

"I just find it amusing how badly you manage to scrape yourself up, like, over and over again. Will and I have made a game out of guessing what you'll injure next."

I can't help laughing. It sounds brittle and ugly. "Glad it's amusing to you, at least."

"Yeah. Just so you know, I wouldn't mind not playing that one anymore. In fact I'd really appreciate it if you'd stop now, Dual. Give my nerves a rest."

I nod and meet her blue, blue eyes. "That's the plan."

She nods and we share a brief, true moment.

"So I guess you're dying for an update, huh?" She goes on to explain about how the resistance have been brought safely out of hiding and moved temporarily into the enormously oversized mansions of the Gates, which has rather amusingly horrified its original occupants. She tells me stories of the filthy sewer people playing pranks on the prim and proper families of the ministers and I laugh so much my eyes water. The wall around the Gates is already being pulled down – that was one of the first things Luke ordered, after the chaos had subsided. He hasn't tackled the actual wall around the city yet, obviously, but he's sent people to block off the tunnels until we work out what to do about the Furies and the poor Blood agents sent down there to be slaughtered. He's now also writing up a motion to abolish the administering of the cure to all sixteen-year-olds. It's a huge start.

"I can't believe I've slept through it all."

"Yes, it's extremely lazy of you."

Hal's fallen quiet and is simply looking around tranquilly.

"Can I have a cuddle?"

As Pace hands her son to me and I cradle him on the bed, she asks, "Was it all … all that stuff underground, was it part of your plan? I mean, were you just acting all distant?"

Limerence

I should lie, but find that I can't.

She sees the truth in my eyes and can't help a fleeting expression of pain. "You'll be okay now, though. It's all over. You'll get back to normal."

I nod, but my eyes are drawn to the window.

"What will you do now?" I ask Pace.

"God knows. All I've ever done is training and chores, when you think about it."

"Pace, you've been working in Dodge's lab for years. Your understanding of chemical science is amazing."

"Yeah, but I dunno if I want to do that. I only helped out because it was necessary, you know?"

"So don't. Don't ever do anything you don't want to do, and never compromise on that. Find the things you love and hold onto them. Let the rest fall away."

"Why does it sound like you're saying goodbye?"

I answer without sound. *Because I am.*

*

Being in hospital is a bit like being in prison, I've discovered. You get visitor after visitor trailing in to see if you're okay and neither you nor they really want to be there. It's the pits.

As Pace and Hal are leaving there is a bit of a commotion in the hallway. I hear her chatting to someone, hear several voices in response and then I see a flock of bodies press themselves into my room.

At their head is tiny little Sienn. Which means behind her are the rest of her gargantuan family, all seven of them including grandma.

"Hello," the father, Guillaume says, leaning on his crutches.

"*Bonjour*," Sienn says brightly.

So they *are* French. I thought I caught Shadow chatting away to them in another language. Intriguing.

"Hi."

All seven of their faces beam happily at me.

"How are you guys?" I ask awkwardly.

"Oh, we're fine, we've been trying to find you for aaaaaaages but every time we see you in the tunnels you vanish and we never ever get to talk to you!" This has come out of Sienn's mouth in the space of about half a second.

"Sorry about that." I look down at Guillaume's missing foot and grimace. "I'm sorry about that, too."

"You're mad!" the mother exclaims. "A foot for seven lives – *bon métier*!"

The children all laugh.

"Okay, yeah," I chuckle.

"There are no words," Guillaume says. "We can never hope to repay what you've done, not with one thousand lifetimes. But any need or any wish – until the day even our youngest has passed – is our duty to provide you with."

"*Cela est une dette de sang*," the grandmother says.

"This is a blood debt," Guillaume translates, nodding.

This seems to hang heavy in the air. I'm not sure what to say, so I just say, "Thank you. I appreciate that."

"And if you need anyone to do any chores for you or whatever I could come over to your house in the daytime and do stuff for you, just like to help you out with whatever you need, I can do whatever," Sienn breathes, breaking the spell and making everyone laugh.

"She's angling for you to teach her how to fight like you do," one of the older kids says.

I meet Sienn's eyes. This bright light of a child who drew a tiny knife to face hundreds of monsters so that I wouldn't have to face them alone. If anything, I owe her the debt. My throat almost closes. "More than anything, Sienn, I hope you'll never need to."

*

One of my doctors arrives to check on me this evening. She's one I haven't met yet. She has bitchin' red hair and an astonishingly large overbite.

"I'm Liz Taylor, your—"

"Really?"

She flushes. "Yes, I know, it's silly."

"It's great. Sorry, continue."

"I'm the general surgeon who oversaw your surgeries and treatment. Firstly, I just wanted to say what an honor it's been to serve you."

Serve me?

"I mean, not serve you, sorry. Treat you."

I can't help smiling – she's really struggling here.

"Because of what you've done," she presses awkwardly.

My smile goes. What I've done is cause the deaths of four hundred people. Not to mention the rest of it ...

"You had several other key physicians working on you – your orthopedic surgeon, Dr. Landry, is the top in the city, and he says your bones are all healing beautifully."

I wait patiently for her to get to the point.

"But I wanted to come in and talk to you more generally about your health and the condition of your body."

"I'm aware of what's wrong with me. Dual chemicals battling it out, holding me at a precarious balance, etc., etc."

"Yes, well, I've been discussing your case with several biochemical scientists and stem cell doctors who all agree there might be a way to stabilize what's going on at your cellular levels."

"I don't want to put any more shit in my body," I tell her calmly. "I don't want injections, pills, treatments, experiments. I just want to be left alone."

"But Josephine—"

"There's literally nothing you can say. I don't want to hear anything else."

"But there's something—"

"Nope! Uh-uh! Shh!"

She gives up and leaves me alone. I enjoy a moment of satisfaction as I reach for my book. I don't allow my eyes to go to the door, as they have been doing every ten seconds for the last two days, waiting, waiting, waiting for him to come. I don't allow them, but they go there anyway.

*

April 18th, 2068

Josephine

I think remaining in bed for ten days is well and truly enough. I'm still bandaged up and I make sure to take a hefty dose of pain meds before I attempt to get dressed. It's not too bad. Huh. Hooray for real doctors. Bending over to tie my boots is the worst bit, but I manage it by counting loudly.

I check myself out "against all your doctor's strong advisements" and stride out into the sunshine.

It's so bright I don't see him at first. I just hear his voice. "Hey."

Blink blink blink, wait for him to materialize in the glare.

"Hi. Were you on your way in?" I flinch inwardly at the sound of my voice.

"Nah."

I see him now. He's sitting on a bench in the sunshine, looking up at a nearby tree.

"How long have you been out here?"

"'Bout an hour."

I sit beside him. There's a stretch of lawn before us, lined with flower gardens. "Why didn't you come in?"

Luke shrugs.

We sit in silence for about half an hour. I know because I count the seconds.

"It's strange, being out here like this," I point out eventually. "Legally."

"Thanks to you." He gestures at the world. "This is all thanks to you."

I shake my head. It was just a plan, and it was lucky to work.

"You look better," he says.

I haven't looked in a mirror in months. Literally. All I have to go on are the never-ending Frankenstein jokes, so I'm not inclined to believe him.

There's a persistent ache in me. There are hundreds, actually. Even my aches have aches. And they're all for him. For what he's lost. For what I did to him and the impossibility of time travel.

"If I'd just confronted him instead of trying to sniff him out then maybe—"

"No," Luke says softly. "I can't go near the *if onlys* and the *shoulds* and the *what ifs*. They'll be the end of me."

After a while he adds, "You were right."

"I wish I wasn't." God, how empty. Words are worth so little. "How are your parents?"

"I dunno. Battling on, I guess. I don't know how they find the energy to bother."

"How are you?"

He doesn't answer that one. I sneak a peek at his face and see how tired he looks.

"I heard what you've been doing. For everyone."

"You wanted me to lead, right?" There's bitterness there. He shakes his head to get rid of it. "I don't know what I'm doing."

"Yes, you do."

"What if I fuck up?"

"You'll be forgiven."

"What if I make the wrong choices?"

"You won't."

"What about the Furies?"

"I trust you to know what to do. You understand better than anyone about the preciousness of life."

He clears his throat and then asks, "When are you leaving?"

I look at him, mouth opening. "You know?"

"Of course."

Abruptly the needle in my lung is back, piercing me with every breath. "I just can't stay inside the wall …"

"I know, Jose. You don't have to explain. You don't belong here. I understand."

I swallow but there are tears swimming in my eyes. "Let me … I need to …" Frustrated, I dash them from my cheeks. "I lied, when I told you I didn't love you anymore. I didn't know I was lying but I was, very much. I came back for you, only you. This was all for you."

Our hands are resting on the bench between us, his with a cast around it. He moves his bruised fingers so they can entwine with mine and we sit this way for a while.

"I wish I could have helped you," he admits.

"No force can help this." There's no penance in the world that would be enough for what I've done. Turns out there *is* a line. It's a big one, and when you cross it you can never get back. All that's left is retreat.

Luke laughs a little. "This is weird, but I brought …" Out of his backpack he sheepishly pulls a hairbrush.

I laugh and wipe my tears again, nodding.

"I thought it'd be getting pretty bad," he explains as I crawl onto the ground between his legs so he can start untangling the mess of knots on my scalp. It's so generous of him that I sit here crying silently the whole time.

When he's finished he tucks it behind my ears and lets his fingers linger on the burns. Next he touches my throat.

"My voice," I say shakily, almost like a question.

He turns my chin toward him and runs his thumb over my lips. A silent goodbye.

When the moment becomes too unbearable to keep, he says, "There."

I climb back onto the seat, not knowing what else to say but not wanting this to end.

An ocean tide drags me away. The quiet calls.

Luke says, "I've lost my center." He holds his cast up. "My whole life feels like this. Like that poem you read me once. And when you go I won't be able to bear it."

"*Lifeache*."

"I can never remember the end of that poem. How do you survive it?"

I take his hand and lead him onto the grass. We lie flat on our backs and tilt our faces to the speckled canopy above. "With trees, and grass, and the sky."

He squeezes my hand and soon the only sound is the rustle of the breeze through the leaves and the undetectable path of his tears into the ground.

*

April 25th, 2068

Josephine

The pack feels heavy on my back. I've crammed it full of all sorts of things. Warm layers, for starters. Water canteens, packets of seedlings, dry food, matches, a compass, sunscreen ... A tin-opener. I'm not making the same mistake twice.

As I set off I feel like a character in one of Will's paintings, like I'm walking straight out and into the bewitching wilds of his landscapes. I have become one of his smudges on the horizon.

Shielding the midday sun from my face, I turn and call, "Hurry up, old man!"

Shadow mutters something about thinking the trip was meant to bring quiet. He has a different kind of pack on his back, one shaped much more awkwardly. It's the second time someone has carried that cello for me, only this time it was Shadow who refused to leave it behind, instead of me. I have no intention of ever playing it again, but still he carries it.

He catches up to me and passes me the water bottle. Together we watch Intirri flying out over the long stretch of desert plane.

"There are trees up ahead. We just have to make it past the hard bit."

"Whatever you want, my girl," he murmurs. "Wherever you wander, I'll follow."

"While we wander can we talk about Mom?"

"Of course."

"Also – question … are we French?"

He bursts out laughing. It's the first time I've ever heard him do so. Which I guess means yes.

And away we wander.

Chapter 32

September 16th, 2068

Josephine

The moon has always known my secrets. She's the one who tells me the truth, in the end.

*

It's difficult to keep track of time when you're waiting to die. Shadow works in the garden he's planted and finds ways to feed us. We don't hunt animals – I will never again kill a living thing, never eat something that once had a heartbeat. He repairs our little abandoned (no longer) hut, keeping it standing and clean. We have no power or water, but we have a stream outside, and the ocean beneath the cliff, and we have as much fire as we can make.

We don't talk much. I sleep a lot, waiting for it all to be over. Sometimes I go walking with Intirri, and if I see Furies in the distance I find ways to divert them from where we are. Not for me, but for my father. I think about joining them. I do. I long for it, some nights, remembering Medusa and Astro Boy and Washington. I miss them so much. But there's another person here with me now, and that's what matters. It matters not being alone, even at the end.

It's the night of the blood moon when I first realize how much time has passed, or how little. And I think to myself that I haven't felt … right in quite a few months. Stomach flus have plagued me. My body's way of purging itself of the poison within, I thought. I've changed shape, but I've only been vaguely aware of this. I can't stand my body, you see. So I never get naked, not even to wash. There are no mirrors, and I don't look at myself: I can't stand the skin I live in.

It's not possible, anyway. It's never been possible. I've grown so accustomed to that knowledge that it's made up a huge portion of who I am. The absence of what I want most is what makes me, *me*.

Which all explains how I missed it, I guess. It's quite possible I should have listened to what Doctor Overbite was trying to tell me.

Because as the red hue of the moon shines above and I feel no desire to hunt or kill, I feel something else instead. I feel something inside me.

And as I lift my hands to my swollen stomach I know.

The tough, leathery skin I sewed for myself falls away, the past falling with it. I sink to the grass and I cry and cry and cry because even when you think you've checked out, even when you think you understand the world, it still finds a way to save you from yourself. It finds a way to forgive.

With the armor gone the wounds in my spirit are finally revealed; the salt air of the sea gets inside them and I feel them start to heal.

*

September 16th, 2067

Luke

I could smash my fist through the world if I wanted to. I could rip it open and gaze into the burning hot sun at its core, and I wouldn't even be burned. This is how powerful I've become. This is what the moon makes me.

Josi's convoy is up ahead. Driving straight for the wall with the new kids in tow. She's going to abseil them down the outside of the city. I'm meant to follow and protect the back, like I always do. But I'm getting hungry. I'm so hungry I can hardly think straight. And that's the turnoff to where he's been hiding, crawling underfoot like the enduring cockroach he is.

I make my choice; with the approaching sunset and rise of the blood moon it's an easy one to make. This was why I kept the virus in my veins, after all. This was what the blood moon was for: killing Falon Shay. So I peel off, away from the others, from my wife, and I rev my bike fast down the highway.

I have to find him. I *will* find him before the night is through. It matters more than anything else, than everything else. And when I find him I will tear the heart from his chest and dev—

*

January 1st, 2069

Luke

"Townsend!"

I wake in a cold sweat, gasping air into my lungs. Someone is sitting on the couch beside me, resting his hand on my heaving chest. In the flickering firelight I see that it's Zach. Of course it is.

I sit up and slump against the back of the couch. "Fuuuuck."

"Same again?"

I nod.

"This is getting worse. You only fell asleep for like five seconds."

He's right – the movie we were watching is still playing. I don't know what to tell him. Every time I drift off I dream of the same day, I remember my missing chunk of time.

Zach's far too concerned so I look away from his face, taking in the sprawling living room we share. I've been staying in one of the houses in the Gates these last few months, and when it became clear that neither Zach nor I particularly wanted to rattle around in an enormous mansion on our own, he moved into the second bedroom. He's been invaluable with the running of the city – I couldn't have done any of this without him. And sometimes, late at night, when we've both had nightmares about the deeds that plague us, we meet in the dark to share the silence. To make it a little more bearable.

"What is it?" he asks.

"It's ..." I shake my head. "It's my choice. The worst one I ever made. It won't leave me alone."

"What did you choose?"

"I chose death. I followed the moon instead of my wife and she was the one who paid the price."

I'll never leave that behind. It will be a weight around my ankle until the day I die.

Zach doesn't say anything, but he pats my shoulder once more. And I think yet again how much people matter. They're all that matter.

*

It's sunset. My parents and I are drinking a beer on the top of the wall when I finally understand what's to become of my life.

We do this often now, when Dad's well enough. He's got better medication, so he's in much better shape than he used to be. But the disease is degenerative, and there's still no cure to be found. One day it will take him from us, but not before it steals his dignity from him.

"It's the way of flesh, kid," he told me once. A far more graceful way of looking at it than I'd be able.

Tonight the sun sets golden over the red earth and crystal over the far distant sea that snakes up our peripheral. Each time I sit up here I imagine where she is: somewhere in the wilds. I imagine her walking out and out and out until she vanishes inside them, never to be seen again.

The Furies are out there with her now, her Furies. There was pressure from every side to use Dodge's gas to exterminate them while they were trapped in our tunnels, but instead I opened the gates and set them free into the world beyond, just as they were before Josie brought them here to save us. Come what may, I set them free.

"Georgie wanted you to know she got top marks on her history test," Mom says. They adopted her a few months ago, after it was clear that no distant relatives were coming forward to claim her. It's been a saving grace for all three of them.

I make sure I see all the kids a lot. Instead of punishing me for having kidnapped their children, the parents all went out of their way to show their gratitude for having spared them the cure, and agreed to let their kids come over to my place for movies once a week. We try to talk about the people we miss, the ones who were taken from us, but often this is too hard. Mostly we just chat and watch whatever Teddy brings us – he says he's working his way through Lawrence's list of favorite films. It's a sweet way to remember him.

Henrietta and Will are still together, but so quiet about it you'd never know. I saw them once, standing in the kitchen together where they thought no one would notice them. She reached to touch the corner of his mouth so gently, and he spoke something softly to her, and she smiled such a smile … Their quiet tenderness made my heart ache.

Alo, on the other hand, isn't as private about his enduring love for Eric, which he proclaims at the drop of a hat. As far as I know they haven't broken my rule, but thankfully for everyone who has to hear about it, Alo will be eighteen soon and free to do as he pleases. I wonder sometimes if their connection will survive beyond the tunnels, or if it was something made of fear and excitement and the need for comfort. I guess we'll find out.

Coin shaved all his golden hair off to stop himself from obsessively touching it when he speaks. I still see his hands moving sometimes though, as if to the ghost of his old anxieties.

We are all slowly trying to put our pieces back together, even if they make a different whole.

"Brilliant!" I say now, about Georgie's test marks. I'm not surprised she's acing all her subjects – her memory for detail reminds me of someone I used to know.

"She also wanted you to tell Josi."

"Mom, she knows I don't know where Josi is. Which makes me think it wasn't her suggestion, but yours."

Mom spreads her hands in an innocent way. "Don't shoot the messenger."

Dad snorts.

"Jesus, do I have to get this from you on a daily basis, now?"

"Queries about where our daughter-in-law is?" she replies. "Why, yes, you do."

"If I receive a message via falcon I will let you know," I snap. There are no messages via falcon, for obvious reasons.

"Why did she leave?" Dad asks for the eight hundredth time. I suppose since I never try to answer him it's more my fault than anyone's. "It's not safe out there."

"Josi's safe anywhere. She's the only one of us who's *not* fragile."

"But ..."

"She was sad, Dad," I say softly. "She didn't want to be her anymore. She wanted to be free."

They don't ask any more questions about Josi after that. I get the feeling they might never.

What Dad does ask me is this: "And what do you want to be?"

Not this, my heart sings. *Not whatever this is.*

Without me having to answer Mom says, "Being good at something doesn't mean you have to do it, Lukey. It was us who taught you to believe otherwise. You were good at so many things as a boy. I thought it meant you needed a bigger life."

I can understand that, but I never needed a big life. I've only ever wanted small. Half a dozen people and nothing more.

Or even just one, really.

"Do you remember how poor we were?" she asks.

"We weren't that bad off."

"Do you remember how we occasionally punished you with no dinner?"

"Do I ever."

"What you didn't see was that when you didn't eat, we didn't. And often when you ate, we didn't. Your father got sick years before we told you, he was fired from his job and we couldn't afford his medicine. It was … worse than you knew. So when that woman came for you … it was like a sign. That you would be okay. Whatever we couldn't give you, your own talent would provide. That's why we let her take you. We didn't *know*."

"Oh, Mom," I breathe. "Why didn't you *tell* me?"

"Wasn't for you to worry about," Dad says gruffly.

"Then Dave went and money was the furthest thing from our minds."

"Dave went, and I went," I say, ashamed. I fucking ran away and left my parents to deal with his death alone. "I'm not doing that again," I warn. "I'm not leaving you and I'm not leaving Dave."

"Darling," Mom says gently, "we're okay now. Truly. Just as this city is okay. Seeing you in a cage is like a punishment for us. As for Dave … there's no leaving him. He's everywhere."

I look between them both and feel my heart start to pound.

They are clipping the bindings free of my feet.

Will whispered it to me that night in the silo, with Josi handcuffed behind us. He leaned in close to my ear and asked, "You always go in after her, so why have you stopped now?"

My eyes go back to the distant horizon. And I know. If this version of me chooses death or responsibility over love, then I will stop being this version. I will be the Luke Townsend who knows how to do love better. Who was taught first by his brother and his parents, and then by the girl with the dual eyes. I'll be the one who follows her into the wild, no matter how deep she goes.

*

Josephine

With my back bent over the row of potatoes and my hands deep in the earth I feel a kick. I straighten slowly and rest my hand on it, smiling.

There's a whistle and I turn to see Shadow in the door of our hut. He nods for me to join him inside, so I climb to my feet and walk slowly through the veggie patch. The hills all around are windswept and cold this afternoon. This morning I found ice on the stream and tapped it until I felt the delightful cracking of it. We're close enough to the sea here that I can hear its waves at all hours of the day and night.

Inside the hut the fireplace is raging, filling the little wooden space with smoky warmth. I don't sleep inside except during these cold months. Mostly I sleep under the stars, still unable to be within walls for long.

But I'm not the only one to consider anymore.

Shadow stands beside the wooden cradle he's finished building.

I grin. "Pretty darn good, Phillipe."

"Don't you think it's time to go and get him?"

I shake my head. "I told you, we don't have to."

"Josi, you're nearly—"

"He's coming." Every day I say this, and every day I believe it. "He'll find us."

I rest my hands on my belly and feel the kick again.

Can I just say that it's very, very difficult to play the cello while heavily pregnant? It's also fun to try.

*

January 7th, 2069

Luke

Two days I've been walking without water now. There seems to be no end to this barren land. I can't find my way out of it. Even when I follow the sun I get turned around, lost in the endlessness of it.

Five days with the burning hot sun and the freezing cold nights. Two without water. I'm done for.

I realize it almost abstractly. It hasn't occurred to me before now that I might actually die out here. It seems almost funny. Almost.

*

January 10th, 2069

Luke

On the fifth day without water my legs give out. I've been walking too fast, searching for a stream or river or even a bloody mud puddle. Anything to moisten the desert of my mouth. But I don't find anything. I see a tree I've passed twice already and I sit down at its roots.

"Lukey, you moron," a voice says from somewhere in the very corner of my eye. "All those years digging holes and you still haven't worked out where water comes from?"

I sit up a little straighter. "Dave?"

Oh dear. I'm delirious.

But my hallucinated brother has a point.

I lunge at the earth, realizing the tree must be living off some sort of moisture. I dig and dig but the earth is so hard I can't get through it. My fingers crack and bleed. I'm nine years old, digging in my backyard, my brother playing his guitar beside me. I'm digging to find an answer but it's not here. I can't get to it.

"Dave," I say again. Just to have his name on my lips. Just to feel him near.

I lie down under the shade of the tree and watch the sky through its leaves. And just as my eyes are drifting shut, I see a shape move in the distance. It circles around and grows bigger and then it lands on the branch above me. Her eyes are black and bottomless as she gazes at me.

"Hello," I whisper with a smile, thinking how sweet the world is.

*

It's amazing what a burst of hope will do to your adrenalin glands. I'm on my feet in no time, following Intirri across the plains and into a stretch of grassy hills. She leads me to a river, where I gorge myself on water and feel life return to my body.

And then she leads me over the hills toward the sea, to where I see a cliff in the distance, and on that hill a small wooden hut.

As I draw nearer I hear Elgar's cello concerto drifting from the window and stop to listen.

I'm smiling as it cuts off halfway through a note and a figure flings herself out the front door. She sprints down the hill and I hurry up it until there's no longer any space between our bodies and her lips are on mine and her smile and her eyes and her hands.

"How could you take so long?" she breathes and I say, "Because I'm the biggest idiot on the planet," and kiss her again and again but then she's pulling away and dragging me up the hill and saying "Quick, hurry, come—" and I might think something was wrong if not for the sky splitting joy in every pore of her, if not for the music throbbing from her spirit, the absolute love in every one of her atoms and then we are passing a grinning Shadow who I have never witnessed grinning like that and then we're inside and I see—

A child in a cradle. A child with enormous wide eyes, one of which is the color of Josi's darkest brown eye, the other the color of my green ones.

I look at Josephine; she swims in my tears and then I'm reaching for my daughter. She is so tiny in my hands; all along, this was the purpose of them, even broken as they are, especially broken as they are. This is the only thing my hands were ever made for.

I thought I knew love.

*

Josephine

Life finds a way. Even when the rest of her kind was killed, there came a last, lonely bird, brave enough to fly alone.

Even when the earth all around it had been scorched away by blight and disease, the great redwood forest remained steadfast. Even when my body was too ravaged to create life, even when every piece of my spirit had been cut away by my own atrocities and the seemingly endless burden of shame, even when I'd limped into the wilderness to await my inevitable death – even then there came the most precious miracle of all. A powerful denial of the dark, a bursting throbbing explosion of beautiful new life, the strongest kind there is.

I think the secret to how this happens, time and again, is love.

Here Ends The Cure Series

Acknowledgments

I've been thinking about and writing the story of Josephine and Luke for so many years now that it feels surreal – and very sad – for it to be coming to an end. Such a big part of my life has gone into this story, but it takes a village to get a series of books out into the world, and The Cure couldn't have happened without the support of some wonderful people.

First I'd like to thank my first agent, Sophie Hamley, who took a chance on me at eighteen, and found an amazing home for The Cure. I can't express how grateful I am for your support, kindness and patience – I'd be nowhere without you, Sophie!

I'd like to thank the amazing team at Momentum, led by Joel Naoum. Ashley Thomson, Mark Harding, Patrick Lenton and Michelle Cameron, your hard work and dedication is hugely appreciated.

Thank you to the incredible team of editors who've worked on the three novels: Deonie Fiford, Jo Lyons, and Tara Goedjen.

Your insights and wisdom made all the difference and helped the novels fulfil their potential.

Last I'd like to thank my friends and family, especially my mum. It can be a lonely endeavour, writing a novel, but you've all surrounded me with love and support, put up with crazed months in the lead up to deadlines, chatted through ideas, helped problem solve, read countless rough drafts, made four billion cups of tea and inspired me endlessly. For that I'll always be grateful.

This book holds a very special place in my heart, and it's a joyous thing to share it with the world. It belongs to you, now.

www.ingramcontent.com/pod-product-compliance
Ingram Content Group UK Ltd.
Pitfield, Milton Keynes, MK11 3LW, UK
UKHW011351081225
9449UKWH00027B/270